DES

Allie stumbled ...   ...e,
you scared me ha...

"I told you, Allie, you don't have to be my keeper. I don't need . . . I don't want . . . "

Anger replaced her concern, and despite being fully clothed, she waded into the water to confront him. She slipped on the last step and caught at him to save herself from falling. Automatically he steadied her, and they were nearly toe to toe, him stark naked and grinning like a 'possum.

"I don't care what you don't want," she said.

Tiny rivulets poured from his dark hair that lay plastered over broad shoulders. Stricken speechless, she gazed at the water's path down his bare chest, over the laddering of ribs and flat belly into the swirling torrent at his waist. The warmth of his breath caressed her cheeks, and neither of them moved.

Tendrils of ghostly mist rose into the cooling night air; she shivered and the heat off his body enticed her. A passionate need to love and be loved thrummed deep in her belly. Without moving her gaze from his smoky blue eyes, she rested one hand on his hip just beneath the stream's surface. The contact sent a bright sensation through her, and his eyes batted in surprise, turning even smokier. Desire blossomed between them, a palpable, writhing entity that couldn't be denied.

IMAGES IN SCARLET

SAMANTHA LEE

LEISURE BOOKS   NEW YORK CITY

To my husband, Don, who keeps romance in my life.

A LEISURE BOOK®

September 1999

Published by

Dorchester Publishing Co., Inc.
276 Fifth Avenue
New York, NY 10001

ISBN 0-8439-4578-8

ACKNOWLEDGMENTS

I would like to thank my cousin Edna Hiller, who led me to see the true beauty of New Mexico; computer guru Bob Sprague, who is tireless and so patient; and my wonderful agent Jake Elwell, who never gave up on this book.

IMAGES IN
SCARLET

Chapter One

The man lay across the trail on his back, one arm curled above his head, the other crooked over his chest. He looked so peaceful he might have been asleep. A long-legged bay mare waited patiently nearby, as if she were used to such unusual antics.

Allie reined in the mules. With a deep ditch on one side of the road, an incline on the other, she couldn't drive around him. He could be dead, shot maybe. Or it might be a trap, someone else waiting in the bushes to spring out at her. Wrapping the fistful of leather reins around the brake handle, she hopped down and studied the man.

He hadn't even twitched.

Beneath the duster, a Navy Colt hung heavy on her belt. She tucked the coat back to clear the butt of the revolver and glanced around cautiously. Ringo, her spirited palomino stallion, pawed up dust and tugged at the line that held him to the back of the wagon. Clearly he liked the looks of the man's fine mare.

"Hush up, you randy old stud," she said, and approached the man with caution.

His chest rose and fell in the rhythm of sleep. No blood, no visible bullet holes. No one else around. She eyed him once again, shrugged. If he wanted to sleep in such a strange place that was his business, but blocking the road was not.

Expecting bandits to spring out of nowhere, she took another quick look around. A light wind stirred the early spring leaves; the only other sound was the swishing of the animals' tails. She hunkered down, shoved her Stetson back with her thumb, skinned off one glove and touched his forehead. A sheen of sweat there, but he felt cool.

He didn't move.

In repose, he had a pleasant face. Fine dark brows, gently sculptured cheekbones and a high-bridged nose. A battered brown felt hat lay smashed under one shoulder, ebony hair powdered with dust spread around his head in waves. He was beautiful in a wicked sort of way, a little gaunt, as if he hadn't eaten much lately, or slept.

Despite the frustration of the moment, she grinned. He was certainly making up for that. For a while longer confusion kept her from acting.

The truth was, she didn't know quite what to do. She didn't need the trouble this might bring. Let someone else come along and help him out, if he needed help. Maybe he was just a bit strange and liked to sleep in odd places. She could go back a ways, get off the road and bypass him; but leave him lying in the middle of the trail like this? It didn't seem right.

Ahead, the mare moved uncertainly, eyed the rambunctious stallion, then trotted off, eyes rolling. She was clearly not in the mood for romance, even if Ringo was. If the mare ran off, she would be faced with yet another dilemma. Worse to leave a man afoot and lying across the trail than to simply leave him and his horse to their own weird business.

Despite her inclination to escape the situation, she stomped back to the wagon for a canteen of water. "The last thing you need, Allie Caine, is some stray to take care of." She untied the bandanna from around her neck and returned to the slumbering man, still grumbling under her breath.

When she knelt beside him, he made a small noise down in his throat that startled her, brought her up short. She waited. He slept on, and finally she wet the cloth and began to bathe his face.

Long dark lashes shadowed his stubbled cheeks and they fluttered when she wiped his brow. The hand flung across his chest moved, brushed lightly over the swell of her breast and grabbed at her arm.

It had been a long time since a man had touched her, and pleasant memories feathered through her mind, delicious as a river breeze on a hot summer night.

Without opening his eyes he ran his tongue over dry lips, and she tipped the canteen, letting a few drops dribble into his mouth. He licked the moisture away, rolled his head, groaned.

She could kiss him or kill him; he was that vulnerable.

Smoky blue eyes batted open, flared.

"Lorena?" His voice rasped dry as corn husks in a July wind. "Lorena?"

Unexpectedly, energy pulsed through him, catching her off guard. His muscles bunched and he scrambled to his knees, pushing her away.

"Leave me be. Who the hell are you? Get off, get away from me. Go. I'm all right, dammit. Just get the hell away from me." The words crackled in the silence of the warm afternoon.

She remained there on her knees a moment longer. Shock at his violent reaction kept her from responding until he staggered to his feet.

The mare whinnied, trotted toward him, still keeping an eye on Ringo and his male shenanigans.

The man nailed her with a wild stare, swayed as if he wasn't sure where the ground was, then limped backward, one hand reaching for the dangling reins.

Something was definitely wrong with him. She rose, lifted one hand. The wet bandanna drooled down her arm. "You

11

don't have to act like such a jackass. I was only trying to help you."

A dust devil whipped at her coat tails and lifted the hat from her head. She grabbed at it, flinging an epithet into the swirling grit.

Jake hesitated, mesmerized by long strands of blond hair that danced crazily around the woman's face, reminding him of something he couldn't quite grasp. The flash of memory disappeared, lost in the dark caverns of his mind with all the other images. Dammit, why couldn't he keep them long enough to reconstruct even one complete scene from his past? The mare nudged him between the shoulder blades, but he continued to stare at the woman. She wore a black duster that billowed out like great bird's wings when she chased down the hat. Behind her a strange contraption. Some sort of wagon with dark curtains all around. He'd seen one like it once, but couldn't recall where. A graceful palomino, its mane and tail the color of her hair, stood beside the wagon; two mules waited in harness.

The entire episode made him feel disconnected, as if he were dreaming, yet that couldn't be, for he sensed the terrifyingly familiar emptiness of reality. If he knew what he was doing out here, he would ask her the same. But he didn't, so he kept quiet. Whatever her agenda, it was none of his business.

She stood there scowling at him and absently brushed dirt from the hat with the sleeve of her coat. Even as he readied to mount the bay, who had grown used to him using the stirrup on the right to favor his bad leg, he fought the urge to go back, talk to her, grab her by those bird wings and shout into that lovely face, "Who am I? Who the hell am I?"

With the questions burning in his mind, Jake settled into the saddle, and toed the left stirrup onto his boot.

Fear had boiled into his throat when he'd first opened his eyes and looked up at her, dressed all in black, the wide brim of her hat shadowing those finely etched features. The pounding of his heart had nearly choked him. Why he should have been afraid he couldn't say. He only knew that terror gripped him with a steely fist. One would think he'd be used to it, coming to consciousness not knowing what had happened or where he was. It should be old hat by now, but it wasn't. Each time the panic was the same. God help him.

And so he set the mare in motion without saying a word, because he had so few choices. He didn't understand the things that had happened to him, so how could he possibly explain them to someone else? Besides, there was no need. Riding away was too simple. As the mare moved off, Jake turned his head to catch a last glimpse of the woman.

She stood in the middle of the road, arms gesturing. The wind blew her words at him. "Well, you're welcome, you ungrateful wretch. Next time sleep in the ditch, not in the middle of the danged road. Don't you know someone could run over you?"

By the time she finished shouting she had risen to her toes, one hand jamming the hat down tight, as if it might explode off her head with the eruption of her temper.

He stopped looking back and kicked the mare into a canter.

Allie stomped toward the wagon. "Next time I find somebody passed out in the damned road I'll leave him right there and drive right over the son of a bitch." Immediately she realized how ridiculous the statement was and laughed at herself. How often would she find a man lying in the middle of the trail?

She climbed back aboard the what's-it wagon and uncoiled the reins. As the mules moved off, something on the ground glimmered in the sunlight. She reined in the team and hopped down. Half buried in the red powdery dust was a small mounted picture of a beautiful young woman, a *carte de visite* once very popular but now somewhat out of date. She picked it up, rubbed her fingertips over the image to clean it and saw scratched into the corner, *Love,. Lorena. 1861*.

She turned it over, studied the back closely, looked once again at the lovely visage, features indistinct like the popular impressionistic paintings. It was Matthew Brady's work, no mistaking that. What was some down-in-the-heels drifter doing with such a lovely Brady *carte de visite*? He probably stole it. Or maybe someone else had lost it on the trail. Yet hadn't that been the name on the drifter's lips as she bent over him?

"Lorena," he'd said, like a question. "Lorena?"

No, it belonged to him all right, that was for sure. Too much of a coincidence to go any other way.

Off in the distance a fine trail of dust rose from the hooves of his mount. She ought to chase him down, but to hell with him—him and his attitude. Finally she shrugged and tucked the likeness in her pocket. The next time she saw Brady she'd ask him about it. Chances are he would remember the sitting, having an eye for such beauty as the girl Lorena possessed.

Leaving behind the Missouri Ozarks, she rode on north toward Westport and the Santa Fe Trace. Behind her lay only the ragtag remnants of home. Nothing left there but bad memories. Up ahead, out West somewhere, waited her future, and she had no patience with remembering what had gone before. That life was buried along with her mother and sister, and finally her father. Everything she had known and loved was gone, leaving her alone and on her own.

She propped one boot on the footboard and slapped the mules' behinds with the thick reins. Half the day had vanished, and she was through wasting time on thoughts of some stranger who had passed out in an inconvenient place.

But the expression in his eyes when she'd awakened him stayed with her, a haunting glimpse of poignant hope washed away by despair. She scolded herself for being so romantic. Anyway, one couldn't tell that much from a single brief glance. Such fanciful notions came from being alone too much.

That evening Jake made camp beside a creek. He untied his bedroll, emptied both saddlebags and filled a small tin with water, which he shoved into the fire. Restlessly he prowled the perimeter, rubbing at his aching thigh until the damaged muscles loosened up some. When the water began to simmer he tossed in the last of the Arbuckle coffee. Unrolling a greasy cloth, he scraped thick mold off a slice of fatback with his hunting knife, threaded the meat onto a green stick and propped it out over the flames. His stomach rolled with hunger.

In the next town he'd have to find work for a few days to replenish his supply of ammunition and food. Not that cartridges for the Spencer would do him much good; half the time he couldn't hit the broad side of a barn, let alone a fleeing rabbit or scolding squirrel. Hunger had been his companion for so long he ought to be used to it.

After eating the rancid meat, he propped his head on the saddle that smelled of leather blended with the mare's sweat and his own, and sipped at the coffee. He'd save some for breakfast, though it wouldn't taste very good after sitting near the fire all night. Overhead, stars twinkled faintly through a drift of clouds. An owl called in the warm night air. Everything he smelled or heard or touched evoked bittersweet but fleeting visions from his past.

Dammit, why couldn't he hold on to them? Pain wrenched at his heart, for a man with no past could hardly be expected to dream of a future, could he? And so he just rode on and on, one way to go being as good as another. The chance he'd run across somebody who recognized him was slim, yet in every town hope rose anew.

That woman who'd found him back there on the trail, her dark gaze as velvety as this night, reminded him more of a time than of a person. For just an instant, when he'd opened his eyes to find her leaning over him, he'd thought he was back home and the nightmare had ended. But of course that had been stupid. How could he go home when he didn't know where home was?

Hoping at least for soothing dreams from a subconscious that seemed shut off permanently, he let his eyes drift closed.

The rattling of a wagon, the clip-clop of hooves aroused him; a god-awful crash followed by explosive feminine cussing cut the darkness. Someone sure knew some dandy words. Even as he went in search of the origin of the commotion, he admired the imaginative string of expletives.

He figured he knew who was out there even before he spotted the magnificent stallion glimmering in the starlight and the black hulk of a wagon, canted at an odd angle. He could make out the woman, busily unhitching the team, having turned her verbal wrath on the two mules. They took it pretty well, considering that she was calling them slab-sided, devil-eared critters that couldn't keep their ugly eyes on the trail but had to go gawking off like cross-eyed jack rabbits with their butts on fire, dragging her and the wagon through a damned hole, for God's sake.

Jake chuckled. Lord, she had a vocabulary that would shame a drunken bull whacker. And she also had herself a major problem. It appeared that she'd lost a wheel on that strange-looking wagon she drove. Replacing a wheel was no mean feat for two strong men, let alone a woman, even though she did look and act like she could handle herself. Big gal, tough and stringy, he'd guess, though he couldn't tell much for that duster she wore over all those men's duds.

He decided to make his presence known so she wouldn't take a shot at him. "Ma'am? Ho, lady. If you'd hush up that cussing, them mules'd stand."

"What in tarnation do you know about it?" Her shout caused both animals to tauten their hindsides, and one kicked out, barely missing her.

What she said under her breath, he had a hunch was better left unheard.

He limped to their heads, talking low and sweet, and got hold of the leather harness.

"Ho, girls. Sweet girls, you don't want to make such a fuss." He held the back of a hand to one soft nose, then the other, let the animals sniff at his skin, get acquainted.

Both of the creatures huffed and dropped their heads in submission. He rubbed their noses in turn.

"Got 'em eating out of your hand, don't you?" the woman said with some sarcasm.

Jake scratched one of the mules between the eyes and she actually groaned in ecstasy. "Just got to know how to treat the ladies, I reckon," he said. "I expect you can finish what you started now without any more trouble."

"That's plumb disgusting the way they're lollygagging over you."

"Watch what you say. You'll have 'em all riled up again."

She went to work on the hitches, chains rattled and she loosed the team from the wagon. "I can handle it now, thank you. Better not have broken any of my plates."

"Oh, you're welcome. But I thought I might just stick around and see how you figure on getting that wheel back on, if it ain't busted, that is. 'Course if it is, that's another story."

She moved up beside him till he could smell the womanly fragrance in her hair and clothes, and something else he couldn't quite place, a chemical odor of some kind. Her proximity was disturbing and he took a quick step back. And what was that she'd said about her plates? She had more to worry about than a few broken dishes.

Apparently, she took her first good look at him in the darkness. "You're the man from before."

"Before what?"

"The one I found sprawled all over the road. The one who rode off without so much as a thank you after I saved his bacon."

"Was there a stage coming, or maybe a stampede?"

"Smart ass."

Jake laughed again. That was twice in one evening. He'd have to be careful. Too much jocularity wasn't good for a man in his condition.

"You were very rude," she said.

"I beg your pardon, I truly do. I guess I just don't know how to act around folks. I thank you for saving my bacon, ma'am." He touched the brim of his hat but didn't remove it.

"You don't have to be such a smart mouth."

"Smart ass. Smart mouth. Anything else about me you find intelligent?"

"You know, it wouldn't bother me much if you just went back to wherever you came from and left me the hell alone."

He shrugged and leaned forward to steady the singletree while she unhooked one of the mules.

"What day is it?" he asked.

"You mean, day of the week?"

"No, date, month, year."

"You don't know?"

"I'm just trying to see if you're in your right mind. Humor me."

"May 3, 1866."

He nodded. That was a relief. At least he'd quit losing time. For a while there days, sometimes whole weeks, would disappear into the void of his faulty memory.

"Well, is that right?" she asked impatiently.

"I reckon it is. Look, ma'am, it's awful dark out here to try and fix that wheel tonight. I've got me a little camp just yonder by the creek. I'll share my last cup of coffee with you and you can bed down across the fire. I'm harmless, I promise you, and in the morning I'll help you get that wheel back on."

"No man is harmless. That's why I carry this," she said, and whipped out a wicked-looking revolver, just like she might know how to use it. Thankfully, she didn't point it at him, but simply held it up so he could see its black barrel gleam in the starlight.

"Your point is well taken, ma'am. Join me or not, as you wish."

The owl hooted again and something scurried through the underbrush. Her stallion danced and whinnied before she finally replied.

"Just let me get a light and check inside the wagon, make sure none of my chemicals have spilled." She poked around inside the thing for a while, he saw a match flare and a lantern glowing. After a few minutes, she climbed down carrying the light. "Everything's fine. Packed those plates real good. Don't know how long it'd take to get some more sent out from back East."

"Feller could always just buy an old common plate in a general store. They might be nearly as good as those you could get from back East."

She chuckled. "Not that kind of plate. Photographic plates. I'm a photographer. I take pictures."

"Ah." He was dumbstruck. He'd seen some men photographers toting around those big awkward cameras, but never thought about a woman doing it. Before he could ask, she spoke again.

"Help me lead these dumb animals down there, or one of 'em is apt to fall in a hole and break its leg," she said.

Cheerfully he took hold of the two mules and left her to fetch the stallion. It was nice having someone around, brief though it would probably be. Once she saw him at his worst she'd light out.

Together they staked the animals out near feed and water. The mare he called Molly kicked up such a ruckus they tied her out of reach of Ringo.

"Sorry about that," he said. "I'm afraid she isn't broke to company, especially the male variety."

Allie thought the same of herself, but didn't say so. Instead she produced supplies from the wagon, and said, "Oh, Ringo's randy all the time, like most men." Immediately she wanted to bite her tongue. She didn't even know this man's name, and to say a thing like that to him embarrassed her. She did the only thing she could think of and asked him who the hell he was.

"Jake," he told her tersely.

"Just Jake."

"No, not Just Jake. Jake. My name is Jake."

"Jake what?"

"Not Jake What, either."

"Smart ass."

"You told me so once already. Look, Jake is enough, and what's yours?"

"Allie. Allison Caine." She glared at him across the fire.

"Well, Allison Caine, I'll tell you something if you won't breathe a word of it to anyone."

She looked all around to emphasize that there was no one to tell. "Agreed."

"I'm on a secret mission for the government and that's why I can't reveal my identity."

"Bull hockey."

He threw back his head and laughed again.

She liked the sound of that, yet thought he surprised himself each time it happened, like he hadn't laughed in a very long time.

"You're not going to tell me, are you?" she finally asked after his laughter died away.

"Nope, can't."

"Can't?"

"Nope."

"Okay, then, fine. I'll just call you Jake, then."

He looked at her a long time across the fire, tiny flames dancing in the brilliant blue of his eyes. "That'll be good, Allie."

A vague, frightening desire passed through her, and she replied in a sharp, biting tone. "You can call me Miss Caine."

He grinned, one corner of his full lips quirking. "Miss Caine. I'll be happy to do that. And thanks for the extra grub. My supplies have run a mite low."

"Always happy to share. You'll pay me back tomorrow when we fix that wheel."

Allie snuggled down in the bedroll and pulled the wool blanket up under her chin. Dammit to hell, she hadn't wanted to take up with anyone, much less a man. She needed time to recover from her father's death and the sense of guilt that weighed so heavily on her soul. And just as much, she needed to forget Eli and his betrayal, just when she'd needed him most. Yet she felt a companionship with this man. He had a peculiar sense of humor, even though he was a bit rough around the edges. She wondered if he was on the run from the law, but dismissed that possibility. That tended to make a man jumpy, and Jake was certainly well relaxed. He didn't even have a revolver, and the Spencer he carried remained in its scabbard alongside his saddle, not at hand like he might anticipate using it.

He had jumped and run from her earlier, and that had been suspicious. Something had changed his mind, though, and he appeared almost happy to have her company. She was pleased to have his, at least temporarily, for replacing the wheel was not a job one man could do, and certainly not a woman alone.

She feared that wasn't the only reason, but decided not to investigate those feelings. As soon as the wheel was fixed, she'd send him on his way.

Sighing, she turned over and drifted into sleep.

Jake, his saddle and mare were gone when she awoke. She stormed about the camp awhile. He was glad enough to wolf down her food the night before, only to slip off like a blamed coward when he sensed hard work ahead. She should have expected it. Men tended to desert women. She supposed that was just bred into them.

Tears burned her eyes and she moved to the creek to splash cold water over her face.

As she rose she heard a great clamor coming from the direction of her wagon. She hurried back to camp, snatched up her Colt and went to investigate.

She found Jake aboard the mare, and he had rigged up the darndest contraption. A rope hung over the highest branch of a nearby tree and was looped around the rear axle assembly. The mules were harnessed and tied to the other end of the rope.

"Hey, wait a minute," she shouted.

"Morning, ma'am. I was wondering if you were going to join us. I may need your help." He kicked free of the stirrups and slid off the mare. The wheel that had fallen into the ditch leaned up against the side of the wagon. He limped toward it, grinning at her.

21

"Broke the pin. Only damage I can see. Spindle and hub both seem okay. No busted spokes either. Don't suppose you've got any spare parts and tools?"

"As a matter of fact, I do. Up under the seat. Fella advised me about what to carry. Being a woman, I couldn't be expected to know." She started to swing up onto the wagon.

"Careful there, I wouldn't make any startling moves. Those mules are anxious to do their job. Ho, girls. Steady," he crooned in the animals' direction.

She eyed the setup. "You sure this'll work?"

"Nope, but it ought to. See, as the mules move forward, pulling on the rope, it'll have to lift the wagon up off the ground. And when it does, we'll just slip that thing right back where she belongs, slick as can be. Blamed pin just came loose and fell out, no telling where, and so the wheel worked its way off. Need to check 'em occasionally in the future. That's for your edification, being a woman and all."

She glared at him, thought about hurling the tool kit at his head, but reconsidered when she realized how heavy it was.

He reached up, swung it easily to the ground and opened the lid.

Studying the dangerous contraption he'd rigged, a fleeting fear rippled through her. Did he fall flat on his face very often like he had back there on the road? And if so, suppose he did it just as everything was moving into place. There he'd lie, leaving her to figure out what to do next. He didn't give her time to ponder, but made his way to the mules. Bunching up their reins, he urged them forward.

"Easy now, girls. Don't overdo it. Giddy up there, whoa. How's it doing?"

Allie dragged her fascinated gaze from him and glanced at the wagon. "It's working—it's coming up."

"Watch it, then, and tell me when it's good. Then roll that wheel over. Soon as you can, ease her on and give me a shout."

She nodded.

"Did you hear me?"

"Yes." She rolled the wheel closer. It was heavy and took all her strength to move but she got the job done. Inch by slow inch the mules lifted the rear corner of the wagon until she could slide the cumbersome wheel into place.

"How you doing?" he shouted.

"It's there, but I can't get it all the way on—it's too heavy."

Immediately he was at her back, his own arms spanning her and the large wheel, and with a final mighty heave they shoved it onto the spindle. He lurched against her, transferring heat and strength from his body. Taut thighs rippled against hers, his arms remained around her and she wanted loose, wanted away from his embrace because she didn't like what she was feeling, not one bit.

He appeared not to notice, but said, "Okay, you go hold their heads. Keep 'em standing till I get the pin in place and the washer and nut on. We don't want 'em taking off on us. No telling what might happen."

She was forced to slide under his arm and steadied herself by putting one hand on his bulging muscle. It was like touching bands of iron fresh from a forge.

"Ma'am," he said as she ducked free. "Don't rush up on those mules or you might be digging me a grave."

"No, I won't. And you don't take a dive right now, either."

He grinned, eyes as bright a blue as cornflowers, with a sparkle like sunlight on a creek. A rivulet of sweat trickled from under his hair and ran through the dark stubble along his jaw. His maleness filled her nostrils, his breath washed over her face. Danger—and his enjoyment of it—sent thrills of excitement through her.

She had almost forgotten her warning when he replied in a light and sassy tone, "I'll do my best not to. Go on, now. But real, real easy."

Lips tight, she nodded and moved cautiously toward the mules, talking to them like he did, even mimicking the words he used.

Rope held taut as a bowstring, the animals stood fast and rolled their eyes as she eased to where they could see her well.

Perspiration broke out on her face, even though the morning was cool and dew-kissed. She heard a dull thunk from behind, and was afraid to look. One of the mules twitched an ear and shuffled her front feet.

Allie's heart lurched in her chest. "Ho, sweetheart. Stand easy. Whoa, girl." She held out a hand slowly so that the animal would lean forward to investigate, and wished she'd thought to pull some grass. Then she wound her fingers firmly around the leather and steadied their heads.

It seemed forever before he shouted, "Okay, Miss Caine, you can back 'em down."

Her breath came out in a whoosh! And she did as he'd said, then leaned forward onto the nearest mule's back because her knees were trembling so badly they wouldn't hold her up.

Jake came up behind her, and she whirled and threw her arms around his neck. "We did it! We did it!"

He tensed against the embrace, as if she'd struck him, then firmly removed her arms. "We surely did, but we'd better get these ropes undone before these mules take off and flip that wagon over on its back. Then we'd have us a real dilemma." He sent her a quick grin. "That would break your plates for sure."

As much embarrassed by hugging him as by his reaction to the gesture, she took a fast step backward. Together they untied the rope and hitched the mules to the wagon.

Eyes dancing, he glanced at her and asked, "Reckon we broke any of your plates?"

She sensed he wanted something from her, but wasn't sure what it was. It didn't matter, though, for no matter what he needed, she didn't have it to give. Where men were concerned, she was all used up.

Chapter Two

All morning he rode far out ahead of her on the trail, but always in sight. Without consulting her, he found a suitable nooning spot, and she came upon him leaning against a tree. She wanted to ride on, not even look his way, yet she reined in the team and gratefully climbed down, as if he had cast some kind of spell on her. He grinned, but said nothing, just fetched wood and water and built a fire.

Going about her own chores, Allie couldn't help but glance his way. In spite of the limp he accomplished a lot with little effort. He was so pitifully thin that she pulled out all the stops preparing their noon meal, trying to ignore the familiar lecture running through her head.

Just like a woman to take pleasure in waiting on a man. And what had she just told herself? That she wanted nothing to do with him, that he could be on his way. But what did she do but open one of her precious jars of canned peaches brought from home. After that morning's work with the wagon wheel, he deserved a meal that would stick to his bones.

Samantha Lee

"Go ahead, Allie," she muttered to herself even as she did so. "Pick up a stray and see where it gets you."

To add to the disgust she felt, she mixed up biscuits, nested them in the Dutch oven, and piled hot coals over its cast-iron top. Then she peeled the last of the potatoes salvaged from her cellar and sliced them into sizzling grease. While that cooked she cut several thick chunks off a cured, smoked ham and spread them on top of the potatoes to heat. She decided she ought to be proud of her own foolishness, and wondered where Jake had gotten to.

He had been down at the creek for a long time, and she began to wonder if he might have fallen in when she heard him coming back, whistling "When Johnny Comes Marching Home." A Union song. She and her family had been caught up between the two sides in the war, and merely surviving had curtailed any sympathy she might have felt for either the Yankees or Johnny Reb. She had watched bushwhackers murder her mother and sister. They'd worn no uniforms at all, yet that evil war had birthed them.

The song cut off midway, and she glanced up to see him sniffing the air. "Tell me I'm not dreaming. Is that ham and biscuits I smell?"

"You'd better like it, too."

He ignored her grumpy mood. "Oh, I'll like it. This is kind of you. I think I've died and gone to heaven." He squatted awkwardly beside the fire and gazed into the skillet of potatoes and meat.

"There's some coffee left over from breakfast. Want some red-eye gravy?" The look on his face when she asked the question was all the answer she needed. It was difficult to stay annoyed at someone so easy to please.

With some effort he stood and rubbed his leg from the thigh down to the knee. "Good thing you come along when you did, or I'd a gone without coffee today. Figure, next town I'll do some work for supplies."

Allie studied him closely. He'd bathed and scrubbed his neck until it was red. His dark hair shimmered with blue highlights and was still damp and curled at the ends. The thin shirt hugged his shoulders, beads of dampness holding the fabric tightly. Before she could stop herself she thought of him naked in the cold water. She rubbed at her flushed throat and turned quickly away.

Nervously she wiped both hands down the sides of her jeans and felt her thighs trembling. This had to stop. She struggled with her next words. No telling what might happen if she didn't keep the conversation going. "You live hand-to-mouth like this all the time?"

"What do you mean?"

"Well, man like you, looks like you could get permanent work somewhere. Get a decent place to live and fill your larder."

"I gotta be on the move."

She couldn't keep her eyes off him. There was a sadness in his expression that no amount of bantering could disguise. She wondered what terrible things had happened to him. There were plenty of men wandering around just like him. Returning from the war, some with nowhere to go because the home place had been burned or ransacked by the other side. Some turned to bushwhacking or robbing banks, others just roamed around, lost and bereft. She could sympathize; none had suffered worse than her own family.

She must have stared at him too long, for he shifted nervously, glanced at her wagon, attempted to change the subject. "I never thought I'd meet a woman photographer."

It was fine with her if he wanted to talk about something else. "Oh, there's quite a few of us really. Some do it because they're bored, their husbands are rich and they need something to keep them occupied. Others are serious—we want to make a difference, take pictures of things that folks might be interested in looking at, something that will last long after we've passed on.

"I'm headed west to open a studio. Plenty of people back East want to enjoy photographs in the comfort of their own parlors. I understand there's a real need and I intend to fill it. Besides, I can earn my way along the trail without anyone's help. Always someone somewhere with coin enough to pay for having their picture taken." She grinned. "Sometimes I sell a picture for a cured ham or some eggs or a chicken."

"And you aren't afraid to go it alone?" He leaned forward, inspecting the potatoes. "Reckon these need to be turned? Wouldn't want them to burn."

"Oh, don't worry, they won't. I don't have much choice about being alone. That's the situation, and for a long time it's what I needed." Without admitting that meeting him might have changed what she wanted, she fetched a large spatula and turned the potatoes, letting the ham go to the bottom to brown. "Sorry there's no cream for the red-eye."

When she turned to look at him, he was staring at her as if in a daze, his blue eyes clouded and distant. "Hey, you okay?" she asked.

He twitched, came back from wherever it was he had gone. "Sorry, what did you say?"

"Never mind. I'll just use pure coffee. Father always preferred it that way. I like a splash of thick cream as well."

She blinked her eyes quickly, for the reference to her father had brought unexpected tears. She'd thought them all cried out, after having spent weeks breaking into sobs at the most unlikely times. The tears hadn't begun when he had died, but rather later as she stood beside the grave while clods of earth thunked down on his coffin. Finally they had stopped and she had felt wrung out, as if nothing in the world could ever make her weep again.

"I suppose we all have memories," she murmured, and blinked the moisture away to smile at Jake. This man was having the oddest effect on her emotions.

"Wish we did," he said, then turned and limped away before she could ask for an explanation of the strange statement.

When the meal was ready, Jake fell to the food like a starving man. Fork in one hand, knife in the other, he cut up the ham, split a biscuit and poured red-eye gravy over it, then proceeded to clean the tin plate of every morsel. He didn't say a word, but uttered little sounds of pleasure occasionally. She was so entranced by watching him that she ignored her own food.

"My God, that was good," he finally said when he'd swallowed the last bite. His gaze darted toward the skillet perched on a rock near the fire, a double handful of potatoes still in it.

"Take them," she urged. "And another biscuit, too. I made plenty." Actually she'd hoped to have enough for supper so she wouldn't have to cook again that evening, but since she had started going soft in the head over this man, she could deny him nothing. She had planned to take some photographs that afternoon while the light was good, then travel late into the evening. Instead she said, "Save yourself one last biscuit for the peaches. They're juicy and sweet, just right for sopping."

Had she gone quite mad? Considering her recent actions, it was a distinct possibility.

Bent over, dishing the potatoes onto his plate, he paused and gazed at her. "Peaches?"

She nodded and laughed, suddenly very content. How wonderful to come alive again. "You look like you just saw a naked woman," she told him.

To her amazement he turned bright red. That made her laugh some more. "Why, Jake, I do think I've embarrassed you."

"I'll just eat these here potatoes and clean up for you. No need you cooking and cleaning both." He went to shoveling potatoes into his mouth and wouldn't look at her. With the last bite swallowed, though, he looked her right in the eye. "But not till I eat me some of those peaches, if you wouldn't mind."

He finished off the entire quart.

While he cleaned the dishes and packed everything away, she set up the heavy camera on its wooden legs and ducked beneath the black cloth to take a look through the lens. The view up the creek was irresistible—white water shimmering in afternoon sunlight and trees bowed as if they were drinking. After she lined up just the shot she wanted, she came out from under the cloth to prepare a glass plate in the portable dark box. The tangy smell of chemicals transported her into her very own world where everything was orderly and precise, undisturbed by sadness or anger or the tragedies of life.

Jake had finished his work and sauntered over to stand beside her.

"When we first met I thought that was your perfume," he said after a while.

Both hands thrust into the black sleeves of the dark box, she nodded. "Oh, yes, I suppose in a way it is. It helps me remember how much I've always enjoyed doing this. Makes me think of how my father taught me, how patient he was, how loving, how much we went through together. He was so proud that I wanted to follow in his footsteps. He had no sons, you see, and my sister and mother had . . . well, they . . . " She swallowed harshly.

Jake leaned over to peer through the small red window down into the box. Her hands were trembling as they held the glass plate. "Hey, don't drop it. You okay?"

"Sure, silly of me. What's past is gone. What's done is done. Foolish to cry over it."

He remained quiet for a moment, then asked. "Did they die?"

"Yes." She dipped the treated plate into a deep bath of silver nitrate, pulled one arm free and drew her father's watch from her vest to time the immersion.

He remained silent as she watched the minute hand advance past three. She glanced up, caught him staring at her with a sober expression and grinned so he would, too. "Done, now sit right over there, on that rock." She slipped the plate into its light-free box.

He spread a hand over his chest. "Me?"

"You see anyone else? I want you in the picture and there's where you'll sit. Come on, move it or this won't be any good."

"I don't know why you'd want a picture of me," he grumbled, but went nevertheless to perch on the rock as if it were a wild mustang that might buck him off at any moment. He frowned in her direction.

"Well, I don't want you looking like such an old sourpuss. Look at me the way you did when I told you I had peaches."

"I don't know how I looked."

"Like this," she said, and tried to show him.

"Good God, that's about as silly as anything I ever saw."

"Well, come to think of it you did look sort of goofy. Just look over yonder as if you've just seen the most wonderful sight in the world. Maybe someone you haven't seen in a long time just walked up and you're catching a first glimpse of her."

"Her?"

"Yes, her. Quit being so stubborn." She slipped the plate into the camera and ducked under the black cloth. "Okay, are you ready?"

He smiled and turned a little toward her. She stuck her hand out from under the drape and removed the lens covering. "Sit still now, don't move till I tell you or it'll blur." She watched him through the lens for a few seconds longer, then slipped the cap back on. "Done. It'll be perfect."

"I don't see how."

She came out from under the cloth and glanced at him. "Because you are a perfect subject, that's how."

Jake stared blankly at her, then fell off the rock.

For a moment she stood locked in place and gaped at him, not believing what had happened. Then she ran to where he lay, curled up on the ground as if he were asleep. She knelt beside him and touched his face.

"Jake, what is it? What's wrong? Are you all right? Jake." She shook him, but he was limp as an old rag. What had caused this?

He appeared much as he had the very first time she'd ever seen him passed out cold in the middle of the road. A thin sheen of sweat covered his face and he felt cool. He didn't react to either her voice or touch. What in the world could be wrong with him?

The exposed glass plate waited. She had to get it into its chemical bath. He could lie there. Obviously he did this frequently with no lasting consequences. She cast a final look at him and made up her mind.

"Well, I'm no nursemaid, so what does he expect?" she grumbled, then pulled the plate from the black box, treated it and headed for the creek to get a pan of water to wash it. She spared a quick glance in Jake's direction. He slept on as if retired for the night.

While she washed the plate thoroughly in the pan she'd filled, the cold water biting at her hands, she imagined the situations her companion might find himself in. He could fall off a bar stool in a saloon and they'd only think him drunk and sweep him out with others of the same persuasion. Suppose he was riding that long-legged bay through a river and took a header. Would the water bring him around or would he just float merrily along until he washed up somewhere or drowned? The possibilities of dire results were numerous. He ought to be in a hospital or at least under a doctor's care.

She carried the plate carefully back to the wagon where she got busy developing the glass negative onto albumen-coated paper. Jake would just have to lie there awhile. He did, after all, look quite comfortable. And she had to come to her senses and stop worrying about him.

She had several pictures hanging to dry when she heard him stumbling about outside.

"I see your legs. Can I come in?" he asked.

"Too crowded, I'll come out. I'm finished."

"Is it a picture yet?" He acted as if nothing had happened.

"Oh, yes."

She lifted the cloth and ducked under it, narrowing her eyes against the bright sunlight. "You okay? I'm sorry if I just let you lie there. It was you or the photo and the photo won. I haven't ever been around to take care of you before this."

He blinked at her. "Is it a good likeness? Could I see it?"

"Yes, of course." She touched his arm. "Jake, what happened to you?"

"When? Yesterday, last week or last month?"

"Let's make it simple. Thirty minutes ago would do, for starters."

"What difference does it make? You don't know me. I helped you fix a wagon wheel, you didn't take me to raise. Let's just forget it, all right? You were right to leave me there. Nothing you could do anyway. I want to see the picture."

"All right, I'll show it to you. And then I'm going to show you another one you might be interested in. That's only because you helped me out when you could have just ridden on. And then maybe that's what you ought to do: Ride on. It makes me nervous to be around a man who just pitches over on his face at the drop of a hat, and then won't talk to me about it." She squared her shoulders, determined to stick to her guns no matter what her heart told her.

"Fine, all right. I didn't intend to stick with you anyway. I've got places to be."

The tone in his voice made her ashamed but she stuck with her decision. This man would only be trouble, she could see that, yet . . . Annoyed, she lifted the dark curtain on the wagon and took out a piece of wet paper. On it was a fine black-and-white likeness of Jake. The wind had touched his hair so that it blurred a little around his face, but the crooked grin, the damnably attractive gauntness and the distant gaze in his smoky eyes were all captured to perfection. Behind him, moving tree leaves left more blurs, but the view along the creek bank, with its plays of shadows and light, had been recreated as if by the hand of a talented artist.

He studied his own face for a long while. "Is that really me— what I truly look like?"

"Yes, of course. Don't you know that?"

"I guess not." He seemed awe-stricken.

She had seen that reaction before from men on the battlefield who had been exposed to horrors that had forever changed their countenances. Until her father took their photographs they had no idea what the war had done to them. Could it be possible that he had not seen his own reflection in so long a while that he had no idea what he looked like?

"Where have you been? My God, Jake, where have you been?"

He flicked his gaze away from the black-and-white image of himself and his blue eyes filled with moisture. "I wish I knew, Miss Caine. I wish to hell I knew," he said, his hand trembling.

She took the picture from him, closed her other hand over his to still its shaking, and damned herself in the process. She wanted to run. God, how she wanted to run. Instead she whispered, "Call me Allie. Please call me Allie." She let his hand slide from hers and took the picture inside the wagon.

Inside, surrounded by darkness and the soothing odors of her trade, she squeezed her eyes over hot tears, refusing to let them flow. This time she would not let herself love. This time she would be wise and hard. Hard as nails. How she planned to manage that she had no idea.

All the rest of that day they moved briskly along the trail, stopping when it intersected with another and studying the map she carried.

"This road we're on leads to Westport on the Missouri River." She pointed to the black line that marked Santa Fe Trace.

Jake squinted at the map. "It begins right there, the trace?"

"Actually, back East. It's the longest trail in this country and the oldest, too. A leg comes down from Fort Leavenworth to the Oregon Trail Junction."

"And you're going to Santa Fe?"

"Yes."

"Why?"

She smiled and rolled up the thick brown paper, tying a string around it as she considered his question. "I'm not sure I know what you mean. Why am I going to Santa Fe, as opposed to what?"

"Why would you take off by yourself and pick that particular place? Do you know someone there? Did someone go there and come back and tell you how wonderful it is? Why pick that settlement over others?"

"Actually, someone did tell me about Santa Fe. A traveling photographer who had passed through there. He showed me some of his early photographs of the desert, and they haunt me still. There's something spiritual about the land. It's the light. Streaks of color—scarlets, golds, pinks—can almost be seen in the black-and-white reproductions.

"He told me of the need for my line of work in that part of the country. I want to open up a business, make my home there, get a fresh start away from all the memories of the war, the killings, the stench of blood. It's soaked into the land here in Missouri so that it may never wash away. I can smell it in every breath I take—the death and the senseless destruction. I just can't stand to live here anymore, beautiful as it is. In my mind it will forever be tainted by that awful war."

She hadn't intended to reveal so much to this stranger who apparently had enough problems of his own, and because the outburst embarrassed her, she tried to move back onto the wagon seat away from his searching gaze.

He touched her arm and she let his hand remain there a moment before jerking free.

"Let's get moving. I'd like to make the Osage River by the end of the week." She felt angry, sounded angry, and so he moved off to mount up without saying anything.

It was none of his business anyway, what had happened to her. And telling him just formed another bond she didn't welcome. Why didn't he just ride on ahead? He had no wagon to slow him down, and could make much better time than she.

Why was he tagging along with her in the first place? She would ask him if her throat weren't so clogged with emotion.

Jake dropped back to ride behind the odd wagon. He couldn't bear the sensation of her eyes stabbing into his back. Perhaps he would go his own way soon, leave her to make her way as best she could. It was foolish, anyway, how he had latched on to the woman after riding alone for all these months. He hated to admit it, but she gave him purpose. She had a specific thing to do and a place to go, and as long as he remained with her, he could pretend that was his goal, as well. Once he rode away all he had was his blind search for Lorena or someone who might recognize him.

Idly he moved his fingers to the pocket of his jacket. Strange how he hadn't felt the urge to look at the picture since meeting Allie Caine. His finger stirred around in the empty pocket. It was gone! He halted the mare, searched some more.

It wasn't there. The picture of Lorena, the woman he couldn't remember but was sure he had loved. The only thing he had left of his previous existence. What could have happened to it? Dammit, he'd lost it back on the trail. He tried to remember the last time he'd looked at it but couldn't.

Of course you can't, fool. How could you remember something like that when you don't even know your own damn name? Or what day it is. Or what the hell you're going to do with the rest of your life.

He leaned his head back, stared up into the afternoon sky and sensed it begin to whirl around him, and then night closed in and the last thing he remembered thinking was, "Maybe this time I'll break my damn fool neck."

The stallion snorted and Allie leaned out to glance back. Jake was no longer riding behind her. Far back on the trail, she saw his bay mare, and lying beside her on the ground, a crumpled heap. He'd done it again.

She sighed and reined in the mules. Up ahead the empty trail beckoned. She should just ride on, leave him there. Obviously he'd been doing this for a long while. He acted as if he was unaware of his plunges into unconsciousness, but she was pretty sure that wasn't true. Nobody passed out with regularity and didn't know it. He must have his own reasons for ignoring such unusual behavior.

Maybe there would be a doctor in Westport and she could talk Jake into seeing him. What she'd thought at first, that the man was suffering from lack of food, could no longer be true. He'd been eating well since they joined up. And, since they were together, she couldn't bring herself to just ride off and leave him helpless like that. So she fetched the canteen, hopped down and trudged back to where he lay.

He had landed on his stomach and one side of his face. When she turned him over, there was a cut on his cheek and some blood coagulated in the coating of dust.

"Oh, you poor thing," she murmured as she cleaned the wound. He was like a child, wandering around in the wilderness, letting what happened happen, as if he were helpless to do anything about it, as indeed it seemed he was.

She had seen men wounded and out of their heads, milling about in search of home after the war was over. Some would never be the same because of that terrible conflict. Perhaps that was what had happened to Jake. A desire to help him didn't really surprise her, considering the past few days. There might be, after all, some caring left in her soul. He wasn't Eli Martin, and she must continue to remind herself of that, lest she take out her hatred on Jake. His vulnerability made him easy pickings for a vengeful woman.

The object of her thoughts groaned and opened his eyes.

She lifted his head, put the canteen to his mouth. "Here, drink."

"Aw, hell," he said, and took a deep swallow. He shifted and sat up.

"Want me to help you?"

"I'll just sit a minute."

She nodded, bit at her lip and capped the canteen. "You need to see someone about that."

"Did, no one has any idea."

"Doctors?"

"Three different ones in as many places. I'm not illiterate, just stubborn. Their best guess is it's something pressing on my brain and it'll probably kill me one of these days. But hell, in this country there's lots of things that will probably kill me one of these days." He grinned up at her, and the expression tugged at her heart. Then, when he reached out a hand so she could help him stand, she was truly overcome with emotion. Something about the gesture, him being so trusting, so wholly dependent upon her willingness to lend him a hand, broke through her earlier resolution to be rid of him.

On his feet, he favored the bad leg for a moment and she steadied him by stepping under his arm.

"I guess I'm kind of battered," he said. "Could have done better for yourself than picking up a drifter like me."

"You fix a hell of a wagon wheel, though. You gonna get on that horse or you want to hop back and ride in the wagon with me for a while?"

"Truth be known, I don't think I can do either. Sorry, must have twisted my leg." He doubled up his fist and she thought for a moment that he would strike the bothersome leg, but he just rubbed it. The muscles in his arm that hung across her shoulder tensed with the effort of trying to walk, and from deep down in his throat came a husky string of curses.

She faced him, put her other arm around him and rested her head against his shoulder. For an instant he leaned into her, his breath coming hot against her neck, strands of his hair tickling her cheek.

Neither of them said anything during that brief embrace, but something passed between them. Allie sensed the moment and was frightened by it, for it was not the earlier pity, nor even her

38

considered compassion, but another deeper emotion that could very well bind them together if she wasn't very careful.

"Allie," he whispered against her skin, then forcefully pushed himself away, as if he, too, sensed the danger of what had happened.

She wiped her face with the wet bandanna she'd used to clean his cheek. "I'll bring the wagon back. Let's just get you over there on that rock in the shade."

He nodded and let her support him, grunting with each careful step on the injured leg.

When she moved away from him, he said, "Allie, I'm sorry about this. Come tomorrow, I'll just move on. No need to hold you up. It'll be best."

She didn't reply, knowing he was right but not sure she could let him go. Until only a few moments ago, she would have been relieved at his plan to leave. Now, because something had happened that she couldn't even explain, she knew she would never rest an easy minute knowing he was out there plunging around from pillar to post, maybe getting hurt or killed, and her not knowing, never knowing what had become of him.

She remembered then that she hadn't shown him the Brady reproduction of the woman, Lorena, that he'd lost in the dust earlier. It was down in one of the pockets of her coat.

Because of the warmth of the day, she had removed the duster and so she fetched it, then turned the wagon around and headed back to where he waited. As soon as they got him up on the wagon seat, she would show him the thing and have it over with.

She wondered why it might be so important who the woman was and what she meant to this wandering man.

Chapter Three

Waiting for Allie to bring the wagon, Jake pressed the heels of both hands against his temples. His ears roared and the damn leg throbbed until lights flickered on the edge of his vision.

Why didn't this blasted thing just kill him and get it over with?

He heard the muffled clop-clop of the mules' hooves stirring dust as they moved toward him.

She was coming back for him, and he didn't understand why. Best if she just rode like hell in the opposite direction. Obviously she'd had troubles aplenty of her own, and didn't need more. He'd met men in prison who just begged to be punished, on and on forever, like they'd done something terrible and deserved all the ill treatment the fates could dish out. It hadn't mattered that they were guilty only of being on the wrong side. She didn't appear to be one of those, yet she kept touching him and looking at him with those cave-deep eyes, brushing that golden mane of hair away from her face with a gesture so innocently endearing he knew he would never forget it, no matter where he went.

It was ironic—but reassuring—to know there was something he would remember, come what might.

She moved up beside him and he raised his head, opened his eyes. Sunlight framed her like a shimmering halo and cast her face into full shadow; the wind played with her hair. An elusive fragrance worried at the edges of his memory.

"Lorena?" he whispered and reached for her. "Where have you been so long?"

When he put her hand to his warm, moist lips, Allie shivered and dropped to her knees in front of him.

"Oh, Jake, what's wrong with you? Who are you and where have you come from? I can't do this, and yet I can't not do it. Damn you, damn you to hell for needing me so."

She leaned into the circle of his warmth, pulled his head to her shoulder and held on, trying not to think of Papa and willing away the ghost of the man who had once loved her and deserted her when she needed him the most.

Jake wrapped his arms around her until she could scarcely breathe, whispering Lorena's name, panting raggedly against her neck. Then the stubble on his cheek scraped across her tender skin, and he turned ever so slightly, found her lips with his. The kiss was tender, his mouth a silken trap trembling with desire.

For a moment she responded with all the passion she had ever possessed. He had taken her by surprise, as had her unexpected hunger. In that instant she needed him as much as he needed her.

Even as she spiraled into his world she fought against the desire. He would devour her just as Eli had. Devour her and abandon her, leaving a dark, hollow cavern in her soul when he deserted her. Just like Eli . . . just like Papa.

With both hands she shoved hard against his chest. Obviously as shocked as she, he let go and gazed at her with surprise.

Lips agleam with her kiss, he said, "I didn't . . . I don't . . . please forgive me. I didn't mean to do that. My God, what's wrong with me? I'm sorry, Allie. Truly sorry." He licked her taste away.

She touched her mouth with the back of one hand, shook her head vehemently. "No, it's okay. It was my fault, too. My fault. I . . . " The rest of the words washed away in the enormity of her emotions. He had reached deep within her heart, torn at it with such an intensity that she felt ripped free from reality.

He sat there staring at her without saying any more.

She wanted to scream at him to leave her be. Stop looking at her like that, stop, for God's sake, needing her. And never, never kiss her like that again. Shaken, she managed to move out of his reach and stand. "Think you can make it up on the wagon seat?"

He didn't answer, but let her help him to his feet and support him the few steps. With the incredible strength of his arms, he hoisted himself onto the seat. Pale skin and a sweaty brow evidenced the pain he was in, but he made no sound except to breathe harshly.

After tying his mare to the back of the wagon, she climbed up beside him, stole a glance in his direction and decided the photograph of Lorena could wait. He was in no condition to deal with it.

Picking up the reins, she set the mules in motion. "We'll stop soon for the night. It's late anyway, and you're in no shape to travel too far tonight."

"I'm all right. I don't want to hold you up—there's no reason we can't go on till dark."

In truth he did sound stronger, but nevertheless, she stopped at the first good spot that provided grass for the animals, water and some sheltering trees.

He came down off the wagon favoring his good leg, but moving about, though slowly, to help with the chores of unhitching the mules and staking out the animals. Almost as if nothing had ever happened. As if he hadn't been hurt or kissed her or made her grieve inside for love lost. When she began to forage for dry wood for a fire he lent a hand, and she marveled at how tough he was.

"You know, that might get to feeling better if you'd let your leg rest awhile," she told him.

"Just the opposite, I sit around too long the damn thing won't work at all. It'll loosen back up. This isn't the first time I've taken a header off a horse."

She couldn't help but laugh. Perhaps it was simply a release of tension because he was being so casual.

His curious glance made her ashamed.

"I'm sorry, I didn't mean to laugh at your problems. It's just that you say that so casually, like saying your feet are big or something equally unimportant."

He dropped a stick of wood and leaned down to retrieve it, looking with mock exaggeration at his scuffed boots. "I reckon I do have big feet, too, but it never caused me much concern."

"Obviously neither does this thing that happens to you. You just go on like it didn't exist. I'd think you'd be careful and not put yourself in a position where you could be hurt when it happens."

He considered her thoughtfully. "One doc wanted to send me to some big medical hospital in St. Louis so they could study me, poke around and find out what was going on up there." He pointed to his head with a stick of wood. "I said no. I'd rather fall off a horse and die than lie in one of their beds for years with them sticking me with needles and finally killing me anyway.

"The way I look at it, when it comes it comes. I'll be sorry if it causes anyone any undue stress, but hell, someone could shoot me right in front of you this very minute and that'd be bad as well. On you, I mean."

She laughed. "And on you too, I'd wager. But you're right, of course. And don't worry about causing me stress. I think I must have been made to care for someone else. I've been doing it most of my life, and I haven't exactly run the other way." She looked down at the ground for a long while, then lifted her head to catch him studying her. "I'm not running now, but I'm not exactly sure why not."

"Maybe you ought to. I don't need you taking care of me like a damned nurse."

"Don't use that tone with me. I haven't done anything but be decent to you, a total stranger. Next time you end up on your face I'll just leave you to lie in the hot sun and bake." The quiver in her voice made her angrier.

Why didn't she walk away? They stood toe to toe, carrying on the verbal battle without either of them raising their voices. It was as if she couldn't possibly stop dealing with this man, couldn't just leave him where he stood and go on with her life.

Even as she considered the option, his tone softened. "It would be okay if you did, but I thank you all the same . . . for what you've done. All I'm saying is don't feel beholden just 'cause we happen to be traveling the same direction at the same time. I've got along just fine since they turned me out of Andersonville, and I reckon I'll just keep doing fine."

A surge of horror washed through her. "Andersonville? You were in that hell hole?" She'd heard tales of the conditions at the infamous Confederate prison where thousands of Yankee prisoners were crammed into squalid, mud-choked pens and literally starved. Johnny Reb had done well to feed his own, let alone the enemy, and he hadn't been too concerned about doing so. Even worse things were said to have gone on at Andersonville, some admittedly caused by the prisoners themselves. Men could be brutal when the circumstances warranted.

He broke into her reverie. "It was a while back, not worth remembering." Again that ironic grin that popped dimples into his gaunt cheeks.

They headed back toward camp, arms loaded with wood.

"Want to build the fire or fetch water?" she asked.

"Both or either, doesn't matter to me."

She nodded and watched him take out a Barlow knife and whittle a small pile of creamy kindling from one of the smaller limbs.

"How long were you there?"

He looked up quickly. "Where?"

"Andersonville. You said—"

"Oh, I don't know. It seemed like an eternity. I don't remember going there—I just woke up one day and there I was with my head all wrapped in filthy rags, a headache that made me sure I'd been struck blind and a leg so torn up I couldn't walk."

"And how did that happen?"

He shrugged, stared past her.

"You don't know?"

"Ma'am, I don't know anything. I don't know where I was born and raised, I don't know when I joined the army, I don't know what battle I was wounded in. Hell, all I knew when I came around was how to put on my boots and shirt; how to wash and eat, and . . . well, never mind, you know, bodily functions. The rest was gone. Still is. And, oh, yeah, I can read and write for all the good it's done me."

She couldn't imagine such a thing, and even to think about all her past, bad as some of it might have been, being wiped out with such finality was horrifying. "My God, that's terrible."

He took out a match and coaxed the small pile of shavings into smoking flames, then broke up some small limbs and tented them over the fire. "Oh, it could be worse." He tilted his head and glanced up at her, eyes flashing.

She glimpsed again that mischievous little boy she'd noticed the first day they met up. "How's that?"

"I could be ugly, to boot."

"Or modest."

"Yeah, or that. I could use some coffee. Let me get some water."

"I'm getting it," she said, and plucked a wooden bucket off the side of the wagon. She was halfway to the creek before the

45

tears came, and they poured hotly down her cheeks until she was sobbing.

She had no idea whom she cried for, but guessed it was most probably herself as much as him. The loss of her family was tragic, but she remembered her momma's hands caressing her cheek, her sister's childish giggle when they played in the fields at home, her father's patience when she ruined one photographic plate after another before getting everything right. Eli's mouth on hers, his hands . . . his. . . . She forced away those memories, for they made her long to be held and touched, and in that way lay futility.

On the other hand, Jake had nothing he could hold on to when the days were longer and harder than they should be, no remembered love and laughter, no memories. Only blackness where love and compassion and desire should have been. For surely someone must have loved him, the kind of man he was.

Falling to her knees on the bank of the creek, she cried as if at any moment her heart might crack apart. Finally, when the tears ceased, she took off her bandanna, washed her face and hands and filled the bucket.

She met him coming to find her. He took one look at her swollen eyes, grasped her free hand in his and accompanied her back to camp in silence, letting her carry the water. The warmth of his strong fingers wrapped around hers soothed the chaos in her heart. He was indeed a strange man.

Losing his memory had taken away all normal inhibitions, and Jake tended to do and say what he thought and felt without stopping to consider all the ramifications. Too bad she was growing to like him so much. Her plans didn't include a man, and certainly not an invalid.

After supper, which he ate with as much enthusiasm as he had the first meal she cooked him, he cleaned up the dishes and scoured the frying pan quite thoroughly with a handful of sand. He rinsed it and shoved it into the hot coals to dry.

It was time to show him the picture of Lorena and ask about her. Yet she hesitated, for she was unsure of what his reaction might be.

He settled gingerly on the ground near the fire and picked up a stick to chew on. "Feels like rain, no stars and the air's wet."

"Rains a lot in Missouri. That's why everything's so green." She tried to think of more to say to prolong the moment, but failed.

"Gets tiresome sometimes, though, especially when you're sleeping out in the open."

She sighed and rose. "I've got something I want to show you."

At the wagon she felt around in her duster pockets until she came up with the delicate photograph she'd picked up on the trail where he'd fallen.

Returning to where he lay propped on one elbow watching the fire, she handed it to him.

Without a word he took it and shifted so that the firelight wavered over the face of the beautiful girl.

"Lorena." He breathed the word with such adoration that it made her shiver. "Where did you find it?"

"You dropped it."

"When?" He touched the hazy image with the trembling tip of one finger. "I thought it was lost for good when I couldn't find it."

"I meant to give it back to you earlier, then you fell and got hurt and I forgot all about it." She winced at the white lie, but hated to tell him the real reason, that she was afraid of what he might do. Something was wrong in his head, and though he exhibited no violent tendencies, one could never tell for sure.

He didn't reply, just kept looking at the beautiful girl.

"Who is she?"

Shifting, he lifted a shoulder. "I don't know."

"You don't?"

He shook his head. "But I must have loved her, and she me. Or why would she give me this? She signed it, *Love, Lorena.* Maybe she loved me very much. Can you imagine what it must be like for her, waiting for me to come home from the war? Wondering if I'm still alive, or maybe she thinks I'm dead. My God, how awful it must be for her. I keep thinking I'll find her or someone who knows her one of these days if I wander around long enough."

"But you don't even know where you come from. Suppose you're from back East somewhere. You were in the Yankee army, so you must—"

"Aw, hell. I know that." He shrugged and put the small picture carefully in his pocket. "I'll be more careful with it from now on. I could have lost it for good, then I wouldn't have anything from my past."

Silence gripped her, then she asked softly, "Jake?"

"Yeah?"

"You think she might have been your . . . your wife?" She hated that his answer was so terribly important to her.

He spoke thoughtfully. "Or sweetheart."

"I'm sorry. It must be awful not knowing."

After a moment of staring into the fire, he asked, "You going to sleep out?"

"Think I'll put up my canvas shelter in case it rains. Want to help?"

"Sure, why not."

She didn't watch him struggle to his feet—it made her hurt just to do so—but went to the wagon and lifted out the heavy, water-proofed canvas. By then he was beside her.

As they worked she made idle conversation. "It makes a pretty good roof, even if it rains hard. I work under it sometimes when I stop for a few days to take photographs. It gets mighty hot in the wagon. That's when the portable dark box comes in handy."

"It's interesting, what you do."

"You think so?"

"Yes, but then I don't have much to base my judgment on, do I?" He said it more or less as a joke, and chuckled when she did, but she sensed the melancholy behind the words.

"Maybe you'd like to help me out sometime." The words escaped before she thought about them, before she realized that she had made up her mind about the two of them remaining together.

He was quiet for so long, she glanced toward him to see what was up. In the glow from the fire, his features danced in shadows and light, his eyes bright and wet. No man she'd ever known had been so willing to show his emotions. It was quite refreshing, though somewhat disturbing.

He cleared his throat and turned away.

She hoped she hadn't embarrassed him, but didn't say so.

"I'll get my bedroll, think I'll just sleep beside the fire," he said, and moved away before she could reply.

Under the shelter of canvas she peeled off her clothes quickly, buttoned up a soft linsey shirt and crawled into the bedroll. For a long while she moved from one position to another, unable to settle her emotions. In the distance, thunder grumbled like fighting bears. The approaching storm grew in intensity and lit up the sky. She raised on an elbow to see if Jake had taken shelter under the wagon, but the silent hump remained unmoving beside the glowing coals. The first drops of rain clattered on the canvas above her head, lightning cracked open the night like the firing of gigantic cannons and the sky opened up.

The air turned cold and she shivered, wishing she'd put on a flannel gown. She wrapped up in a blanket and peered through the heavy rain toward where Jake had been sleeping. Incredibly, he still lay there.

Suppose he had suffered one of his spells and was unconscious? He could drown or die of pneumonia.

She cupped both hands around her mouth and shouted his name through the tumult of the storm. He didn't reply, and the rain was now so heavy she could no longer see him. It had put out what had remained of the fire and a thick blackness hovered around the camp like a cloak.

Preferring a wet shirt to a wet blanket, she shed the latter and darted through puddles of water to where she thought he lay. "Jake, damn it, don't you know enough to come in out of the rain?"

She practically stumbled over him, fell into the wet grass on her knees. Fumbling at an opening in the blanket, she was startled when her cold hands touched his face. He jerked, making a gawking sound, and grabbed at her.

"It's me, Jake. Allie. My God, you're sleeping in the rain."

"And it's damn cold, too," he mumbled. "Thought it was gunfire."

"Well, why didn't you take shelter?"

He shivered under her touch. "Couldn't move . . . just couldn't move. I thought I was dreaming."

"Your blanket is soaked. Come on, get in the shelter."

He lurched to his feet, stumbled and staggered around, caught up in the blanket, and finally kicked free, almost falling when he did. "Hell and damnation. Ought to've stayed where I was."

"Oh, stop your fussing. You're worse than a kid."

"Oh, yeah?"

"Yeah. Now come on, I'm getting soaked too."

In the shelter, she felt for the lantern and pouch of matches, struck one and lit the wick. What the light revealed made her sorry she'd bothered. Her shirt clung to her skin; cold nipples pointed at Jake like rigid fingers.

He pretended not to notice, and for an instant they stared at each other, then began to laugh.

"You look like a drowned rat," she said.

"Same back at you, only, well . . . " He gestured with one hand. "I've never seen a rat look precisely like that. Damn, I'm freezing."

"I've got two dry blankets. You can have one of them, but you'd better take off those clothes first."

He leered at her. "Just trying to get me in a compromising position, woman?"

She nearly choked on laughter. "Right. If I had a mirror I'd show you why that probably would not have occurred to me."

He leaned over, wrung out a handful of his hair. "That bad, huh?"

She glanced down at herself. "No worse than me, I'm sure. I'll blow out the light, then we can both undress and wrap up. How's that?"

"Don't bother me if it don't bother you. I'd like to get some sleep sometime tonight."

The rain had slackened a bit, the violence of the storm abated, so they no longer had to shout at each other to be heard.

"It's about to stop, I think."

"Could be," she replied tartly and blew out the lantern.

"Hey!"

"What?"

"It's dark."

"What's the matter, can't find your own butt in the dark?"

"You've got some mouth on you, Allie."

The way he said her name gave her a shivery sensation that she tried to pass off to the wet and cold. She could only imagine the contortions he was going through to get out of his heavy, wet clothing. He probably would have a hard time of it, hopping around on one leg then the other with the sopping denim of his jeans hanging to his skin stubbornly. She quickly thought better of offering to help him. He'd just have to handle the job as best he could. As for herself, she skinned out of the dripping shirt and wrapped up in the blanket, then lowered herself to the ground near her saddle and curled up into a tight ball.

He continued to mutter and stomp around.

"Can I help you?"

"I don't think so."

"Well, then quiet down. I'm trying to go back to sleep."

After a while, "Allie?"

"What?"

"I'm cold."

She swallowed hard and shivered. "Me, too."

"What?"

"Can I trust you?"

"Hell, no. Remember what you said about no man being harmless?"

"Well, maybe I ought to get my Colt."

"Most of my parts are too cold to move. Come on, Allie, two blankets are warmer than one. Two bodies are warmer than one."

"Great logic, Jake. Just great. That isn't exactly what I'm pondering here, but thanks for the opinion."

More silence broken by the chattering of teeth.

"Allie? I'm really cold. I'm shaking so hard my teeth are rattling. Suppose I black out just as you need me for something? It could happen, you know."

"Yes, Jake, but that's not fair."

"I know, that's what I've said all along, but I'll be damned if fair ever came into it."

"Okay, stop your whining. I've got an idea."

"Finally."

"You wrap up in your blanket and turn over so your back is to me. I'll wrap up and cuddle up to your backside. That way we'll keep each other warm. And if you so much as make a move toward me you'll black out all right, but it'll be 'cause I lobbed you upside the head."

He chuckled. "Allie, you wouldn't do that. But I'll tell you something you can count on."

"What?"

"I won't ever do anything to you you don't want me to, and that's a promise."

"That's what I'm afraid of," she whispered, and hoped he didn't hear her, for she knew it wasn't him she didn't trust, but herself.

"What? I didn't hear."

"I said, I'll be right there. Are you ready?"

"Indeed I am," he replied in a lecherous voice. "Come and get it."

"Jake, stop that."

"Okay, I'm teasing. Come on before you freeze, to say nothing of myself. Hurry."

"Keep talking. It's so dark I can't see my own hand in front of my face, let alone you."

Instead he began to whistle the tune she'd heard him singing earlier, "When Johnny Comes Marching Home Again," and she moved cautiously toward him. The grass under her bare knees was damp and cool, its fragrance heavy in the rain-drenched air. Rain fell steadily and softly on the canvas above them and back in the woods frogs set up a tentative, questioning serenade.

Her grappling hands touched him and he stopped whistling abruptly.

"Is that you, Allie?"

"Stop that. Now lie still, don't turn over."

"Never."

She curled around the curve of his body, knees following the line of his thighs to tuck up against his backside. Then she pulled the blanket away from her breasts and put it and one arm up over his shoulder.

He sighed deeply. "Ah, that's better already."

She had to admit it was.

Once he awoke, or thought he did, to find himself lying in a soft, warm bed, and when he turned over to take the woman in his arms, he saw he slept with Lorena. She whispered a name, her breath warm and sweet against his lips. Desire ran through him, flames licking through his gut. He tightened his hold, lowered his lips to the pearl-white mound of her breast. Hot tears coursed down his cheeks when he realized that his arms were empty, the sheets drenched in crimson. Terror gripped his heart and he tried to scream, struggled to get away, but tangled sheets bound him to the bed and no sound came from his aching throat.

When finally he could move, he wrapped both arms around the woman in his bed, tears drying tightly on his cheeks as the fear slowly faded.

When Allie awoke in the morning her head lay on his arm, her nose buried against his chest. His dark hair tangled with hers in the grass and his warm breath fanned her bare shoulder.

For a moment she lay very still, afraid to open her eyes. When she did he was watching her, his gaze as deep a blue as a mountain lake after a summer storm.

"See, I told you you could trust me," he said very softly and touched her hair where it spread over his arm.

One bare breast peeked from under the blanket, but she couldn't bring herself to stir. The trees, the silvery light of dawn, a wisp of rain-kissed breeze embraced her. He embraced her, and she felt on the verge of a fantasy. For just that brief instant she did not wish to disturb the magic.

He glanced at her rosy nipple, then gently pulled the blanket over it. "Did you sleep well?"

Unable to speak, she could only nod.

His back to her, he dressed, and she gazed at his bare skin, the curve of his spine disappearing into long blades of green grass. Watched the ripple of muscles across his shoulders as he fought with the damp britches. She could count the laddering of his ribs and wanted to touch him, do something that would instantly make him whole again. She tried to look away, but couldn't, and was embarrassed when a sob jerked down in her throat.

"Get dressed, Allie, while I've got my back turned. This is your chance. Hurry now, girl. We've got miles to go today. Lots and lots of miles, and you mustn't waste them staring at my bony backside."

An insatiable urge to throw her arms around his neck and hug him frightened her into silence. How could this be happening when all she wanted was the freedom to find her own way? If only she could simply walk off and leave him standing there. But she couldn't, and she was terribly afraid of what would happen because of it.

Chapter Four

Jake and Allie had covered plenty of ground by noon the next day. At their backs the sloping foothills of the Ozarks grew faint in a distant haze as the land ahead rose and fell gently. The warm air soon dried their damp clothing. When they stopped for a break, they lay in a patch of new grass on a rise above a chattering creek. In companionable silence they gazed into the bright, rain-washed sky, watched a red hawk swoop down not a hundred feet away and snare a young rabbit that had strayed too far from its den.

"If I was much of a hunter I'd do that, and we'd have rabbit stew."

Allie turned to him. "Fly, do you?"

He hesitated a moment, then laughed. "No, I mean go out and stalk my prey and shoot the poor helpless thing."

"How do you know you're not?"

"Not what?" His voice drummed deep and lazy, as if he really weren't there with her at all.

"How do you know if you've ever hunted?"

"Oh. I've tried it already. I can't seem to hit the broad side of a barn with that rifle I carry."

"Spencer. All the Yankees carried them toward the end of the war. It was said they could load up in the morning and go into battle and shoot all day without reloading. Probably turned the tide of the war, what with most of the Johnny Rebs still using outdated muskets and single-shot rifles."

Before she finished he had propped his head up on one hand to stare at her. "How does a woman know about weapons and the strategy of war?"

"You hang around with men, especially soldiers, for very long and you pick up things. I don't know, I've always been interested in things like that. I like the feeling of power carrying a gun gives me. It almost makes me equal to a man." She knew, but kept it to herself, that he wasn't turned out of Andersonville with that Spencer. He'd gotten it somewhere else later.

He interrupted her musings with a question. "When did you hang around soldiers?"

"I was in the war myself, in a manner of speaking. I guess you'd say I served as a neutral."

"Allie, my God, what did you do in the war? What were you thinking? You must have been a child."

She shrugged, pulled a blade of grass and worried it with her thumbnail. "I had no place else to go but with my father after my mother and sister were killed by bushwhackers in '63. He came and got me as soon as he heard. The way things were in Missouri, he was afraid something bad would happen to me and he'd never see me again. So I went to war with him and he taught me to use the cameras and develop plates. Matthew Brady wasn't the only photographer to shoot the war."

"My God, Allie. But a woman, a girl you must have been then. Weren't you frightened? I mean of what could happen to you because you were . . . I mean . . . God, Allie."

"Don't be so surprised, Jake. I was sixteen and dressed like a boy—who could know? We hacked my hair off to the shoulders and I wore a slouchy old hat. No one ever looked twice at me. And I learned a lot. I learned that I loved using the camera to transport myself into an altogether different world. Its eye shut out everything but precisely what I wanted to see. Even the worst things we photographed were narrowed down, made more pristine and somehow manageable. Those boys fighting and dying. Those boys and the look in their eyes. Captured forever on a piece of paper. Imagine that."

"Black and white doesn't record the color of blood," he said, a bitterness in his voice she'd not heard before.

Caught up by a rush of her own memories, she looked away. "It got to where I didn't even mind the stink of the chemicals, considering what death smells like. They were purifying in contrast. Of course, the best thing was that my father and I were together. I loved him very much."

Jake reached out to finger a lock of her hair. "You could have been killed."

"I suppose, but I wasn't, was I? Besides, there's a kind of thrill to knowing that. Surely you understand. I didn't die in the war and neither did you, and so here we both are, gallivanting around out here where we could still be killed. And you with that thing in your head, waiting to go off. Don't lecture me about taking chances."

He held up a hand, then sat up and wrapped both arms around bent knees. "Sorry, it's none of my business. You're right. I need to go for a walk over there." He gestured toward the trees.

"Okay, don't get lost."

He walked off, chuckling. She rolled to her stomach and closed her eyes against the glare of brilliant sunlight. They would have to leave soon, but it felt so good to stretch out and relax.

Time drifted, languid and remote, and she wondered fleetingly if indeed he had gotten lost. The thought no more than occurred to her when a shadow loomed above her.

"Back at last," she murmured without opening her eyes.

A deep, cultured voice she didn't recognize said, "Ma'am, I'd appreciate it if you stood up real slow and easy."

She yelped, tried to scramble away, but the man grabbed her arm. "I give you my word of honor as a gentleman that we won't do you any harm."

Struggling did no good. His strong fingers bit into her flesh. The Colt lay out of reach under the seat of the wagon. How could she have been so careless?

"Here, now," he said. "I told you we won't hurt you. We just want you to bring your camera box wagon and come with us. For just a spell. It's just to make us some of those pictures like you been taking."

"Let me go. I'm not doing any such thing. I'll call my—"

"And we'll shoot him before he can get here. Now, be sensible, little gal."

He jerked her roughly against his chest, and she looked up into an indescribably handsome face. He had intelligent dark eyes, great dimples in both cheeks, generous, well-formed lips. When he smiled, which he was doing now as if he were thoroughly enjoying the confrontation, he revealed straight white teeth.

"Who are you and what do you want?"

"I believe I've told you what we want. My name is Cole Younger, and that gentleman is my brother Bob. Say hello to the lady, Bob."

The air literally whooshed out of her lungs. Bushwhackers and outlaws! She knew all about them. They or someone like them had murdered her mother and sister and now were going to kill her as well. For all she knew the notorious Quantrill could be nearby.

"You lower-than-skunks, filthy killers. Turn me loose this instant."

"Bob, get over here and help me settle this wildcat down. We don't want to hurt you, miss. Jesse and Frank just want their pictures made and so do we. You have to understand this is very important to all of us."

"Jesse and Frank? Jesse and Frank James? You . . . they . . . dear God." She swallowed hard, her heart boomed until she couldn't hear or catch her breath, leaving her dizzy.

"You're talking too much," Bob said. He was neither cultured nor kind like his brother.

Cole cast him a quick, harsh look. It shut up the younger man, and he turned back to Allie.

"Don't you go fainting on us, now. It's a simple thing and when you're done we'll set you back on your way, no harm done, just like I said. We don't want to hurt anyone. You make a fuss and that feller gets in on it, we'll have no choice but to kill him. You don't want that, do you?"

She shook her head and tried to tear her arm loose from his grip. "You're hurting me already."

"It isn't my intention. Stop struggling. Time's running out. He'll be coming back. Just relax and let's get in that what's-it wagon and ride out. That way, there'll be no trouble."

Bob took her other arm, but hadn't yet said another word. Cole seemed in charge and far the more talkative of the two. Indeed, he spoke much like an actor on a stage. He was also better looking. Surely he wouldn't do anything bad to anyone, even though he did have a fierce hold on her.

She thought she saw movement in the woods where Jake had disappeared, and made up her mind quickly. "Okay, let's go. I won't give you any more trouble." At least not till she could get her hands on the Colt. Then they'd see what trouble was.

However, Bob climbed on board ahead of her, immediately found the weapon and stuck it in his belt with a wide grin. His teeth weren't as pretty as his brother's. Amazing that she even noticed a thing like that at a time like this. It came from having the eye of a photographer, she supposed.

It occurred to her that they might kill her, and belatedly she wondered what Jake would do when he returned and found her gone.

They rode for what seemed like hours, and she kept glancing over her shoulder. Surely Jake had returned and would follow, if he wasn't lying back there, out cold. If he did succeed in tagging along, he could get them both killed. He wasn't exactly her idea of a rescuer, anyway. It would be best if she got herself out of this without any help. Hooking up with a man just so he could come to her aid hadn't been in the plan anyway. The idea annoyed her.

It was almost sunset when they emerged from a thick grove of trees into a small clearing where a cabin stood. Smoke drifted from the chimney and chickens scratched around in the yard.

"Hey, there's Jesse," Cole said when a rider appeared on their right flank.

"Well, well, if she isn't a pretty one," the notorious gang leader said. " 'Rough winds do shake the darling buds of May.' " With that eloquent quotation, he dismounted and gallantly offered his hand to her.

She ignored it and jumped to the ground beside him, a little shaken by his quoting of Shakespeare. Up close she saw that he was little more than a baby.

He laughed at her discomfort and the two Youngers joined in.

"Spirited. Reckon she gave you plenty of trouble, this fair damsel."

Younger grinned broadly. "Not any more than we could handle, but she's spry and mouthy."

"I haven't said two words to you," she said.

The men laughed again.

Anger bolstered her courage. "I don't know how you think I can capture your likenesses. It's far too dark for picture-taking. So why don't you just let me go back and leave me be. Maybe someone will take pictures of you when you're shot down robbing some bank or train. They can lay you out on doors and put your rifles beside you."

Cole glanced at Jesse. "See what I said? Mouthy."

Once again the men laughed, and the boy who was Jesse James tugged playfully at a lock of her hair. "You'll stay the night, take our pictures tomorrow, then be on your way. We have no reason to hurt you."

Samantha Lee

How young he was! She didn't know if that was good or bad for her.

"You're sure being all-fired polite for having kidnaped me," she said. "Why would you let me go? Suppose I go to the law and lead them back here?"

"We're generally all-fired polite," Jessie said. "Unless someone crosses us. Then we get right nasty. Besides, we didn't kidnap you, we just borrowed you for a while. Won't take much of your time.

"As for leading the law here, we aren't staying long, so don't bother."

She nearly sputtered with frustration. They had her and it was evident that they would keep her until they were ready to turn her loose. The realization effectively shut her up, and when Younger took her arm she followed along with no more protest.

Inside the cabin, a sturdy, middle-aged woman hustled around a cook stove. Allie's stomach turned over at the smell of coffee and frying meat. It had been a while since she'd eaten and she was starved. When scared she had the appetite of a horse.

She was happy to see the woman, however. That made her believe that none of the men would try anything bad.

Besides the aroma of food and wood smoke, the cabin smelled like men, but the place was not at all as unpleasant as she had expected. The room they were in served as kitchen and living space and a door covered by a ragged curtain led off to another. An assortment of rifles and pistols were scattered about, and a pile of saddlebags and bedrolls formed an unruly hump against a wall. She counted at least a dozen weapons on the table and the floor. A carbine lay across the bed near the only window.

The woman put a large, steaming pot on the table. "Jesse," she said, "move these guns so I can serve your supper."

The boy said, "Sure, maw," and obeyed the command like the child he was.

The five men bellied up to the table and left Allie standing in the center of the room. The fifth man must be the other notorious Younger brother, Allie thought.

The woman addressed Allie in a pleasant voice, but the words were issued as a command. "Come fix you a plate, dear. These boys won't do you any harm, or I'll lay a board upside their heads. Jesse, set that pot over this a way."

He did so and the woman filled a plate with stew and gestured toward Allie. "Stand with me over here at the dry sink and we'll eat together." She filled another plate and glanced impatiently at Allie, who hadn't budged.

"She ain't deaf, is she?" she asked the room.

"Join my mother to eat," Jesse ordered.

Allie looked into the agate-hard eyes of the young outlaw, ancient far beyond his years, and experienced a mesmerizing fear. Little wonder that bank tellers quietly handed over the cash when he pointed a gun at them.

She did his bidding. She might be mouthy but she was no fool. Besides, the stew looked and smelled delicious and her stomach was so empty it hurt. Or maybe that was terror crawling around in her gut like a caged animal.

When Jake sauntered out of the woods sometime later, he discovered Allie and her wagon gone. The palomino grazed placidly alongside the bay mare, who had finally learned to tolerate his male bossiness.

He knew some time had passed because he'd come to lying in a pile of dry leaves. She couldn't have tired of waiting and gone on, not leaving that palomino stallion.

He knelt and examined the wagon tracks in the rain-soaked earth, headed back the way they'd come. He only took the time to saddle the palomino before mounting his own bay and riding back down the trail.

The sun slipped across the sky as he rode, eyes on the trail for any sign of the wagon turning off. He almost missed the track when he came upon it. Several horses had ridden over slabs of flat slate, kicking up chunks of rock, and when he moved on a short distance, he picked up the wagon tracks sunk into the soft earth of a nearly hidden path that wound along the bench of the hill. He blessed the previous night's rain.

Soon he passed through a growth of oak so dense the heavy foliage left the trail in deep shadow so that he didn't see the lone rider until he moved from the trees out into the open.

"Private property, sir," the man said. The words were polite enough, but the voice held an edge.

"Folks don't take to visitors?" he asked. Danger lurked around the man, prickling the hair on Jake's neck, but he held his tone steady.

"Not so's you'd notice. You about got to be expected."

Jake raised his shoulders and tried another tack. "I'm looking for a friend, might have come this way."

"Uh-huh." The rough looking young man maneuvered his horse crosswise of the road and slipped a rifle from its scabbard.

Jake kept an eye on the man's dirty finger, curled within the trigger guard of the weapon. "Was told I could find him here."

"Nobody here expecting anyone. Like I said . . . "

"I know, you got to be expected."

The man grinned tightly and thumbed at the rifle's hammer.

Jake touched the brim of his hat and pulled the bay's head around. She kicked at Ringo in passing and he gentled her. He knew how she felt, but there was no use in either of them starting something. He'd obviously stumbled on some two-bit hideout. Missouri was thick with would-be robbers, mimicking their hero, Jesse James. Still, he had no intention of retreating very far, because the what's-it wagon tracks led right on past where that fellow sat his horse. After dark he'd go in on foot. One thing he'd learned was patience, and so he rode out of sight of the man, left Molly and Ringo in the woods and settled back against a tree to wait.

There would be no moon till late, near midnight, and by then he would have reached his target. The presence of a guard proved he was close to something secretive, but why had Allie ridden in here?

The obvious conclusion was that someone she knew had come into their camp and she had accompanied him, willingly or not, back to this place for a good reason. Hell, maybe she even went to take one of her pictures. That would explain why she left in the wagon instead of riding the palomino. The only thing he couldn't figure out was, why sneak off and not tell him? Maybe she thought she'd be back soon, or maybe she had no choice.

Either way, he had no intention of leaving until he found out.

Long gleaming fingers of evening light prodded through the thick foliage, splashing on a carpet of last year's leaves. One beam crept toward his foot. He reached a hand out as if to capture it, and fell into a vision as if he'd stepped through a door into a room.

A golden-haired woman stood by the window across that room, back to the light so that her features were in shadow. A man moved toward her. A tall man with midnight-black hair, dressed in powder gray britches and a morning coat, a cravat bunched around the stiff white collar of his shirt.

The man lifted one hand and cupped her face; she leaned into the touch.

"When will you tell him?" he asked, lips against her lovely flesh.

She stiffened, pulled away. "I can't. I won't. He needs me too much."

"Nonsense. He needs no one, never has. I should know."

"I love him. He means everything to me. I want—"

"To. Hell. With. That!"

Jake twitched at the ferocity of the staccato words.

An expression of dark anger clouded her features. She appeared to stare directly at Jake where he stood inside the door, and held up a hand in a gesture he couldn't interpret.

65

He spoke to her, his tongue and mouth so dry he could hardly utter the words. "Lorena? Lorena, is that you?" He struggled to move, go to her, take her in his arms and fill the empty void around his heart, but he couldn't.

The man across the room repeated her name, sounding as desperate as Jake felt. "Lorena, don't ruin your life over this, or so help me God, I'll kill him. I won't let this happen."

"Leave. Leave now," she said, and moved to stare out the window once more, shoulders hunched in stiff defiance.

The man strode past Jake so close his hair stirred. In that instant he got a look at the man's face, and saw that it was his own. Younger with a thick mustache, but his nevertheless. Dizziness fogged his sight.

When the door slammed behind the man, Lorena sank to the settee and cried into her hands. Shock held Jake captive, though he ached to go to her. Instead he tumbled away into thick darkness, the sound of her voice chasing him, calling a name.

He lifted his head from where it rested on upraised knees and blinked. He struggled to remember the name Lorena had spoken, but it hadn't followed him back into reality. It was very still in the woods except for the gentle songs of night creatures and the ragged sound of his breathing. Only a few lavender streaks lingered in the gunmetal sky.

A persistent throbbing made his eyeballs ache and he rubbed at them with the tips of his fingers. Wearily he recalled what he had seen. Something was out of whack in the odd vision. He thought about it awhile and filed the scene away; a trick he had learned in order to recollect happenings. One day he hoped there would be enough of such memories in his foolish brain to put the pieces of his life back together.

Right now he had to find Allie and make sure she was all right.

He decided not to take the Spencer with him. It would get in the way, and he had no intention of shooting anyone anyway. All he wanted was to see for himself what she was up to. If she

was in trouble, he'd have to get her out as best he could. Not
with some cumbersome rifle that would only slow them down
if they had to run. He never was very good with the damn thing
in the first place, and didn't even remember where he'd gotten
it. Wouldn't have had it from the war, not coming out of
Andersonville.

Impatiently, he made his way quietly along the road, keeping
under the shadowy trees. Night vision kept him from running
smack into the trees, but it sure was damn black out there. It
would make it hard for them to see him coming.

Up ahead an orange glow flickered like a distant lightning
bug, then grew larger and more distinct as he moved forward
with caution. It was lamp glow from the window of a cabin. He
smelled a fire burning and the pungent odor of horses.

There was no sign of the what's-it wagon or the mules, but
they could be around back. Best to wait till the lamp went out to
do any moving around. There didn't seem to be a dog about, a
break in his favor.

Patiently, carefully, he worked his way around back of the
cabin to take a better look at the situation.

To Allie's immense relief the men had all bedded down in the
main room. Wide awake, she lay on a pallet on the floor near a
narrow bed in which Jesse and Frank's mother slept. Outside
the glassless, curtainless window a waning moon rose through
the trees. As she gazed at it a head raised slowly above the sill.
Heart racing, she clutched both hands over her mouth to keep
from screaming. Had one of the men decided to grab her?

The figure leaned forward, hesitated.

She held her breath, waited.

The older woman snorted, turned over.

Just let this fellow come a little closer and she'd punch him
in the mouth.

Moonlight tumbled past the tree tops to puddle across the
floor and bed. Finally the man made up his mind and scrambled
over the sill. She made her move, hammering on him with both

fists, kicking and yelling. The intruder began to shout as well, and then Jesse James' mother started screeching to add to the melee. From the other room, an explosion of noise joined in.

"Allie, dammit, stop hitting me," a familiar voice rasped.

Too late she sorted out the request from all the other clamor, but she did stop pounding on Jake, who had come through the window. By that time, though, Jesse, Frank, Cole, Bob and the other man were all crowded into the room. Someone fired a shot that thunked into a wall.

Over by the bed a match flared and the lamp spluttered. Jesse's mother, in a voluminous nightgown, stood on the sagging mattress with her back against the wall, a burning lamp held high above her head.

"Stop shooting, you'll hit someone. Now everyone just settle down." The command came from Cole Younger.

Allie, all wound up with Jake on the floor, hissed in his ear, "What were you doing?"

"Trying to rescue you."

"I could have done without it."

"You're welcome."

"You two shut up," Jesse ordered in a flat, ominous voice. "Who is this?"

Cole answered. "He was with her earlier. Husband, brother. I don't know."

"Well, why didn't you bring him along, too? It would've saved all this hubbub."

"Figured it was just easier to grab her and leave. Thought she'd be less trouble by herself. Never thought he'd track us here. Must have eyes like a damned eagle."

Clearly, Jesse had reached the end of his patience. "Get his gun, then. Good God, what a lot of trouble to go to just to get some pictures made. I'd rather have robbed a bank."

"He ain't got one," Bob muttered, after poking around over Jake, who by then had climbed to his feet and helped Allie stand.

68

Jesse laughed, then Frank and the rest joined in, including the older woman, who by that time had crawled down off the bed and placed the lamp on the table.

"Reckon what he thought he'd do, coming in here without even a danged gun?" Bob asked.

"They weren't going to hurt me," Allie told Jake.

"And how was I supposed to know that? I didn't know it was going to be a picnic."

"Don't be mad. I appreciate your caring. They want their pictures made before they go off somewhere to rob and plunder someone but us poor Missourians, who've had just about enough of robbing and killing."

"Just who the hell are they?" Jake whispered.

The outlaws had stopped laughing to glare at Allie.

"We don't kill Missourians," Frank said.

"That's Jesse and Frank James and the Youngers," Allie said, almost on top of Frank's declaration.

"Aw, hell," Jake said.

"Now don't anyone get in an uproar," Jesse said. "I know only too well what the little lady means, and she's right. We hadn't ought to add to their troubles. Looks like these two might be in love." Despite the nature of the statement, Jesse's eyes held an expression of mockery that he masked quickly enough when he noticed her staring at him.

"We've tried not to add to any poor folks' troubles," he told her. "Most of what we take ends up back in the pockets of those the government's robbed."

"Hah!" Jake said, and tried to get past Allie to continue the argument with the outlaw.

She poked him in the ribs. "Hush. How would you know anyway?"

"An outlaw is an outlaw," he persisted.

"Keep that up and they'll tie and gag you," she hissed.

"I'd like to go back to bed," Jesse's mother said. "That is, if you'd all get out of my room."

69

"What'll we do with him, Dingus?" Frank asked as the men filed through the door.

"Tie him up," Jesse replied. "And if he don't keep his mouth shut, stuff a sock in it. I'm going to get me some sleep." With that Jesse went to his bedroll, flung out on the floor and lay down, hugging his rifle. "Hell, I don't see he poses any danger, man who'd go after his gal without even a gun." He chuckled some more before drifting off to sleep.

Allie went back to her pallet, feeling a little sorry for Jake because he would have to sleep tied to a chair all night. But he had brought it on himself.

Even so, after everyone started snoring, she sneaked into the room and untied him, led him quietly to her pallet and pulled him down beside her. She settled her head on his arm and fell asleep before he could start any further arguments.

Chapter Five

Allie awoke with a case of the shakes, reassured somewhat by Jake's arm cradling her head. A strand of ebony hair tickled her nose and lay like a veil over his face as he slept. She fingered it back and he opened his eyes, the intense blue smoked by lingering dreams.

To keep him from speaking too loudly, she touched the tips of her fingers to his lips and whispered, "Good morning."

Still half asleep, he captured her hand, kissed the warm flesh and murmured, "Morning, Lorena."

"Allie, I'm Allie. Who are you, Jake?"

He blinked, shook his head. "Sorry, I wasn't awake. I don't know, Allie. I don't know who I am this morning any more than I did yesterday." Dimples flashed; he blinked and grinned broadly. "Nothing like waking up to a new world every day."

He continued to hold her fingers and she let him, amazed at his ability to cope with any situation.

"I thought maybe I'd catch you unawares and you'd remember something." Distracted from her fears by the exchange, she answered his grin with one of her own.

His forehead wrinkled in thought, and he gazed into her eyes. "What's wrong, Allie? I'm sorry I called you Lorena."

"No, it's not that. I was just thinking how dangerous it is for us to be here. Men like these murdered my mother and sister. Rode in and dragged them from the house, stripped them naked, did God only knows what to them and shot them before looting our farm of everything that was there. And they want me to take their pictures."

He put his other arm around her. "I'm sorry, Allie. That's a terrible thing to remember. Sometimes I think it's better that I can't remember anything." His warm breath fanned her cheek. "Where were you when they came? Did you see it?"

She bit at her lips to keep from crying. The loss was still a raw wound that throbbed when touched.

"I'd gone to the privy." Her tone revealed a buried disbelief. "They didn't even look in there or I'd be dead, too. It was the war, and bushwhackers were everywhere. Momma had told us girls what to do, only she and Sara didn't have a chance. I was so scared." Her voice quavered. "I was willing to crawl down in one of those stinking holes if I had to to stay alive. I let little Sara die alone. I'll never forgive myself. They didn't even look for me, Jake, they just . . . just butchered them and what they didn't steal they destroyed, burned the house . . . and. . . . "

He rubbed the back of her head with one hand. "Ssh, Allie. Ssh. I'm so sorry." He kissed her ear through a fall of hair and held her close. "Did you see them, was it—?"

"No. No, I was too afraid. I never want to be that frightened again. Never. I've always felt like I should have done something."

He closed his eyes and held her. There was nothing he could say that would quiet that guilt, and so he offered silent understanding and a shoulder.

72

After a while she stopped crying and pulled from his arms. Such weak moments were rare. How annoying to break down in front of Jake. She said gruffly, "Don't cause trouble with these men. They might kill us both. They're not going to hurt us if we do what they say."

Her moods swung like a hanging rope in a high wind, and sometimes he had trouble keeping up with them. "I hope you're right. Sometimes you're a mite naive, for the life you've led."

"And you're a little too sarcastic for the one you can't remember."

They grinned at each other, both understanding the need for such brash repartee.

When he grabbed the windowsill to pull himself to his feet, she resisted helping him. He wouldn't have appreciated the gesture, she was sure. He leaned against the wall a moment, rubbing his thigh.

"Okay?"

"Fine." His lips twitched into a grin. "A bit embarrassed is all."

"It doesn't matter—they aren't going to hurt us. And you did come after me. I thank you for caring."

Just then someone in the other room yelled, "Well, where did he go?"

"Hell, I don't know," another voice answered. "I tied him up real good."

"Well, damn, they're probably both gone."

Jesse burst into the room, pulled up short when he saw Jake and Allie. He was silent for a moment, then called over his shoulder, "Never mind, the two of 'em are in here." He aimed a savvy look at Allie. "Guess the lady didn't want to sleep alone. Soon as we eat breakfast you'll take those pictures for us. How long will it take?"

"If everything goes well, I can have you some prints before the midday meal."

Jesse raised his brows. "That soon? Durn, that's almost like magic, isn't it?"

73

Already anticipating with pleasure the poses she planned, she replied absently, "Yes, it is." Laid to rest were her memories, the sorrow and fear they had recalled. This was business, something she was good at.

Excitement stirred her blood. She was about to take pictures of the most infamous outlaws of their time. Jesse and Frank James and the Younger brothers, and she would capture their images forever. She could make copies to keep herself. Wouldn't it be something if she one day became as famous as Matthew Brady?

"I'm starved," she told Jesse brashly, took Jake's hand and dragged him into the other room where they joined everyone else for breakfast.

"I'll help clear up the dishes, Mrs. James," Jake said.

"Samuel. The name's Mrs. Samuel. Zerelda Cole James Simms Samuel, to be exact. I've outlasted me a passel of men."

It was the first time Allie had noted humor in the woman's dour personality.

"Well, Mrs. Samuel, I'll wash, you dry," Jake said and rolled up his sleeves.

Her amusement changed to amazement. Allie decided the woman had likely never had a man do such a thing before. The truth be known, she had probably never met a man quite like Jake, either.

Allie turned her thoughts to the work ahead. She would ready one plate at a time in the total darkness of her specially constructed wagon. It being close at hand, she wouldn't bother with the portable darkroom. The quality of each picture depended on good light and timing. The morning sun would be perfect on the east side of the cabin, an ideal backdrop for the photographs.

She dragged out the camera, set up the tripod and began gauging the distance and sliding the box to focus. The gang must have been photographed before. She was sure she could remember seeing earlier calotypes of Jesse and Frank.

After a while Jesse burst from the house carrying a Winchester repeating rifle. Frank followed on his heels, belting a Colt to each hip and complaining.

"I ain't wearing a morning coat, Dingus. Cole is dressing all up like some bank president. He's in there tying on a cravat, for God's sake. And where did he get that silly little black hat?"

"That's a bowler. You know Cole, always the gentleman. Don't worry about it."

"But we're gonna look goofy next to him in that outfit."

"A rose is a rose, Frank. If anyone looks goofy, it'll be Cole." Jesse buttoned his shirt up under his throat and stuffed in the tail clear around. "How's my hair look? Does it need to be slicked down?" He looked at Allie, and appeared to blush. " 'As after sunset fadeth in the west, which by and by black night doth take away,/Death's second self doth seal up all the rest.' "

Frank stared at the brother he fondly referred to as Dingus, and Allie did too. Then the younger brother tipped his head. "Always quoting Shakespeare, you'd think he was putting on airs or the like," he said to no one in particular.

Jesse cleared his throat and Allie ducked quickly under the drape to take one last look through the camera lens. Frank backed away from his brother and eyed him critically.

"Douse it with water, I'd say," he finally replied to Jesse's question about his hair. "Say, why don't we pose with our guns pulled? Pointing them right at that doodad she's got."

Allie came out from under the cloth. "Camera, it's called a camera, and if you're going to point those guns at me, kindly unload them first. I'm going to treat the first plate now. I want everyone ready so there won't be any delays. Who's first?"

Frank stepped forward, drawing his Colts one at a time and extracting the bullets. "Me, I'm ready. The rest are still fooling around."

Allie grinned at their childish demeanor and quickly slipped back under the drape. "Okay, move to your right a bit. Take a step forward. That's good. Now just stand there till I'm ready."

Frank bent both knees slightly, glowered and pointed the revolvers. He froze in that position, staring with wide eyes at the round lens.

"You can relax till I get back, just don't go anywhere." Smiling, she stepped up into the darkroom. The window was treated and let in only "safe" light so the plates wouldn't be exposed prematurely. First she coated the 18-by-21 glass with syrupy collodion, then treated it with light-sensitive silver nitrate and immediately slid it into a light-tight holder. Each plate had to be exposed while still moist, thus the method was referred to as "wet plate process." The coating's sensitivity to light deteriorated as it dried.

She carried the holder to the camera, shoved it in and took another look through the lens. Frank had not moved a muscle since she posed him.

"Hold it, hold it," she said from beneath the cloth, and removed the lens cover. "Don't move, don't move. Okay, that's it."

Quickly she removed the plate and headed for the wagon. Inside she bathed the glass in developers and washed it in water Frank had carried for her earlier.

By the time Mrs. Samuel and Jake came out of the house Allie had taken and developed several shots and was preparing another plate for a group shot. Jesse and Frank wanted one of their mother alone as well.

It was past dinner time before the last picture was taken, a group shot of Frank, Jesse, Bob, Jim and Cole Younger and Zerelda Samuel, and each developed onto albumen-coated paper. Allie's extra prints were hung to dry in the small wagon.

When she presented the others to the gang Jesse was the most impressed, and studied each print carefully.

"Now, when we die folks'll have something to look at and remember us by," he said, his eyes glowing with savagery.

Frank attempted to act as if this was an everyday occurrence for him, but Allie could tell he, too, was pleased.

Images in Scarlet

The handsome Cole Younger stared at his picture as if it were a mirror, rearranging his hair and tilting his bowler at a rakish angle while he studied it. Bob and Jim strutted and clowned.

Jake moved over beside Allie to help her with the forty-pound camera and tripod.

He said in a low voice, "I'm gonna go fetch the team and get them harnessed up. You climb up on that wagon soon as this is loaded and get everything tied down, cause we're getting out of here quick as we can. These guys may change their minds about letting us go and I want to be ready."

"Where's our horses?" Allie asked as they stowed the camera and tripod.

"Back up the trail. Now listen, you don't worry about me. Soon as this wagon's hitched, you get on out of here."

She eyed him. "Yeah, and what're you going to do, outrun them on foot? I'm not leaving here without you. Besides, they're going to let us go. They said so."

"Allie, dammit." He grabbed her arm, tried to turn her in the cramped space of the wagon.

Her fingers clamped around his wrist, and she spoke through gritted teeth. "Don't do that. Don't yank me around like that. I've not needed anyone to take care of me since my father died, and I sure don't need a man pushing me around. I won't start it now. I won't." To her embarrassment, tears welled in her eyes. A bad time to cry, when you were trying to appear strong. Maybe he wouldn't notice. With only the back curtain flung open it was pretty dark in the wagon.

Jake let go as if he'd stuck his hand in a flame. He hadn't hurt her. He would never do such a thing. He hadn't even meant to grab her, but she did so try his patience. So sweet and caring one minute, stubborn as one of her damn mules the next. With her it wasn't simply a matter of rubbing her nose to settle her down, either. And this thing with her father wasn't finished yet. She had a long way to go, and her way of dealing with it

77

appeared to be refusing help even when she could use it. He figured there was a lot more to Miss Allie Caine than he'd yet learned.

"Okay, I'm sorry. I didn't mean anything, except that I'm worried about your hide and my own too, that's all."

She nodded, but didn't speak. He would rather it was from anger at him, something she could handle, but guessed she couldn't quite talk yet because she was still trying to swallow the crying jag she needed so badly. He hoped someone was around to pick up the pieces when she finally did fall apart.

"I'll get the team," he said, and lowered himself carefully from the wagon on his good leg.

Jesse and Frank glanced at Jake when he led the mules out to hitch them up. He just kept right on moving, but the hair on the back of his neck prickled. If they were of a mind, they could plug him in the back, and then God knows what they would do to Allie.

"You get shot in that leg?" Frank asked from right next to him. Jake's skin crawled like he'd stepped on a rattler.

"Something like that."

"In the war?"

"Yeah."

"Hurt still?"

"Some. I get by."

"War's a damn poor excuse for a man getting rid of his mad, ain't it? Especially when the ones starting it and the ones that really get hurt aren't one and the same."

Taken aback by the man's insight, Jake chuckled to cover his surprise.

Frank filled in the void. "I'll give you a hand with that." He backed the mules into the traces while Jake hitched them up.

If the man asked him which side he'd fought on, Jake knew he might be in trouble. During his stay in the area he'd learned that folks in Missouri were just about divided in half on the issue, but he was sure the James boys had fought for the Confederacy, if they were in the army at all. He didn't know much about them except from others' conversations over the past few months. Sometimes his thoughts treated him just like he was normal, till he mulled something over awhile. He'd awakened one morning in that stinking hell hole of a Reb prison, and were it not for that memory he wouldn't even know he'd fought on the side of the North, for Johnny Rebs didn't imprison their own kind. He sighed. He didn't feel like a damned Yankee, but probably that was only because he'd been wandering around in the South for so long.

When he and Frank finished hitching the team, Jesse came sauntering across the yard carrying Allie's Colt. Instead of approaching Jake he went to Allie where she was tying down the back curtain on the wagon.

Quickly, Jake moved in their direction, and so did Frank.

Jessie kept hold of the revolver and pulled a bundle of bills from his waistcoat pocket. "Ma'am, this here'll pay you for the work you did and the pictures. It's a plenty."

Allie eyed the money, but didn't reach for it. "Stolen money, I guess."

Jake cringed and tried to signal her to watch her mouth. Things could decay here real quick.

Jesse favored her with a dark glance, but his voice held steady. "Well, not so's you'd consider it. Belonged to a blamed carpetbagger. Yankees need to be relieved of the money they stole from us during the war, and that's a fact. Wouldn't surprise me if some of it didn't belong to your kin once upon a time."

"All the same, you don't owe me anything."

Jesse frowned. "We don't ask something for nothing. We want you to take it. I didn't steal it from anyone you'd know."

"All the same." She took hold of the Colt, still eyeing the money with distrust.

Jake moved forward. "Allie, thank the man for the day's work and take his money so we can be on our way. We've got a far piece to go and the day's more than half over."

Without turning loose of the gun she shoved her hair back and he saw stubbornness well up all over her. She was about to do them in. He wanted to shout at her. Take the damn money, throw it in a damn ditch somewhere, but just take it. He could see by her eyes she wasn't about to do that, and so he did the only thing he could. He stepped in and took it himself, then turned to Allie.

"I'll give you a hand aboard." He gritted the words out between his teeth so she could see he damn well meant business, for all the good it might do.

She tightened her mouth, her dark eyes sparked. Fixing to fight back. He could see that right away. At that moment Jesse let go of the butt of the Colt, and she stood there a moment gazing at it. Stupid to pull the thing around by its barrel, especially with Jesse James holding on to the trigger end. She put it under the wagon seat, then let Jake hand her up.

Jake's breath whooshed out with relief. He turned to Jesse and Frank, offered his hand. "Pleased to meet you. If anybody asks, we didn't."

Both men shook hands with him, grinning broadly.

"It wouldn't matter anyway," Jesse said when Jake had climbed up beside Allie. "If anyone believed you we'd be gone before they got here. Most folks'll just think you're bragging, anyway, you tell 'em about meeting us famous outlaws. You'all take care of yourselves, and thanks again, ma'am, for the pictures. We're beholden to you."

Stiffly, Allie twisted around. The men stood in the yard waving as if she and Jake had been friendly visitors come to pass some time.

"Throw that money away, Jake," she hissed before they were even out of sight of the cabin.

He drew a long breath of relief, cut the stack evenly and laid half on the seat beside her. "Yours. Do what you please with it. I'm keeping mine. I believe I earned it, and I'm damned tired of being hungry."

"Earned it? What did you do to earn it?"

He noticed she left the money be. He stuffed his inside his shirt. "Got myself knocked out, tied up, and washed all those greasy dishes, that's what."

Allie glanced at him, laughter playing around her set mouth. "Oh, Jake, you are something, aren't you?"

"Yes, maybe I am, at that. Trouble is, I'm not sure what. Why don't you let me drive this team and you relax. You've had a hard day."

The scowl she cut his way shut him up for the time being, and they rode on in silence.

They found Molly grazing in a patch of meadow near where Jake had left her. She raised her head and whinnied when she heard them coming. Allie's stallion, Ringo, came trotting over from a grove of trees nearby.

"Looks like they did okay on their own," Allie said.

Jake noticed that she had stowed her half of the money Jesse had given them in a small valise behind the seat. She might throw it away later, but he doubted it. Real cash was too hard to come by on the trail, and if she were to make it to Santa Fe, she would need all she could get. He, for one, was going to treat himself to a pair of boots and britches and maybe even a new Stetson hat when they got to Westport. And after that, right after that, he planned on bellying up to a cold mug of beer, maybe two.

Since the end of the war the westward movement had overrun the river town of Independence, and Westport had taken over in importance. Everyone headed for the Oregon and California trails passed through there on the Old Santa Fe Trail. Roads branched into the settlement from all directions. Because of rains during the past few weeks the streets ran knee-deep in mud, and the air hung heavy with the stench of animals and humans, the clamor of the crowd almost worse than the stink.

Allie had already had enough before Jake could find a spot to leave the wagon. "I'm not staying here," she told him after he climbed down and reached up a hand to her.

"What do you mean? Where are you going?"

"I don't know, but this is dreadful. How could anyone enjoy a meal or a walk or sleep with all this going on?"

Someone shouted, other voices pitched in, a gun went off. Teams pulled large wagons along the muddy street. Drivers yelled, whips cracked, cargo rattled.

Jake took a wild splatter of mud across the chest from a passing coach and couldn't come up with a sane reply to her objections. He'd put up with almost anything for just one mug of cold brew. These river ports usually had ice, and he'd been dreaming of the cold liquid oozing down his parched throat for the past two nights.

He angled a glance at her. "Maybe it just takes some getting used to."

"Could be, but why would I want to?"

Nearby, the batwing doors of a saloon swung open. Jake could almost taste the beer drawn from its wooden keg immersed in ice.

"Might be worth it for one cold beer."

She made a rude noise, eyed him doubtfully.

He tried one last time. "You could probably drum up some business here. Apt to be plenty of folks with money to pay for one of your pictures. Come on, Allie, join me for a brew, then we'll talk about this some more."

"They'd never let me in a saloon."

That lopsided grin appeared that told her he would soon be up to mischief. "Would if they didn't know you were a lady."

"I'm not a damn lady!"

"Okay, okay." He gestured feebly toward her chest. "You know what I mean."

"I'd never get away with that."

"You've done it before. Just push your hair up under your hat and hunch forward a bit so you . . . so those . . . " Again he swung a hand to indicate her breasts and flushed. "So they don't stand out so—uh, so . . . Can't you lean forward just a bit or something? Wouldn't you like just a taste of that good, cold

ale? Think what it would feel like sliding down your throat, all
frothy and cold."

"Jake, behave yourself. Besides, I was a lot younger then,
not so . . . well, so . . . developed."

"Come on, you know you want to. Dare you, Allie. Bet you
can't get away with it. Bet you a whole dollar."

"Of the money you earned washing all those dirty dishes?"
she teased. "Why, Jake, that was hard-earned money."

He nodded. "And I'm willing to give it up, too, just to have
your company in yonder." His dimples winked and he reached
up for her once again.

"Well, we couldn't stay but a little while. If no one guesses
I'm a woman all the while we're in there, I win a dollar?"

"Yes, a dollar of that money Jesse James stole off some
damned Yankee. A whole dollar. Only one thing."

She arched a brow. "I knew there'd be a catch."

"There is. You win, you got to spend it on something pretty
for yourself. Is it a deal? Just think, you get a pretty and you get
a cold beer, too. I'm buying."

"What makes you so all-fired free with your money all of a
sudden? Feeling flush or something? You ought to put that
money back, Jake. Save it for something special."

She gave him her hand as she finished speaking and when
he lifted her down into the mud, he said, "This is something
special."

Her heart kicked at her rib cage. He was the damndest man
and if, just if, she were looking, maybe . . . she groaned
inwardly and put a stop to that nonsense.

He helped Allie poke all her long blonde hair up under her
hat, captured her hand and led her toward the saloon.

"Don't forget to slouch forward," he said out of the corner of
his mouth before shoving open the batwing doors. "Stay behind
me and do what I do."

She squeezed his hand, then let go and followed him, eyes on
a spot between his shoulder blades. He worked them out a

space at the bar, several raw cut boards supported by large wooden barrels, and ordered two brews.

The place was a madhouse, a cacophony of sounds and smells. The only women in the place were nearly naked. Allie had never seen so much bare feminine flesh, and certainly not in public.

A singer performing on a table finished the ribald lyrics of a tune and leaned forward so that what part of her breasts had been covered were exposed. The bartender slid two brimming mugs in front of Allie and Jake. With relief she turned away from the scene. The man next to her jostled her arm just as she lifted the mug, and liquid and foam poured down her chin and dripped onto her shirt.

"Look out, you clumsy oaf." She gave him a shove with her shoulder and hip.

"What'd you say, kid?" He bumped her back, hard enough that she staggered up against Jake and spilled some more of her beer, this time on the bar.

"Wait a minute, you big jackass." Allie slammed the beer down and faced the barrel-chested man.

"Allie, don't do that," Jake said in her ear. "We haven't even finished our beers. He'll clean your plow, and likely mine, too. Can't you be good for five minutes?"

He no more than got the words out before Allie hit the man in the chest with the flats of both hands. "Mind your manners, you great oaf."

"Who's gonna make me? Some scrawny kid like you?" The man wadded up Allie's shirt front in one mammoth fist and lifted her off the floor.

"Aw, hell," Jake muttered, turned up his mug and gulped down the rest of his beer, then stepped into the fracas.

It wasn't easy to get to the man, what with Allie dangling there between them, clawing and spitting and kicking. She actually got in a couple of good punches and kicked her assailant in the knee, but nothing fazed the giant. She managed to make him so mad he roared and tossed her over the bar.

That gave Jake the chance he'd been waiting for, and he butted the man head on in his generous gut. The two of them went flying and cleared the bar of customers for at least ten feet.

Allie came up from behind the bar, hat gone and hair hanging down, the front of her shirt ripped open to reveal her generous endowment and her beribboned camisole. Her clothes were drenched in whiskey and she marveled that she hadn't been cut by the broken bottles lying around. Miraculously, her mug of beer stood on the bar. She grabbed it, gulped down the contents, and without wiping the foam from her mouth dived over the bar with the heavy empty mug in one fist to give Jake a hand.

Four or five men lay sprawled on the floor, moaning and groaning, while Jake and his assailant went at each other. Every time the big man swung, Jake dodged easily from the path of his fist and belted him one in the gut. The blows didn't phase the bear of a man, yet he couldn't seem to connect with any of his own.

Jake was clearly wearing down and getting nowhere except keeping the man from wiping up the floor with him.

Quickly, Allie looked around for a better weapon than an empty mug and settled for a broken chair. She filled both hands with chair rungs and started whamming the giant across the buttocks and back. Under the first few blows he only grunted, but then she began to get his attention. It was a good thing, too, for she didn't have much energy left and Jake was panting, his blows growing weaker and weaker.

Finally the man whirled, grabbed the rungs from her and lifted them above his head. His enormous roar shook the rafters, and at the precise moment when Allie was sure he was going to brain her, Jake cracked him smartly on the head with a half-empty bottle he'd come up with from somewhere. Maybe the only unbroken one in the place.

An immense cheer went up from the spectators, who had formed a ring around the battle and were laying bets.

"You through now, all of you done?" the angry bartender shouted.

A squat, hairy fellow gripped Allie's elbow and shoved her up against the bar. "I'm buying this'n a drink. Okay by you, honey?" He leered at her nipples, which were evident through the beer-and whiskey-soaked camisole.

She nodded wearily and pulled her shirt together. "I'll take a beer. Someone seems to have spilled mine."

A hearty round of laughter filled the place.

"Hell of a fight." A hand slapped her on the back, rattling her back teeth.

She had downed half the beer before she realized that she didn't see Jake anywhere. He hadn't been hurt—the guy had not laid a fist on him—so where had he gone?

Mug in hand, she turned from the bar to see that he had joined a few other unfortunates sprawled out cold on the floor.

"Oh, Jake, not again." She finished the beer, then went to his side and sank wearily to her knees. Adrenaline from the ruckus drained out of her so that her feeble attempts to rouse him brought little results. She began to think he wasn't going to awaken when he finally opened his eyes, the blue clouded with familiar confusion.

After studying her a moment he grinned, and she resisted a temptation to put her arms around him.

If there was a doctor in town, she'd see Jake paid him a visit. He'd do well to just stay here and get some treatment for whatever this strange ailment might be. It was dangerous for him to go with her on the trail to Santa Fe. Besides, she enjoyed his company far too much, and she'd be damned if she'd let a thing like that get out of hand.

Chapter Six

A hand jarred at her shoulder and Allie stopped staring at Jake to turn toward a voice she remembered all too well.

"Allie, my God, it is you. What kind of a mess have you gotten yourself into? Lord, it's good to see you. What are you doing here? And who is this . . . uh . . . this unfortunate fellow?"

Her lips moved over Eli Martin's name, but nothing came out. She tried again, her heart doing flip-flops. She had once loved this man and he had loved her, or so she had thought. Now she couldn't even speak to him..

He took her arm, tried to lift her to her feet. "Allie? Are you hurt? Let me take a look at you."

She stiffened and yanked away from his grip. "Turn me loose, Eli. What are you doing here, anyway? I had hoped never to lay eyes on you again." Him with his shiny mahogany hair and broad shoulders.

"Aw, sweetheart, don't be that way. Think of what we meant to each other."

"That's exactly what I am thinking of."

He laid a hand on her shoulder. "I was real sorry to hear about your father. I intended to come see you while I was in Missouri, but I just got here and haven't had the chance."

"Stop it, Eli. You never cared for my father. You resented him and you know it, so don't . . . " She jerked away from his touch.

He shrugged. "It was your choice, Allie. You know that."

"You insisted I choose between my father and you. If you had loved me you wouldn't have done that."

"If you had loved me, you'd have come with me." His hazel eyes hardened, his broad jaw clenched.

Jake groaned and the bartender interrupted. "Ma'am, I reckon it would be a good idea if you got your friend out of here before Lem wakes up. He's gonna be mighty fierce. What's wrong with this fella, you figger? No one laid a hand on him. I seen it. He just went down like he was poleaxed, and me standing there lookin' right at him. Put up one hell of a good fight. I've seen Lem beat the waddin' out of many a good man, but he never laid a hand on this 'un. Never laid a hand on him. Lem, he's whupped big 'uns too, bigger'n him."

Allie pulled her gaze from Eli's. His sensual mouth and mesmerizing, changeable eyes still held a fierce power over her, though hatred for him turned her stomach.

She bent over Jake, shook his shoulder.

Eli stepped around to his other side. "Let me give you a hand."

A shiver set her insides to quaking. "No, you get away. Don't touch him, don't come near me. Just leave us be."

Caught by a fierce anger, she couldn't move, but then Jake reached toward her, and she took his hand in hers while he struggled to his feet. Looking only at him, she kept her back to Eli and took deep breaths to control an urge to race from the place as if all the furies of hell stood there instead of the man she'd almost married.

"Allie?" Two voices in cadence. Jake's concerned; Eli's demanding, and she whirled, as furious as she'd ever been in her life.

"What are you doing here, Eli? I thought you went to California."

Before Eli could reply, Jake asked, "You know this yahoo?"

Eli answered the question for her. "Yes, indeed she does. Let me buy you both a drink. That is if there's any whiskey left in the place that's not on the floor."

Jake tugged at her arm. "Allie?"

"Let's go, now," she said.

"I'm surprised at you, Allison," Eli said. "I certainly never thought I'd see you in such a condition."

Allie yanked away from Jake's grasp. "What do you know about me? What do you care? I told you once, and I'll tell you again. I don't ever want to set eyes on you, in this world or the next. Get away from me. Far away."

Eli shook his head, clucked his tongue and retreated a few steps from her venomous charge. She was surprised to see he wore a pistol in a holster beneath his neat black jacket.

Jake put an arm around her shoulders in a protective gesture, even though he seemed to be leaning on her more than holding her up. His courage renewed her own, and the weakness she'd felt under Eli's stare faded.

"Come on, Jake. I want to go now." Immediately she changed her mind, turned and attacked Eli once again. "It was your idea to leave, and now that my father's dead I suppose you think you can just . . . that I'll take . . . take you back. Well, you're wrong. Wrong."

Jake felt a raw tension pouring through her. "Come on, honey. Let's get out of here."

In a blaze of anger, she turned on him. "Don't you 'honey' me. I don't need either one of you, so just leave me be." She shoved her way through the crowd and out the door.

Jake gathered her hat and his without giving the man she'd called Eli another glance. Whatever was going on between the two of them, he wanted no part of it. He found her sitting on the end of the boardwalk, legs dangling over the muddy alleyway.

89

Samantha Lee

Without saying a word he lowered himself down beside her, handed her one beer-soaked hat and crammed the other down on his head. Then he took it off, peered inside and traded with her.

"Thanks," she said after a while.

"Nothing to it."

Tilting a quick grin at him, she added, "Well, not much to it anyway. Only about got yourself killed."

More silence, then he said softly, "You lost, you know."

"I lost? You were the one on the floor."

"The bet." He fingered her camisole with a delicate touch that sent shivers through her.

She nodded, pulled the shirt together. "Damn him, I hate the bastard."

"Yeah, I could see that right away."

He waited for her to say something else, and when she didn't, asked, "Who is he?" It startled him that he was jealous of the man for what he and Allie must have once had. For her to hate him so much, she must have loved him deeply at one time.

"I don't want to talk about him."

He nodded curtly. "Hmm, okay. That's up to you, I suppose. You gonna pay me now?"

She squinted at him. "Pay you?"

"The dollar you owe me."

"I owe you? I saved your hide in there when that great oaf was beating on you, and now you want me to give you a dollar?"

"I think you've got that all wrong. Who hit him on the head when he came at you? He'd a squashed you flat if I hadn't laid him out. Besides, the bet didn't have anything to do with the fight. I bet you—"

She held up a hand. "I know the bet, Jake. God, I feel dirty." Sniffing the air around him, she pinched her nose. "And you smell bad, real bad. I'm going to find a place to take a bath."

Together they slid off the edge of the boardwalk and made their way through the ankle-deep mud. Jake spotted the bath house and guided her toward it. They slithered across the street.

He gestured at the slab front of the bathhouse. *For Men Only* was hand-painted in crooked black letters on a smaller sign hanging on the crude board door. "Put on your hat and stick your hair up under it, or you'll be washing in the river tonight."

"I tried this once tonight—what makes you think it'll work any better the second time? And they have some nerve. For men only, indeed."

Sensing she was set to go off again, he stuck out a grimy hand. "Double or nothing?"

Tears welled in her eyes for no apparent reason and he wanted to touch her, to hold her again like he had earlier. Doing so had produced an unexpected reaction in his gut, for he had never thought of any other woman except Lorena since the day he'd come to himself in Andersonville, the first day of his life. Up till tonight Allie had been a friend, someone to pass the time with. Someone who made him feel almost normal.

She made a face, pawed away the hot tears and turned from him.

He considered that a very good thing, because it gave him time to come back to his old self. He shouldn't be feeling this way about any woman, not any but the one he loved.

Shoulders hunched, she stared at the sign and began stuffing strands of long hair up under the beer-soaked hat. While doing so she caught a glimpse of her breasts scarcely disguised by the flimsy camisole.

"Oh, Jake, maybe I shouldn't . . . they'll know."

"Don't be silly, of course you should. All you need is a little repair work." He shoved her up against the plank board siding of the building and did the best job he could covering her with what was left of her shirt. It was hard because he kept touching her warm, soft skin.

What a damn fool he'd suddenly become.

He steeled himself and bent closer, said gruffly, "Lord God, Allie, you smell like a brewery." And a delectable woman, he finished silently.

"You don't smell so good yourself."

Spell broken, he made a rude noise down in his throat. "Be quiet and let me do the talking, and we'll both soon smell a whole hell of a lot better."

"They're going to know, Jake. I'll just wait at the wagon and when we make camp I'll find a place to bathe."

"Nonsense, you should be able to take a bath in there same as me."

"You have a point, Jake. But I am structured just a bit differently, and somebody is bound to notice."

"There're curtains, and when they come in with more hot water just scootch down until . . . " He pointed at her chest. "Until those are underneath, you know."

"Oh, Jake, this is ridiculous."

"No, come on, you can do it. I'll betcha a dollar no one finds out, unless you choose to bare your . . . your . . . uh, well, you know, just to win a bet."

She touched his arm. "Make you a deal. I go in with you if you go see a doctor after we come out. No bets."

"Whoa, why should I do that? Hell, you're the one that needs the bath. Sounds like some kind of a crazy deal to me."

"Jake, something is wrong with you and it could be dangerous. Just let someone take a look."

"Bye, Allie." He left her standing there and stepped through the doorway into the bath house.

She shoved in behind him. "Wait."

He grabbed her arm, dragged her along and raised his voice. "Hush, boy. You're taking a bath and that's the end of that." Shoving her against the counter, he said, "Two, please," and spread out a bill from the money Jesse James had given them.

A dimple winked in his cheek and his eyes sparkled when he turned toward her. "Your pa will skin me alive if I let you go out to supper looking like a ragamuffin. You're taking a bath and that's final."

Glaring at him, she made a face and mouthed the word *boy*. Though the idea of a hot bath was inviting, she would get even with him for this.

The attendant gave them each a towel and a sliver of lye soap, then led them into the back where several tin tubs sat in cubicles with the curtains open around them. Two were closed for privacy. She'd never been in a public bath house, had no idea exactly what might go on there.

God, suppose they sent someone in to scrub her back? A beautiful, half-naked woman, perhaps. Or worse, a man.

Jake shoved her playfully into a cubicle and drew the curtain. He took the one next to her. She heard the rustle of his clothing, the clunk of his boots dropping on the floor.

"Hot water coming," a thick masculine voice cried.

Allie gazed down into the tub, which had about a foot of water in it. It looked fairly clean, so she supposed they did scrub out the thing between bathers.

She sat on a crude seat and worked the boots off her feet, then the dirty socks. Stretching out her legs she wiggled her toes and sighed. She heard water being poured into the tub in Jake's cubicle, soon followed by a long, drawn-out "Ahhh."

After a moment he called out, "Boy, you in the tub yet?"

"No," she shouted in a gruff, low voice.

"Well, wait till they bring your hot water. I wouldn't undress if I were—"

The curtain rustled open and a large bare-chested man entered carrying two buckets of steaming water.

Allie crossed both arms over her chest and slouched forward, intent on a bug moving across the floor. The man didn't even glance at her as he filled the tub. She watched the steam for only an instant after he left, then shucked out of her clothes in double time and hopped in. She placed the hat on the floor, and with a sigh lowered herself to her ears into the wonderful hot water. She closed her eyes and groaned with pleasure.

Just as she lathered the soap and began to wash, a cheery voice called out, "Hot water."

Grabbing up the hat, she held it over her breasts.

"This ain't too hot, want I should pour it over your head, rench off all that soap?" he asked with exaggerated good nature.

Scrunching further, she nodded and clenched her eyes shut.

"That feel better, ma'am?" the attendant asked in a low, amused voice, then hightailed it before she could react.

She gasped and sputtered, wiping sudsy water out of her eyes. The hat bobbed in the murky water like a dead fish.

"Jake, I'll kill you when I get my hands on you. You cheated, you told him, didn't you?"

From the other side of the wall came a well-satisfied chuckle but no reply to her question. She really didn't need one.

"All I wish is that I'd had clean clothes to put on," Jake said as he hurried after Allie back toward the what's-it wagon and their horses.

"If you hadn't been in such an all-fired hurry to get me into that place, we could have bought some decent clothes first."

"Aw, come on, Allie. Don't you feel better?"

"Of course, I do, but I could have died when he called me ma'am like that. And me naked down in the water with only this disgusting hat to cover myself with." She gestured with the disreputable wad of felt she had removed from her head as soon as they were out of sight of the bath house. "I had no idea what he was going to do. He might have chosen to toss me out on the sidewalk bare as the day I was born."

By the time she finished the tirade Jake was consumed with laughter.

She tried to remain angry with him while she pawed around in her valise for some money, but couldn't. He had a way of making everything fun. A man like him who had no past he could remember, knew no friends or enemies, had no idea if there was anyone in the world who loved him, and he made each day brighter because he enjoyed every moment. Whatever was causing those blackouts could kill him at any time, and here he stood absurdly amused over such a silly prank.

She couldn't help but join him. Chuckling, she stuffed a wad of bills in her pocket and took his arm. "Come on, let's go buy some clothes."

"I'll be glad to see you get a new hat. I'll bet you pay someone to hold a gun on you while you put that one on every day."

"What's wrong with this hat? It was perfectly respectable until it took a bath in beer and soapy water. Besides, considering that . . . that thing you wear, you're one to talk. For a long time I thought it was a dead animal of some kind."

Laughing, they walked along the boardwalk arm in arm.

While they were paying for their new clothes Allie struck up a conversation with the storekeeper's wife, a round, red-faced woman. It appeared to be her job to worry about every single thing that went on within the crowded mercantile, and she had a hard time concentrating on what Allie was saying while bobbing about trying to keep count of the customers.

"I wonder if I might come back and take pictures of you and your husband here, when you're not so busy," Allie asked once she got the fussing woman's attention.

"Whyever for?" The woman plumped the sagging bun on the back of her head.

"It's my business, and I need samples of my work. I would be glad to take your photograph without charge if I could use a copy of it to show to prospective clients. I believe that if merchants would circulate pictures of their business accommodations, people would remember and shop with them when they have a need for something. Sort of like running an ad in a newspaper."

"Nobody does anything for free," her husband chimed in. "And I wouldn't want them to. You want to take one of these what-do-you-call-ums, then we'll pay you and you give it to us."

Allie sighed. "Well, of course that would be fine, too. What time do you open in the morning?"

"Around eight or so."

"If I were to come by earlier, and we set up something, then perhaps we could talk about the rest. The service will cost you nothing unless you want to purchase the prints. How will that be?"

The man's wife glanced nervously around the store, then back at Allie. She smiled tentatively and looked up at her husband.

He nodded a silent agreement and waited on a teamster with an armful of purchases.

Allie thanked them and moved away from the counter to where Jake stood, the large brown-paper parcel in both arms. She pushed aside dark thoughts of the sudden appearance of Eli Martin and let excitement fill her. She had actually made her first business contact.

If this storekeeper agreed, others might follow suit. She also hoped to take some portraits of the women and children heading West. Their dreams and motivations would be far different from the men's. Fear of the unknown, what might happen to their children, and birthing babies along the trail surely would affect the countenance of these women. No man could understand, but Allie hoped to capture forever the feelings that those women must be experiencing. She was eager to go to work with the camera.

As they came out of the store, she spotted Eli Martin on the opposite side of the street. He leaned casually against a post smoking a long black cigar, and she could have sworn he had been waiting for them. Something about the way he tipped his hat, looked right at her, then moved off down the sidewalk told her so.

What did he want? And why now, after all this time? She searched around within herself for even an inkling of the love she had once felt for him, but could find nothing but resentment and a hate she had succeeded in stifling for a long while. How dare he bring all that back when she had learned to live with it?

"Let's go, Jake. I don't want to stay here any longer."

"Okay by me. A little bit of this place goes a long way."

They slopped back to the wagon and climbed aboard, boots carrying great globs of mud onto the floor boards. She was glad they had not put on their new ones.

Later that evening they were camped along the trail west of town, preparing their first good meal in days.

While Jake peeled and fried potatoes Allie mixed up thick cornmeal batter for johnny cakes and set them to cooking on the lid of the Dutch oven. She cut a few slices from the butt end of a cured ham and watched Jake slide the frying pan onto a bed of coals and cover it. He caught her looking at him and held her gaze for a somber moment before smiling quizzically.

"I'm just wondering where you learned to cook," she explained.

He shrugged. "Beats me."

They were both silent for a long while; then he spoke. "Tell me about that fella."

"No. I'd rather hear about your . . . about Lorena."

He touched his pocket.

"Yes, her." Allie nodded toward his hand, cupped over his chest. She had seen him carefully transfer Lorena's likeness to the pocket of his new shirt.

He picked up a stick and stirred it around in the coals till it caught fire, then lifted it and stared into the flickering flames.

She breathed in the pungent odor of burning hickory and the smell of the good supper cooking before them. He wasn't going to tell her, but then, perhaps he didn't know.

"Lorena is her name," he said unexpectedly, the words blurred by emotion.

"Yes, I know that much."

"Then you know all I know."

"Oh, Jake. If that's all you knew, you wouldn't continue to carry her picture around. You murmur her name in your sleep, or when you're coming out of one of your . . . your . . . "

"Call them what everyone else does. Fits." Abruptly he laughed, an unnatural and loud sound in the still air.

97

"Dammit, Jake, can't you take this seriously?"

His gaze flicked from the burning twig to catch hers. Reflections of the flames danced in the moisture that filled his eyes.

"If I did, Allie, I'd surely die."

The tone of his voice reached down deep in her belly and awoke an emotion she'd thought dead and gone. A deep need to love someone, to be loved once again.

Softly, he asked, "Who is he? If you don't talk about him, it'll just keep eating at you, you know."

She nodded, rubbed at her nose. "Yes, I do know, but I can't. I'm afraid."

"Of what?"

"My foolish self. There's so much and I try to keep it all hidden away. Don't pick at it, please."

But he had gone too far to let it be. Her tone told him more than the words themselves. "Allie, what you're doing is worse than what's happened to me. You can't keep denying the things that have happened to you. It won't make them go away, and soon they'll turn on you. Tell me, you know you can tell me anything. Hell, I don't have a bunch of stuff cluttering up my mind. Let me help you, Allie, before this destroys you."

"Damn you. I was fine until you came along!"

He moved closer to her, wrapped a large hand around her clenched fist. "No, you weren't." But I was fine, Jake admitted silently. No visions of blood around his sweet Lorena; no nightmarish memories of a man who looked like himself, perhaps hurting her. Only great black holes lurked in his mind until he met this woman who awoke his emotions like no one else had. He dragged his attention back to Allie and away from what awful images might await him should he close his eyes.

She dragged in a sob-ridden breath. "No, you're right, I wasn't. I will not cry. I won't."

"It's okay if you do."

She pulled her hand away, clenched it with the other hard against her stomach.

"I adored my father, even if he did desert us so he could follow the war with his camera. I felt so abandoned when he left, and God help me, so righteous when Mama and Sara were killed and he had to take me with him. I had survived a horrible thing and now my father had to love me because I was all he had left.

"We worked in that hell day and night for two years with death all around us. I trusted him, and he couldn't have chosen anything I loved more than what we were doing. Those haunted, brave faces, captured forever with light and chemicals. And we were doing it together. I guess . . . I guess I was able to hide the guilt I felt because I couldn't save Mama and Sara because my father loved me and I loved him."

She stopped, watched Jake stir the potatoes and ham, then set the skillet on a hot stone beside the flames.

"Go ahead, it'll keep," he said and settled beside her. He had a feeling that if she stopped now he'd never get her started again. And she still hadn't once mentioned Eli Martin.

"There's not much more to tell. We came back home, set up a studio . . . and . . . then he died. I just can't come to terms with it yet. It's the worst thing that's ever happened to me, losing my entire family."

He nodded, understanding, because in an odd way he had lost his, too, and sometimes felt such empty loneliness he thought he might go mad.

"And Eli Martin?"

"Oh, him." She shrugged. "Let's eat."

"Tell me about Eli."

She swung on him, jaw set. "I can't." Her voice shivered over the two words, spitting them out letter by letter. "Don't you understand?"

"Oh, yes, Allie, I do. Tell me. Talk about him before he destroys you."

"I was fine . . . fine, till you . . . "

"No, you were fine till he . . . And you know that."

99

"I . . . loved . . . him."

"Yes." He put an arm around her shoulder, drew her head down. And way down inside, she still did. The realization jarred him to his very bones.

"He said that if I loved him I would go to California with him, but I wouldn't because my father was so ill. I couldn't desert him . . . like he . . . like he did me. Eli couldn't see that. He said if my father loved me he would want me to be happy, to go with him. My father . . . my father hated Eli. Said he was not good enough for me, but Eli said all fathers were that way, and if I didn't go with him, he would go alone." She took a deep breath, but didn't move out of Jake's embrace. "And so he did."

"And so you remained with your father until his death?"

She nodded against his chest.

"And even that didn't take away the guilt, did it?"

Her silence scared him, as if he had opened up a big, deep, empty cavern and she had fallen in. He thought he'd gone too far, till she said very softly, "What makes you so smart?"

"I'm not. It's just easy for me to see because I'm not involved. It's not your fault your father went away, and your mother and sister were killed and you weren't. It's not your fault your father died. It's not even your fault Eli Martin went away and deserted you just like your father once did."

"Maybe not, Jake. But all the same, it feels that way. And most of the time I get along okay with it. He's not coming back into my life, I won't let him. I won't let anybody ever make me feel that way again."

Yet, even as she said the words, sitting there with Jake's arm around her, she realized that she cared deeply about what happened to him, this man who didn't even know who he was. And that thing in his head would kill him one day soon.

After supper she again brought up her suggestion about him seeing a doctor.

"Since you are so bent on nosing into my business, Jake, I'm going to do the same. I think you should see a doctor, and the sooner the better."

He became almost as indignant as she had earlier. "What do you think they're going to do to me if I do? Huh, Allie? Do you have any idea? They'll stick me in a hospital someplace where they can put their needles in me and worse, poke and prod and call in more doctors who don't know any more than they do. Do you think I want to spend what's left of my life letting those medical geniuses make me miserable? I'm not going to do it, and I wish you'd let it go. Now. Or I swear I'll just ride out and be rid of your yammering about this."

"Then that's what you'll have to do, because I don't want to watch you die. I'm tired of wondering every time you pass out if this time you'll be dead when I go to wake you up."

"Aw, hell, Allie. Why should you care anyway? We're good company for each other. Can't you just let it go at that? We're both going the same direction, why not travel together? Hell, we don't fight, I haven't made any passes at you, you're safe with me."

"What do you call what we're doing now but fighting?"

"This?" He swung an arm around to include her. "This isn't fighting. We're just having a slight difference of opinion."

She stared at him for a minute and he grinned.

"A slight difference of opinion," she muttered.

He gazed into the dying fire for a moment. "You suppose old Jesse James knows he financed us such a good supper? Did you ever take pictures of anyone that famous before, Allie?"

"No, I never did."

"Then I've brought you good luck."

"Jake, you are the strangest man I've ever met."

"And you've met plenty, huh, Allie."

"No, I guess I haven't, but you're sure a new experience. When I set out I was prepared to run off any man who came within a hundred feet of me, and what do I do? Fall in with the first one I come across."

"Or in this case fall over the first one you come across." He chuckled. "You've got to admit, I do have a rather unique way of meeting up with strangers on the trail."

"Oh, Jake, you are totally hopeless."

She realized only after they had gone to bed how adroitly Jake had turned the subject away from seeing a doctor before it could become a full-blown argument.

Chapter Seven

Jake awoke from a mysterious dream that vanished before he could examine its meaning. He recalled Lorena's face, streaked with tears and begging something of a shadowy man, the name Ethan like an echo in the gleam of early dawn as he opened his eyes to the real world. He didn't know what to do with this piece of the puzzle. Sometimes he wished everything had remained a blank, for so far all he remembered only brought him pain.

Allie stood by the fire sipping a cup of coffee. She wore a long-tailed man's shirt and a pair of faded red longjohn britches. Her pale hair hung loose, the early morning light streaking it with gold and silver. He smelled ham frying, coffee perking, bread baking. Contentment replaced his earlier apprehension. For an instant he'd stepped into real life, and it felt good. Too bad it was a fleeting experience.

He raked his fingers through his tangled hair.

She grinned at him. "You look like you've been wrestling a bear."

"Feel like it. I was having the strangest dream, and now I can't remember a damn thing about it. Funny, at the time it was all-consuming. Urgent, like I'd left something unfinished I had to fix at all cost."

"Was it about Lorena?"

He hated to admit it, for she probably got tired of his forays into that dark past, but he nodded and fetched himself a cup of the black coffee.

"After breakfast I'm going in to town to take some pictures. Want to come along?"

"Sure, I'll help with the equipment. It's too heavy for a woman to lug around, anyway."

The corners of her mouth quirked in amusement. "Obviously not. Plenty of us do it."

He raised an eyebrow. "I ought to be fixing breakfast, seeing as how you're the one who works all the time."

"That's not the kind of work a man ought to do."

He glanced up quickly to see that she was teasing him, getting back at him for what he'd said about her carrying the heavy equipment. "Touché," he said with a broad grin. There came that normal feeling again. He could get used to this, if he dared.

After breakfast she crawled in the cramped wagon to dress while he cleaned up the leavings. When she came from behind the black curtain, he glanced up casually, then took a long look. She wore a dress the color of sweet cream butter. It was cut simply, with no trim. The neckline caressed the hollow of her throat, the bodice hugged her full breasts and tiny waist; the skirt, delicately gathered, kissed the grass and disguised her supple leanness. She'd pulled her palomino-blond hair into a tail high on the back of her head.

Jake guessed she looked much like that sixteen-year-old who had gone off to war with her father, and the idea left him totally speechless. Something stirred in his groin, surprising him, and he looked away quickly. Only in his dreams did he desire a woman, and he always supposed that woman to be Lorena, yet who wouldn't want this vision that stood before him?

Obviously aware of the effect she was having on him, she smiled and her eyes lit precociously. He turned so abruptly he dropped the black skillet before he could put it where it belonged. Physically and emotionally starved for so long, his body tended to betray him at the most inopportune of times, and he wasn't about to pay any attention to this latest deceit. It would pass and his hands would stop trembling if he concentrated on something besides the beauty of this woman early on such a bright spring morning—besides the fragrance of wild honeysuckle and smoke from the fire, the lingering breakfast smells and the lilting sound of her voice. Dear God, don't let him start wanting something else he couldn't have. Not now, when his life was consumed with such an impossible quest.

Allie felt a keen disappointment when Jake turned from her. She had deliberately set out to make him desire her more than Lorena, to forget his unhealthy obsession with a woman he didn't even know anymore, if he ever had. He might well have found that photograph on the battlefield, or on the corpse of one of his comrades in Andersonville.

But he didn't react at all, other than to fall silent—which was probably simply from the shock of learning that she owned a dress. He could have said something, told her how beautiful she looked.

Considering her own motives, she chided herself for being all kinds of a fool. Did she really want to travel with a man who would scheme and woo her, put his hands on her at every chance? The answer was a definite no, yet she had gone out of her way to attract him. She wasn't sure why.

An awkward silence rode between them on the drive to town.

Nell, the storekeeper's wife, turned out to be a willing ally. She and Allie chatted amiably while setting up a perfect background for the photograph that would depict the mercantile at its most advantageous.

As the morning sunlight spread across town, Allie posed the storekeeper and his wife in front of the store, the sign in full view behind them. Jake fetched planks for them to stand on in the muddy ruts. Deep shadows and contrasting light framed the scene perfectly.

Carrying yet another long plank as well as the heavy camera, Jake helped Allie set up the equipment in the center of the main thoroughfare. He noticed when she lifted her dress to keep it out of the mud that she was wearing her old boots, the ones she had carefully cleaned the previous evening. She was saving the new pair for something special, no doubt.

He hired two tow-headed youngsters to watch for oncoming traffic, then slogged through the mud to stand beside Allie. When she loaded the first plate and moved under the drape, he raised his hat high to signal the boys to see that the street remained safe until she finished the shot.

Eli Martin eased his mount forward from the shadow of the alleyway. "That's it, fella. You take good care of our little Allison," he muttered. He studied the lean, beardless man Allie called Jake, then looked once again at the wanted poster he'd picked up in a sheriff's office in some town east of the Mississippi. It was one of many he carried, and he couldn't remember where he'd gotten this particular one. Looking at the drawing, he imagined the beard gone, the neat dark hair in the picture shaggy like this Jake wore his. Sure as shooting it was him, no matter who the hell he said he was.

He read the man's name over again, but his eye was caught by the bold black letters beneath. $10,000 REWARD, BROUGHT BACK ALIVE. The biggest he'd gone after since taking up this thankless job. But he knew the murdered woman's father had put up the lion's share. No one was worth that to a government recovering from a civil war. He guessed that was why being a bounty hunter paid better than being a lawman. It was a damn fool way to make a few bucks, but he enjoyed the feeling of power it gave him.

After a moment's thought, Eli folded the poster carefully and stuffed it back in the pocket of his jacket. The unusual stipulation that this fella be brought back alive might cause some complications. And then there was Allison and the way he still felt about her. Even so, if he was careful he could make it work out for everyone. Everyone but Ethan Hollingsworth.

Jake watched with good humor when the two boys came racing back, laughing and shouting, grubby hands held out for the rest of their pay.

Allie watched, then asked, "What was that all about?"

"Just making sure you weren't disturbed. Do you think it's a good idea to work out in the middle of a busy street without any protection at all?"

She laughed merrily. "For a man who tempts fate on such a regular basis, you sure do worry about what I do. No one would run over me."

"Well, maybe not, but I wish you'd be more careful."

"Nonsense, you're an old worry wart."

Despite the words she patted the back of his hand. He wished she hadn't touched him, the way he was feeling about her. It was probably just that damned dress coupled with his strange dream about Lorena that brought on his desire.

He wanted Allie to go back to wearing jeans and loose shirts, maybe even that ratty black duster. That way he could continue to think of her as his buddy and forget this man/woman nonsense that left him more confused than one of his blackouts.

When Allie headed off to talk to Nell, he drew a great sigh of relief and remained several paces behind her while lugging the heavy equipment. By the time he reached the counter in the store, the two women were chattering.

"Right out in front would be fine," Nell said. "We'll rope off a section along the hitching rail and put up a sign, that way you won't have to go all over town."

"Oh, but won't that get in the way of your customers? You could lose business."

Nell glanced at her husband. "Not if I take some sweets out, maybe for the kiddies to buy while they wait to have their picture made. It'll attract more folks than it will turn away, won't it, Clem?"

"If you say so, Nell." Her patient husband grinned at Allie. "She always has the better ideas anyway, and somehow they always work. I'd be a fool to naysay her. I'll just remain in here and handle store business."

"Jake will help us, won't you, Jake?" Allie said, and grabbed his arm to pull him into the conversation. Her soft breast brushed against him and he tried to ignore the way his gut lurched. Prolonged celibacy was taking its toll all at once, he thought with wry surprise.

"Sure, you tell me what you need, I'll do it." He was relieved when she moved away.

A scant half-hour later, an area had been roped off for the camera and portable dark box, and planks rearranged to accommodate chairs for those who would pose for their portraits. By the time they finished the preparations a crowd had gathered, and the chairs quickly filled for the first sittings.

As the morning wore on, Jake proved to be very adept at composing the shots, and when children were involved, managed not only to get the little rascals to remain still but to get a smile out of them at the proper moment.

Nell displayed her acumen for business by selling bags filled with candy among the crowd. The arrangement turned out to be lucrative for everyone. Allie refused to take payment for her picture of Clem and Nell, for they had brought her a very profitable day. The storekeeper reluctantly acquiesced.

The sun slipped quickly toward the horizon as Allie moved under the black drape for what would be the final shot of the day. She was startled to spy Eli Martin through the lens of her camera, cockily posed with his hat held over his chest, his other hand in a pocket so that his expensive suit jacket was swept back to reveal a gold watch chain. What was Jake thinking allowing such a thing when he knew how she felt?

She threw back the cloth to glare at Eli. "I'm sorry, the light is gone. We're finished for the day."

Jake, who had failed to notice Martin take his place in the chair because he'd been talking to Nell, turned at the sound of

Allie's irritation. The handsome Martin, all duded up, strode toward her, a determined expression on his face. Darkness clouded Jake's vision for an instant, then cleared. There was no time for that; he had to stand beside Allie.

Trembling, Allie took a couple of quick steps backward to put space between her and Eli. "I told you to stay away from me. I meant it." She could hardly speak, her teeth were clenched so tightly.

With a roar Jake leapt between them. He grabbed Martin and flung him aside with such ferocity that the man staggered, almost fell in the mud.

"Hey, keep your hands off me," he shouted, and brushed at his suit as if Jake had soiled the material.

"Leave her alone. She's told you."

Sensing the threat in Jake's tone, Allie took his arm. It was like grabbing a hunk of iron. "It's okay," she told him. "Come on, let's go."

Jake shook free and lunged forward. "You come near her again, you son of a bitch, and I'll feed you your heart."

Allie gasped. The voice was not Jake's, nor were the words, and they so filled her with terror that she couldn't speak.

Eli Martin obviously felt the same, because his hand, quick to grip the butt of the revolver on his hip, dropped to his side and he hurried off without so much as another glance in her direction.

For a moment she remained at Jake's back unable to move or speak. When Martin disappeared around a corner down the street, Jake's shoulders raised, and she sensed the tension flowing out of him. But when he turned, a granite hardness in his blue eyes made her shudder. Almost as if by magic, the ice melted and he held out a hand, smiling.

"You okay?" he asked softly.

Still speechless, she nodded, and busied herself packing the equipment. Jake helped her, and neither mentioned the episode again.

He didn't forget it, though. A glimpse of something evil had surfaced from the darkness of his mind, and it had scared hell out of him. He made every effort not to touch Allie as they worked. She was having some kind of strange influence on him. Being with someone who truly cared about his welfare was the best and the worst thing that had happened to him. Furthermore, she trusted him and there wasn't anything he wouldn't do to keep that trust, even if it meant leaving to ensure her safety. He feared the darkness that sometimes eclipsed his soul, tried not to ponder too much what he had said to Eli Martin. For a moment there he had been willing to kill the man, and it scared him to death to think he might actually have been capable of doing so. But the mood passed quickly, and he was happy to forget about it and think only of Allie, who looked so exceptionally beautiful.

While they worked he stole quick glances at her. The creamy fabric of her dress set off her dark eyes; her golden hair, tousled by the wind, escaped in untamed curls to frame her face, which had a peach-colored flush dusting the tan of her cheeks. She took to the sun well despite her pale hair. The skin at her throat glowed above the fabric that lay across the swell of her breasts. He tried not to gawk, but God she was gorgeous.

In an effort to keep from staring, he glanced quickly down at his hands and saw they were trembling. Clenching them into fists, he limped to the front of the wagon, where he busied himself with the team. By the time Allie was ready to leave he had the unwelcome desires firmly in hand, and was able to climb up on the seat beside her without playing the fool.

The next morning at breakfast, which he arose early to cook, Allie brought up the subject of joining a caravan.

"Much as I hate to say it, Jake, it would probably be best if you made the arrangements. They don't tend to take a woman too seriously. I think since we've got the money, we ought to pay for a spot with one of the trader's caravans, rather than going it alone to Santa Fe. Though I would rather not be tied to their schedule, being with them will keep us safe from any Indians or outlaws who might be lying in wait for lone travelers."

Since their arrival in Westport he had expected her to tell him she would continue on alone—had thought she would literally kick him out of her camp. Now she wanted him to make the arrangements, as if his going with her were all settled.

His relief was so immense he could barely speak. "Much as I hate crowds, I think you're right." He took a bite of potatoes and chewed, and chewed some more. He didn't know what to say next, resisted the temptation to kiss her in gratitude, and was surprised to find her studying him intently. "What? Something wrong?"

"Wrong? No, nothing. Of course not." She didn't want to tell him what she was thinking; it would be too embarrassing. But she had noticed that since they'd been together he'd begun to fill out some, the sinewy muscles that had once resembled knots in rawhide now rippled beneath skin turned golden by the sun. She could no longer count his ribs when he stood shirtless at the mirror to shave. He was a damn fine-looking man with that mane of black hair and those blue eyes fringed by long black lashes.

She regarded him for so long in silence that he was afraid she wasn't telling the truth. "Is it that Martin fellow? Are you afraid of him?" he asked when she continued to stare at him.

She batted her eyes. "Who? No. I mean, well, yes, I suppose a little, but that wasn't what I was thinking."

"What then?"

She shrugged and wanted desperately to change the subject but felt at a loss. How did you tell a man you wished he would treat you as more than his long-lost buddy?

"You sure are acting peculiar this morning," he said with a grin, then scooped up a spoonful of potatoes.

Allie studied her fork until her heart stopped kicking around in her chest. If he had looked up he might have seen her feelings written all over her face, but he didn't, and she quickly took a bite of ham and gazed beyond him into the early morning haze. Renewed emotions stirred deep inside her. Not too long ago Eli Martin had erupted young love in her in a whirl-

111

wind courtship that had left her breathless, longing for more. Then he had gone away and broken her heart. This attraction to Jake ran much deeper and was rapidly getting more complicated. Worse, it was the last thing in the world she wanted, not with this man who didn't even know who he was or where he came from.

The next day Jake made some inquiries in town and was directed to Harrison Defoe, a wagon master of one of the traders' caravans due to pull out soon. A spot for him and Allie was easily secured, and less than an hour later they were buying supplies. Other needs could be filled along the trail, either purchased at forts where they would stop, or from the traders themselves who were taking goods to Santa Fe. There would never be a shortage of food traveling with a caravan.

While Jake made those arrangements, Allie went in search of a wagon belonging to a man who had come to her the day before and asked if she would take a picture of his wife, who was confined to their wagon. She was expecting a child and feeling poorly.

Allie wanted to ask the man why in the world he would drag her west in her condition, but knew it was none of her business. Besides, when a man got a notion, nothing was likely to stop him. Especially nothing a woman had to say about it. She knew that from experience, didn't she?

However, she had agreed to take the photograph, and when she arrived at the designated area, a wagon yard on the outskirts of town where those looking to join a train were camped, she had no trouble finding the man. He waited for her at the entrance to the yard, hat in hand.

"She's not real happy about you coming. Says she would rather have a picture done when she's pretty, but ma'am, I have to tell you, I don't expect her to survive this trip, and I want something to remember her by."

Fury thick in her throat, Allie glared at the man. She wanted to scream at him, throw something at the fool, tell him to take his wife to a doctor, not drag her across the country in a covered wagon. She only nodded curtly and he crawled up beside her to guide her to his waiting wagon.

He yammered on about taking his family to Oregon where they could begin a new life, and about how women had babies on the trail all the time and it was nothing. His wife, however, had something else wrong with her. She wasn't strong.

Allie wanted to punch him in the mouth. When she met his wife, she wanted to do worse than that.

The girl was no older than fifteen. If she was with child it didn't show yet, but she had great dark circles under her eyes, her hair hung lank and dull and she was rail thin. Not exactly a good subject for her camera, yet Allie found when she got everything set up and peered through the lens at the image of the girl, something happened to her heart and she knew she had to take this picture. It was important to capture the sheer hopelessness of the girl's existence in the light of her husband's desires. Such a photo would speak volumes about the conditions awaiting some women who traveled to the frontier. The girl sat in a chair her husband had placed beside the front wheel of the wagon, and when she looked up at the camera, eyes filled with melancholy, Allie exposed the shot while tears rolled down her cheeks.

She could scarcely see to develop a print for the husband, which he took eagerly to show to his young wife and other members of his family. She quickly made another print and hung it inside the wagon to dry. It would be the first of many shots for what she intended to be a pictorial essay on women traveling west. She hoped the sorrow in that young woman's eyes didn't portend the contents of that essay.

One of the younger men in the family helped her store her equipment. "You took a good picture of Emma," he said equably.

"Thank you. She . . . uh, she doesn't look well."

"No, she's always been a puny little thing. She'll be okay." The statement sounded like a plea for help, made from the need to believe what he was saying.

"I don't think she will," Allie said, unable any longer to control her fury. "Why don't you tell him to take her to a doctor instead of dragging her out across the wilderness?"

"Wouldn't do no good," the young man said. "She'll be better when she gets out to Oregon. We all will be." Again the same tone.

"She'll never reach Oregon," Allie muttered.

Nothing she could do would make the girl's life any easier. She would only stir things up and likely make more trouble for her. She cursed herself for a coward because she did nothing but drive away, fuming.

Jake sensed her foul mood, but all he said was, "Why don't we go into town and eat tonight, spend some of that dirty money old Jesse gave us?"

"Is that all you think of, money?"

The tone of her question stopped him in his tracks. "Well, Allie, I don't think so. No, that's not all I think of."

"Women. Do you ever think of women, Jake?"

She wasn't going to let this be. He knew it. "I guess, sometimes. What is it, Allie? What happened to get you so upset?"

"I'm not upset. Do I sound upset? Do I look upset? I'm not upset."

"Yes, you sound upset, you look upset. I don't like it when you're upset."

She strode across the space between them and stuck her square chin high, glaring up at him with fire in her eyes. "So what are you going to do about it? Put me in my place?"

He was glad she didn't have on that pretty dress, or he might have found a few places right away, but in her jeans and shirt and her fists punched into her sides, like a kid challenging the bully he just knows is going to beat the snot out of him, she was too vulnerable for that. As far as that was concerned, he was too. If he touched her it might be way too late for rational thought. He tried mightily to conjure up an image of Lorena, but for the first time, failed.

"Just like all men," she sneered when he didn't answer her. "When push comes to shove you don't have any answers."

"I don't have any answers most of the time, Allie. But if you'll tell me what's wrong, what happened to get you so het up, I'd be glad to listen. However, if you intend to keep talking in riddles and acting like I just shot your pet dog, why then I think I'll just take me a ride into town all by myself and find me something to eat."

He turned from her and the world whirled around him, the sun rotating faster and faster until it dimmed and went out.

Allie stood over the unconscious Jake for several seconds, fury draining from her. Inside she felt empty, foolish and sorry.

"I swear, Jake, if I thought you did that on purpose I'd box your ears," she muttered, then sank down beside him, lifted his head and put it in her lap. "You poor thing, poor, poor baby."

She brushed the hair off his forehead. "You make me so mad, damn you. Why won't you take care of yourself?"

He made a gurgling sound down in his throat that frightened her. Suppose he died this time?

A tear ran from the corner of one of his eyes and she wiped it with a finger. What was going on in there? What madness had he locked up so that he wouldn't have to look at it? And what might happen the day it escaped? Would it kill him? Would it kill her?

She had no idea, yet couldn't bring herself to tell him to ride on, leave her be. There must be a reason for her reluctance. Since her father's death she hadn't much use for men. They tended to be too much like pitiful Emma's husband or Eli Martin. Or her father, whispered a nasty little voice. She quelled it. Most men were self-absorbed, hateful and egotistical. Jake was not any of those. Despite what had gone on in his life, he put her needs ahead of his own at every turn.

He stirred, took a few deep breaths and his eyes popped open. She glimpsed again the confusion and despair that he quickly covered.

"Heck of a way to get out of an argument," she teased.

His head lay in the warmth of her lap, nested in her soothing feminine essence. He couldn't have moved if he'd been on fire. And then she leaned over and kissed him very gently on the mouth and his world tilted as it never had, not even in the worst of the blackouts.

When Jake's warm lips parted in a passionate response to her kiss, Allie jerked away, eyes wide and heart pounding. She uttered a tiny, perplexing sound and felt a tremor like the caress of butterfly wings down in her belly.

The experience so shocked her that she scrambled away from him, letting his head bump onto the ground. He lay there for a moment, staring up at her with cloudy eyes.

"What are you doing?" she said, and rubbed at her mouth with the back of one hand.

Without a word he rolled over and crawled to his feet. It took a while for him to regain his balance. Once he did he touched his lips with the tips of his trembling fingers, his eyes a dangerous ice blue. He had never looked at her in quite that way, though she well remembered the expression turned on Eli Martin earlier. For a moment she was more frightened by his gaze than dismayed by what had happened. He might have been someone she didn't know at all.

Before she could stop him, or even try to explain her actions, he fetched his hat and saddle and headed for the mare.

"Jake, what's wrong? Where are you going? Are you all right?"

In silence he spread a blanket over Molly's back and tossed the saddle up. Draping the stirrup over the seat, he hitched in the girth, grunting as he pulled it snug.

Allie didn't know what to say. She had never seen him angered into silence like this. He'd always been so easy going, so ready to laugh away his troubles. She didn't know if it was the kiss or her reaction to it that had set him off. She had, after all, accused him of initiating the incident when it had been her doing.

He forced the mare's nose up out of the grass and slipped a bit between her teeth. After he eased the bridle over her ears, he lay his face against her jaw and stood there immobile for a long while. Allie watched his shoulders rise and fall in great breaths.

She moved to touch him. Under her palm, his muscles tightened into knots, and she jerked away when he whirled to face her.

"Don't . . . don't do that again."

"What? I don't—"

"Don't kiss me. Don't pet around on me and pity me and look at me with those bottomless eyes. I'm not a little wounded puppy you dragged in on a leash. I'm a full grown man with desires and secrets too deep for you to understand. You don't like men. You distrust them. And with me, Allie, that's very wise. Since even I don't know what the hell I might do to you."

She remained standing there in silence until he rode out of sight up the road toward Westport. He probably wasn't coming back, and she didn't know whether to be relieved or sorry. A part of her said that she was going to miss him very much; another echoed that she was better off alone.

Jake rode the trail as if a baying wolf nipped at his heels. He had seen, in that moment when her lips touched his and he stirred back into consciousness, the most frightening thing he could ever have imagined, and he would not subject her to what it meant.

It was Lorena, the girl in the picture he carried in his pocket. Only she didn't look like that anymore. She lay sprawled across a deep red velveteen settee, her throat slit and her eyes open in horror at the last thing she had seen.

And what she saw . . . dear God, what she saw, he saw too, and he couldn't bear it.

The moon rose before him, enormous and white as milk. He spurred the mare on, terror gripping his throat until he could scarcely breathe. Pale silver light spread across the land, silhouetting great blackened trees against the dark sky. The mare

117

laid back her ears and galloped, the rhythmic chuffing of her breath loud in the night.

A dreadful black silence swallowed his soul, bite by bite, until there was nothing left of it.

For what he had seen, standing over the dead Lorena, was himself, and in his hand a blood-stained knife.

Chapter Eight

When Jake didn't return by morning, Allie decided he had left for good. Her first reaction was that she was better off without him. She could quit imagining him dying on her. He had left and that was no big surprise, was it? Like Eli, like her father. Thank God, she hadn't let herself love him.

Then she remembered how hard he had worked the day they had put the wheel back on the wagon, and her a stranger. And later, the way he had thrown caution to the wind to rescue her from the clutches of Jesse and Frank James. And how funny he could be just when she was feeling at her worst. And his gentleness with the children she was taking pictures of.

Even though she was loath to admit it, her lonely heart would miss Jake, but at least she hadn't loved him.

She could go to Santa Fe without him, and without anyone's help if Defoe wouldn't allow her to join the caravan alone. She saddled the palomino and headed for town to find the wagon master. They were scheduled to leave the following day, and it was almost a thousand miles to Santa Fe. She had never

119

intended to ride out unaccompanied, even before she met Jake, but she would if she had to.

She found Defoe at the wagon yard surrounded by the men who would keep the train together for the long trip. When she asked for Defoe they moved apart, making an aisle to a tall and imposing man with a crop of hair the color of ginger and chin whiskers to match. His ruddy skin was splashed freely with freckles. He wore leather chaps over his britches, a faded blue shirt and a vest of deer skin. A large knife was strapped to his hip. He wore a black hat with a wide brim and silver conchos around the crown. He didn't remove it nor did he smile when she introduced herself.

When he spoke she saw he had a canine tooth missing. It gave him a sinister look, but his voice was melodious. "Have we had the pleasure, ma'am?"

"No, and I won't take but a moment of your time. A friend of mine, Jake . . . " She stopped, realized she didn't have a full name to give him, and was stymied.

Defoe arched one red brow and narrowed the other eye. It made her extremely nervous that he was regarding her as if he were taking aim.

Clearing her throat, she stumbled into an explanation. "Jake, well, he paid for our passage, his and mine, with your caravan to Santa Fe. Now, I'm sorry to say, Jake has . . . uh . . . been called away on other business, but I would like to continue with the bargain."

"Sorry, no refunds. His money's paid," Defoe said, and made to turn away.

"I don't want a refund. I simply want to make sure that I can . . . well, that you won't . . . I have a small wagon, a team of mules and that stallion." She gestured toward Ringo, who had trailed along behind her after she dismounted.

One of the men in the group approached the palomino and ran a gloved hand across his withers. "Would you sell him, then?" he asked in a thick Irish brogue. "A lass such as yourself has no business on a great huge beast like this one, and a stallion to boot."

Allie's glance darted from the man to Defoe, who simply waited. He was gauging her mettle, and she sensed her acceptance might rest on her reaction to the Irishman's cheeky remark.

"The day I can't handle a mere male, man or horse, will be a cold day in hell," she said. "You'd not stay on his back more than the time it takes to spit."

The Irishman did just that, aiming right between her boots, but made no reply.

She smiled, turned back to Defoe and said, "Sir, chain your pet before he forces me to defend myself and my honor." She rubbed a gloved palm lovingly over the curved butt of the Colt at her hip.

Defoe shook his head at her tormentor, nodded at Allie and did that trick with his eyebrows again. She thought he might have practiced it in front of a mirror, it appeared so calculated.

"I apologize for McKearney. He learned his manners in a barnyard. Would you really have shot him?"

She shrugged. "Depends."

"On?"

"How far he wanted to take it."

Defoe regarded her without raising his brow, his gunmetal eyes bright and sharp. Then he nodded as if satisfied. "What kind of a wagon are you driving?"

"It's a dark box, a what's-it wagon. I'm a photographer, and I plan to set up a business in Santa Fe. I also hope to ply my trade along the trail. Plenty of folks enjoy possessing their likeness, or would like to send a picture back home."

"Is that right?" Defoe asked. "Would you take mine? It's a thing I've never done."

"I . . . well, of course. Does that mean I still have a place in the caravan?"

A man sitting nearby flipped open a leather-bound book.

Samantha Lee

"Caine, Jake Caine?" he hollered at her. "Paid yesterday?"

Caine. In lieu of no name of his own he'd used her last name. That brought a knot to her throat. "Yes, that's it. My name is Allison Caine."

Defoe scratched at his beard. "I thought you said he was a friend. You're his wife? He run off and left you to go alone?"

Allie stumbled over a reply. She couldn't let them think that Jake would go off and abandon his wife in a strange town, although it was very possible he had left behind a wife he didn't even remember. What an odd situation she'd gotten herself into.

Oh, well, Jake was gone now, so she could get back to her own itinerary.

"Wife? No, not at all. Jake and I are . . . we're cousins, only distant cousins, and his . . . his mother is very ill. He had to rush to her side."

A chillingly familiar voice chimed in. "Isn't that a shame? Leaving a lovely lady like you to fend for herself. Cousin, you say?"

With dread growing in her heart, she turned to see her handsome ex-fiancé beaming at her as if he'd just struck gold.

Coldly, she replied, "Yes, cousin, and I expect him to rejoin me as soon as he can."

"Well, of course we can't have you traveling alone until such time as he does." Martin turned to address Defoe. "I'll see the little lady has everything she needs, and she can pull that funny little wagon of hers right in behind mine. In fact, if she wishes, we can tie it on and she can ride with me. I have plenty of room. Miss Caine and I have a previous acquaintance."

Allie's heart did sink then. Martin would be along on the trail to Santa Fe? If it hadn't been for Defoe's "no refund" policy, she would have backed out right then. Instead, she appealed to Defoe.

"That's not at all necessary. I prefer being on my own."

The wagon master obviously did not care for Martin and showed it in his reply. "I think we can handle this without your

122

assistance, Martin. You should remember you're only along because I have no choice. Left to me, I'd shoot you and leave you for the coyotes. I've no use for bounty hunters at all, and I don't need much of an excuse to stretch your mangy hide high in a tree, no matter who your friends are."

Allie gave Martin a savage glare and thanked Defoe. Despite being grateful, she couldn't overcome her dismay at learning that Eli would be accompanying the caravan and that he was a bounty hunter.

"I'm camped about two miles west of town near the trace. Should I plan on joining you then as you pass by in the morning?" she asked Defoe.

He nodded and studied her hard. "We'll expect you to pull your own weight, we'll lend a hand when we can, but our main objective is trade with the Mexicans, not taking settlers west, and we don't let that out of our sight. You should, however, be perfectly safe. The Indians don't usually bother with us because we're so many and so well-armed. One of the reasons homesteaders prefer to travel with us. If you have any problems with Mr. Martin, one of my men will be more than glad to shoot him for you, should you not want to do it yourself." He grinned, showing the feral teeth.

She shivered, left quite speechless by his remark. Defoe turned away before she could judge if he was serious. A quick glance at Eli revealed a hard-edged stare that should have bored a hole in Defoe's back.

She would like to know more about the foul deeds that had alienated Eli to Defoe, but clearly these men had other things to do, and she certainly couldn't ask right in front of him.

Again she rubbed the butt of the Colt, placed her new Stetson firmly on her head and swung onto Ringo's back. Men who rode with the trading caravans were a strange breed, tough and uncompromising, but she felt she could trust Defoe to keep his word. He wouldn't have remained long in this business if he were not an honorable man. Still, she didn't look forward to traveling in Eli's company and would remain as distant from him as possible.

Eli narrowed his eyes and watched Allie ride off. Where had that fellow gotten to? Suppose he didn't return? Eli damned himself for not keeping closer tabs on the two, but he hadn't expected such a turn of events. They had seemed so tightly bound to each other. Now he didn't know whether to ride out in search of the so-called Jake, or hang around Allie.

She was an awfully sweet pot of honey for any sane man to leave for very long, though he himself had been foolish enough to do so once. That wouldn't happen again. He made up his mind quickly. The man would be back, and it would be foolish to run willy-nilly in search of him. Eli had no idea where Jake had gone, but he sure as hell knew where Allie was.

"Keep your eye on the bait, old son," he said aloud, and returned to his own wagon.

It rained during the night and, under the canvas shelter, Allie snuggled deeper into her bedroll. In the brilliant lightning flashes she had a sudden recollection of Jake lying beside a drowned fire in the rain until she'd fetched him to sleep under her canvas. And later waking to find her head on his arm. The muscles rippling beneath her cheek as she moved against him, his hand trailing across her shoulder to enclose her in an unconscious embrace. It was a warm memory, and she had too few of those. There were times when she wished her own past would take leave like his had, for she was reminded too often of that horrible day she had hidden in the privy and watched through a crack while her mother and sister were attacked and butchered. But then she would remember some sweet and poignant family moment and know that to lose all those precious memories would be devastating. How horrible to carry around a black void, endlessly searching for someone, something, that would trigger a vision from the past.

What had she said or done that made Jake so angry he ran away? She couldn't recall anything specific, and he was usually so easy going. Perhaps he felt he had betrayed the mysterious Lorena when they'd kissed.

124

Sometime in the night, as the storm moved to the northeast and a cool wet breeze tossed great drops of water onto the canvas above her head, Allie thought she heard the thud of horse's hooves. She looked but could see nothing in the darkness. Automatically she checked the Colt, which was draped over the saddle at her head, but heard nothing more. She dozed off gazing at long fingers of moonlight creeping across shimmering puddles of rainwater.

Rubbing at his aching leg, Jake sat the mare for quite a while after Allie settled back down into her bedroll. Would she think him a complete fool?

The farther he had ridden away from her, the more miserable he had become. Allie was his one connection to reality, and what they did together remained something to cling to. As the miles between them rolled out behind him, the hideous nightmare of himself standing over Lorena's murdered body grew vague. It had been a dream and nothing more, and he had been foolish to let it send him running. At first, he had thought it a true memory from his past. But after spending a restless night on the trail, his fear of the reality of the dream faded. His mind had simply dredged something he feared up out of his subconscious. Nothing more than that. And as for his apprehensions about hurting Allie, he had probably done that by leaving. He wished never to do anything to harm her, and he would kill anyone who tried. She needed him. She had no business traveling alone, even if she could take care of herself. Women were vulnerable to almost any evil desires certain men could imagine, and no matter what anyone said, a man was more capable of defending a woman than she herself could ever be.

So he'd returned. Wearily he crawled off the horse and settled into the shadows, propped upright by a tree so he wouldn't doze off. While he watched her sleep, an apparition moved from the uneasy recesses of his mind.

"I will not listen to you," a woman said. "You are lying to me. Lying. I've loved you all my life, trusted you. How can you do this to me?" Her soft, broken sobs tore at his heart.

125

"Lorena?" he whispered.

The vague form vanished and he doubled a fist and slammed it into the spongy ground. Dammit, why couldn't he hold on to these brief flashes until one of them led him somewhere?

What did the accusation mean? Had Lorena spoken those words to him? Dear God, had he been untrue to her and she found out? Had he done such a horrible thing to the woman he loved? Betrayed her, for God's sake? He didn't feel like that kind of man, but no one could truly know what the total loss of memory could do to a person. Perhaps he was no longer even the same man he had been. Could he have been someone brutal and uncaring?

An outlaw, a killer perhaps? A dull ache throbbed between his temples.

Allie awoke to the fragrant aroma of coffee perking, raised to see flames crackling merrily, and came up with the Colt in her fist. Though the sky glowed pink and silver, beneath the trees the camp lay in dark shadows, lit only by the fire. She could see no one.

Beyond the trees Ringo nickered and she looked to see him and Jake's mare silhouetted against the shimmering metallic sky, rubbing shoulders like old friends.

"Jake?" she called softly. "Is that you, Jake?"

When she received no reply, her heart fluttered. Someone could have found Jake in a state of unconsciousness and stolen Molly. Yet why would he ride back here? It didn't make sense.

A figure emerged from behind a clump of brush nearby and she aimed the Colt but didn't thumb back the hammer.

"It's me," he said. "Just me."

She stood there a moment, the pistol still pointed. Part of her was overjoyed at Jake's return, while her sensible self sounded a warning. Beware, it cautioned, beware a foolish heart.

"If you're going to shoot me with that thing, let's get it over with," he finally said when she continued to point the gun at him.

"For God's sake, you scared the devil out of me." She lowered the barrel, glanced down at her bare legs. The shirt didn't

126

even come to her knees, and the breaking morning light quickly revealed her state of undress.

"I thought . . . I mean, you were gone. I didn't expect you to come back, and so I and so I—"

"Me either. I mean, I wasn't going to. Don't worry, I'm not looking." But he was, and they both knew it. Her long shapely legs tapered to fine ankles, the ankles of a thoroughbred. And he did appreciate that. His imagination supplied visions of the supple curves under the shirt. He kicked the thought out of his head. He would behave himself. Allie was a friend, a buddy, a pal, nothing more. He would not be untrue to Lorena, in thought, word or deed, even though it was possible he once had been.

Though pleased about Jake's return, Allie fought the urge to let him know. There were things that remained unsettled between them, and she had to be very careful. When he turned his back she hurried to her bedroll to replace the Colt in its holster and slip on jeans, socks and boots.

He busied himself with breakfast, chattering away to fill the silence. Allie took down the canvas and folded and rolled it, letting him talk. He didn't seem to be saying anything that required a reply.

"I guess I got about five miles down the road out of Westport before I started to miss your fussing, in another five I was going nuts and talking to myself. That's when I figured the only way I would keep my sanity was to come back here so you could holler at me some more."

She glanced up to argue the point with him, then decided not to, since she saw he was having such a good time relating this tale.

He paused, gestured at Ringo and Molly rubbing noses contentedly. "Besides, she got to pining so bad for him I couldn't get her to do anything. I'd say whoa and she'd trot, I'd holler gee and she'd haw. Damndest thing you ever saw."

With an unexpected sense of relief Allie moved toward the fire where he had finished cooking and was dipping up food

127

into tin plates. He set them on a flat rock near the fire and filled two tin cups with coffee.

She took hers and sat beside him, ready at last to hold up her end of the conversation. "You're so full of bull. I never holler at you, and you know it. The rest of that probably isn't true either."

She picked up her plate, embracing her relief at having him back. She'd be more careful and not go kissing him anymore, for both their sakes. That's probably what had spooked him. He had responded to the kiss, she knew he had. The memory made her dizzy, and at that very moment it took all her willpower not to throw her arms around his neck and plant a good one right on that lopsided grin. See if he did it again, see if he moved those full lips over hers so languidly it made her heart ache. He glanced up at her, blue eyes dancing, and she turned away quickly, embarrassed.

Allie knew in that instant that she was falling in love with this man, no matter how her head might protest. And for that matter, no matter how he did protest. There was no getting around it, and she figured she would be in a heap of trouble before this thing was all sorted out. Jake might never find out who he was or where he belonged. And he could go on loving the phantom Lorena the rest of his life. Or he could fall over dead tomorrow from that insidious beast in his head. It looked like it wasn't going to make a bit of difference, where her feelings were concerned. Somehow she would just have to deal with it.

Meanwhile, he was here and so was she, and she intended him to stay, so she relaxed beside him companionably and let him lead the conversation.

"Train leaves this morning," he said.

"Yes, I made sure they'd let me go on without you."

He nodded and glanced at her. "What'd you think of Defoe?"

"A fair man, sort of full of himself, but I guess sometimes that's necessary. Did you know Eli Martin is going, too?"

He glanced sharply at her. "Why?"

"Why? I don't know why. What I do know is that I'll never understand how I could possibly have thought I loved him, and I also know he is about the oiliest son of a—"

"Allie," he scolded.

"Well, he is."

"What'd he say to you?"

"That 'the little lady' could ride with him and he'd take care of me."

"I'll bet that impressed you."

Allie laughed. "Defoe offered to shoot him for me."

"If he don't, maybe I will."

In the pause before Jake laughed deep down in his throat, she glimpsed the frightening man who had threatened Eli earlier, but then the hard reflection in his azure eyes faded, and she was able to smile. Despite her doubts, it was good to have him back.

They dropped the subject and packed the wagon. Allie double-checked the glass plates and various chemicals to make sure all were secure, and just as Jake finished harnessing the team, they heard the rattle and clang and shouts of the approaching caravan in the distance.

She climbed up onto the seat, urged the mules to the edge of the trail and craned her neck so she could catch first sight of the trading caravan. It was time to go at last. Anticipation made her heart beat faster as the lead riders came abreast. She spotted the wagon master Defoe, and he slowed his prancing black, touching the brim of his hat. Silver conchos on both bridle and saddle gleamed with every high step of the proud horse.

"Tuck in behind the third wagon, ma'am. They'll make room. Keep up, though, or fall out." He glanced toward Jake on his mare. "Guess your cousin's mother has recovered. Just as well. Even with us, no woman should travel alone. Good luck, the both of you."

Allie watched in amazement as the enormous boxy wagons approached. What a sight they were, like a Fourth of July parade. Painted blue, with red trim and white Osnaburg canvas fluttering in the wind, they moved in a line that stretched along the road as far as she could see back toward Westport. She could have parked two of the what's-it wagons inside one of them. As she fitted into the space allotted for her she noticed a copper plate on the freight wagon ahead that read Studebaker. These were not the boat-style Conestogas used East of the Mississippi, or even those smaller replicas following the Oregon Trail. All were referred to as prairie schooners. These huge freight wagons were modeled more after earlier farm wagons, only much larger and with the typical hooped canvas covering similar to a Conestoga. Often they were all lumped together and referred to incorrectly as Conestogas,

Because of the rain the night before and a wet spring, the wagons lumbered along hub-deep in mud for most of the day. Jake was gone a lot of the time lending a hand when one of the heavily loaded wagons became hopelessly bogged down. Allie's team of mules had little trouble moving the lighter what's-it wagon through the mire. She didn't see Jake until they nooned to allow the animals to rest and graze. With mud to his knees and splattered over his face, he still wore a wide grin. Only during unguarded moments did his eyes reveal the ghosts that haunted him.

For a few days, travel proved to be relatively easy. There was plenty of water and shade. The first night they made camp at a place called Lone Elm. If there had ever been a lone elm there, it was gone now, as were most of the trees. It was said they had all been cut to supply firewood during the years since the Santa Fe had been blazed over forty years earlier. As if to make up for the lack of trees, glorious wildflowers painted the land with brilliant brush strokes of purples, reds, blues and yellows.

Allie imagined what it would be like to capture the wonderful colors with her camera, but remained solemnly content with the black-and-white photos she took. She would learn to make this country come alive on paper, despite the lack of color.

During the long nooning rests, she had taken to setting up her dark tent and camera. Word soon got around the caravan, and each day someone would show up to have pictures taken, so she was busy with portraits as well as landscapes. She learned that more than a dozen families of homesteaders traveled with the caravan, in half again as many wagons. Some had as many as two or three wagons to a family. The caravan, in all, contained upwards of sixty wagons in a line that stretched out for miles. When they stopped for the night, they formed three circle-ups adjacent to one another.

It was no wonder the Indians left them alone. Allie noticed all manner of weapons carried by men who looked tough enough to stand against the meanest savage in hand-to-hand combat.

Spring rains soon tapered off and the warm sun began to dry the prairie. Unlike the mountains of Missouri, this air did not kiss the grass with dew each night, and so they slept out under the stars on pallets spread outside the circle, leaving the inner area as a corral for the oxen and other beasts. The freight wagons were so heavily loaded there was no room to sleep inside them, and so teamsters slept in the open. They were just out of luck when it rained hard and flooded the ground beneath their wagons. Some of the homesteaders had tents, but most of the teamsters did not.

Defoe himself possessed an elaborate tent where he held council and dealt with any problems that arose among the travelers or working men.

As for Allie and Jake, they slept several yards apart, and he did not offer his arm as a pillow for her head anymore. She toyed with all kinds of possibilities to regain their former camaraderie. Perhaps she could pretend she was frightened of the dark, or of the lonely sound of coyotes and owls. Trick him into doing something he clearly was trying to avoid. But that would have been childish, maybe even harmful to their tentative relationship, for she sensed he walked a very thin line between dealing with his memory loss and falling into the abyss of despair.

There were nights when she ached to put her arms around him and comfort him, but she dared not. She would not chase him away again.

Life on the trail suited her. She liked the excitement of never knowing what each day would bring. The more life challenged her, the happier she was. When Jake asked if she would teach him photography, she was ecstatic. It was difficult work keeping that many wagons moving along the trail, and he had pitched in from the start without being drafted, so they saw very little of each other. She missed that. At night he would return to camp in time to be of help to her, then they would eat and he would fall asleep almost immediately. Despite the hard labor he glowed with good health, his muscles thickening and his limping gait growing less discernible with each passing day. His tortured body was healing, but she wasn't sure about his mind.

He interrupted her train of thought. "I asked if you would teach me more about photography. What is it, Allie? You're acting like you're miles away."

"Sorry, just wool-gathering. You ought to rest when we stop at noon. You work much too hard." She was afraid he'd think her too eager, and so she approached the request by playing the devil's advocate.

"Nonsense. I prefer it. I could be more help to you if I knew how to mix the chemicals and treat the plates. I could even learn how to develop the prints. I want to pull my own weight. Don't treat me like an invalid."

At his harsh tone, she glanced up to see his eyes gleaming hard and cold. For a moment it frightened her, and she could think of nothing to say. Another man still lurked within him, and once in a while he allowed her a brief glimpse at him before covering up with that boyish grin she'd grown so fond of. Suppose that man should one day escape and drive away the Jake she knew? What then?

Abruptly he became his old self. "Allie, I help out anyway, when you're taking pictures."

His abrupt mood changes were puzzling, yet she welcomed his interest. Beneath that black drape she could create an image either good or bad, overexposed or unfocused, clear and crisp as the camera would allow. Under there the world of color became one of blacks and whites, contrasts that she manipulated so that crimsons and scarlets were only blacks of varying degrees, blue skies and pale green leaves and soft sienna earths developed into shades of white tinted with splashes of gray.

When she faced reality, its cruelties were revealed in vivid hues. The brutality of men, the weaknesses of women and children, the harshness of nature, were all slashes of reds and purples and ghastly greens that bled all over each other to create a menage of images.

"Allie?" Jake said and touched her arm. "You okay?"

"Oh, I'm sorry." She glanced at his hand curved around her wrist with the lightest touch, and imagined him caressing her, then closed her eyes and shook her head.

"You were a million miles away."

She smiled to ease the tension. "Sorry. Are you sure you want to mess with all those stinking chemicals?"

Before she could object he raised her hand to his mouth, lips whispering over her flesh as he sniffed. He glanced up and grinned. Suddenly she wanted to muss his hair and kiss him; she wanted to laugh and cry, and didn't know why.

"Doesn't smell so bad. I guess I'm used to it," he said softly, still holding her hand.

It would be a way to have him near her, and he seemed very sure, so she pretended to reluctantly capitulate. "Okay, then, I'll teach you on one condition."

He let her hand go, raised a brow. "No conditions, Allie. That's not the way it works. No conditions."

As if to get away from her, he took a quick step backward. A strange look passed through his eyes and was gone. She wasn't sure what it meant, but she nodded and agreed with him. She had wanted to bargain with him, beg him to take better care of himself, but saw how foolish such a request would sound. Of course, one didn't make deals with something like this. It was a gesture of friendship, something one person did for another because she liked him, trusted him. *Loved him,* came an insidious whisper. She brushed it away.

She must be very careful, for this man, like Eli, like her father, would manage to hurt her sooner or later. That she knew. And worst of all, he was never going to love her.

Chapter Nine

A military freight caravan overtook them eight days out of Westport, and moved past in the second set of ruts, the uniformed drivers shouting friendly insults at the teamsters, who returned them in kind.

Some of the bull whackers, intent on showing off for the military drivers, got in a contest with their panaches, monster whips with three to four-foot stocks made of heavy wood onto which was fastened a braided rawhide lash, often measuring up to twenty feet. At the tip of that lash was an eight-inch piece of rawhide that could be replaced when it wore out. The idea was to "pop" that rawhide at just the right spot near an animal's left or right ear, a friendly reminder that would guide and inspire the oxen pulling the heavily loaded freight wagons. The winner of the contest was the one who caused the loudest crack, and some sounded like the shot from Allie's Colt. Any man who drew blood from an animal lost the bet.

All day the going had been easy and Jake rode along beside Allie while the military caravan passed. The antics and byplay between the teamsters and the army men and the cracking of the gigantic whips grew unnerving. He found himself flinching with each leather "shot" until he could no longer endure the racket.

In his mind cannons fired, the screams of downed horses and wounded men echoed, one who lay dying called his name over and over. In the mist of memory he could not make out the man's face, but he wore the gray uniform of the enemy.

He spoke in a voice so familiar Jake groaned with the effort to remember. "I didn't mean to do it, Lanse. You gotta forgive me. Dear God, forgive me before I die. Lorena, she was . . . she is . . . oh, God, I'm sorry."

The vague images faded, but the word *sorry* echoed until he repeated it over and over. In defense he dropped back and took a place on the far side of Allie's wagon to escape being caught between the two trains. The increased and abrupt flashes of memory were driving him crazy. He concentrated on the vast green plains rolling like a green ocean into his future.

Allie leaned from the wagon seat, called his name and jogged him back to the present.

He raised a hand to her.

"You okay?"

He nodded. "Fine, I'm fine. Don't worry."

She didn't say anything, and he noticed that for a while she sent quick glances his way every few minutes. She would not be deterred from her concern, no matter how much he grumbled and scowled. In truth, having someone like her caring about him was not all bad. As long as she didn't get too carried away. It must be hell for her, though, not knowing when he might have one of his falling-down fits. Several days had gone by without one, though flashes of memory continued. Did he dare hope?

He glanced once more at Allie. The wind had loosened long strands of golden hair from under her Stetson, her dark eyes gleamed like river stones in her sun-bronzed skin. She had one

136

long leg propped on the wagon box with the handful of reins threaded through her gloved fingers. He saw all this so clearly that she could have been one of her photographs frozen so he could lovingly study each detail. His throat tightened and he felt an unexpected urge to touch her, make sure she was real and not a part of that elusive past he groped for with such greed. Perhaps he ought to pay more attention to this day and those yet to come and not worry so much about what he couldn't remember.

In a burst of high spirits, he shouted her name.

She turned, renewed anxiety clouding her features.

"I just . . . aw, hell. I just wanted to say . . . how beautiful you are today. How glad I am to be with you."

He swept off his hat, used it to smack the mare smartly on the rump and let out a wild yell. The long-legged bay took off across the prairie. A cooling wind plastered his shirt against his flesh, kissed his hot cheeks, tore through his long, sweat-dampened hair. Sunlight warmed his bones, and he wondered what it would be like to never be cold and lonely again. Allie kept him from being lonely, and if he would let her, he sensed she would keep him from ever being cold. To hold her every night, to love her, to give in to normal male desires that daily he was able to ignore but nightly was forced to endure, would be a wonderful thing. Yet, as long as the ghost of Lorena haunted him, he couldn't do that. He was surprised to find that he wanted Allison Caine, for since leaving Andersonville he had wanted only one thing: to get his old life back, and that included Lorena.

Jake's antics filled Allie with newfound delight. One day he just might turn away from his clouded past and right into her arms. God only knew what she would do if he did, though. What a dilemma.

She turned her attention back to the horseplay between the men. The drivers in the military caravan had mule teams, and

137

so weren't accomplished bull whackers. They were the brunt of ribald jokes about that, as well.

"How's your ass, private?" one of the teamsters yelled.

"In better shape than your'n," the kid replied.

"You ever want to become a real man, come see me. I'll teach you how to use one of these."

A uniformed man on horseback called back, "Don't need me one of those to be a real man, Rowdy."

Allie was relieved when the last of the military wagons passed them by, for the constant noisy give and take grew tiresome, though she realized these men all needed a rest from the back-breaking jobs they performed. It was, however, nice to get back to the peace and relative quiet of the slow-moving caravan—the sing-song jangle of chains in the traces, the squeak and thud of wheels passing along the worn trail, the sounds and smells of the animals.

She couldn't help but notice that Jake never entered into any such ribaldry with other men, but preferred to remain off on his own. For all his joking around with her, he was a very lonely man.

When they stopped for the night, he was nowhere in sight. Darkness fell and still he didn't show.

Damn, where was he? Suppose the mare had stumbled in a hole and thrown him off; or he had taken a header with one of his seizures?

She couldn't settle down to making camp without going in search of him, though she had no idea where to start. As soon as the team was taken care of, she saddled the stallion and rode to the crest of a rise. Holding Ringo back from his natural inclination to gallop, she carefully checked out the terrain. The huge animal danced and pawed air, eager to race the wind.

Night crept up on her there. A sliver of moon followed the trail of the sun across the western sky. Ahead the terrain dropped imperceptibly, and every clump of shrubbery and trees formed an inky, impenetrable mass. Sometimes the caravan traveled into the night when the moonlight was bright, but this night they had bedded down early.

She stared into the dusky glow. "Dammit, Jake, where are you?"

Nothing stirred as far as she could see, and she reined Ringo around to move toward the dying flares of the setting sun. The sound of hoof beats approached from behind and her heart leaped. She whirled, but instead of Jake, she saw the tall, rakish figure of Eli Martin.

Her heart swelled in her throat until she thought she would be sick. She wanted to dig her heels into Ringo's sides, make him rear and race away with her, rescue her from facing Eli out here alone.

Eli anticipated her, grabbed her mount's bridle and forced his head down. "Allison, don't run away. We have to talk. Sooner or later, you have to face me. Let's get it out of the way here, where there's no one to interrupt."

"I'm not . . . that is, I don't care to talk to you. We have nothing to say to each other. Now, if you don't mind." Ringo danced, threatened to bolt and she brought him under control with both knees and a firm hand.

"Allison, talk to me."

"Why should I do that?"

"Maybe because you loved me once. Or at least I thought you did."

"You thought I . . . ? That's rich, Eli. What about what I thought?" She hadn't wanted to get into this. It could lead in only one direction, and she did not want him to ever know how badly he had hurt her.

"I asked you to go with me. Begged you, in fact. But you turned away from me. Chose your father instead. A man you deeply resented. Hadn't you told me so often enough?"

She swallowed painfully. "I didn't . . . that is, I was too young . . . I loved my father, Eli. You should have seen through my hurt and known that. I had to stay with him. I had to . . . take care of him."

"To salve your guilty conscience? Allison, be realistic. We both know why you picked him over me. You thought you had to make up for the death of your mother and sister."

"That's not true. I know a lot of things now that I didn't then. But you don't know anything about me or my father. He's dead now, and I suppose you think I'll just forget that you abandoned me when I needed you most, just like he did." That admission, made aloud and in front of this man, fueled her anger. "Damn you, Eli. Why are you here? How did you know where to find me, and why are you following me?"

He shrugged, stared off into the ashy evening. "And so you showed him you were better than him, didn't you? Allison, I didn't even know where you were. Running across you was an accident, pure and simple. I had other things on my mind."

"Then why don't you get to them and leave me alone?"

Eli yanked at his horse's reins, swung its head away from her. Before he rode off, he answered her question. "Because, ridiculous as it might seem, seeing you has made me realize that I still love you. I didn't even know it. Isn't that a good one? And I intend to have time to prove it to you. It's a long way to Santa Fe, Allison, and I'll be around."

Eli's admission brought unwanted memories of the youthful and all-consuming desire he had once awakened in her. He had been the first man to touch her intimately, and recalling it kindled a fire within her. She was so stunned by the reaction that for a moment she forgot why she had ridden out there in the first place. Watching Eli ride away, she shook those unwanted memories and scanned the surrounding land for Jake's long-legged mare, and saw her stroll from the shadows below.

Ringo nickered and started forward without urging. The mare answered and Allie could see that no one sat the saddle.

Something had happened to Jake!

At her urging Ringo broke into a trot, yet it seemed to take forever to reach Molly. Apprehension dried her mouth, the beat of her heart quickened, then nearly stopped when she dropped from the saddle and could find no sign of Jake.

Abruptly, a voice raised in song broke the stillness. " 'When Johnnie comes marching home again, hurrah, hurrah. We'll give him a mighty welcome then, hurrah, hurrah.' Duh da da da duh da. . . . "

A loud *wahoo* followed by a huge splash interrupted the tune, and she broke through the trees to see Jake playing in the water like a kid, shaking his head so that great drops flew out around him, forming miniature rainbows in the dying light.

She stumbled to the edge of the creek, shouted, "Damn you, Jake, you scared me half to death."

He let out a joyful roar, high-stepped toward her. "Allie. Holy Hannah. I scared you? You just turned my hair gray. Don't sneak up on a man like that. 'Specially not when he's bare ass deep in water. What are you doing here?"

"Looking for you. I was frantic . . . uh, worried that something had happened when you didn't come back."

"I told you, Allie, you don't have to be my keeper. I don't need . . . I don't want . . . "

Anger replaced her concern, and despite being fully clothed, she waded into the water to confront him. She slipped on the last step and caught at him to save herself from falling. Automatically he steadied her, and they were nearly toe to toe, him stark naked and grinning like a 'possum.

"I don't care what you don't want," she said.

Tiny rivulets poured from his dark hair that lay plastered over broad shoulders. Stricken speechless, she gazed at the water's path down his bare chest, over the laddering of ribs and flat belly into the swirling torrent at his waist. The warmth of his breath caressed her cheeks, and neither moved.

Biting at her lip to steady its quavering, she managed to speak almost coherently. "Jake, I . . . God, I was so scared something had happened to you." Tears came to her eyes, making her angry and embarrassed at the same time. She could no more stop them than she could force herself to move away from him.

Tendrils of ghostly mist rose into the cooling night air; she shivered and the heat off his body enticed her. A passionate need to love and be loved thrummed deep in her belly. She ached to touch Jake in all his secret, bare places. If she looked closely she might see every part of him, for the water was crystal clear. Instead, without moving her gaze from his smoky blue eyes, she rested one hand on his hip just beneath the stream's surface.

The contact sent a bright sensation through her, and his eyes batted in surprise, turning even smokier. Desire blossomed between them, a palpable, writhing entity that couldn't be denied.

He rubbed at her cheek with his thumb, said under his breath, "Dammit, dammit, dammit," then tilted her chin up and placed his mouth over hers so gently she could hardly bear it. He tasted every inch of her mouth, then moved inside where his tongue lapped ever so slowly. She could hardly contain the burning desire that exploded within her.

He swayed with the rhythms of her hunger, grew hard against her belly. A jagged breath passed from his mouth to hers. She suppressed an overpowering desire to claw and bite and scratch at him, to beg him to rip off her clothes and take her right there, both of them naked and wet as the day they were born. An aching need like none she had ever known shot through her and she coiled her arms around his neck. He still hadn't touched her with his hands, but his mouth claimed hers in a way that held her as fast as the tightest embrace. At her frenzied response his lips trembled under hers, went slack. A small sound came from deep within him, like a far off melancholy cry.

With an unexpected, harsh movement he grabbed her arms and shoved her backward violently, a steely grip keeping her from falling. The cry became a grating, hoarse moan.

She sagged and cried out involuntarily. If he had let her go she would have tumbled backward into the water, but he supported her at arm's length, as if he too might lose his balance. His breath came in great gasps that prevented him saying anything for a long while.

She clenched her fists and waited. If she could have found her voice she would have cursed him with every breath. Why couldn't he just hold her like they both wanted? What was the matter with him? But of course that was a stupid question. Stupid, stupid. And she ached inside so badly she wanted to clutch at her stomach and cry and moan like women did who had lost all they held dear. Instead she yanked her arms from his grip and stumbled out onto the bank, tears blurring her vision.

No woman would be fool enough to want a man who didn't want her.

And she'd had her fill of that anyway, hadn't she?

What was wrong with her that she could not make the right choices? She had known she didn't need the heartache loving this man would surely bring, yet she had let this happen. Made it happen. Had she learned nothing from Eli Martin? From her father? Maybe she liked being punished. Maybe she thought she deserved it.

There was no doubt in her mind that Jake would continue to look for Lorena until he found her, and when he did, he wouldn't hesitate to go to her, sparing Allie not even a backward glance. She had lost everyone in her life who she ever loved. Why set herself up for such pain once more? Better not to ever love again than go through that.

She stood on the bank for a moment with her back to him, hoping he would call out to her, praying he would not. If she didn't walk away that very minute, he would surely break her heart.

"Allie?"

That soft, husky way he had of saying her name sent shivers through her, but perhaps the reaction was only from being soaked to the skin.

Her boots squished as she fled at last into the darkness. The wet jeans dripped down Ringo's sides when she climbed into the saddle. Jake waded out of the water, and it took every ounce of strength not to turn around. Shameless of her, but she wanted to see him in the silvery twilight emerging from the creek wet and sleek and bare. Instead, she hunkered on Ringo and dug in her knees, the only sign the great stallion needed to send him into the night, carrying her up over the rise and down again, out of sight and hearing of the man she both loved and despised.

Back at camp she peeled out of the wet boots and clothing, draped pants and shirt on nearby brush and crawled into her bedroll without building a fire or fixing supper. She lay there for a long time gazing at stars that flared in the purpling sky. She had dozed into a restless sleep when he returned, and awoke immediately but didn't move.

She hoped he would leave, prayed he would not.

Jake built a fire and put on some coffee. Once in a while he glanced at her still form, sensed that she was not asleep but instead lay listening, waiting. He wanted to say something to her, had to, but it would take a while to figure out how to get started. All he knew about women was what he knew about her, and that didn't give him much to go on.

He breathed deeply of wood smoke laced with the fragrance of boiling coffee and the lingering tang of photographic chemicals. And Allie. He could smell her all around, enclosing him, reaching out. He regretted what he had done, for now he feared she would want him to leave. Allie was not ready to give her heart to a man—her father's death was too near—and even though she had made the first move, he should have backed away immediately, not let it go so far.

He sat there for a while thinking about that, and knew it wasn't entirely the truth. The truth, of course, when he would admit it, was that he wanted her desperately, but could not bring himself to be unfaithful to Lorena. And yet tonight a passion had been awakened, had sprung from the void he had lived with for so long. He had wanted Allie with all of his body and soul, his mind and heart. He ached for her, but still he would never betray Lorena. Surely Allie could understand that and forgive him.

Images in Scarlet

He remembered nothing, knew nothing for sure about the man who had once lived in this shell he now inhabited. Didn't even know if the occasional memories were any more than fantasies, dreams, nightmares. Hell, he might as well be a damned virgin for all he knew about making love to a woman. The way his body had responded to Allie, though, it hadn't forgotten anything even if his mind had, and he'd been just a step from taking her, loving her, forgetting all about Lorena.

That was a laugh. He knew nothing about Lorena except that he carried her picture, he had done something unforgivable to her, maybe even killed her, and she had probably loved another man. Why in God's name didn't he just put it all behind him?

He sat there with his regrets, gazing into the fire while he drank two cups of very hot black coffee. Finally he went to bed fully clothed, head propped on his saddle.

Allie lay still for a long while listening to Jake's breathing smooth out. She must have fallen asleep, for she was next aware that she walked in a graveyard. She moved from the graves of her mother and sister to that of her father, much as she had the day she buried him at their side and left Missouri for good. In one hand she carried rose petals, which she sprinkled over each grave. On and on the petals fell until great mounds were heaped at each stone. Then she knelt at her father's grave—strangely thick grass covered the raw earth as if he had been buried there for years—and began to beat at the ground.

"Why?" she screamed. "Why did you do it? Why, why?" She pounded until her fists were raw and bloody, and awoke sobbing.

Once fully awake, she considered the dream. Clearly she was still very angry with her father over his leaving the family to go off to the war and shoot his pictures. Yet, that had been forgiven when he returned for her, hadn't it? From that moment on they had never had so much as a harsh word. He had been a gentle man, a successful man, who provided well for his family, yet clearly she hadn't resolved her anger, still blamed him as well as herself for what had happened to her mother and sister.

Wiping night tears from her eyes, she sat up and hugged both knees. Then she saw Jake's still form, head propped on his saddle, boots lying near his stockinged feet where he could pull them on at a moment's notice.

Her heartbeat quickened. She had expected him to be gone when she awoke—actually had thought that's what she wanted, but seeing him lying there so peacefully, she knew it wasn't.

As they moved on along the trail, Allie found herself wondering about Emma, the girl who had been so ill her husband had wanted her picture made before she died. They rode in a train of about thirty civilian wagons that trailed out behind the trading caravan. The California-bound train would soon branch off from the trace and head northwest. She had not forgotten the look in Emma's eyes when her husband carried her out and put her in a chair for her picture. Before the trails separated Allie decided she would visit with the girl.

Perhaps it would take her mind off the situation between her and Jake. They had been polite but cool to each other since the incident at the creek, but he stayed and for that she was grateful. He wasn't one to pick a fight, nor respond if she did, so they had left it at that and moved on. He kept his distance, day and night, and she supposed he no longer wanted to learn the photographic trade from her.

It was probably just as well. Such duties would cause them to work together in very close quarters. Arms brushing, thighs touching, foreheads against one another in deep concentration.

In an effort to stop thinking about him, she asked one of the outriders to drive her wagon for a spell so she could visit with the Nichols family. When she found them and their two wagons about a mile behind the traders, she offered Isaac Nichols several thick slices of pink, sugar-cured ham as a calling gift. He welcomed her and she dismounted, tied Ringo to the back

146

of his wagon and climbed inside to sit with the frail young woman.

Emma rode propped up in a bed that had been fashioned for her in the middle of a large load of goods. She remembered Allie and appeared happy to have company.

Allie sat on the edge of the feather bed ticking and held the girl's thin, pale hand in her own. It was warm and damp. The wagon smelled of illness.

"How are you feeling?"

"I'm well. I'll be fine. I'm so happy to have someone to talk to."

Allie couldn't imagine that the girl would ever be fine. Her cheeks were sunken, her eyes huge and underlined by shadows, her voice quavery.

"Don't any of the women from the train ever visit with you?"

"Sometimes, but they are all very busy. It's hard work, seeing to a man and young'uns on the trail. Maw has no time to trade words with me, either."

"Oh, is she your mother?" Allie had noticed the woman, who looked to be not much older than Isaac.

"Not really, no. My mother and father are in Ohio. She is the mother of my husband's first wife, the grandmother of the boys."

"The boys? Oh, I thought they were you or your husband's younger brothers."

"The biggest one, Jacob, is my elder brother. He's strong and works very hard. He will pay our passage and then some."

Allie lifted a brow. "Pay your passage?"

Emma gazed at the blue sky peeking through the oval opening in the canvas. "We are indentured. If it weren't for him, Mr. Nichols would have not kept me when I fell ill. But because Jacob is so big and strong, so valuable to him, he is letting me go with the family to California."

Allie swallowed the knot in her throat. "Dear God," she murmured.

"Oh, it's all right. Mr. Nichols is a righteous man, and it was unfair to him after he paid all my parent's debts to find he had a weakling who may not even live to bear him a child."

"Your parents sold you and your brother to . . . to some man because he would pay their debts?"

Emma nodded. "Jacob and I have eight younger brothers and sisters—they could spare us." Her thin lips tightened. "Things were hard after the war. Everyone has to do what they can to survive. It's not uncommon."

"Yes, but you're only a child yourself."

"I'm fourteen." Emma shot a defensive glance at Allie and whispered, "She hates me."

"Hates you? Who hates you?"

"Maw." The girl's lip trembled and tears floated in her enormous eyes.

"Oh, surely not. Why would she hate a sweet little thing like you?"

"Because of Aaron."

"Aaron?"

The girl nodded and turned her head away. It was obvious that she needed someone to talk to so badly that she was willing to tell a total stranger her innermost secrets. Allie knew the feeling, and felt a great deal of empathy for this girl. She was carrying the child of a man probably three times her age; worse, she was much too ill to do any work, and was left alone all day every day in the back of a wagon where all she could see of the world was an oval of sky. She probably would not live to bear the child or see California. How dreadful. And now this further complication of someone named Aaron.

"Honey, who is Aaron?"

"Aaron is my husband's oldest son. He's sixteen and . . . and . . . he says he loves me and we can run away together as soon as the baby is born and I'm well again." The words tumbled out, one over the other and the girl didn't look at her, but kept her head turned toward a large wooden crate.

"Have you and he . . . I mean, is this child your husband's?"

148

"It will be, of course. I'm only carrying it for him."

Allie stared dumbfounded at the girl. Surely she knew . . . understood how women . . . Dear God. Allie smoothed a lock of the child's hair.

"No, I mean, did you let Aaron do . . . you know . . . what you let your husband do with you?"

Emma appeared puzzled, then she began to cry softly. In between ragged breaths, she told her story. "He's so sweet to me, he's like a little boy. Not like Mr. Nichols, mean and rough and big. Aaron never hurts me, you know, like that. I want to go with him, but I'm so afraid. And now Maw knows and she'll tell Mr. Nichols, I know she will. She'll tell and he'll beat Aaron and probably Jacob, too. He's done that before, beat both of them for just the tiniest of things. And Aaron works so hard he can hardly crawl out of bed every morning. And Jacob, too. What am I going to do?"

Allie leaned forward and put her arms around the girl's bony shoulders. "Oh, child. Dear child." How could this tiny thing have gotten herself in so much trouble so early in life?

"Will you help us?" Emma whispered, her hot teary breath wetting Allie's cheek. "I know it isn't right to take the baby away from Mr. Nichols, but I'm so afraid Maw will tell. We were going to wait, truly we were, until the baby came. He and Maw would be happy then, what with the new young'un, and we could sneak away. Maybe they wouldn't even come after us. But now . . . she saw Aaron . . . Aaron leaving . . . leaving after we . . . He only comes to stay with me for a while at night, after everyone is asleep, and he holds me and . . . and loves me a little. He doesn't do the other thing, you know, because he's afraid he'll hurt me and the baby. He kisses me . . . oh, and touches me . . . and his hands are so gentle and his mouth so warm . . . I'll die if anything happens to him. I truly will."

Allie believed Emma would probably die soon in any case, yet the girl's story was heartbreaking. How could she walk away without doing something?

From outside, a woman's harsh voice called the girl's name. She stiffened in Allie's arms, and quickly they dried the tears on her face and tried to appear normal by the time Maw stuck her head in the opening.

"Think you can get up for your supper tonight, or are you just going to lie there and let someone bring it to you? Plenty enough I have to do with you in this condition, without toting food to you."

Emma raised her head and managed a bright smile aimed at Maw. "I'll come out if one of the boys can help me down from the wagon."

Maw leered at her. "And I suspect you'd be wantin' that to be Aaron, would you? Little slut." The last was muttered as the woman turned away, but Allie had no trouble hearing her and was sure Emma did, too.

As she rode back toward her own wagon, Allie vowed that somehow she would help Emma and Aaron escape the terrible situation they were caught up in. She had no notion how but knew it would have to be soon, for tomorrow they would reach the cut-off for the Oregon Trail and it would be too late.

Chapter Ten

All afternoon the train moved closer to the cutoff of the Oregon Trail. Still, Allie had not come up with a plan. She wanted to approach Jake about it, but his attitude lately left her feeling as if any decisions were hers to make. She eyed him as they cleaned up after supper that evening. Someone had to break this silence that hung between them like a granite wall. Neither was angry, it was just that they couldn't seem to get back to the old friendliness they'd enjoyed before "Jake's water dance," as Allie had come to think of that night at the creek. She hoped that something would happen soon to smooth things over a bit, for she missed the old camaraderie. It was difficult to tell if Jake felt the same. He had a unique ability to enclose himself in a solitary cocoon that allowed no one in. Meanwhile he went about his business, whistled his tunes, grinned when he found something amusing and did his work. He continued to be polite but not warm and effusive, and he did not communicate any feelings. She hated it, but he appeared not to mind, one way or another.

If she had any doubts about helping Emma, they were ended later that night when Aaron paid a visit. She had noticed the boy hanging around just after dark, but didn't recognize him. He approached after Jake had stretched out on his bedroll, placed his hat over his face and appeared to be sleeping. Allie sat beside the fire, poking a stick into the dying flames and then watching it burn itself out.

At the sound of footsteps, she glanced up, expecting Eli Martin, for he had taken to strolling by, tipping his hat, passing a few words and moving on. Maybe he thought that would eventually break down her defenses. Instead of Eli, though, she saw the boy she'd noticed earlier.

He swept off a worn felt hat and said, "Ma'am, I'm sorry to bother you. My name's Aaron Nichols. Ain't you Miz Caine?"

Caught unaware, she blurted out, "Ohmigosh. Yes, yes, I'm Allison Caine. Is Emma all right?"

"Oh, yes, that is, she's as fine as she can be right now. But I . . . that is, she told me that she . . . uh, spoke to you about us. And I . . . well, that is, we don't have anywhere to turn. I'd just grab her up and take her out of that wagon and run off with her if she wasn't . . . well, sick and . . . uh, the baby. I'm afraid I'd hurt her, make her worse. But I swear, if she has to stay there much longer, she might as well be dead, and me too, ma'am. Oh, Lordy, me too."

Allie had risen as Aaron talked. In the firelight she saw that he was a rawboned young man. Her father would have said he had not yet grown off. He seemed all arms and legs, but his chest and shoulders showed signs of maturity. He had an unruly thatch of sandy hair that he occasionally raked at with splayed fingers. In his other hand he held an old brown felt hat. He smelled of trail dust and sweat and had the sweetest smile.

"Aaron, do you have any idea what could happen to you two if you go it alone?"

"Yes'm, I'm afraid I do. Do you know what will happen to us if we don't? Maw knows what's going on. Thousand wonders she hasn't told Paw already. 'Sides, Jacob says he'll go with us to help out."

Allie nodded, tilted her head. "Aaron, the woman you call Maw, she's your grandmother, isn't she? I mean, I understood that she is your mama's mama."

Aaron nodded miserably. "But we all have called her Maw since she took over our raising when our real maw died birthing Ishmael, the least one. Maw didn't want Paw to bring 'those two pieces of trash'—that's what she calls Emma and Jacob— into the family. She's got her heart set on Emma's baby, but she'd be content to take my maw's place in every way, if you know what I mean."

"You mean with your father?"

The boy didn't answer, just stared into the fire. "Emma said she asked you to help us. Are you going to, or should Jacob and I just pick her up out of that there wagon and walk off with her? We'll get as far as we get, I reckon."

"Oh, Aaron, don't do that. Please don't do that."

He nodded miserably. "Then what am I to do?"

"Aaron, is the child yours? I asked Emma but she didn't understand."

"No, ma'am. I never touched her that way. I wouldn't. She's too frail. But I love her with all my heart and I'll take care of the young'un as if he was mine. Till then I just want to see to her, get her away from Paw before he kills her. Then she'll get well, I know she will. He still goes to her, and I hear her crying afterwards. Even though Maw. . . . " The boy broke off. Obviously he wasn't quite willing to reveal some of the shameful things that were going on within his family.

"Aaron, your paw is going to be livid if the three of you run away. You know that, don't you? She's carrying his child, she's indentured to him and so is Jacob. Running off is breaking the law, don't you see, and not only can he come after you, he can get the law after you."

"But that's not right, him owning her like that. Isn't that just like slavery? And didn't we just fight a big war about that?"

153

"Yes, it is and yes, we did. But there are a lot of things not right in this world. And wars don't always make them right, either. Believe me, I know."

"What are we going to do?"

Allie stared into the fire for a long while, thinking of a lonely little girl left homeless after the brutal murder of her mother and sister. What would have happened to her had it not been for the kindness of others who cared for her until her father returned? She touched Aaron's arm. "Don't worry, I'll think of something. But it will have to be soon. Tomorrow night we'll be camped near the Oregon Trail cut-off. The three of you put some things together. A little food, some clothes and water. Do you have a horse, an animal that you can take with you?"

Aaron shook his head. "We sold all the horses and mules to buy the two teams of oxen for the wagons, but I could steal one for Emma. Me and Jacob can walk."

"No," Allie said softly, "don't steal one. Let's not start out that way. I'll figure something out. You just be ready after everyone is asleep. There won't be a moon. Don't worry, I'll think of something."

Even as she said it, Allie had no idea what she would do. She simply could not let these children go off on their own. They wouldn't last a day without help, and it looked like she was going to have to be the one to give that help. There was no way of getting around it, she would have to ask Jake to lend a hand, if she could get him to talk to her.

She spent most of the night trying to come up with a solution. Before dawn she was already busy coaxing flames from coals for a breakfast fire and waiting for Jake to rouse himself. Even though what she had to say to him was not good, she was excited that at last she had a clear reason to renew their relationship. She had been looking for an excuse to break the silence that hung between her and Jake, and now she had one.

As soon as Jake returned from his morning trek to the woods and splashed his face with cold water, she approached him with the sorry tale.

In silence he poured their first cups of coffee from the steaming pot while she finished her story, all the while watching him closely. If he said no she didn't know what she was going to do, for she couldn't possibly carry this out without his help, yet she would not desert those children.

His solemn stare lasted through most of her recitation, but his expression softened at her declaration that she would help the youngsters. When she finished, he asked, "You're absolutely sure you want to get involved?"

Immediately defensive, she replied, "Yes, I do. Whether you help me or not. So just say you will or you won't, and don't try to talk me out of it. Oh, Jake, if you could see these two kids, talk to them, then you'd know."

He sighed and blew on the steaming black liquid. "What do you think we should do, then?" he asked, and she could have kissed him.

"Use some of the money Jesse gave us, all if that's what it takes, to buy them horses and supplies. Jake, they have to have a fighting chance. As it is, the girl is going to die. I just know she is. But better in Aaron's arms than in the back of that wagon with those miserable people hovering about like vultures."

He nodded, rose and went to his saddle bags where he took out what was left of his share of the money. He returned, bills clutched in one fist, and sat on the log he had dragged up beside the fire the evening before.

"I have another idea, Allie."

Relief spread through her. "Oh, Jake, thank you. I was so afraid you'd be against doing anything. It won't be easy slipping them away without Mr. Nichols or that dreadful woman catching us. I didn't want to do it alone."

Belatedly she realized what he had said. "What's your idea?"

"That's a lot of money, especially when you put yours with it. Probably more than Nichols or his clan have ever seen in one place. Why don't we just buy the kids out of their indenturement? Then they won't have to run away. They can go where they want without having to worry about him chasing after them."

155

She thought about that awhile. "Well, Jake, that might work. The way I read this basta . . . uh, Nichols, though, I'm afraid he'll say no. She is carrying his child."

"A man like that, he might not care about an unborn baby."

"True. But Aaron says his grandmother is counting on having the baby for herself. And if we give him all the money to get them free, then what will they do? They won't have anything. They'll be lucky if he lets them take their own clothes along. They'll have no food, no pack animals, nothing."

"Wait a minute. You said the woman they call Maw, she hates the girl. She wants her son-in-law all to herself? That's sick, still, it might be a solution. Suppose we get her to help us get them away? She'd be rid of her competition, we could maybe give her a bit for her trouble, then there'd be money left for the kids."

Allie squinted into an errant finger of early sunlight. "That's pretty tricky, and it just might work. I guess it would depend on how much she's counting on the girl living to have the child. I don't think she will, but . . . I'd rather not let her in on it unless we have no choice, and then only if she thinks what we offer is all the money we have. If she guesses that we have enough to buy supplies and horses, she'll hold out for all of it."

"Damn, these are not very nice people."

She nodded thoughtfully. "It comes from living through such terrible times. Some folks just can't handle it and have been pressed to do things they'd never do under ordinary circumstances, but these two are really the scum of the earth. I doubt they'd be any different, no matter what the circumstances."

Jake remembered the gang of cutthroat prisoners in Andersonville and nodded. She was right about what circumstances did to some people. His stomach rumbled and he glanced at her with a grin. "I'm starved. I cooked yesterday—it's your turn. And while you're doing that I'll nose around for mounts for those kids. Surely there's some extras in the remuda that Defoe would be willing to let go of. Reckon we'd better not pass the word around what we're doing."

Seeing the old grin on Jake's face, Allie could almost forget the frightening task that lay before them. She smiled back at him and fetched her half of the money Jesse James had given them.

She handed it to Jake and as he started to walk away, said, "Jake, thank you for helping. I was afraid you might fight me on this."

"Fight you? No, I wouldn't fight you. You ought to know that about me by now."

He grinned and she bit her lip to keep from running to him and giving him a hug.

Allie didn't dare contact Emma or Aaron to let them know the plan for fear Isaac Nichols would suspect something. As it was, if the man found out she and Jake had anything to do with the disappearance of his child-wife, his son and his legally indentured servant, there was no telling what he would do. Instead, as she went about her normal morning chores she tried to come up with a safe place for the kids to go. It wouldn't do for them to take out alone cross-country with no plans at all. And the first place Nichols would check would be the caravan headed for Santa Fe. It would be a logical choice. If her outfit was large enough, she might take the chance of hiding them out, but three full grown runaways would not fit in the small what's-it wagon. What they needed was a destination somewhere off the beaten path where they would be safe. A place where no one would ever think to look for them, would never accidentally find them.

Suddenly she knew where that place was. It was so simple she wondered why she hadn't thought of it sooner. Were there any flaws in her plan? Could the kids find the well-hidden cabin? After mulling over her idea awhile she decided that with thorough directions they would have no trouble, and Jake could provide those. She couldn't wait to talk to him about it, see what he thought. There really wasn't much time to come up with anything better. It would work, she knew it would, and while the former hideout of the James gang might not be perfect, it would provide a roof over their heads in a hidden location. Certainly more than they had any prospect of otherwise.

She fetched a folded piece of brown wrapping paper and a pencil from her carefully packed supplies and started a map of the route as well as she could remember it, beginning with the road out of Westport. What would the James brothers think if they knew that their money and their hidden cabin would be used by kids on the run? Where had Jesse said they were going? Somewhere out of Missouri, she recalled. Where they could find more banks to rob, no doubt. She shrugged, wondered briefly whatever would become of the many outlaws spawned by that terrible war, and went back to the sketch.

Jake returned leading a gaunt spotted gray and a shaggy but stout pony. "They don't look like prime horseflesh, but I think they're both big-hearted and will give their all. The pony will be fine for the girl. I couldn't talk them out of a third mount from the remuda, but Defoe said he thought Martin had brought along a couple of extra horses and he might let me buy one. But to tell you the truth, I'm not too excited about dealing with him. He's bound to want to know what we're wanting with the animal, and first rattle out of the box he'll be nosing into our business. Appears to me he hangs around you too much anyway."

The last was said with a surprising amount of fervor.

Though it pleased her to have Jake irate over another man's attentions, Allie was anxious to change the subject. She did not want to rehash Eli Martin's connection to her past, or explain it in more detail.

Rubbing a hand down the flank of the pony she gazed doubtfully at the angular hipbones of the big gray. "Maybe we ought to buy extra food for this one."

Jake nodded. "Defoe said he'd been down with some kind of complaint, but was coming around real good now. Looks healthy in the eyes, and his feet and mouth look fine. I believe he'll do."

Allie leaned up against the gray, felt the animal tense to hold her weight. His head came around and he nuzzled her shoulder.

She rubbed his soft nose, curling back his lip to see strong young teeth. Jake stood close by. She glanced from the horse to him and back again, and smiled widely.

He grinned like he hadn't in days. "What is it?"

"This horse reminds me of you the first time I saw you."

He glanced down at the lead rope and flushed.

Allie laughed aloud. "All skin and bones but ready for anything."

"I was ready for anything, Allie. Still am."

She cocked her head, sensed he wanted to say more, but was holding back. Damn that water dance of his. It had ruined a perfect relationship. Well, nearly perfect.

She glanced up to catch him staring at her.

"Jake, I—"

"Allie, couldn't—"

Their words tumbled all over each other.

"You first," he said.

"I'm so sorry about what happened. I pushed you to do something you didn't want to do, then blamed you for getting upset. I want us to talk together again, I want us to be friends."

"It wasn't your fault, it was mine. I'm the one that kissed you, not the other way around. And I've acted like a blamed jackass about it ever since. Hell, I was the one that was naked." He shot her one of his boyish grins. "Who could blame you for being attracted to such a fine-looking specimen?"

"Oh, for goodness sake." She leaned against the gray and chuckled. "Well, I'm glad that's settled. And I promise, I'll do my best to resist your charms from here on in, even if you are the finest-looking specimen I'm apt to see in my lifetime.

"Now, what are we going to do about another horse? I agree with you about Martin. If Nichols comes around asking questions about the kids, he might let it slip. What about Defoe? What will he say?"

"Nothing. I felt him out and took him into my confidence. I didn't have any other choice. Nichols may question him when he finds the kids gone. What I'm hoping is that the old man just

159

shrugs it off and keeps right on moving toward California, but we can't count on that. Defoe was sympathetic, said he had no patience with such shenanigans anyway and would keep quiet. We can't trust anyone else to do the same."

"You're right," Allie said. "Oh, I thought of the perfect place for the kids to go. Well, as perfect as any place could be, under the circumstances."

Jake perked up.

"The James hideout, back down south in Missouri."

He thought about that. "How will they find it?"

She fetched her sketch. "I started drawing them a map. You look at it and add the landmarks you can remember. Once they find the road, they'll have no trouble."

Jake took the crackling piece of paper, spread it on the tailgate of the wagon and went to work with a pencil. He had an eye for details she hadn't even thought about, like certain shapes of boulders and where unusual trees were in relation to the spot where the route left the main road and wound through the wilderness to the cabin.

She remarked about him coming up with so much information.

"I guess it's because I have lots of room in my head for what's going on around me." He tapped his temple with a finger. "Since there's nothing else rattling around up there, it just stands to reason I'd fill it up with something. Besides, I work extra hard to remember things. I think I'm afraid I'll lose it all again, and that scares me. Do you remember that boulder shaped like a huge lizard just to the right before we headed off the road? I think it was right about here."

He put the pencil point down and drew a rough outline. "If they veer left there and ride into that ridge of scrub oak they should be able to pick up those faint ruts I followed when I came after you."

Excitement coursed through her and she hugged herself to stop the trembling. "Oh, what if something happens to them? What if she starts to have the baby and they don't know what to do?"

"Allie, if we're going to help them do this, we'll have to not think of things like that. We're giving them a chance. From what you've said, they're going to run off anyway. At least this way, they'll have a roof over their heads, some food, and if the boys are quick, they can get work in one of the settlements nearby. It's the best we can do, but I don't want you to stew and fret. It'll just upset you."

Knowing he was right, she nodded. "Okay, now what about another horse?"

He looked up from the map. "I don't think there's any way to get one. Those boys will just have to take turns walking. Hell, there's folks proud to be walking all the way to California. I talked to one or two going to Santa Fe with this train that have walked every step so far and intend to continue to do so. It's the best we can do without putting them in danger.

"If the old man doesn't discover they're gone till morning, he'll spend a good part of the day questioning folks before he actually sets out after them, if he does at all. By then they can be long gone, and I don't think he'll expect them to be going back toward Westport. That was a stroke of genius, thinking of the James cabin. Hope to hell them boys didn't change their minds and are still there."

"I don't think they will be, but even if they are, they didn't strike me as the type that would bring harm down on three youngsters just trying to make do. Did they you?"

"Well, they did tie me up to that blamed chair, but still, you're right. I'm beginning to think they are outlaws not so much because of what they do as what the law thinks about what they do. And, of course, you had to be on the right side coming out of the war. The winning side."

He paused, glanced at her. "Are you going to talk to Emma and Aaron before tonight?"

"No, I told Aaron to be ready as soon as everyone was asleep."

"Fine. I'll go along with you. You can keep the horses on down the trail a ways and I'll sneak in and fetch them."

"Let me get them. They know me."

"And take a chance on you getting caught? I won't do that."

"You're fighting me, and you said you wouldn't. If they catch you in there it'll go real hard on you. Me, there's a chance I can plead my way out of it. No one thinks women can really do anything anyway, and especially not that old fart."

"Allie, I swear."

She tilted her head, said his name in a serious tone.

"Oh, well. Do it your way. You will anyhow. But if you get caught I'm coming in to get you and I promise you it won't be a pretty sight."

She laughed. "Oh, yeah. Like when you fell over the window sill at the James hideout?"

"I figured you'd never let me live that down. Hell, I knew you'd bring it up every chance you got. That was different and you know it. I'm different. Just don't let that 'old fart' catch you, you hear?"

He headed for the corral to fetch the mules and hitch them.

She watched him limp several paces away, then shouted, "Hey." When he turned, she said, "Don't you go falling on your face, you hear me? And thanks."

He grinned and waved.

She tied the two spare horses to the back of the wagon and squatted beside the fire to make johnny cakes for breakfast.

A stagecoach passed the caravan as it got underway that morning. Soon they would move into The Narrows. To the north lay the Wakarusa River, to the south the stream called the Marais de Cygnes, forcing them to travel between. Deep ruts gouged in the earth evidenced the difficulty of the route during rainy weather. A month earlier and they would have been bogged at every turn, but it hadn't rained in a while and a hot sun had parched the ground. Only a few marshy places were in evidence. They were easily bypassed.

They nooned near the intersection of the Oregon Trail, and while they were there, the wagon train in which the Nichols family rode approached.

Allie stood out in the open, one hand shading her eyes, and watched as wagon after wagon rumbled off toward the north. She spotted Aaron walking along beside a team of oxen, about eight wagons back from the lead. Come dark they might be five or six miles up the trail. She and Jake would get no sleep this night.

As she turned to go back to camp and prepare herself a cold meal, she saw Jake approaching on his mare. It looked as if he might be planning on eating with her for the first time since the water dance affair. It looked like something good would come out of this terrible situation, after all. She had missed his company a great deal.

By late that evening, the Santa Fe traders had moved on down the trail toward the southwest probably five miles or more. Once camp was made and folks were settling in, she and Jake packed up their own saddlebags, loaded the gray with the supplies Defoe had put together for Aaron and Emma, and headed back down the trail. Setting a fast pace, they covered in very little time ground they had ridden over once this day, for two on horseback could travel much faster than a caravan of bunglesome wagons.

It was full dark before they spotted the distant campfires of the homesteaders. In silent agreement they veered off into a thick growth of cottonwood trees alongside the encampment. There, it was decided, Jake would wait with the horses, while Allie fetched Emma, Aaron and Jacob.

"But you get in any kind of trouble at all, you skin out of there, you hear?" Jake said, looking down at her. "Cause if you're not back pronto, I'm coming in after you. I don't want Nichols to have a chance to lay his filthy hands on you."

Allie touched the butt of her Colt. "Don't worry, that won't happen. You give me time, now. I'll get in as close as I can, but I'll have to wait till all's quiet, so don't you go jumping the gun on me."

"Will do. You remember, you can holler as good as the next one, and I don't want you to be too proud to yell for help if you need it."

She nodded grimly, but knew that calling for help was the last thing she would do. Getting those kids out quietly without any fuss at all was her goal. She moved off into the darkness.

"Allie?" Jake said just above a whisper.

She stopped, turned, strained to make out his features.

"Be careful."

The tone of the words moved through the night to caress her, charged her with a case of goose bumps. She wished he had hugged her, or she him. After a moment she headed for the flickering campfires that illuminated the huge dark hulks of prairie schooners circled against marauders.

Earlier, when she had spotted Aaron she had marked the wagon in her memory. A large Conestoga-style blue wagon, with a peculiar assortment of tools hooked to one side: a draw knife, three scythes and a two-man saw. All carried tools, but she had memorized this particular arrangement so she could locate the wagon easily. It was on the far side of the circle, and so it took her a while to make her way there. She kept low to the ground. Every sound spooked her, made her freeze into what she hoped would look like a scraggly piece of brush. After what seemed like hours she spotted the Nichols wagons.

Hanging back she watched carefully the comings and goings of the family. Which of the two wagons was Emma in? The woman they referred to as Maw soon carried the smallest boy to the back of one and tucked him inside. With some ribaldry the other boys bedded down on the ground beneath, and then Maw disappeared from sight. Perhaps they had a tent on the far side, for she couldn't imagine the older woman sleeping out in the open. It made her nervous not to see the elder Nichols, for he would be the real danger.

She and Jake had decided that she would try to get the three out without incident, but if it became necessary she would offer to pay Maw to keep quiet. Men were very often occupied with guard duty, or caring for stock, and if they were lucky Nichols wouldn't even be around. Still, Allie decided that the prudent thing to do was to wait a while longer, until only the perimeter guards were out and about. She could dodge them easily with no moon.

Off in the distance a coyote set up a mournful yip, yip, moan, and Allie stirred. It was time to go, for not a sound had come from the camp for a long while. She let the guard on horseback make his slow way past her and as soon as he was out of hearing, crept toward the wagon in which she should find Emma, Aaron and Jacob waiting and ready.

She drew back the curtain and whispered the girl's name. There was no reply. Were they waiting somewhere else? Perhaps in the other wagon, the one in which the younger boy slept. That didn't make sense.

"Emma, Aaron, where are you?"

A hand lashed out of the darkness, grabbed her arm hard, swung her around roughly. "What the hell you think you're doing, little lady?"

She smelled whiskey and body odor, a sour hot breath washed over her face and she swallowed a scream as she stared into the glowering countenance of Isaac Nichols.

Chapter Eleven

Jake hated letting Allie go into the camp alone, and wished he had more spunk when it came to dealing with her. She called the shots and he obeyed, like some dumb dog. Then he would get angry at her for treating him like her pet. Yet he couldn't imagine her putting up with a forceful man who bossed her around and made her toe the line. Somewhere there must be a middle ground.

He shrugged and settled back against the rough bark of a big cottonwood. They were friends, and that was the important thing.

If she got in trouble she couldn't handle, he could damn well wade in and take care of it. Or could he?

Sometimes he wondered just what kind of man he had been and if he would ever find out. Perhaps he was doomed to wander the rest of his days in search of somebody, anybody, who might know who he was and where he belonged. He thought of the confusing dreams or visions or whatever the hell they were.

Was he recalling what had truly happened, or were they something his mind made up to compensate for the lack of memory?

He rubbed at his aching thigh. The flesh was dented with scars from the explosion that had wounded him and put him in the hands of the enemy. Though he had learned to live with the dull throbbing in the weakened muscles, the leg would never be as strong as it once was. It was the damned blackouts that debilitated him, for he never knew when one would come or how severe it would be. It had been a while now since the last one, but he dared not believe they had stopped.

No matter how hard he tried, he could not remember that day on the battlefield. The concussion had wiped out years of memories of personal experiences, yet he could read and write, sing songs from the war, and like he'd told Allie, he hadn't forgotten how to put his own pants on. Odd how selective such a thing could be. The doctors he'd seen when he came out of Andersonville had been as perplexed as he. Though they had observed all kinds of memory losses—amnesia, they called it—its perversities weren't to be explained. Some sufferers recovered, some didn't. Some became totally helpless and couldn't even remember how to feed themselves or walk, others just had blank holes in an otherwise healthy memory. Then there were those like Jake, and he had always considered himself lucky, for it could have been so much worse.

He touched the pocket in which he kept Lorena's picture. If he could only find her, let her know he was alive, he wouldn't mind the rest at all. He could live with it, but dear God, why couldn't he find the woman he loved?

A noise, the rustle of something scurrying through the underbrush, broke into his reverie and he slipped behind the tree. Even with limited night vision, he made out the boy running as he came within a few feet of him. The horses pawed the ground, tugged at their reins.

Jake launched himself at the youngster, brought him down with a thud. The kid kicked and scratched, bit at the hand Jake clamped over his mouth to keep down his indignant cries.

After a brief struggle Jake subdued him and said in his ear, "Quiet, boy. Hush up. Who are you? Where are you going in such a hurry?"

The kid's eyes widened and Jake slipped his hand away so he could speak. "Aaron. They've got her. The lady that came to help me and Emma. Oh, Lord, you've got to help. Paw will hurt them, hurt them both real bad."

"Allie, he's got Allie? Where were you going?"

Aaron rolled his head around wildly. "I didn't know what to do, I was going to the traders to get help."

Jake struggled to his feet. "Get up, now. Show me."

Grabbing his rifle from its scabbard, Jake hurried along behind the boy, cursing the damned leg but keeping up all the same.

Together they circled wide around the encampment. All was so quiet Jake couldn't help but think the boy was mistaken. Wouldn't trouble like this rouse someone, especially those closest by?

The boy signaled him to stop and pointed. "There, in that wagon, he's got them both in there."

"Where's her brother? Jacob, isn't that his name?"

"He tried to help and the old man laid him out with the butt of his rifle. I was smart enough not to get in on it. I can't do Emma any good if the bastard kills me. I knew we had to have help."

"Why not get someone in the train?"

"No . . . no, they won't help. Everyone's terrified of Paw. Besides, what a man does with his family is his own business, right?"

Jake put a hand on Aaron's shoulder. "Okay, calm down. They'll hear us. Allie. Is she hurt?"

"He hit her when she tried to fight back, knocked her out. Emma, she's just huddled in there crying. He's got her so—"

"That's fine, boy. You did good. Now you listen, and do just what I tell you. Understand?"

Aaron nodded his head vigorously. Even in the darkness Jake sensed his determination to conquer the terror and help save the woman he loved. The smell of fear emanated from the boy, and probably from himself, as well.

Placing his lips against Aaron's ear, he whispered, "You go back to the horses, take the big mare, and you ride as fast as you can to the trader's caravan. Tell Defoe, that's the boss, what's happened and tell him to bring some men. If I don't bring this off, he can handle Nichols."

"What're you going to do?"

"Me? Why, I'm going to rescue a couple of ladies. We'll meet you along the trail if all goes well, if not, well, then Defoe can mop up."

"You take care of Emma. Don't you let nothin' happen to her."

"Don't you worry, and boy, don't you ride my horse to death, then you'll be afoot and doing nobody any good. Now quit jawing and get moving."

Jake didn't wait for the boy to do as he was told, but began to slink closer to the wagon in which Allie was being kept prisoner. His heart beat thunderously, the back of his throat clogged and he felt as if he might shoot off in all directions at once. All sensations he could not remember ever feeling. If that bastard hurt Allie, he'd kill him. It was an unexpected, razor-sharp vow, not unlike the one he'd expressed to Eli Martin. What a terrible feeling to contemplate taking a life, worse to realize that Allie was in danger of losing hers if he didn't do something.

Clearing his mind for the task ahead, he crept to the side of the wagon the boy had pointed out, placed an ear to the canvas. From inside came weak sobbing. Placing the Spencer carefully on the ground near the wheel where he could find it, he stepped up on the frame and peered into the darkness. The rifle would do him little good in such close quarters, and might get someone innocent killed.

He waited a moment, heard nothing but the incessant sobbing. Just as he decided to move inside and damn the consequences, a rough feminine voice blurted literally on top of him, "Shut up the damn caterwauling, now."

It was all he could do to muffle a stunned cry of his own. She'd scared the living wits out of him. Inside someone groaned, then mumbled enough words for him to recognize Allie. He had three women to deal with, one definitely hostile, and it was so damned dark he couldn't see his own hand in front of his face.

Cautiously, he raised one leg and eased inside, one boot coming right down on the middle of a soft body. All hell cut loose. One of the women let out a startled, godawful screech, another pounded him across his back and a third locked her arms around his waist.

"Allie? Allie, dammit, answer me."

"Jake?" It was the one squeezing the breath out of him. He gasped and grabbed at the fist that continued to hammer him soundly.

"Is that Emma yelling? Tell her to be quiet."

"Yes. Hush, Emma, help has come." Allie let go of Jake, he heard a grunt of pain and the woman pummeling him stopped. "Bitch," Allie muttered under her breath. "You'll have to carry Emma, she's too weak to run. Honey, this is Jake, and he's here to help us."

"Where's Aaron?" The voice was that of a very young, very frightened girl.

"He's safe," he told her. "Come on, let's get you out of here."

From outside came shouts. Allie scrambled up on the seat and pawed around under it. She brought out her Colt that Isaac had taken when he caught her, pointed it skyward and fired a quick shot. She thumbed the hammer back a second time, pointed the gun at a gang of men.

"Get her out, Jake. Me and these fellows are going to come to a quick understanding, isn't that right?" Her glare at the group momentarily hushed their clamor.

Jake moved Emma to the wagon seat, lowered himself to the ground and reached up for her. "Just put your arms around my neck, honey, I'll do the rest. And don't you cry anymore, you hear?"

The girl obeyed and rested her head against his shoulder with a sob-laden sigh. She was light as a whispering breeze.

"Allie, come on. Get my Spencer, there on the ground by the front wheel."

A younger male voice said, "I've got the rifle. High tail it, I'll cover your flank."

"Jacob, oh, thank God, I thought he'd killed you," Emma said.

Allie called down from her perch, "I'll be coming, you just get her out of here and I'll persuade these gentlemen to leave you be if I have to deposit some lead in their butts. I'm right behind you."

From out of the crowd, someone shouted, "You bastard, that's my wife you're stealing. I'll have the law after you."

"Hush up, Nichols, or I'll have the law after you for what you did to me," Allie said.

"Goddammit, that's my wife he's hauling out of here. Do something. You gonna let some puny woman with a pea shooter stop you?"

Isaac Nichols lurched out of the throng, and the men around him set up a grumbling. Sensing she was about to lose control, Allie planted a shot between Nichols' feet, spraying dirt and gravel up the insides of his trouser legs.

He cupped his genitals and made a bawling sound.

"I can come closer. Any of you want to see?" The Navy Colt gleamed as she raised the sights.

From the other side of the wagon, Jacob moved to where the crowd could see him and the powerful Spencer. It froze them all in their tracks.

"Allie, get down from there and come on. I'm not leaving till you do," Jake shouted from the nearby trees.

He put the girl in Ringo's saddle and swung up behind her. Leading the gray and the pony, he rode toward Allie. By this

171

time she had backed away from the dangerous gathering of men, Jacob right beside her carrying the rifle.

Allie fired another shot, then turned and ran, vaulting onto the pony's back. He carried double saddle bags and she squeezed her legs between them, hugging the pony's sides with both knees, one fist wrapped in the thick mane. Jacob scrambled onto the big gray, sharing room with bedrolls and bags of supplies. The three horses thundered off into the night. It would take the men a while to saddle up and ride after them. It was certain Nichols would be on their trail, though, so they weren't out of the woods yet.

Where the Oregon met the Santa Fe, Jake hauled up.

Allie joined him. "What is it?"

"We need a place to hide out here for a while."

"Why? Shouldn't we get back to the caravan, convince them that those yahoos are up to no good so they'll help us fight them off?" Allie spoke between long, deep breaths.

"That's what they'll expect us to do. Head for the caravan, and with any luck they'll catch us. This girl can't take this rough riding much longer."

Emma's reply proved his point, despite her words, for she was weak with fatigue and pain. "No, no, I'm all right. I only want to get to Aaron. Did you find my brother Jacob?" She sagged back against Jake.

"I'm right here, sis," piped up the boy.

Emma tried to raise her head from where it rested against Jake's chest, but sighed with defeat. "Where's Aaron?"

"She'll never make it, Allie," he said softly.

"Okay, let's put the horses over there in those trees, and I'll look around for a place to rest awhile. With any luck they'll ride right on by us."

"It has to be within sight of the trail so we can stop Aaron when he comes back with Defoe."

She nodded, but thought that was a mighty tall order, in the dark and all. Several minutes later, on a rise about five hundred yards southwest of the junction she rode up on two large boulders at an angle to each other. Their position formed a natural shelter surrounded by some scraggly Osage orange, a few scrub oak and plum bushes. She hurried to fetch the others, and they were soon in the hideout, the horses tied some distance away and completely out of sight of the trail.

Jake had brought his canteen and each took a long swig of the tepid water. Allie helped Emma stretch out on the ground and Jacob lay down next to her.

"You okay, sweet pea?" she asked when the girl had settled back and closed her eyes.

"Fine, just fine. Thank you."

Jacob said softly, "I'll keep count of her, don't you worry."

Allie smiled at the tone of the young man's voice, so brave and self-assured. He could be no more than sixteen. She crawled to Jake's side and together they leaned against one of the large boulders, still warm from the afternoon sunlight.

He touched her arm. "How about you, you okay?"

She nodded, covered his hand with hers.

Instead of pulling away from her touch, he was silent a moment, then chuckled.

"What?"

"You were pretty impressive out there. Just like a—"

"If you say just like a man, I'll smack you."

He laughed softly. "I was about to say just like a blamed wild outlaw. Didn't have man or woman in mind."

"Uh huh."

"Honest, hope to die."

She shuddered. "Oh, don't say that, not even in jest."

For a moment both were so quiet they could hear the youngsters breathing. Allie grew intensely conscious of Jake's hip and thigh touching hers and she squeezed his hand.

"You weren't so bad yourself."

"Yeah, I did pretty good up against a woman, didn't I?"

Another silence, then, "Jake?"

173

"Mmmm?"

"You ever think about settling down, stopping this search of yours, letting go the past and living for today . . . tomorrow?"

"Sometimes, sure, but then I'll look at Lorena's picture and think of her not knowing what happened to me, and I just have to go on."

"It's so fruitless. It's such a big country, and you could have come from anywhere. Have you ever tried to search the army's records?"

"For who? I don't have a name. Hell, even those who did, some were never identified and were buried in mass graves. I don't even know what regiment I was in."

"But you were in the Union army?"

"Almost certain, unless I was a turncoat Reb and my own kind put me in Andersonville for treason. There's not much reason to suspect that.

"What about you, Allie? Why are you out searching for another place to be? Don't you ever think about settling down? Finding you someone to hold you and let you rest your head on his shoulder now and again?"

"Not really. I don't regret the time I spent with my father, but I cared for him so long and he was so ill, I'm afraid I've nothing left to give. I wouldn't be able to be considerate and kind to a man who would most certainly make demands on me." She could not bring herself to mention Eli and his broken promises. Some other time, perhaps.

"That's crazy, and you know it. Look how you are with me. Hell, you pet around on me and take care of me like I was some—"

"Yeah, I know, puppy. You told me. You're different, Jake. You . . . well, you're so fiercely determined to do everything yourself, and yet it doesn't bother you to let me do what I have to do. I didn't know there were men like that. I honestly didn't. I've always thought they were like my father or . . . "

She stopped. "I don't want to talk about this. I haven't sorted out all my feelings yet. I loved my father, but sometimes when I think about what he did, I hate him. Is that possible?"

Jake didn't answer, and after a while she asked, "What was Andersonville like?"

He shuddered, lifted her hand and began to trace along her fingers clasped through his. He swallowed harshly.

"It's the one thing I wish I didn't remember. I was . . . I came to myself on a grubby blanket with dozens of others like me, all laid out in the open, side by side, some of them moaning and already dying. It must have been raining, 'cause I was wet and those walking around were calf-deep in mud. Someone had taken my uniform and left me in longjohns that were shredded where my leg was wounded. I couldn't walk, and the guards would bring some sort of sloppy mess they called soup in a big vat and leave it to sit out in the open. It was every man for himself and some didn't even have a vessel to dip out the horrid stuff, so we'd cup our hands and fill them, then lap at it like a dog."

He stopped, kissed her fingertips. "You don't want to hear this."

What she wanted was for him to take her in his arms, put those warm lips now resting on her hand over her mouth. She wanted, dear God, for him to make love to her, on the ground with the small pregnant girl and her brother sleeping nearby. Despite the danger she wanted Jake's arms around her, she wanted him to love her.

Instead, she said softly, "You need to tell it to someone before it drives you crazy."

And so he told her about the filth and the degradation, about the men caged there who managed to make the place even worse than it had to be by becoming predators themselves, feeding on the weaker of their own kind. And he told her about drifting in and out of consciousness. And how he discovered that he could escape into another world and leave behind the

175

hopelessness. After a while he welcomed the blackouts. They somehow sustained him until the war was over. By that time many of the men who hadn't killed each other had starved to death. When the Yankees rode in to rescue them most could barely crawl from the hovels in which they huddled, naked, bug infested and half-mad.

She listened in utter, stupefied silence while hot tears rolled down her cheeks, and when he had finished she lay her head on his chest and cried. She was certain then that she loved him. Loved him for the unbelievable strength it took to survive such a hideous ordeal, for the way he went on with his life, his consideration of her and his undaunted courage to discover his past, no matter the barriers or possible consequences. And she felt so damned hopeless in that love.

His arm crept around her shoulders, a finger brushed hair from her tear-stained face. "Don't cry. It's over and done with. I shouldn't have told you. All this time I've only wanted to forget. Funny, isn't it? How I search so hard for my past, yet what I can remember I wish I could forget. Who knows? Maybe all my past is better off forgotten."

She glanced up to find him gazing at her, eyes gleaming in the darkness.

"Tell me, Allie Caine," he whispered, his lips close to hers. "Tell me why you aren't married and off somewhere far from me. Very far so that you don't tempt me. God, how you tempt me."

She leaned forward and touched his lips with hers, all the while knowing she should not do this thing. She would only push him away again, and she wanted him near her no matter what rules he set down.

Yet, because she could do nothing less at that moment, caught there in the serene aftermath of violence, she moved one leg over his hips and settled on his lap facing him. The hardness of his body set off a hot flow of desire she could not quench, and she molded herself to him, arms twined about his neck.

He wrapped her up within the circle of his embrace, passion blinding him to anything but her exquisite body. He feared such untamed yearnings, hated being out of control. The unbridled desire sent him spiraling into darkness, helpless to stop what was to come. It was too much like the way he felt before one of his spells came upon him. Yet a joyous expectation swallowed him up, his body responded quite vigorously, and he was totally unprepared to resist.

He spread his hands over her back, inched them under her arms to cup the gentle swell of her breasts. His mouth yearned to touch her there, to kindle her fire as she had his. She leaned backward and bared her throat. His lips and tongue belonged there against the frantic pulsing and he bent to savor the tantalizing flavors of wild flowers, wind and rain. Between her breasts, a taste piquant and earthy nourished his growing desire. Every muscle, all flesh and bone, ached to take what she offered. Take and take and take until they both dropped from exhaustion.

She moved against him, and he yearned to be free of the binding fabrics of their clothes to feel her delicious flesh against his, to plunge deep into her warmth and drown there. Had any man ever felt such primitive, wanton desire? He thought not.

An all-too-familiar voice whispered in his head. *You will not do this, I won't allow it.*

Lorena!

Before he could react, Allie yanked at the buttons of his shirt, jerking him back to reality. In the distance a wolf howled, the mournful cries ululating over and around them. He shivered, lay trembling fingers along the swell of her breast.

There, where his mouth belonged, her flesh rose to his touch.

If you do this to me, I'll never forgive you. Never, the voice insisted.

Go away, Lorena. Please, leave me in peace.

He drew in his breath, worked another button loose on Allie's shirt and lowered his eager mouth. Had anything ever tasted so sweet?

She moaned deep in her throat, her pulse vibrating a soothing rhythm against his cheek. She worked at his belt buckle, moving her body languidly against his, a sensual urging to his growing arousal.

Her life and his coming together were all that mattered. Together they could fill the black void in his mind, his soul, his very heart.

He could remember praying but he didn't know when and thought he had forgotten how. Now it came back to him, and he asked only that he be allowed this one, joyous experience. Loneliness had seared his heart, quelled any passion he might once have possessed. How would he know? For since leaving the prison no woman had aroused him. Had he always been such a man? He ached all over with longing for her, a need so deep it writhed to be satisfied.

Allie opened his buttons, shifting her warm buttocks down his thighs. The pressure of her weight sent a vicious throbbing right to the bone of his bad leg. Pain flared like fire through his brain, and he moved her to one side with a groan.

She halted her work at the opening of his pants, but said nothing.

Perhaps she thought he didn't want her. He had to reassure her so she wouldn't go away. If he lost her this very minute, he would die. "It's all right, I . . . please don't stop."

Ethan, if you leave me I'll die. It's all his fault. I didn't mean it, please forgive me, Ethan. He'll never come between us again.

He stiffened. The voice. The damned voice again. Why didn't she go away, shut up, leave him be? "Stop . . . stop it, now."

"No, no I won't. I won't." Allie leaned forward and put her warm, moist lips on his bare belly, then worked her way upward, kissing and nibbling at his warm skin.

This time she would make him want her. Want her so badly he would forget all about his ghost woman. No matter what he said, she wouldn't stop. She reached the fine c`urly hair of his chest, took another nip. "You don't want me to stop. Not now." She ran her tongue around one nipple.

His breath came in gasps. "Not you, Allie. Her. I want you, I do. Oh, God, God please let—"

Immediately she stopped his plea with her mouth, giving him her tongue.

The nourishment opened within him an anticipation of such magnitude he could not contain the hunger.

He ripped the remaining buttons from her shirt, gathered her breasts in his hands, never taking his lips from hers.

She cried out into his mouth; desire jagged through his gut like a bolt of white-hot lightning. A taste sweeter than drops of the honeysuckle flower poured over his tongue.

Beneath her palms, Allie felt his rigid desire throbbing like a pounding heart. She imagined him inside her where no man had been before. He shifted, lay on his back, hands cupping her breasts. She moved over him.

A breeze rustled through the surrounding trees and cooled the moisture his kisses had left on her flesh. For an instant they remained motionless, studying each other in the velvety darkness. Star shine glinted in his eyes.

In a husky, faraway voice she would not have recognized as his, he said, "Oh, God, Lorena, it's been so long. I thought I'd never see you again. I want you. So much, so much."

With a coldness in her heart, she lashed out at him. "I'm not Lorena, damn you, I'm not." The denial slipped through stiff lips but her body's desire betrayed her, wouldn't let go, kept wanting him no matter what. He was making love to a ghost woman, while she desired him here and now in the flesh.

Let it happen, she thought almost dreamily, as she leaned forward and offered her bare breast. Let him think he made love to his precious Lorena.

Jake moved to take her, slipping her loosened pants down around her hips, shifting her so that once more she was straddling his hips. He pulled her forward to kiss her breasts, riding toward a blaze of crimson light that beckoned. He reached the rampart of her desire, made ready to breach it, heard her cry out. Her fists pounded against his chest as hot, wet tears fell on his bare skin.

"I've always loved you, and I'll never hurt you," he said, and pulled away, an incredible sadness engulfing him. Of course, it was only a dream, and he was foolish enough to let himself be aroused.

"Jake, damn you. Damn you," she said, and the words fell over him like bitter rain.

He wrapped one hand around the back of her head, held her there a moment as reality drove away the vividness of the erotic illusion.

"Allie, my God, I'm sorry. Allie, please forgive me."

An ache grew in her breast until she could scarcely breathe. "Don't you be sorry. Don't you ever be sorry for loving me."

She had misunderstood him, but he dared not tell her so. He was sorry he had been unable to love her, to finish the mind-numbing, glorious love-making. His entire body throbbed with the loss, and Lorena lingered in the nether world, mocking him.

He cradled Allie against his chest, rocked her, crooned to her. Their perspiring bare skin clung together.

God help her, she still wanted him. She stopped crying, put her arms around his neck and pulled his head to the hollow of her shoulder. They remained that way for a long while before she spoke.

"It's I who should be sorry. I know you want to stay true to Lorena, and I didn't mean to trick you into making love to me. But I'm here and she's not. You don't know her. You don't know where she is or who she is. And I don't understand why you can't let her go. She's no more than a ghost. Oh, Jake, maybe she doesn't even exist." She took in a deep, ragged breath, then hurriedly went on before he could speak.

"I don't want you to leave me because of this, but I'm afraid you will. I promise, Jake. Promise faithfully, that if you'll stay I won't let this happen again. Never, never."

When he did finally reply, there was a harshness in his tone she'd not heard before. "Why in the hell would you want me to stay with you when I do the things to you that I do? I don't understand, Allie. Are you punishing yourself for something you think you've done? You don't deserve this kind of treatment. It was you I held, but my brain just does the damndest stuff. Honestly, I was making love to you. I didn't mean to call you Lorena. Dammit, she won't leave me alone."

"No, Jake. Don't lie to me to save my feelings. You're not an ordinary man, Jake whatever-your-name-is, and I can't bear the thought of you wandering around out there alone doing God-knows-what to yourself. And worse, I can't bear the thought of going on by myself after having your company this far."

Suddenly, out of the darkness, Jacob cried out his sister's name. "Wake up. Come on, wake up, Emma," he begged.

Allie and Jake struggled to button up their clothing and moved to the girl's side. Allie touched the frail arm, ran her hand up to the girls neck to feel for a heartbeat. Nothing stirred beneath the gossamer skin, though it was still warm to the touch.

"Oh, dear God," Allie said. "Oh, Jake, she's dead. Poor, poor little mite." She began to cry, and he took her once again into his arms, but this time only to console her, and perhaps himself as well.

Chapter Twelve

A silvery dawn crept across the land as the sad trio set out to transport Emma's body to the trader's caravan. Her brother Jacob had understandably insisted they not return to the Nichols' wagon, and he led the pony that carried the small pitiful bundle wrapped in a blanket. Jake rode bareback on the gray and Allie was on Ringo. They had only gone a mile or so when they heard riders approaching. Aaron had returned with help.

Allie had no idea what Aaron would do when he saw the body of the young girl he loved so desperately. Just thinking of it made her own tears start anew.

The group drew up in the center of the trail and as Jake explained to Defoe what had happened, Aaron leaped from his horse with a mournful cry and ran to the blanket-draped body. Before anyone could stop him, he tugged the slight form from the pony's back, slid to the ground with her cradled in his arms. Holding her close he rocked back and forth, crying so pitifully the men stopped discussing the escape in reverence to the boy's loss.

So engrossed was everyone in Aaron and his grief that when Isaac Nichols appeared, riding hard, he had bailed off his horse and began punching and kicking Aaron before anyone could stop him.

Allie, still mounted and the closest to the fray, slid to the ground and grabbed the large man by the belt. She intended to pull him off the helpless boy, but found she had tackled a bit more than she could handle.

With scarcely a pause in his punishment of the boy, Nichols backhanded her as if she were no more than a pesky insect. The blow sent her flying. She landed flat on her back, the wind knocked out of her. Nichols kept pummeling the boy, who tried to cling to the body of his beloved and loudly mourn Emma's death as if the beating were no more than a mere distraction.

Jake ran to Allie, pulled her to a sitting position and saw that blood trickled from the corner of her mouth. He touched it with a thumb, eyes flaring from blue to vivid green, a fire out of control. Before Allie could stop him, he jerked the Colt from her holster, pivoted into a crouch, thumbed back the hammer and shot Nichols.

It happened so quickly that even after the blast of the weapon had died away, no one moved or spoke. Jake's action had struck them dumb. Not even Jake had a word to say, but remained in position, pistol still pointed as a thin trail of smoke leaked from the barrel.

Nichols sprawled somewhat awkwardly over Aaron, who continued to hold Emma's tiny body. The grieving boy shoved the heavy man away and fussed with Emma until he had the blanket wrapped tightly around her once again. On his knees he brushed a smear of dirt from her cheek, bent forward and kissed her, then leaped to his feet, spat in the inert Nichols' face and kicked him over and over. All the while he continued to weep.

A terrible sadness enveloped Jake. He could not bear to look upon the body of the girl, nor the weeping boy. He desperately wanted someone's arms around him and turned to gaze at Allie.

Samantha Lee

Not yet sure what had taken place, only that Jake had shot
Nichols, she rubbed her aching jaw and tried to shake away the
ringing in her ears. Her head swam and she couldn't quite concentrate on the scene before her. She reached a hand toward
Jake, who still held the Colt in his fist, but he misunderstood
the gesture and handed it to her, butt first. His eyes looked right
through her and she could only stare back at him.

At last Defoe came to his senses enough to bring some order
to the chaos. First he ordered Jacob to take care of his friend,
Aaron.

"Now, you and you," he pointed at two others, "you get this
poor child's body back on that pony." He moved to inspect the
wound high on Nichols' shoulder. By this time, the wounded
man had come around and was howling like a banshee how he
was going to see they all paid, every dadblasted one of them.

"And especially that son of a bitch what shot me. And in the
back, too." He tried to lunge to his feet, but the .36 caliber shell
had torn a sizeable hole where it had exited the front of his
shoulder and he was in no shape to move around much.

Flabbergasted, Allie gazed at Jake. The man who had told
her he couldn't hit the broad side of a barn with the rifle, had
drilled a hole in that bastard Nichols faster than lightning and
without taking aim. Just pointed and shot, like a gunfighter. She
climbed shakily to her feet, and Jake hurried to help her. He
limped along beside her, one arm around her waist.

She jammed the pistol back in its holster. "Jake? Are you all
right?"

Eyes holding a look of stunned surprise, he wrapped his
arms around her and held on. She swayed, braced herself.

"It's all right. You did what you had to."

"It's not that. I think . . . I remember, oh, God, Allie, I think
I remember shooting someone before. With the Spencer. I took
it off a dead man . . . someone was shooting at me . . . I think I
killed him . . . but I . . . I just can't put it all together."

He released her, lightly touched her swollen jaw with the tips
of his fingers. "I should have killed that bastard, too."

184

The distant hard look in his eyes frightened her, and she shivered and hugged herself, wishing she were still in his arms but afraid at the same time. Something was dreadfully wrong, but before she could question him or offer solace, he strode past her.

He found his mare milling with the other horses, mounted up and rode away. Allie watched him until long, early morning shadows from a grove of huge cottonwoods swallowed him up. At least he was headed toward the caravan, but she was worried about him. He had appeared stricken beyond his own understanding. She recalled the expression that had obscured his handsome features just before he pulled the Colt from her holster. It was the face of a man she didn't recognize at all. A man intent on only one thing. Killing. Obviously, he recognized it as well as she.

When the entourage arrived back at the trader's caravan, Allie left the efficient Defoe in charge of arrangements for poor little Emma's burial and went in search of Jake. Aaron submitted to Jacob's ministrations, the wounded Nichols was being tended by both a doctor and a guard, and a funeral would be held for poor little Emma before the wagons pulled out.

She found Jake sitting beside her campfire while a coffeepot of water boiled merrily. She fetched a bag of coffee and went to sit beside him.

"You make it, I never put enough in," she said and held out the cloth bag.

Without a word, he poured the grounds into the water until there was nothing left in the bag. He grunted in surprise and handed it back to her.

"Well, I guess that'll be strong enough," he said with a slight trace of his old humor.

She marveled at his ability to bounce back from just about anything, and tried to match his tone. "A spoonful of that in a cup of hot water ought to just about do it, if the stuff isn't too thick to dip. You may have invented something new."

He nodded, let her attempt at levity fall between them and silently played in the glowing coals with a stick for a few moments. "How's the boy?"

"Devastated." Allie turned to meet Jake's somber gaze, and a great sadness washed over her. "That poor little girl. Oh, God, why do things like that have to happen?"

She lowered her face in both hands and sobbed. Like her dear little sister Sara, poor Emma had never been given the chance to grow up and have a life. Unwanted memories of that horrible day came back with a vengeance. Sara sprawled in the dirt, her skirt hiked up to reveal stained white stockings, one small shoe lying in the bloody grass beside her. Eyes closed forever, while behind her their mother lay, defiled by the bush-whackers. And the blackened ruins of their home smoldered, filling the air with a thick, acrid smoke that Allie still imagined she could taste in the back of her throat. All around the woods had been quiet, the violence stilling the birdsongs. The only sound the crying of one lone child. Herself.

Jake wrapped an arm around her, touched his head to hers.

"Ssh, Allie. Ssh," he said, but he wanted her to cry it out because she always kept too much bottled up inside.

Her voice muffled by wracking sobs, she said, "I couldn't save my sister or my mother, and I couldn't save Emma either. Why, Jake? Why?"

Her sorrow ripped at his heart. He couldn't answer her question, because there was no answer. Enclosed in her grief he had forgotten his own frightening reaction to Isaac's brutality. Such consideration would come later. Now he must soothe Allie.

"You did all you could. At least she was looking forward to her life with Aaron. You gave her hope when she had nothing. The world is filled with tragedy. You can't save everyone."

"I can't save anyone. Not anyone." She buried her face in his chest. His other arm closed around her. She rested there letting the steady throbbing of his heart comfort her.

Even in her sorrow for the tragedy of Emma's death, she couldn't help the small, creeping fear that one day Jake, too, would go away. If not taken by death from that malicious demon in his head, then he would simply ride off down the trail in continued pursuit of his phantom lover. He might as well be married, whether he actually was or not, and she knew better than to let herself care for him, yet she couldn't stop this attraction, this all-consuming need. She had never wanted it to happen, but there was no way on earth she could move from his embrace and face this heart-wrenching grief alone.

Strange, how all along she had thought him the needy one to whom she would have to offer sustenance. She had never realized that he would give as much as he took, perhaps more. Every time she reached out he was there.

"Jake?"

He stirred but didn't take his arms from around her.

"Did it frighten you, shooting Nichols?"

He cupped the back of her head with one hand. She would never know how frightened he had been, but not at the prospect of killing that son of a bitch. When Nichols hit her and knocked her to the ground, when he saw her lying there, momentarily stunned, he had faced the possibility that somehow the man had killed her. He hadn't suspected such a rage lived within him, but it had risen to crowd out all good sense. He really didn't remember taking her Colt and shooting the man, but he knew he had done it. Just as he knew he had fought in the war, though he remembered nothing.

"Jake, were you?"

"What?"

"Frightened?"

"I thought he had killed you. Of course, I was frightened. Terrified. Furious."

"But I thought you . . . I mean, I just supposed you did it because of what he did to those kids. What he might continue to do if he wasn't stopped. And Jake, my God, it was like you

187

knew precisely what you were doing with the Colt. Like you had done it a hundred times before."

She stirred from her nest against his shoulder to gaze up into his eyes. Her words hammered him like a brutal rush of icy wind, but he tried not to let her see.

Pushing a strand of hair away from her face, he shook his head. "What I did was instinct, that's all. And it wasn't as noble as you make it sound. All I could think of was killing him because he had hit you. I don't know, I've never felt anything quite like that. Not in this lifetime, at least."

"You love me, Jake. I think you love me."

He closed his eyes and stiffened. Refused to say the words. For then, what about Lorena? What about his past and all it meant? Could he simply turn his back on it and walk away?

She kissed his taut jaw line. "I think someone needs to teach you how to love. What it feels like."

He actually chuckled softly. "Oh, yeah? It seems we've tried that."

Leaning away from her, he gently knuckled her cheeks. "Oh, Allie, I'm sorry. You make me feel so damn good. But I must have loved Lorena. Until I know, I just can't betray that love. It brought me through a terrible time, still sustains me when I think about my past. I won't give it up."

"Oh, Jake. You've clung to that for so long because it was all you had. It's not Lorena you seek, but the memory, because there's absolutely nothing else for you to hang on to. Can't you let it go? Forget someone who may not exist in exchange for this. For me. For us. I'm real, this is real." She lay flat palms against his warm chest. "Today and tomorrow are real. Yesterday . . . well, it's no longer anything but fleeting memories. Some we keep because we cherish them, the rest we have to discard, like worn-out old shoes, like that hat you made me throw away."

The corner of his lips twitched and he opened his eyes, cornflower blue and bright with moisture. "And look how you howled."

"Yes, look how I howled. I love you, and I won't give up. The only way you can stop me is to ride away, leave me here alone. Can you do that?"

"Hell, no. And you know I can't."

"Well, then, let's have some of that godawful coffee before it turns as thick as molasses."

He would admit his love soon enough, of that she was sure. Meanwhile, despite his fears of that mysterious other life, she could trust him, and that was worth more than just about anything she could imagine.

Before holding Emma's funeral service, everyone made ready to pull out. Defoe had sent one of the men to escort the patched-up Nichols back to his own wagon train. He dispatched a note to the wagon master recommending that Nichols be sent back to Westport under guard, but voiced his doubts aloud about that happening as he walked beside Jake and Allie up the hill to the spot they had chosen for Emma's resting place.

"He has a family and those folks'd rather see him take care of them, even poorly, then to have him put in jail and leave them abandoned. A woman and children on the trail with no man means someone has to look out for them. It's a lot of additional trouble for everyone."

"What about Jacob and Aaron?" Allie asked Defoe as they watched the two young men support each other while Emma's grave was dug.

"Teamsters can always use some good strong backs and they'll work for food. They won't go hungry and they'll have a place to sleep where no one'll beat them. It's the best I could do."

Allie warmed to the stoic leader. She had been right about his being a fair-minded man. He moved away to stand beside the hole that yawned darkly in the lush green prairie grass. She saw he held a Bible in one hand, and a lump grew in her throat. She thought of her camera and what a picture the gathering would make.

Sensing Allie's sorrow, Jake grasped her elbow, then changed his mind and slipped an arm around her small waist.

He knew he'd be better off if he never touched her, but it just wasn't in him to leave her to face hardships alone. She was probably right about him loving her, but he could scarcely admit it to himself. Not only did Lorena beckon him, but the snatches of vivid memories threatened to reveal something he didn't want to know. He might well be a killer. Every time he tried to think of making love to Allie, murderous images joined Lorena's features to come between them. He felt possessed by what he didn't know, as well as by Lorena herself. He could not let her go, no matter how much sense it made to do so. Her very essence filled his mind and he could not go even one day without looking at her picture. Yet holding Allie while Defoe read sonorously from the Good Book, he knew that this woman was all he could ever want or need.

What was wrong with him that he couldn't just forget the past? That he continued to pursue memories he didn't even wish to remember?

Allie's shoulders heaved and she sobbed softly, but Jake supported her, kept her strong, even when they placed the wrapped body of poor little Emma in the ground and shoveled clods of earth onto her.

She recalled going half-crazy beside the graves of her mother and sister, and spending weeks in a darkened bedroom while kindly neighbors saw to her needs. Only when her father had shown up had she been able to recover. After the war, when he fell ill, at least she had him to care for. But then he had died and left her world stark and empty.

After losing everyone she loved, she had vowed never to love anyone that deeply again, but here she was crying over a child she had grown terribly fond of and doing it in the arms of a man, God help her, that she loved fiercely.

The traders moved on immediately after the funeral. Except for a short nooning, they pressed on for thirty-five miles before stopping to camp along the banks of a clear creek. Man and beast luxuriated, for there was plenty of timber, good grass and a running stream.

Everyone bathed and filled water casks, some washed clothes. Allie noticed that Jacob and Aaron gathered up britches and shirts and underwear from many of the traders and washed them in the creek, beating each piece of clothing viciously. She thought perhaps in that way, the boys were venting some of their tremendous anger and sorrow. There were many times after her family died when she had wanted to beat on something.

Nearly everyone who did bathe left their underclothing on to do so, the women separating from the men and going upstream around a bend. Since there were only a few homesteaders in the trader's caravan, there weren't many women, and Allie was content to get acquainted with them as they lolled neck-deep in cold water. Once submerged, she removed her underclothes, rubbed each item briskly with a silver of lye soap and then washed herself. The other women tried not to watch, and she grinned at their shyness. If only they would let her, she would set up her camera on shore and preserve their modesty for all time. Of course, it was too dark for that, but she couldn't help considering it. She would call it "Virgin Wives."

Later that night, she told Jake about the experience and he teased her.

"Why, Allie, I'd be more than happy to frame you in the lens of that camera while you bathe. Just say the word, I didn't know you wanted pictures like that."

"And I had no idea you were interested in seeing me in the buff."

He chuckled, and she was pleased that things had gotten back to some semblance of normalcy between them, even though she wished for so much more. She hated it when something disturbed the easy rapport they enjoyed.

"Tomorrow, if we take a long nooning, would you teach me something about your work? I'd really like to learn more than composition and toting equipment around."

For supper Jake had fried potatoes and they had eaten beans left over from the previous night, so she credited him with cooking and did the clean-up. She glanced up from washing the plates and saw he was entirely sincere in his request.

"I guess I can do that. And then I suppose we'll have to take turns toting that forty-pound camera around," she said.

He shrugged. "Well, all's fair. You wouldn't be complaining, would you?"

"Heavens no. I carried it around before you came along, I can do it again."

"Tell you what. I'll carry the camera full time if you'll cook full time. I'm not very good at it, and I'd much rather eat what you fix."

She held up a dripping plate. "That means this is yours every night."

He grinned widely, cheeks denting with dimples and eyes sparkling. Her heart flip-flopped, like it always did when he looked at her that way.

"You're a tough woman, very tough."

"Not nearly tough enough, Jake. I wish I were." Tough enough to compete against your precious Lorena, she finished silently.

If she wasn't afraid he'd cut and run, she'd seduce him that very minute, she wanted him so badly. Instead, she joined him in easy banter and kept her desires to herself, at least for the time being.

The following day everything that could go wrong did. A wagon loaded with more than a ton of supplies lost a wheel when it dropped into a crevice hidden by tall grass. The wagon tilted precariously, the load shifted and laid it on its side.

While riding back to help, a teamster was thrown from his horse, saddle and all, when the cinch broke.

To top it all off, a band of renegade Pawnee appeared and demanded a share of the dumped supplies. They might have been watching for something like this to happen.

Defoe went into a confab with the leader of the ragged bunch and Allie fetched her camera. It was too good a chance to miss.

Not taking time to unload the portable dark box, she worked in the what's-it wagon. After sensitizing the collodion covered plate by lowering it into a narrow bath containing silver nitrate, she hurriedly loaded the wet plate into its light-tight holder.

Afraid the Indians would do their business and leave before she could get at least one exposure, she had looked around for Jake, but he was nowhere. Probably helping with those dumped supplies, along with almost everyone else. She dragged the heavy camera and tripod out, set them up with a clear view of the Indians and Defoe, then ran back to the wagon, grabbed the box containing the plate and hurried to slide it into the camera. Quickly she slipped under the black drape and exposed the shot. Since the picture wasn't posed there was, of course, the danger that someone would move and blur his own image, but she took the chance because she was absolutely thrilled to be so close to real Indians, even though they were rather scraggly and not at all what she had expected.

The Pawnee continued to argue with Defoe, and she decided to try for another exposure. Back in the darkness of the wagon she quickly treated and washed the exposed plate and placed it carefully aside before treating another and repeating the entire process once again.

By the time she developed the pictures and came out of the blackness of the small, cramped wagon; she was drenched with perspiration, but she had her pictures. Later she would bring them out in a better light and take a good look, but she was satisfied that she had some good prints.

Eventually, things sorted themselves out somewhat. The fellow who had been thrown from his horse had a broken arm, which had to be splinted and wrapped. The Indians rode off happily with a few feed sacks loaded with corn meal, flour, salt, sugar and coffee. One had insisted on a cup of rendered lard, which he ate by dipping in a finger, removing a great dollop, sprinkling sugar over it and licking it like a lollipop.

It was so late in the afternoon when the men finished unloading the wagon, replacing the broken wheel and repacking all the supplies that Defoe decided to spend the night at Cotton-wood Creek. That day they had put only eight miles behind them. They were one hundred ninety miles out of Westport according to the mileage counter attached to a wheel of Defoe's wagon.

Jake showed up after dark, exhausted and limping badly. He lowered himself with a groan onto his bedroll, which Allie had spread for him when she made camp.

She watched him rub the leg, face contorted with pain. Searching through the wagon, she located a small stone jar of rose-scented cream. She poured him a cup of coffee and carried both to where he sat propped against a fallen log.

"Drink this," she said, handed him the coffee and knelt beside him. She placed the small pot of cream on the ground and began to undo his belt buckle.

"Hey," he said, sloshing hot coffee over his hand and cursing.

"Be still and drink. I'll handle this." She unbuttoned the dusty, stiffened jeans. "Lift your butt."

"Allie, dammit, you're undressing me."

"Exactly. Now be still and cooperate, or do I have to haul these off you the hard way?"

He swallowed the last of the hot coffee and shifted so she could pull the pants down. "Now what are you going to do?" he asked.

"You're always rubbing your leg, so I guess it wouldn't hurt if I did it. You just lean back and relax and let me see if I can't get some of the soreness out.

"Why did you just keep working till you nearly dropped? No one would have thought the less of you if you'd quit when you became totally stove up."

"I'm not stove up, not by a long shot." He watched as she fingered cream into her palm, rubbed her hands briskly, then lay them both on his scarred thigh.

The sweet scent of roses drifted between them, and he had a quick vision of a crystal vase reflecting shards of lamplight, scarlet roses dropping petals onto the rich patina of a walnut table. Long, delicate fingertips . . .

Allie's voice shattered the illusion. "Men are always so tough, aren't they? Relax, you're taut as a bow string."

Her hands, warm from the rubbing, moved gently, smoothly over the aching muscles. Tension flowed from him; he sighed and relaxed. Once in a while she would hit a tender spot where one of the splinters of metal remained embedded in flesh, sending a bright, sharp pain skittering through his leg. Gladly he endured that to have her touch him like this. The cream's fragrance mixed with Allie's own. He licked his lips and could taste her, the way she had tasted when he held her in the dark the night Emma died.

He wanted badly to reach out, touch her. She leaned so close that once in a while one of her breasts brushed against him. Her hand moved to the inside of his thigh and she massaged in small circular motions.

He felt himself growing hard, and was frightened by the desire he couldn't seem to control when it came to this beautiful young woman. As far as his mind was concerned, his body was virginal, though he doubted that to be true. Still if you couldn't remember a thing, wasn't it the same as if it had never happened? Or suppose he had only made love to Lorena? Wouldn't she want him to continue to be true to her even if he couldn't remember?

He closed his eyes, drifted. . . . A woman sat in a high-backed chair, turned away from him so that all he could make out was streaked blonde hair piled high on her head. Red roses were on the table beside her. He moved carefully across a carpet that dulled his footsteps. He didn't want to look at her face, yet he couldn't stop himself.

He touched her shoulder, stepped in front of her. Blood the color of the roses smeared her features and he roared with terror. Tried to run, but his feet wouldn't move. He thought his heart might burst.

"Jake? What is it? Wake up, wake up."

The urgent plea jerked him upright. He gasped, clawed for something to hold on to to keep him in this world away from that other. He touched her hand, clasped it hard.

She soothed him. "It's all right."

"Killed her. Killed her." He bucked and fought.

Allie threw herself across him. "Stop. Stop it, Jake."

His arms went around her. He breathed heavily, chest heaving under her.

"Take it easy now. You're okay. Ssh, Jake." She rubbed absently at his shoulder, and across the back of his neck. He began to relax under her fingers, but didn't let go.

He held her and held her, thinking irrationally that maybe he could drag her with him into the dark world where anything they did could be forgiven, for it wasn't real. Was it? Her mouth captured his. She tasted of all his hopes, everything sweet he'd ever known. If Lorena saw them here, then she would be angry. But it was dark, very dark.

He dragged in a ragged breath, she slid her tongue between his lips. This was wrong, unfair, but it was too late to stop. A deep hunger opened within him, a hunger for her love that would only be satisfied by the act itself. They hadn't finished what they'd started the night before and he felt hollow, incomplete.

Bidding Lorena to leave them alone, he responded to Allie's demanding kiss, rolled her over so that he lay on top of her. Without taking his mouth from hers, he pulled at her shirt, clawed at the belt of her pants, fingered the buttons loose.

He would not call her Lorena this time, and they wouldn't stop, no matter what. She would simply pretend to be the woman he thought he loved and give herself to him. This time he would take what she offered.

She moaned as his hand moved inside her pants, warm and demanding.

He would never forgive her or himself, and tomorrow when he rode away, the memory of this would be all he would have left. But it didn't matter. At this moment nothing but loving her made any difference at all.

As she moved with him, he reached toward the eagerly awaited ecstasy, deep into the place where he would at last find release. As if from far back in the darkness of his mind, he watched himself take her by the shoulder, pull her warm, sweet mouth back to his. Felt her rigid nipples against his chest, her breath fanning his face, her hands caressing him in all those places that ached for her. He entered her in a blaze of glory.

But none of that happened in reality, and he kept his eyes closed, feigning sleep until she stopped massaging his leg and moved away. Then he turned his head so she couldn't see a warm, wet tear slip from the corner of one eye.

Chapter Thirteen

The earlier dream returned when at last he slept. He saw himself poised above the woman, a knee on either side of her. His thigh hurt like hell, but he ignored it to raise up and fumble with the fastenings of his own pants. He had waited so long to be with her, to touch her, to kiss her, he could hardly contain his desire.

In the light from the fire, her eyes flared open; dark, dark eyes shimmering with tears.

They were the wrong color! Not Lorena's eyes, not at all.

What was he doing? Who was this woman?

"Damn you, what have you done with her?" He spat the words at her, wondering who she was, what she was doing there beneath him.

She shook her head, confusion clouding her features. "No, Jake, no. No, Jake, no," she kept repeating.

Why did she keep calling him Jake? That wasn't his name, it was . . . it was . . . Fool, everything was a blank.

Furious, he shouted, "Tell me where she is."

The shriek echoed through the dark caves of his memory. The roar of a cannon, a bright flash of debris-strewn smoke, a vivid pain that jagged through his temples like a bolt of lightning. Agony so severe, so all-encompassing, that he wrapped both arms over his head and roared like a wounded animal. Then he collapsed on her and was still.

Even after Jake's cries rang out and all grew quiet again, Allie lay stiff and unmoving, listening, waiting. She wanted to go to him, yet seemed unable to move, her limbs frozen as if a great blue norther had swooped down during the night.

His cry of despair, so far removed from the frightening animal-like roar of a few minutes earlier, was a plea she could not ignore.

Wrapping a blanket around her shoulders, she crept to where he lay and knelt beside him. Her hand flashed pale in the moonlight as she touched his bare shoulder, soaked with perspiration.

"Jake? Are you awake?"

He did not respond. Dear God, suppose he was dead. That beast lurking in his brain had finally come to life and destroyed him. Frantically she moved her fingers to his neck, felt for a pulse, subconsciously holding her breath until she located the steady beat.

He was alive, but dear God, what had happened to him? He lay on his stomach, head tucked beneath the curl of one arm so that she couldn't see his features. Gently, she fingered hair from his damp cheek. The skin twitched under her touch.

"Oh, Jake. My dear Jake. Where have you gone? I wish I could help you." She leaned forward and kissed his earlobe, whispered softly, "I do love you so. I promise I do."

At that moment she remembered the doctor who had set the teamster's broken arm, and decided to fetch him. Perhaps if he could actually observe one of these fugues of Jake's he might have some answers.

"Jake, oh, Jake," she said aloud as she danced on one foot then the other, pulling on her pants and shirt but not stopping to put on boots. "I'll be right back. Right back." She patted at his shoulder, touched his cheek, moved away and then turned to glance at him once more. She hated to leave him alone.

He murmured something she couldn't understand.

She ran back, knelt beside him once more. "What? What did you say?"

Teeth grinding, he said, "He's a bastard and if you aren't careful . . . he'll . . . I'll . . . "

The words faded. She leaned closer, trying to make out the words muted by his arm.

"Goddammit," he roared, flinging her arm away and turning over onto his side so that he was facing her. His eyes glimmered in the firelight.

Unable to move, she listened in horror to the unfamiliar voice.

"Touch her and I'll kill you," he vowed.

"Jake, wake up." She shook him gently.

"Could I have a drink?" he asked abruptly, and he sounded almost normal.

She moved to fetch water, and as she did, the other voice from within him said very clearly, "Or maybe I'll just kill the both of you and be done with it."

At the menacing tone that did not remotely sound like him, she stopped dead in her tracks. Goose bumps skittered up her spine and her teeth chattered. She wanted only to run off into the night howling like some demented being. Had he gone mad, and had she joined him in that madness?

Up to now she had felt safe with him, but at this moment she wished she had the Colt strapped to her hip instead of wrapped in its belt beside her saddle. That voice, stone cold with deadly menace, terrified her. It was almost as if another person lived within him and threatened to burst free like some ugly monster. If he came after her what would she do?

Hand shaking, she drained water from the cedar barrel into a tin cup and turned, found him standing right behind her. He wore jeans, pulled on but unfastened, and no shirt. Heat poured

200

off him, but she shivered as if a cold wind had passed between them.

In her fright she spilled most of the water. Her heart hammered, muffled her own cry from a throat so raw it burned.

His hand covered hers, guided the cup to his mouth and he drank the few remaining swallows.

"More," he said gruffly and let go so she could refill the cup.

She shook so badly she couldn't hold it under the stream, and once again his hand encased hers. He shoved her into the nook where the barrel was tied to the wagon so she could not escape, remained against her while he drank again. She felt the movement of his chest and stomach when the water went down.

This man smelled and looked like Jake, but something about his eyes, his voice, was unnerving. She concentrated on the bobbing of his Adam's apple as he swallowed, and tried not to think what he might do next. He had so frightened her that she could scarcely remember the compassion she'd experienced only moments earlier. She had told him she loved him, and now she feared his slightest touch and searched frantically for a way to escape.

"Now," he said, dropping the cup to the ground. "Where were we?" He slid an arm around her waist.

"Let me go, please." The steadiness of her voice surprised her, considering that she felt as if she were being held by a total stranger, or worse, some kind of unnatural being.

His grip loosened, and he shook his head, shuddered. "Allie? God, my head hurts. What did you hit me with?"

She still couldn't escape his trap. "I didn't hit you. Listen to me. Carefully. You—"

He took his arm away, pressed the heels of both hands into his eyeballs and staggered backward a few steps.

Quickly she slipped from the confining enclosure in which he'd trapped her. She wanted to run—run as fast as she could to get help, to get away. He slumped against the wagon, fingers spread across his head, obviously in acute agony. She couldn't leave him like that, hurting and confused. Hesitating only for a second, she ran back to his side and slipped deftly under his shoulder, wrapping an arm around his waist.

"Come on, let's get you off your feet, then I'll fetch the doctor. Something terrible is going on inside your head. We've got to find out what."

He let her support him to the bedroll where he collapsed to the ground. She spoke in a low, comforting voice while covering him to the waist with a blanket, then ran to find Defoe. She couldn't remember the name of the doctor who had tended the man with the broken arm. All she knew was that he was with the train and maybe he could help Jake. Someone had to.

She reached Defoe's wagon sobbing, and it took a while to make herself understood. Finally Defoe told her he would fetch Doc Tremaine, and she was to return to her wagon and see to her charge until they arrived.

Before Allie ran off, Defoe muttered something about this being a dark, bad-luck day. It was true. Only that morning they had buried Emma, then the wagon had turned over and dumped supplies, one of the men had broken his arm, and now this. What else could happen? She was almost afraid to wonder.

When she arrived back at camp, Jake lay as she had left him, but he was awake, for he called out her name. She hurried to his side, no longer frightened of the stranger he had become. This was Jake, the man she loved. He would never hurt her.

She knelt at his side. He reached out without opening his eyes, and she took his hand, bent to touch his forehead with her lips. His skin felt cooler, drier.

"Are you all right?" she whispered.

"I'm better. Sore. My head is sore, but it doesn't hurt so bad anymore."

"Just lie still and don't move. Defoe is bringing Doctor Tremaine."

"Aw, Allie. Why'd you go and do that? I don't need a damned doctor poking around on me." Still obviously in some pain he cringed with the difficult utterance, then fell silent.

She was so relieved to find him the old Jake again, she nearly forgot her earlier terror. But not quite. Watching him change from one personality to the other had badly shaken her. Would he do it again? And if he did would it be worse the next time?

"Jake, you . . . you had a terrible seizure of some kind. It was awful, worse than any of the others, and it terrified me. Then you acted so strange, so like someone else. I had to get some help. Now stop fussing and lie still until Tremaine gets here."

His fingers tightened in hers. "I didn't . . . didn't hurt you, did I?"

She nibbled at her lip, then reassured him that he hadn't. Not really. He'd just come too close for comfort, was all. "No, of course not. You just scared me."

He sighed, still not opening his eyes, but she noticed that he relaxed a bit. His hand clasping hers released some of the pressure and his breathing evened out. She thought he might have dozed off but when she tried to pull away from his lax grip he hung on and wouldn't let her go.

Defoe and Tremaine arrived in a few minutes, the latter carrying a small black bag that served to reassure her. At least the man acted as if he knew what he was doing.

He knelt on the other side of his patient. "What's his name?" he asked in a velvety voice.

Allie relaxed even more. "Jake . . . just Jake."

The doctor addressed his patient. "You take it easy now, Jake. We're going to help you." He looked at Allie, "What happened?"

As she began to tell him a little of Jake's background and recent behavior, he removed a candle from the bag and lit the wick.

"Jake, could you open your eyes?" he asked, interrupting her tale.

Jake did so without hesitation. Tremaine had a way about him that was mesmerizing. He moved the candle slowly back and forth before Jake's eyes. "Ahh," he said, after a while, and it was almost like a sigh.

"What?" Allie asked.

"Well, he's not dead," Tremaine said in that same enticing voice.

Jake chuckled, then groaned.

"Well," said Tremaine, "at least he has a sense of humor."

Allie wasn't amused, and let the doctor know it by giving him a disgruntled look.

He ignored her. "That hurt, then?" he asked Jake, as if it were an encouraging sign that his patient felt pain.

Without waiting for a reply, he placed his fingers on Jake's temples and held them there awhile. "Took quite a knock on the head, did you?"

"A long time ago."

"Has anyone taken a look at you since?"

"A few."

"And is this the first time this particular thing has occurred, this sort of attack, I mean?"

"It was the worst, but there've been others. Look, doc, there's no use in this. By morning I'll be fit as a fiddle. And I'm not going to some hospital, so you might just as well close your little black bag and go take care of someone that can use your help." Jake made to rise, but Tremaine easily held him down by the shoulders.

"Well, of course, it's entirely up to you. And you're right, young man, we don't know much about head injuries, so you would probably be wasting your time in a hospital, but I'd take it easy for a few days if I were you. And I would look for a profession that doesn't involve bucking horses or fisticuffs. Otherwise, it's a crap shoot, pure and simple.

"Now, get some sleep. You and the little lady look like you could use it."

Tremaine moved his head in a curt nod and led Allie away from Jake. His eyes were the brown of muddy water, his face lank almost to ugliness, but the tender voice made up for his shortcomings in looks.

"Was he violent?"

Allie considered lying to the man, but when she met his gaze, was unable to. "Yes, for a short while. He seemed utterly confused, acted like two different people."

"You'd do well to consider separating yourself from him."

"He didn't hurt me."

"But you were frightened, yes?"

"Well, of course I was. Anyone would be. He became someone I didn't know, another person. He thought I was someone else. Doctor, Jake lost his memory from something that happened to him during the war. I think he is simply restructuring those memories and he is as frightened as I am."

Tremaine raised his eyebrows. "Only fools claim to understand the workings of the mind, of thought processes. There are hospitals—we call them asylums—for people who are confused and cannot function in this world."

He leaned closer to Allie. "Personally, I would shoot that man or throw him off a cliff before I would send him to one. There is a woman named Dix who has been attempting to change the way the insane are treated, but she has a long, arduous task, since we have no medication for such afflictions. It's simply a matter of tying them down and letting them rage on. For the most part they languish in their own filth and . . . well, never mind, it's not a pretty picture."

Allie raised herself to full height and glared at Tremaine. "If you're telling me he's insane, you can forget it. I will not believe it. He had an injury and it's taking him a long time to recover, that's all. Doctor, I've seen a little of what this man went through when I spent time alongside my father as a photographer during the war. Believe me, the horrors we saw were nothing compared to what went on in Andersonville. From what Jake has told me, that was pure hell . . . worse than hell. I will not condemn him to the life of a madman as payment in kind after he fought for this country. He deserves better than that."

"That is very commendable of you, madame. However, you are at risk and it is a foolish risk. Just what do you owe this man? I understand you are not married."

"What do any of us owe another human being, doctor? He is a kind and gentle man who wants desperately to recover his humanity."

Tremaine shrugged. "I'm very sorry, but I must suggest to Captain Defoe that he request this man leave the caravan. It is not in his best interest to continue to allow him passage."

"That's outrageous," Allie said.

"You would do well to protect yourself in the same way, madame. I will take your leave."

The bastard had never raised his voice, right to the end. His tone no longer comforted her. Tears of frustration filled her eyes as she watched him walk away.

They were days past Council Grove and traveled on the true frontier. Despite the army's concerted efforts to put down the Indians, it was still not safe to travel across that country alone. And that was not to mention the bands of cutthroat whites who had roamed the area since the end of the war. And this inhuman doctor suggested that Jake be banished into that wilderness alone. She couldn't allow that. What could they do? She had left Missouri because of its bloody history. Had she stepped into worse by taking up with Jake? They would only be safe traveling to Santa Fe with a caravan.

After putting another stick of wood on the fire, she moved wearily to sit within the circle of its warmth. Despite the balmy night, she felt chilled to the bone by Doctor Tremaine's visit and his damning declaration. Why had she fetched the man? Would Defoe literally kick them out?

At last she grew sleepy and went to check on Jake before bedding down for what was left of the night. He lay on his back, one arm stretched out, the other crooked above his head. This night she did not dare put her head on that arm that had served her so well as a pillow on other nights. Cautiously she tugged off his jeans and covered him. Then she dragged her bedroll over near the wagon and spread it out. It saddened her to think that she might never feel his arms around her again.

206

Yet did she dare allow her love for him to flourish after what had happened? All the same, she would not abandon him.

Jake moved across a familiar room. At the windows, burgundy drapes kept out the early morning sunlight. Underfoot a rich, intricately woven rug muted his footsteps. A man stood near the fireplace, the crackling flames reflected in a half-filled glass of red wine. He gazed in awe past the man at a portrait hanging above him. A portrait of Lorena.

"Ah, she is a wonder, that beautiful girl," the man said.

A disgusting, lustful tone.

"You didn't tell me she was so beautiful. Perhaps I would have come to meet her sooner if you had."

The man was clearly talking to him. Odd how he couldn't find any words to reply. His lips moved, but they felt numb and his tongue lay useless, like a dead slug.

Ethan chuckled. Ethan? Yes, that was his name. But who Ethan was, where he had come from, he had no idea. He felt a dark foreboding of what was yet to come between this Ethan and his lovely Lorena.

As if he had summoned her, she appeared in the doorway, taking his breath away. She wore a dress the very same color as her eyes, the blue satiny fabric hugging her lush breasts and billowing out from her narrow waist. It whispered when she moved across the floor, one graceful hand extended toward Ethan.

He took it, put it to his lips. "It is a pleasure indeed. Lanse has told me so much about you. I've never before believed his ravings, but in the future I shall. He could have added to his praise in this case, however."

Lorena tilted her head; curls that hung from the upswept golden hair danced with the movement.

From his dark corner, he drew a deep breath, spoke her name, but she ignored him and gazed up into Ethan's beautifully sculpted, dark features.

Much darker than she would ever know. He wanted to halt the scenario, but they appeared not to hear anything he said, even though Ethan had addressed him earlier. It was as if he were no longer in the room.

If Ethan put his hands on her, he would find out who else was in the room, and fast.

"And where is Lanse?" Ethan asked.

Lorena gestured vaguely. "Oh, who knows? He's been acting strange lately. It's sometimes a real bore being around him."

Ethan nodded. "Yes, well, I guess I understand that. Don't I live with him all the time? But let's not waste anymore precious moments discussing him. He isn't here, and I am. So, how would you like to come for a carriage ride with me, and we'll find someplace quite elegant to take supper."

"That would be wonderful."

No. Lorena. No, don't go with him. Jake could not make the words come out, though he shouted them with all his heart and soul. His tongue, his lips, in truth his entire body, refused to move. At last he realized that he was not really a part of what he watched.

A light slashed across his eyelids and awoke him, dragged him from the room and into a star-strewn night. Above his head hung a golden moon.

"Beware, Lorena. Beware." he mumbled, then touched his head, remembering Allie and the doctor. The other had been a dream. Or had it? Perhaps it was a memory. He would have to think about it some more. Ethan. Dammit, where did he remember that name from? And only recently.

He moved gingerly, wary of the pain coming back. The debilitating headache was gone, but he felt completely exhausted. So much so that he wondered if he could make his way to the water bucket to slake the monstrous thirst that filled his mouth like a great wad of cotton. He might well have eaten sand for supper.

He turned on his side, expecting to see Allie sleeping within arm's reach. She wasn't there. He was momentarily thrown off balance. What had gone on the evening before? All he could recall was her bringing the doctor and the ensuing examination.

He sat up carefully, for he well remembered the brutal pain that had threatened to split his head wide open, and he had no wish to bring it on again. Only a brief, dull throb matched the beating of his heart, but it faded.

Thank God for that.

He looked around some more for Allie, saw a dark form on the ground near the wagon. Moonlight turned the vehicle into a looming shadow, the water barrel a mere lump clinging to its side. He would have drooled if he could have summoned up any moisture. When he crawled carefully to his feet, he noticed that he wore no pants, just his thigh-length under drawers.

Odd. He could have sworn he went to bed fully clothed the previous night.

Knees wobbling, he moved toward the beckoning water barrel.

He was halfway there when he remembered something. A woman under him on the ground, shirt torn open, tears in her dark eyes.

No, he wouldn't have done such a thing. It was a dream. A dream of Allie, and she had been crying.

Dammit to hell, what had he done?

He stood in the silvery moonlight, fists clenched at his sides. After a while he continued his search for water, carefully stepping around Allie's sleeping form to fill up a cup and drink deeply. He filled it again and took it with him back to his bedroll, where he propped his back against a fallen log. He remained here the rest of the night, wide awake, examining the scene he had relived between Lorena and the man called Ethan. His mind kept landing back on the name Lanse. They had both spoken of him, that third person missing from the room. He could make absolutely no sense of it. It was amazing how difficult it was to piece such things together when he had no memory to go on.

He removed the picture of Lorena from his shirt pocket and held it where the moonlight shined across her features. After a while, he touched a thumb to the lovely face and put the picture away. To her he was probably dead. The way she had acted, she had probably married that Ethan person a long while ago. And why not? Why couldn't he let it be?

He knew the answer to that question before he even formed it in his mind. Because he wasn't at all sure, but what if he had done something terrible to her? Caught her in Ethan's arms, killed her? And what of Ethan? Jake was afraid that if he stayed with Allie he might do something equally bad to her.

If before he had resisted Allie's love, his own for her, because he did not want to betray Lorena, now he added to that the fear that he would bring harm to Allie. Finally and irrevocably he knew that he loved her and would do anything to protect her. What had brought about that knowledge, he wasn't sure. Perhaps last night when she had put him to bed and held his hand, terrified as she had seemed of something he must have done to her, perhaps then he'd known. That love had been a long time coming on, denied over and over as he yearned for something he could never have. He might never stop thinking of Lorena, but he loved Allie. Even as he realized his feelings, he also realized that, sadly, it was too late. He would leave as soon as possible, and protect her from the ultimate danger—what lay hidden deep inside himself.

He must have dozed off sitting there, for the rattle of pots and pans, the shout of teamsters, the braying and bawling of animals, awoke him near dawn.

He climbed to his feet and felt surprisingly refreshed, though ravenous as a bear, just out of hibernation.

Before he could pull on his jeans, Allie came from the wagon with a fresh pair.

She held them out, didn't meet his gaze. "Feeling better?"

"Yes. Allie?" He moved toward her.

She waved a hand, backed away a few steps, turned and went to the fire to start breakfast. Disturbed by her actions, he put on the stiff britches and answered nature's early morning call in the nearby woods without saying more to her. She was obviously in no mood to talk.

When he returned a filled plate waited on a rock near the hot coals. He could hear her rattling around inside the what's-it wagon. His heart ached worse than his head had; the pain nearly made him sick. He must have done something terrible last night to have upset her this much. He couldn't bear the idea that he had hurt her. Every bite he swallowed caught in his throat.

She still hadn't come out of the wagon when he went to fetch the team. When he returned, though, she was there waiting and silently helped him hitch the mules. She carefully avoided touching him and said nothing. He saw that she had been crying and he wanted desperately to take her in his arms. Then he remembered the dream, his stomach clenched and he turned away until the feeling passed.

He let Allie drive and rode a little ways behind her so that she couldn't see him, but he could watch her.

The teamsters pushed hard that day, only allowing an hour for nooning, and that for the safety of everyone because they feared wearing the animals down. During that hour, Defoe approached Jake, who had tied the mules, each on a length of rope that would allow good grazing, and then sat down with his back against a tree away from the others.

The wagon master removed his fancy Mexican hat and sat beside him. Jake thought him unusually nervous for a man who always seemed to have himself well in hand. He knew something was coming he probably wouldn't like.

Finally Defoe got around to the point after remarking on all sorts of things from the weather to the state of grass, wood and water.

"I reckon Miss Caine has spoke to you about last night. I'm all-fired sorry, but I have to harken to the doc's suggestions."

"What about last night?" Jake said gruffly. He was loath to admit Allie hadn't spoken to him at all except to inquire about his health.

Defoe stared at him, obviously bewildered. "You don't remember?"

Jake met the stare with one of his own, but waited for the man to go on without answering.

"I . . . well, as a matter of fact, we are all concerned about your . . . uh, your unusual behavior. Doc says you could be an extreme danger to the other folks on the train, and most especially Miss Caine. I can't fathom why she hasn't spoke to you. Doc told her . . . told me as well . . . that it would be to our best interests if y'all left the train."

Odd, he wasn't surprised. "Allie too? Why does she have to go?"

Defoe cleared his throat. "Because, frankly Mr. uh . . . Jake, she threw herself in with you when Doc made the announcement. I think you ought to talk to the young lady about this, sir. Convince her she's not being wise in her choice. If the dangers out there are bad for a man alone, they are worse for a woman. I'm right sorry as hell to be doing this to you, but I have a duty to the folks on this train." Defoe climbed to his feet, twisted the hat round and round by the brim. The silver conchos gleamed in the sunlight.

Jake thought the wagon master probably had never been so at a loss for words, and wondered why. They weren't friends, he and this man. Yet Defoe appeared to hate this chore much more than would seem normal.

The man found his voice, though. "Sir, we'd appreciate it if y'all went your own way. There's no use in you continuing with us when we hit the trail this afternoon. I'll refund that portion of your travel fee that seems equitable. I'm real sorry about this, you being, well, sick and all."

"I'm hardly sick, sir," Jake said, and struggled to his feet, leaning on the tree to do so. As if to belie the movement, he said, "I do as much if not more work than the next man. But never you mind, I get the drift of what you're saying, and I'll be riding out. I'd appreciate it if you let Miss Caine continue on. I'll not be staying with her. You can give her any refund that's coming to me."

Jake limped away from the amazed Defoe before he could reply. He fetched his mare, who was grazing contentedly and rode her down to a nearby creek where he filled his canteen and let her drink. Then he went to the wagon to pack his bedroll and enough supplies to see him back to Westport. From there he would go east in his search. It had been foolish of him to head west anyway. Most likely, he had lived east of the Mississippi, and that's where he should be searching. He would simply pretend that he had never met Allie Caine, never held her in his arms, never looked into her beautiful dark eyes and seen himself there. He had denied that love so long, it shouldn't be difficult to continue the charade. After all, his memory was pretty faulty anyway.

Chapter Fourteen

While he hovered over a pot of coffee Eli heard of the previous night's events and Defoe's request that Ethan Hollingsworth, who called himself Jake, leave the caravan. Tossing the dregs, he mounted quickly and rode a full perimeter around the circled wagons, but found no sign of the man anywhere.

Damn. Where would Hollingsworth have gone? Prospects of the ten-thousanddollar reward grew dim. Eli rode back to his own camp with no idea what in the hell he was going to do. Stick with the train in the hopes Hollingsworth would meet up with Allison in Santa Fe, or go in search of the man. The latter made little sense, because he had no idea which way the fool had ridden. He decided to keep her in sight, for the way Hollingsworth acted, he wouldn't be too far away.

If the ten thousand dollars slipped through his grasp, so would the chance to make a killing in the land deal in Santa Fe.

When Allie returned from the portrait shoot on the other side of the circle-up she knew Jake was gone. There lurked an aura of emptiness about the camp. She was alone, as alone as she'd been after her father died. It was a feeling she'd almost forgotten in the time since she'd found Jake sprawled in the middle of the trail. She should be relieved, but she wasn't.

While she fetched the mules, hitched them to the wagon and packed her equipment, she missed him more for his company than for the help he had been. She found herself thinking of something funny or sad and turning to tell him, only to find no one there. One moment she would tell herself she was better off without him, the next recall that boyish smile, his touching gentleness, the humor he brought to the simplest of chores, and knew it wasn't true. Despite his tragic background and the terrible things that were happening to him, Jake had remained courageous and gentle, always protective of her. She was in love with him, missed him dreadfully. Being lonely was no fun at all.

When the caravan stopped for the night, she fetched her camera and went in search of a subject, dragging along the little wheeled dark box. It was a heavy load and one Jake had handled with ease and equanimity. Tears burned her eyes. She never did get to teach him how to mix the chemicals and coat the plates and develop the pictures. Now she never would, for she feared that this time he had gone for good.

Grumpily, she concentrated on business. This day she would offer to take photographs of Defoe and his men, show him he wouldn't make a mistake if he allowed her to remain with the train after the way she had smarted off when he suggested Jake leave. She really couldn't blame him, and he had asked a long while back for photographs. It was time she held up her end of the deal, and in the process she would firm up the earlier agreement that she could tag along, with or without Jake.

Very pleased with Allie's proposal, Defoe posed with his magnificent black stallion, and he wore the silver-banded Mexican hat tilted to the back of his head as she suggested, so the wide brim wouldn't cast a shadow over his eyes.

A rider approached as she worked, but she didn't look up until she had finished developing the first picture in the dark box. Defoe and several of his men hovered around waiting to see the result.

"I ain't doing this 'less she makes you look a whole lot better than you do," one of them joked. "Fer my ugly mug could well ruin her whole apparatus there. If she can make you pretty, she can do anything. Right?" The fellow laughed and punched one of his buddies.

"How about including me in on this?" a pleasant voice asked.

Defoe looked up, shouted a greeting. "Well, Clay, you old scudder, what're you doing in these parts? I'd a thought they'd a hung you by your scrawny neck by this time."

"Would if they could catch me," Clay said, dismounting and shaking hands heartily with Defoe. "I've been meaning to settle down a bit, buy me a ranch. Retire from my thievin' ways, but they won't quit shipping gold and let me be."

Defoe cackled. "You old hoss, you. Blamed if it ain't good to see you. Well, you say you want your picture made? This little lady can do it. Take a look at this." He held a damp photo up gingerly by one corner.

"Why, that is you. Look at that."

The man called Clay tipped his hat toward Allie. "Clay Allison, ma'am, and who might you be?"

Allie stared at the man's proffered hand, throat as dry as shucks. Even in Missouri everyone knew about the notorious outlaw, Clay Allison. And here he stood before her in the very flesh.

He was tall and broad-shouldered with a shock of black hair and eyes the color of a spring sky. The clean-shaven face was angular and square jawed. He wore a pair of pearl-handled pistols belted on over a loose jacket and buckskin pants. The horse he rode in on was a big black that made Defoe's look minuscule by comparison. When the affable outlaw moved, his spurs jangled merrily.

216

What a fine specimen of a man he was, and certainly a perfect subject for her camera. Excitement flickered through her. After taking pictures of the James gang, wouldn't a few of this man be a welcome addition to her collection? She could imagine displaying them in the window of her photography shop in Santa Fe. That was positive thinking, and she enjoyed the idea a moment longer before raising a trembling hand to his. His glittering gaze resting on her, he lifted the hand to his lips and tasted her flesh with the warm tip of his tongue.

"Lord, you're a beauty if I ever saw one. And out here in the wilds taking pictures of this scruffy bunch. Ma'am, you belong in satins and lace with diamonds about your throat and gold on your fingers. That you do. And I'm just the man who could give you all that."

She laughed. "I'm sure you could, Mr. Allison, but at what price for the both of us?"

He threw back his head and guffawed. "I'd settle for looking at your pretty face while you fix me up with one of those, and would pay handsomely for it, too." He gestured at the dripping picture Defoe held.

"I'd be only too happy to oblige, if you would agree to my making some copies for myself. Why, when I tell people I've taken pictures of the famous Clay Allison and lived to tell it, I'll be the most popular photographer in Santa Fe." She waited to see if he would take the statement in the teasing manner in which it was meant, and wasn't disappointed.

"And when I tell all my rowdy friends about you, ma'am, why they'll be flocking to your door. So much so that all your respectable clientele will run from you in horror. Now, tell me what to do. I'm in your hands."

Allie smiled. She liked bantering with this man, and it helped somewhat her efforts to forget about Jake riding alone along whatever trail he had chosen for himself.

She ended in taking three separate shots of the agreeable outlaw, more from his urging than her own. Not satisfied with a standard pose, he wanted to try some that were rather dramatic, and even talked Defoe into letting him point his pistol at him while he "clawed for sky."

In between shots, while she was busy developing one plate and preparing the next, Allison stood nearby and kept an eye on her while he sipped from a silver flask. He offered it to Defoe, who declined politely.

"That rotgut you drink'd cause me to lead these folks off into the hills and we'd be so lost we'd never get to Fort Union, let alone Santa Fe. And worse yet, I wouldn't give a damn."

"You weren't always such a stickler. Goin' soft in your old age?"

"As we all are. What was that I heard you mumble about retiring to some ranch?" Defoe grew suddenly serious. "I would keep a low profile around here if I was you, Clay. We got us a real live bounty hunter in our midst, the son of a bitch."

Allison caressed the butt of one of his pistols. "Point him out and I'll solve your problem. What's he doing riding with you anyways?"

"Danged if I know. Hell, maybe he's going to New Mexico to look for you."

Allison cawed heartily. "Won't find me there, will he?"

"Reckon he won't. Just watch yourself, is all." Defoe signaled a nearby teamster. "We've got to confab for a spell, Clay. If Miss Caine doesn't mind, she can take the rest of these fellas' pictures tomorrow."

They had been talking about Eli Martin, Allie was sure, but her thoughts were elsewhere, and she gave the conversation little thought as she packed up her equipment.

The handsome outlaw stepped to her side. He smelled of cigar smoke and raw whiskey and the horse he'd been riding. It wasn't all that unpleasant.

"Miss Caine surely doesn't mind. And I'd be ever so pleased to have you join me for supper tonight," he said to her.

She looked around at the empty rolling land. "And just where would that be, Mr. Allison?"

"Why, at your camp, where else? I have an elegant bottle of wine in my saddlebags, and I've been anticipating such a fine lady as you to share it with. In the meantime, allow me to help you tote your equipment back. You know we outlaws on the run learn to cook up some pretty decent food, so I could lend a hand there, too."

She glanced at Defoe and he nodded with a grin.

"Aw, go on and feed the poor feller. He appears to be plumb wore out and half starved. He's harmless, despite what you might have heard. I'll even throw in something for the feast. Cookie is making up some fine sourdough biscuits. I'll send a batch over in a while."

Allie studied the two men for a moment. If she went back to camp alone, she would only brood. And she did enjoy this man. She had spent most of her adult life in the company of men, and in general found herself bored with women. They tended to speak of things that held little interest for her, like the choice of fabrics for draperies, or who would wear what to a dance, or even, God forbid, the whispered vagaries of childbirth.

As they strolled back to camp, Clay Allison talked of the wonders of the southwest, the fascinating mixture of cultures to be found in New Mexico, which he promised would delight as well as amuse her.

"The El Camino Real runs between Santa Fe and Mexico City, linking the white homesteaders and merchants with those from Mexico. It has done so since the 1700s," he told her. "It's a six-month journey between the two cities. Less than a day's ride from Santa Fe is El Rancho de las Golondrinas—the Ranch of the Swallows. It's crowded with travelers. There are enormous cottonwood trees, cool springs and flat farmland— all the weary traveler needs to provide food, water and shelter. But it is lovely beyond words and offers much more, a succor for the soul."

Allie listened in awe to the man who spoke with a pleasant lilting tone that placed the accent on syllables in a way not like any other she'd heard. She was soon to learn he spoke English

219

much like the Pueblo Indians and the Mexicans, giving the words the melodious accents of their own lovely languages. It was an affectation he'd obviously cultivated, for she hadn't noticed it earlier when he was joshing with Defoe.

"And the churches, ah, one does not even have to be religious to experience the blessed tranquility each offers. El Santuario de Chimayo, where people travel to seek the blessed earth, and the St. Francis Parish church, which our good Bishop Jean Baptiste Lamy wishes to turn into a cathedral of exquisite beauty. Ah, yes, you will find Santa Fe much to your liking, senorita, as will your camera. I look forward to seeing what you chose to capture through that magic eye. Perhaps if you decide to settle down there, you can one day take the first photograph of Bishop Lamy's dream cathedral, yes?"

As Clay Allison continued to talk, and he did indeed continue to do so, while they prepared the evening meal together, she found herself only half listening. The fascination of his descriptions brought visions of the studio she would open, the wonderful photographs she would take. Imagining Jake there with her came as naturally as seeing herself in such a setting.

Over the delicious wine that reflected the firelight in its amber hues, Clay spoke of the breathtaking beauty of the high desert. "In the summer the rains come late every afternoon, accompanied by the most thunderous light show. And when they leave, these storms, the land is shafted with light, spilling through the clouds in divine glory. In the evening the air is sometimes so still and clear the sounds of life carry everywhere, making it difficult to sleep. Ah, the horns and drums, the harp and guitar, the violin and banjo. And yes, even the mewing of cats, the barking of dogs, the braying of jacks. You will indeed love it, senorita."

She saw herself riding with Jake through the fragrant *chamisa*, which Clay explained was sage but colored a bright yellow-green, not purple.

She listened and tried to learn, for she was sure this place was going to become her home, this land of which he spoke so lovingly. She already yearned to see it. Yet she couldn't help thinking about Jake. Where he might be, how he was doing. Had he already fallen prey to that beast in his head? Without her to see to him? She admonished herself. He had gotten along quite well before he met her, and she wasn't his keeper.

"Excuse me, Miss Caine. Are you all right? I've asked you the same question twice and you seem to have drifted miles away. Am I boring you? That would certainly put a blotch on my flawless reputation with the ladies, and I am capable of speaking on other subjects that might be more to your liking."

She pulled herself from the reverie. "No, I'm sorry to be so rude. I was thinking about a friend. I'm very worried about him. I do like hearing about Santa Fe, for I intend to make my home there."

"Ah, and this friend. Was he so irresponsible as to run off and leave a beautiful young lady like yourself? Point me in his direction and I shall haul him back to you. This foolish, foolish man."

His light teasing brought a burning to her eyes and throat. Damn it, she couldn't bear thinking of Jake out there alone. She didn't want to wonder the rest of her life what had become of him. If something were to happen, she wanted to be there when it did. It just wasn't going to work, being parted, and if she had to leave the caravan, so be it.

The handsome outlaw watched her closely. "I see I have struck a nerve. I would be more than happy to assist you in your dilemma. Nothing is more satisfying than helping a young woman in distress, even if it is to bring her together with her lover. I fear I am an incurable romantic."

Allie's eyes popped wide. "I never said he was my lover."

"And the way you are blushing, I have indeed hit the peg on its proper end with my clever hammer, have I not? Oh, I'm not

221

averse to playing Cupid. It would please me most fully. Let us say it would just be an additional payment for the wonderful photographs you produced. I don't feel I have reimbursed you enough, for I will treasure them always. It's wonderful to think we can carry into our old age the image of what we once were, so young and beautiful and virile, hand it down to our children and theirs." He laughed outrageously.

"Mr. Allison, you are so gracious. I'm embarrassed to have acted this way, but I can't stop thinking of him."

"Ah, alas, I cannot hope to woo you, for you love him. Does he love you? Stupid question, of course he must, for to be exposed to your beauty for more than a minute, a man would fall deeply in love with you, as I have." He paused and chuckled infectiously. "But then, I do so adore beautiful women. I suppose your friend, he has experienced bad times that caused him to run away."

"It's worse than that. Much worse." And she told him the story, as if it were the most natural thing in the world to spill her innermost feelings and Jake's private hell to this stranger.

He listened without comment until she had finished, then raked his long fingers through his hair. "My friend Defoe has forgotten his compassion, I fear. What this young man does not need is to be cast out. I will speak to Defoe, and of course the doctor can be totally discounted, for what man of medicine has any good sense to speak of? They spent their lives with their noses in books; what can they know of the human condition—of how we all yearn for our heart's desire? Do you know which way your young man went?"

Allie's mind boggled at Clay Allison's willing involvement in her problems. He surely didn't mean to go after Jake, to bring him back here.

"No, but we did talk about him going in the wrong direction to find where he was from, since it would follow he probably lived back East to have served in the Union Army."

"Then he probably headed in that way, and no doubt would stick to the quickest route, the Santa Fe Trace, one would suppose."

"What's the use? You'll never find him. He's had all afternoon and he might ride on into the night."

"Ah, yes, but not, as they say, hell bent for leather. He would want to spare his horse with so many miles to ride. I, on the other hand, can move quite quickly in order to catch up with him before he reaches those wicked cities along the Mississippi."

Allie stared at Clay. "Why would you do this?"

He shrugged. "Perhaps because the excitement has gone out of my . . . shall we say, former life. One can only rob so many banks before it becomes quite boring. I look for something new to do. Perhaps I can make up for some of my earlier transgressions and do something good before I hang up my chaps." He laughed heartily, as if he had told a marvelous joke, and Allie couldn't help joining in. He was a most perplexing, yet likeable, man.

"And would it be too much to hope that you have taken a photograph of this mysterious young man?"

"Yes, yes I did. That's a wonderful idea, but I don't think you'll ever find him. I heard in Westport that the freight caravans and homesteaders taking the Santa Fe Trail number in the thousands. Jake could be anywhere by now." Even dead, she thought silently, but bit her tongue painfully to keep from saying it, lest it be true.

Clay touched the butt of one of his pistols. "Ah, but I have had a lot of experience in running men to ground. You will give me the photograph of your young man, and I'll wager I'll have him back to you within the week. No man ever escaped Clay Allison. He will stop to eat and he will ask his questions. Someone will remember him, and I shall find him."

She glanced quickly at Allison, for the lilt in his voice was gone, replaced by a deliberate harshness that frightened her. His slitted eyes portrayed the killer he was said to be.

A deep shiver raced through her. What was she doing trading stories with such a man? Sitting next to him beside her campfire sharing food and wine? Had she lost her mind? What if he tracked Jake down and killed him? But of course, that was utter nonsense. What would be the point in such a thing? All these thoughts tumbled through her mind as they sat side by side, staring into the dying fire. Clay Allison seemed to have lost his desire for conversation as he quietly sipped wine from his refilled cup.

Eli swung by Allie's camp late that evening. He was surprised and angered to see her with a stranger. The two of them sat side by side near the fire, talking as cozy as could be. Had she already taken up with someone else, and him waiting in the wings for her?

In the darkness he couldn't make out the man's face, but he would be sure to learn it if the man stayed with the train. Meanwhile, he would see that Allie was kept real busy entertaining her old beau, the honorable Eli Martin. He might as well get her used to seeing him, for once he'd turned in that fool Hollingsworth, she would be his again. And this time no one would take her away from him.

In sorrow, Jake retraced every mile he had traveled with Allie, putting more and more space between them. At night he would fall from his horse and sleep a few hours, then ride on, seldom stopping to eat.

He met freighter caravans and homesteaders, he passed plodding caravans returning from Santa Fe loaded with their spicy cargos of Mexican chiles, the Indian corn known as azule, golden pumpkins and exotic fruits, the intricately hand-woven rugs and lovely baskets, beautiful leather saddles and Navajo blankets, all so popular in St. Louis and farther east.

He studied the many faces, searching for a memory, a familiar figure or friendly voice. Occasionally he asked questions, but no one knew him; he knew no one. So on he rode, bereft and no longer the happy man he had been when he traveled with Allie Caine.

Often, accepting the hospitality of someone's campfire, he would remove the picture of Lorena from his pocket and show it around. Some would nod, point, think until he grew hopeful, then shake their heads. Others just gave him a quick no, as if they cared little for a man searching for the woman he loved. Often Jake remembered Allie in that context, but Lorena's ghost would appear and chase away the emotion.

Would he never find out who he truly was?

About four nights into his meanderings, Jake spent an evening with friendly teamsters, sharing much of his story because they were curious. The next morning he took his leave, carrying with him their best wishes. It was a most promising experience for him, because though none of them knew of him or Lorena, they had been generous and helpful. It made him feel as if he were as normal as they and not the madman the doctor saw.

That night he had no more than drawn the blanket up under his chin, the Spencer snugged up beside him, when he heard a rider approaching. Flames spat fretfully from the fire, casting a small circle of light. The stranger hauled up outside its illumination.

Jake ran his hand along the rifle barrel until his fingers found the trigger guard, his thumb the hammer. Otherwise, he remained still, waiting for the man to make his move.

"Ho, the camp. I'm looking for a fella named Jake. Hear he came this way."

Jake eased from under the blanket, crouched low and crept behind the shelter of a cottonwood tree. "Come into the light where I can see you," he called.

A tall, large man led a huge black horse forward into the glow. He wore two sidearms, but held his hands out away from them. "I'm harmless, as you can see. Are you Jake?"

"Could be, depends on what you got in mind." Jake's heart fluttered. Had the men he'd met sent someone to him to tell him who he was, who Lorena was? Curiosity and excitement got the better of his sense of caution, and he stepped from behind the tree. At least he thought to keep the rifle at ready. "Who might you be, and what do you want?" he asked.

"I'm a friend of Allie's. I have the picture she took of you to prove it. Could we talk without that Spencer pointed at my gut? I've lived a long time, like to make it longer."

Allie had sent someone after him. But why? The sudden realization that something might be wrong filled him with terror. "Is she all right? Something hasn't happened to her, has it?"

The stranger approached the campfire, studying Jake's face. "It's you all right, the one who ran off and left that pretty little lady to fret herself half to death. If I had a woman like her, do you think I'd be dragging my tired old butt around on the trail looking for something that probably doesn't even exist anymore?"

"Who the hell are you? And what business is this of yours? I asked if Allie is all right, and you'll by God answer my question or . . . " He raised the barrel of the rifle, clicked back the hammer harshly.

The man held up both hands, his demeanor immediately altered. His voice softened, despite staring down the barrel of the formidable Spencer. "I'm a friend of Defoe's, sir. You don't want to shoot me with that gun. It'd blow a hole in me big enough to put your fist through, and if Miss Allie Caine is any judge of character, you wouldn't be up to such an ugly thing as that.

"We met a few days back, and she told me her tale of woe, or should I say yours. Now before you get your back up, I should explain that I simply have that effect on women. They can't help it, nor can I. But I seldom take advantage, if you know what I mean. She took some photographs of me, very good ones, I might add, and we got to visiting. She is very upset, very concerned about you, and wishes me to bring you back."

"Did she hire you to hogtie me or what?"

The man laughed heartily. "Hardly. Not that I couldn't do so, of course. No, her intentions are, I believe, to leave the caravan's protection and search for you if I don't return with you.

226

That, as you can imagine, would put her in much more danger than you might if you return."

"Has she lost her good sense?"

"No more so than any woman in love, my friend. Does that answer your question?"

Jake shuddered and involuntarily touched the pocket where he kept Lorena's picture. "And what did she pay you to do this?"

The man swept off his hat and offered Jake an exaggerated bow. Jake thought him a little drunk or not quite right in the head. The idea tickled him despite the circumstances. He was the one whose head was supposed to be messed up.

"She paid me nothing, my friend, not in coin or bill or services."

"Well, you're one strange son of a bitch, I'll give you that."

"Then perhaps we'll make good traveling companions, since as I understand it, you are one strange son of a bitch yourself. This woman for whom you search, is she more important to you than Allie Caine? And if so, how could that possibly be?"

Jake eased the rifle down beside his bedroll and sat, gesturing for his companion to join him. The man did, and Jake was glad for the time he had to think over the question. He could see why Allie had shared her confidences with this man. It was easy enough to talk to him, and he had a charm beneath which lurked a sureness of self not often found in drifters.

He thought about Lorena, or the idea of her, for he only had the few vague illusions that might or might not be truths to go by. Then he put those up beside Allie Caine and what he'd had with her. This stranger was right, of course, he would be a fool to continue to pursue a dream and turn his back on Allie.

"There are problems. I have this thing in my head."

The man rapped on his own with his knuckles, making a hollow sound. "As do we all, my friend."

"I could hurt her."

227

Slitted eyes gleamed in the firelight, stared at him. "Has that happened?"

"God, no. I would never . . . dammit, I frightened her."

"Men are forever frightening women, even with the best of intentions. It has something to do with what we could do to them if we wished."

Jake gazed into the dying fire, ashamed of tears that moistened his eyes. "The doctor said I might do anything."

"What the hell does that *pendajo* know? We all might do anything. The point is, we usually don't, not unless we fully intend to. You are hurting her more with your absence than you ever will if you go back to her."

Jake sighed. "Why in the hell do you care so much? What's your game, mister? I don't even know if you're telling me the truth."

"Ah, my friend. What is the truth but an illusive wish?"

"Who are you?" Jake asked, almost convinced that he had lapsed into one of his dream fits.

"Name's Clay Allison, but that no more tells you who I am than your borrowed name does for you, does it?"

"*The* Clay Allison? The outlaw?" Now he knew he was dreaming. Why would a man such as this waste his time trying to reunite what he supposed were two lovers? Wasn't he supposed to be out robbing banks, or stage coaches, or shooting ranchers over water rights?

Jake stared in amazement. "By God, I know who you are. I remembered it just as if I'd always known it."

"Well, I'm pretty infamous." Allison chuckled.

"No, you don't understand. How come I remember you all of a sudden, when I don't even know my own name? Am I . . . do you think maybe it's coming back? It . . . when you told me who you were it just flashed through my mind what you do. I know who you are. Do you understand how that makes me feel? To actually know something from the past? My God." He slapped the outlaw hard on the back, bringing out a grunt.

Allison gaped as if Jake had lost his mind instead of regained some of it. Then he began to laugh and soon Jake joined in.

After a while, he said, "Does this mean I don't have to hogtie you to take you back to that little gal?"

Jake studied the distant darkness for a long while, touched the pocket of his shirt, then said, "Yes, I guess that's exactly what it means. You're welcome to bed down here overnight. We can leave at first light."

Chapter Fifteen

By the time the caravan of freighters had traveled through Fort Larned and headed for Raton Pass, Allie had given up hope of the return of Clay Allison, with or without Jake. Nearly two weeks had passed with no word.

They were deep in hostile Indian country, and the army had sent out an escort to see them safely through. The Indians persisted in their efforts to keep the white man from chewing up their land, and much was heard of the Kiowa Chief Santanta and his daring raids. But no one discounted the infamous Geronimo and his Apaches, or the Comanche, the Arapaho and the Southern Cheyenne. And word was that Colonel Kit Carson continued his pursuit of the Navajos in New Mexico, driving band after band into the Bosque Redondo. The area was a cauldron of Indian problems that bubbled and boiled at every opportunity. Since the end of the war, the army had poured into the Southwest to protect the traders as well as the homesteaders who moved west in droves.

Allie was more concerned for Jake than frightened of the Indian threat to herself. The caravan was large and heavily armed, not a likely target. She worked frenetically, almost as if she had to capture forever with her camera lens every single face, each sunset and lovely vista. It was surprising how eager people were to pose and pay a few coins for their own likeness. Often they met freighters headed back east and she would photograph their wares and the colorful Mexican *cocheros* perched on the seats of their wagons.

Many of the brave frontier women proved ideal subjects for the camera's eye, and when they couldn't pay she gladly took a trinket of little value in return for adding their likenesses to her collection. Her supply of plates dwindled until she feared she might run out before they reached Fort Union, where she hoped the order she had placed in Westport would be waiting.

To her dismay, Eli began to pay regular visits. Though she discouraged him harshly, he brought her flowers and spoke of their time together with fondness until her carefully built defenses began to crumble. Between fending him off and keeping busy with her photography, she was able to endure the days without the man she loved. While she sensed the importance of what went on around her, concern for her own future overrode it all. Jake had become a part of her life for a brief moment, and in that time she had foolishly made plans. Now she had no idea if she would ever see him again. And if she did, how would they feel about each other? How would he seem? Was he getting better or worse? The worry nearly drove her mad.

Eli chose an evening when she felt at her lowest to seriously attempt to break down her defenses. At the end of a hot, exhausting day she sat beside the campfire, sipping at coffee and feeling rather disgruntled. Wind-blown grit lodged in her eyes and mouth. She did not welcome an unexpected visit from Eli Martin.

"You look beat, Allison," he said, moving behind her and massaging her shoulders and neck.

It felt so good that she moaned in appreciation and did not ask him to stop. So of course, he continued, his strong fingers moving expertly down her backbone to the base of her spine.

His breath feathered against the back of her neck. She shivered.

"Lie down," he whispered. "Just stretch out and let me work those kinks out."

She closed her eyes for a moment and let him maneuver her so that she lay in the grass on her stomach.

His palpating fingers trailed across her buttocks, along the ridge of her backbone up to the base of her neck.

He leaned close. "God, Allison, I've missed you so. How many times I wanted to come to you on hands and knees and beg your forgiveness." His lips touched the nape of her neck.

"Eli, please don't."

"Aw, Allison. I'm sure you miss that fellow, Jake. But let's face it, you and he aren't suited. We, on the other hand, are meant to be together. Unless, of course, he's coming back. Is he, Allison? Is he coming back?" He busied himself once again with an innocent massage of her shoulders.

It wouldn't be wise to push her too far, too fast. If he was careful, sooner or later, she'd be his again. All he had to do was play his cards right. But more than that, he wanted that bastard Hollingsworth and the reward on his head. Too bad he had to be alive, or he'd just lay in wait and shoot him. Allison need never know. Once Hollingsworth was sent off to prison, sweet little Allison would be vulnerable and lonely. In no time he would have her, the Warings' ten thousand dollars and his land deal in Santa Fe.

And so, patiently, night after night, he appeared to keep her company, slowly making inroads into her life.

One evening he found her writing a letter to Matthew Brady, and when he asked about it, was immediately sorry, for her reply opened old wounds.

"I had nothing but debts when my father took sick. We hadn't been in business long, you see, and owed everyone.

Then he couldn't work, and I had to care for him and keep up the studio. When he died . . . " She fixed him with an accusatory stare. "I had to sell most of his photography equipment. One was his Latimer Clark Stereoscopic camera. It would have been perfect for the landscapes I want to shoot."

"I've seen the stereoscopic viewers," Eli said, trying to steer the conversation to safer ground. Her silent accusation was all too true. He had left her when she had needed him the most, and somehow he had to make her believe he wanted to atone for that. More than that, he had to find out where Ethan Hollingsworth had gotten to, and soon. He ground his teeth and continued the lame conversation about her blasted stereoscopic photographs.

She warmed to her subject despite memories of Eli's betrayal. "They aren't suitable for portraits, but the twin lenses produce sharp still lifes. The depth of field is incredibly realistic, as if you could walk right into the scene. If my business continues like it has during this trip, I can afford a used one. I'm hoping Matthew Brady will have one he would be willing to sell me. He's so successful, I'm sure he makes regular replacements with newer cameras."

"If you need money, Allison, I'd be glad to—"

She waved an impatient hand. "No, I won't let you do that. You've done quite enough to me already. I won't be beholden to you as well."

Her old bitterness colored the words and Eli sighed. He still had a long way to go with his plan to woo her back into his arms.

He tried one more tack. "Perhaps you should ask your friend, what's his name? Jake, isn't it? He might be able to lend you the money, and you do seem quite close. Did you ever say where he went?"

His ploy didn't work, though. She just drilled him with one of her high and mighty stares and said, "Jake is none of your business, Eli. None at all. Now, if you don't mind, I'd like to finish this letter."

Samantha Lee

Considering the effort a lost cause for the moment, Eli took his leave.

It was dark when she laid aside the finished letter to Matthew Brady and rose to stretch. As she did so two riders appeared out of the night. She couldn't make them out, until Molly rode into the circle of firelight.

When Jake kicked free of the stirrups and slid off the mare, surprise, anger, joy and fury played games with her emotions until she didn't know whether to hug him or scream at him. For a moment she didn't move or speak, but simply gazed into his wonderful face.

He spread both arms wide and laughed. "Well, Allie, say something."

She ran into his embrace, nearly knocking him over. His hat fell to the ground and he buried his face in her neck, holding her so tight she could scarcely breathe.

"I missed you, Allie. I love you. Oh, how I love you."

The declaration, muffled because he was busy planting kisses on her neck and face, drove away her sadness. He loved her and he had come back to her.

The sound of his laughter, the feel of his lips against her flesh, of his windblown hair against her cheek, revitalized her aching heart. She caressed him, kissed him, uttered nonsensical phrases. In the next instant she pulled free, scowled at him. "If you ever run off like that again, I'll skin you alive. Don't ever do that to me again. I thought you weren't coming back. I thought . . . oh, Jake, you scared me half to death." In the next breath back in his arms, she said, "If you ever do that again, I'll come after you myself."

"Rather than send an outlaw to fetch me?" he teased, then cupped her face and gazed into her eyes. "Oh, Allie, how could I have left you? I look at you and touch you and know it was the worst thing I could ever have done to us. Oh, Allie, my sweet."

He kissed her tenderly, tasting languidly of her eager lips.

She would not let him go, not ever again. The kiss grew in intensity until desire throbbed wildly within her. He was back! And she was where she belonged. In his arms.

Behind her someone coughed deliberately, then chuckled. "I'd just ride off and leave the two of you to it, but if I don't get myself a cup of coffee and a place to rest my weary bones, I shall collapse."

Reluctantly they pulled apart, turning to greet Clay Allison.

"I do hope you'll forgive me the interruption, but I trust the two of you will have plenty of time together from now on, and it appears everyone else is asleep. Is that coffee I smell yonder on the fire?"

Allie arranged her tousled hair self-consciously, straightened her shirt and took Jake's arm firmly. "Yes, please do join us. Have a cup. Tell me all about your adventures finding this runaway."

Jake hugged her, and together the three sat around the fire sipping hot coffee and talking into the night.

Clay finally took his leave, promising to see them in the morning before he rode on back toward his ranch. "I'll go bed down in Defoe's tent. He sleeps so hard he won't even know I'm there. You two have a good night now, you hear? And Jake, you better take heed, you leave this pretty little lady again, and I'll have her quicker than you can say Geronimo."

For a moment the two of them quietly listened to the thudding hoof beats of Clay's horse going off into the darkness. Jake squeezed her hand in silence, said nothing. She drew a deep breath. A soft breeze played over her skin, her heart thumped against her breast. Why did he continue to sit there, arm touching hers, thigh warm and hard against hers? She wanted to tell him how she felt. For so long she had waited, thought of what they would do should he return, dreamed of his hands and mouth on her. And now she refused to make the first move. It had to be him, for she couldn't bear it if he turned her away again.

The silence between them grew unbearable and so she turned to speak. He did so as well, and they uttered each other's names simultaneously. He lifted a hand and she thought he would touch her, but it went instead to his shirt pocket where he kept the damnable picture of Lorena. She wanted to grab it from him, toss it in the fire, stomp the cinders into dust, but she sat stiffly as he withdrew it, took one long look and raised his gaze to hers, eyes smoked with passion.

Pain lanced her heart, the pain she would have felt had she been in his place or that of Lorena. She touched the carte de visite, took it from his lax fingers.

"We'll find out who she is, Jake. I promise you. And then she won't be between us any longer."

He shook his head. "No, it's not necessary."

"Yes, it is. For both of us, it is very necessary. I've written to Matthew Brady about some other things, but I think he can help us with this. If you don't mind being parted from this for a while, I'll include it in the letter. I think he may know who she is. I'm sure it's his work."

"But why . . . I mean, if you knew . . . I don't understand why you would want to do this now. Now that I tell you it doesn't matter anymore. Why not before?"

She grazed his stubbled jaw with the tips of her fingers. "Probably for just that very reason. Now that it doesn't matter I can see how unfair it is for you not to know. I'm sorry, Jake. I've done some foolish things where you're concerned. I suppose I was afraid if you found out who she was you'd know who you really were, and you wouldn't . . . well, you wouldn't be my Jake anymore. You wouldn't be the man I love, the man I know loves me. You'd be instead, the man she loves, the man who loves her."

He started to speak but she held up a hand. "I know I should have made the offer right away, for I knew as soon as I saw the likeness that it was Brady's work. At first I thought it probably wouldn't matter, and then later I didn't want you to find her. Then I was simply angry that you couldn't let go of her and love me the way I was growing to love you. I don't want you hurt anymore, Jake. Or myself, for that matter. It's time we put it all behind us. And if that means finding her and getting this settled, then that's what we'll do."

He leaned forward, his forehead touching hers, but said nothing.

"I'm sorry," she whispered. "Whatever you want to do about it is fine with me."

"I love you, Allie," he said against her cheek, sending chills through her heated flesh. "But she'll never let me be, and I'm so afraid I'll do something to you when I'm . . . well, not right. I'm afraid the doctor is right and I'm a madman who needs to be locked up."

She put her arms around his neck once again. "No, no, that can't be true, and I refuse to believe it. You've never tried to do anything to hurt me." She remembered the night he had backed her up against the wagon, ranted frightening words, and acted like someone else entirely. But nothing had happened. Nothing. And he had not tried to hurt her. She had been frightened by his actions for his sake more than her own.

"Don't worry, we'll work things out. I won't let you think like that. Shall I send the carte de visite to Brady? It's up to you."

He held her for a long while before nodding. "Yes, see what you can find out. But Allie, until things are straightened out, until . . . well, until I get my life back, we can't . . . I mean, it wouldn't be right for us to, you know—"

She sagged against his shoulder, shook her head miserably. "I know, I know." Looking up at him, she asked, "Have you been well? I mean, no—"

"Falling-down fits? Not one. I have experienced some more bits and pieces of recollections, but nothing that helps. I think it'll come, Allie. I really do. I'm beginning to remember ordinary everyday things, just as if I'd always known them. We'll just have to be patient."

They held each other for a long, exquisite moment, then separated and sat staring into the fire.

"Hey, it'll be all right," he said. "We're good buddies. We've been friends awhile, Allie, and it's worked out just fine. It won't be for long. Hell, we're civilized."

"I know, and I agree. Just to have you back is enough for now. But I want to tell you, Jake, if you change your mind, decide—well, you know, it's okay with me. I'll be ready any time you are."

"That's a hell of a thing to tell a man feeling like I do right now. Like I might just throw you on the ground and have my way with you this very minute. Forget all the caution."

For a split second, she wished he would, but then he laughed self-consciously and she joined him. A keen sense of satisfaction, a warming comfort, filled her. Everything would work out, she knew it would, and meanwhile, they were together and on their way to a new life in Santa Fe.

The letter containing Lorena's picture went off to Matthew Brady the next morning on a stage they flagged. Just as Clay Allison had predicted, Defoe accepted Jake's return calmly and there was nothing said by the good Doctor Tremaine. The handsome outlaw took his leave, casting a broad wink in the direction of Jake and Allie. She suspected he had probably had a lot to do with Defoe's change of heart. Things would work out. The thought filled her with a pleasant tranquility as the traders' caravan moved onto the trail once more, Jake riding beside her wagon as if he'd never left.

In the days that followed he made her laugh and sometimes made her shed poignant tears for what she feared might never be. But she tried to keep those times to herself. He learned to treat the glass plates, and to transfer the images to paper for the finished print. She taught him to mix the solutions of nitrate and salts. He found it awkward at first working in the dark box, but soon grew quite adept at the procedure.

She educated him about photography, showed him the collection of her father's daguerreotypes that included several presidents, including Abraham Lincoln. She acquainted him with her wooden T. Ottewill sliding-box camera, showed him how to ease the rear section back and forth to focus the subject, how to lock it with the screw that ran in the slot in the baseboard. Explained to him how the awkward shape and size of such a camera had been overcome by making it a folding model with hinged sides that collapsed when the front and back panels were removed. It was a real boon to the traveling photographer, and a big improvement over the bellows that attracted mold and insects.

She told him how some old timers looked back at the daguerreotype process with fondness, even though it required much more bulky equipment be carried in the field.

"The daguerreotype could be gilded, finished and cased while the lady subject put on her bonnet," she explained.

He drank it all in, listened with an intensity she'd learned to expect from him. And many times when he stood close to her, breathing softly on the back of her neck, she would fight an insatiable desire to be in his arms. She wondered if he felt the same, but was afraid to ask, for they walked such a narrow line. She would not scare him off again, no matter what.

As for Jake, he had never known such peace. His dreams were no longer haunted by anything but his passion for Allie, which often awoke him with a hunger he longed to appease. But he stuck to his guns, while they awaited word from Matthew Brady. For then, perhaps, they could go on with their lives.

The caravan moved past the Cimarron Cutoff and the treacherous jornada. Few used the arid, dangerous route anymore. Before Dick Wooten had improved the mountain branch of the Santa Fe, many traders went south at the cutoff to avoid the rugged eight-thousand-foot-high Raton Pass. But Wooten, armed only with his dream and an insatiable ambition, secured a charter that allowed him to construct a decent road through the pass and charge people to use it. The endeavor made him a rich man and opened the way for easier trade with New Mexico. The caravan would cross the mountains on Wooten's improved road and gladly pay the charge. From there it would veer to the southwest toward Fort Union and New Mexico Territory.

During the crossing even the equable Jake showed signs of wear and tear as he tried to lend a hand everywhere at once.

He helped repair broken wheels, replace shattered axles, unload and reload disabled wagons. Many nights at the campfire he worked on damaged leather harnesses until his fingers nearly bled. It was as if he wanted to show his gratitude to everyone in the caravan for allowing him to remain—prove he was no danger to them.

Allie worried that he was pushing himself too hard, and in truth he was. He wished desperately for a change in their status, hoped for a miracle that might clear up his past and let him live at last free of concern over actions of the man who dwelled in shadowy silence within his soul. The man he had once been haunted by, hovered just out of sight with the threat of return—a return that could change him forever, make him a person no one would know. Not even Allie or himself. As time passed he grew to dread Matthew Brady's reply, and wondered why he had allowed Allie to write the letter.

One afternoon, after a particularly harrowing few miles, Defoe circled the wagons early.

As Allie made camp, four magnificent red men, their beautiful near-naked bodies gleaming in the late afternoon sunlight, appeared from out of a grove of trees near the what's-it wagon. She was alone. Jake had taken the team to the corral and he had recently formed the habit of having a cup of coffee with Defoe and some of the teamsters before returning to the supper fire. She suspected it was another of his attempts to prove himself as normal as the rest of them. Nobody trusted loners, he told her, only half in jest.

Allie caught sight of the braves, glanced quickly over her shoulder to see a few folks nearby occupied with unloading and setting up camp. Fright tiptoed through her, but it was followed by a desire to capture those four majestic men forever with the lens of her camera.

They stopped a ways out, regarded her in stony silence. They sat on paint ponies and each held a lance. Wind off the mountains stirred the flashing white manes and tails of their mounts.

She took a few tentative steps away from her wagon and toward them, heart hammering against the back of her throat.

Dear God, how she wanted their likeness in her camera lens. How could she ask them if they would pose? Perhaps they spoke English.

The leader touched his pony's flank with a moccasined foot and rode slowly toward her. She halted and let him approach. The Colt lay under the wagon seat, and she didn't know whether to be relieved or apprehensive. If she were armed they might run away or attack.

The brave pointed at her strange little black-curtained wagon and asked a question.

"You want to see?" she asked, and motioned him forward.

He glanced over his shoulder at the other three who remained stoic and silent, then prodded the pony closer to her. She smelled the wildness of him, probably from the game he ate and the oil he used on his bronze body. It was not at all unpleasant. Her mouth dried out and a warning of danger rode up her spine like a tiny lizard. She ignored it and went to the wagon, not taking her eyes off him.

The brave reined up, made a guttural sound deep in his throat.

"It's okay, see?" She grunted and hefted out the heavy camera, folded up so it was hard to see what it was. Perhaps the Indian wouldn't have known in any case.

Fingers fumbling, she opened out the camera, held it up where he could see.

"I'd like to take your picture," she told him, using hand signals to help him understand.

He looked at her, tilted his head. How very fierce he appeared, but what marvelous bone structure in that face. And his eyes. Dark, mysterious caverns that held secrets she ached

241

to know. The late afternoon light bathed the angularity of his features, casting shadows she wanted so to capture with the camera. When he did not object or make a further move toward her, she fetched the tripod, set it up and fastened the camera to it, all the while keeping a watchful eye on him.

While he waited and the other three continued to sit their horses at a safe distance, she treated a plate in her dark box which she had unloaded earlier. The brave kept an eye on her as if she were prey. In the draped box, her hands trembled when she tilted the plate from side to side to coat it evenly.

At last she was ready, and slid the protected plate into the camera. She kept every movement slow and deliberate so as not to alarm him or the others. Was he going to stand still while she did this? Surely someone would come along and sound the alarm. Did she dare hope to actually take this marvelous creature's picture?

Slowly she ducked under the cloth and focused the camera. There might not be time for a second shot, and she did so want his full figure. That would mean either she backed up or he did, for all she could see was head and shoulders. The others were in view to the back. Should she take it, chance getting another before they bolted?

She moved her hand from under the drape toward the lens to expose the plate, and the brave stepped forward, pushing his face up close so all she could see were lips and nostrils. With a sigh she came out from under the black cloth, slid between him and the camera and placed both hands flat on his broad chest to move him backward. His skin was slick, hairless and hot to the touch, the muscles thick and taut. His heartbeat was that of a wild, threatened animal, and he did not budge.

Dark eyes smoldering, he fingered up a lock of her golden hair and said something just above a whisper, as if he wanted only her to hear. With his breath came the smell of raw meat. Allie stood her ground as the other three laughed. Adrenaline shot through her, sharpening her fear and excitement so that her nerve endings tingled.

From behind her Jake said in a calm, low voice, "Allie, move back this way very slowly."

Her heart kicked harshly, and she tried to carry off the charade of fearlessness awhile longer, turning, grinning. It took every ounce of her strength to make her voice work, for she was suddenly terrified. "Oh, hi, Jake. Come here, you can help. They don't understand that I need them to move back so I can take their picture. He keeps wanting to look into the lens. Quit gaping and come here."

Without warning an arm locked around her neck, choking off her breath and lifting her feet off the ground. Terror stunned her, but she kicked out in reflex, gasping and clawing at the strong bronze arm that held her prisoner.

"Aw hell," Jake said, then demanded, "Let her go. Look, look. I'll give you this, just turn her loose."

She struggled to see, but blackness had begun to close around her. Jake's image wavered and disappeared, appeared again as the pressure at her throat let up a bit.

"I can have her and that," the Indian said in English.

Jake glanced over his shoulder quickly. "I don't think so. You want the rifle, let her go."

"I like her better than the rifle."

Jake made a rude sound, shrugged, and launched himself at the Indian, sent him staggering. In fending off Jake, the huge brave had to turn Allie loose, and she tumbled in a heap to the ground.

For Jake there wasn't an opportunity to see if she was hurt. All he could do was hope someone would spot the ruckus or hear it before these four cleaned his plow. And that's what they set out to do. The one who had wanted Allie tossed Jake away as if he were a pesky fly. He bounced and skidded, came to his feet awkwardly and scrabbled to put himself between them and the fallen woman. The Spencer he'd offered the brave lay in the dirt.

Jake continued to call Allie's name as the first of the four came at him. If he could arouse her, get her moving, she'd be out of danger. She moaned as if she heard, but lay still.

243

"Could have picked someone besides Apaches to mix with," he muttered, and launched himself at the first Indian. He hit the brave hard in the stomach, driving him backward and all the time shouting at the top of his voice. Pain shot through his leg when two more tackled him low.

He grunted, twisted an ear, pummeled a hard belly, bit a hand. Was everyone in camp deaf and blind? Were they going to let these Apaches kill him?

In the midst of the melee, the fourth brave headed for Allie, who was stumbling to her feet.

"No, you son of a bitch, leave her alone," Jake yelled, even while fists pounded him into the ground.

At last a rifle cracked. In the midst of getting the worst of the fight Jake recognized Defoe's voice over an enraged outcry from the Indian who'd gone after Allie.

"Back off or I'll shoot you all," the wagon master bellowed. "Delgado, get your tail up here and speak to these heathens so they understand."

Jake half crawled toward Allie when his attackers abandoned him to face Defoe's more imminent threat. She had fallen backward and sat, legs spread, one hand rubbing her throat, the other propping her up.

The man called Delgado rattled off something to the braves, but Jake was more interested in Allie than anything else. By the time he had crawled to her side and wound both arms around her, the four braves were riding off with Jake's Spencer.

"The one feller, they was Apache, said he'd be back for his picture later," Delgado said in an awed tone as they watched the Indians disappear beyond a pile of red boulders. "Did the senorita really offer to take their picture?"

Defoe shook his head. "Hell, she probably did. Wonder they didn't kill her and Jake both. Tell Lieutenant Riley what happened so he'll post an extra guard around camp tonight. Where the hell are those soldiers when you need 'em, anyway? Them wild'uns just might be crazy enough to come back. Hell, you'd think we had enough troubles without stirring the 'Pache pot to a boil."

Delgado spat in the dirt. "They went out to reconnoiter the perimeter." He used the fanciful soldier words with a trace of a Mexican accent and plenty of derision.

Defoe strode to where Jake and Allie sat in the dust. "You two any the worse for wear?"

"I don't think so," Jake said. He was a bit embarrassed by the situation, now that he saw Allie was not hurt. "I'm sorry about this, Defoe. She didn't understand."

"She did, too," Allie said. "I'm the one who's sorry. I could have gotten myself or someone else killed. I feel so foolish." She touched the corner of Jake's mouth where a rivulet of blood flowed. "Are you hurt? Oh, Jake, you could have been killed, wading into them like you did. I'm sorry, are you okay? Are you sure you're okay?"

The fact that she might have been responsible for his death, or a serious injury, fastened Allie's heart in a cold clasp.

"Oh, Jake, they could have killed you, and you just kept going at them. Why did you . . . ?" She broke off, ran her hands over his head and face, down his shoulders and arms.

Eyes closed, he sighed in relief. She was all right, she was safe. He leaned heavily against her. The throbbing in his leg was nothing compared to the pain he would have felt if they had hurt her or carried her off.

Defoe helped Allie to her feet and Jake stood, turned to say something to her, but was interrupted by a woman screaming. Everyone around him disappeared, and he looked into Lorena's face. She held out a hand, mouth a rictus of hate, and he followed her into the darkness.

Chapter Sixteen

They slept together that night, her holding him close even after he came out of the blackout. He had saved her life, throwing all caution to the wind, caring not that he might be killed. The scene had caused one of his spells, another thing for her to feel guilty about. Stupid enough to walk right up on four Apache braves, but for that to result in him risking his life to save her made matters even worse.

She watched him in the flickering light from the campfire, brushed hair from his damp cheek, kissed his mouth gently.

"Oh, Jake, I wish you wouldn't go away from me like this. Why does she have such a hold on you? It's so damned unfair."

His eyes darted back and forth, as they had done since two of Defoe's men had carried his limp body back to her camp. She touched the closed lids tenderly and tried to imagine what he saw in that other world to which he retreated without warning. He carried terrible scars, the worst of them on his soul. Something so dreadful had happened that he continued to react to certain images or occurrences by leaving the real world. She was caught between hoping he never retrieved the past to praying he would so they could face the enemy and conquer it together.

He moved, moaned and opened his eyes.

"Hello," she said softly.

He didn't answer for a moment. She could see him struggling with the few brief but frightening minutes when he had no memory at all. It was terrifying each time, because he always feared one day waking up to find he could not remember yesterday and never would again.

His hand came up, fending off some invisible monster.

She took his wrist in a gentle grip. "It's okay. It's me, Allie. Everything's fine. How do you feel?"

Scrubbing at his head with spread fingers, he moved a little away from her. "Don't . . . ah, hell, did I get run over by a stampede?"

His withdrawal hurt her, but she tried not to show it. "Just four full-grown Apaches." Her arms ached with emptiness, and she wanted to put them around him again, but resisted the temptation.

"Ah, yes, it seems I remember a tussle." He sat up. "Where are we?"

"Our camp. There's the wagon."

Seeing him move as if to rise, she came to her feet. "What is it? Stay put. You need a drink or some coffee? Are you hungry?"

"I don't need to be waited on. When're you going to start taking care of Allie and stop worrying so much about everyone else?" The edge to his voice faded as quickly as it had come, but didn't fail to cut deeply.

He was angry at her for being so careless, and she didn't blame him. She stepped back, watched him struggle to his feet, stagger, then limp to the wagon and the shadow of the water barrel. He drank two cups, then drew a third and held it out to her.

A faint grin, a tilt of his head asked for a truce.

Moving only close enough to take the cup, she told him thanks and sipped the sweet, cool liquid. "I feel like a fool. I could've gotten both of us killed." She gestured with the cup. "That was a dumb thing to do out there. I put everyone in jeopardy. I realize that. You . . . I don't know what I would've done if they'd hurt you . . . killed you. Jake?"

His eyes smoldered, he gripped her shoulders, pulled her closer, knocking the cup from her hand. As he stared down into her face, she felt the strangest kind of fear. Not of him so much as what might yet happen with this enigmatic man, and worst of all, her own reaction to it.

She shoved herself close to him, forced him into almost the same position he had once put her, wedged back against the wagon and the cedar barrel. "I love you, Jake whatever-the-hell-your-name-is. So stop looking at me like that. You're not going to frighten me away. And being ornery just isn't in your nature, whether you know it or not. We're going to see this through together, unless you tell me this very minute that you don't love me, don't care what happens to me, want rid of me. Tell me that, Jake. Tell me."

He gripped her shoulders even tighter, and she flinched but didn't break eye contact.

"I can't tell you that," he whispered hoarsely, then leaned forward and put his lips hungrily over hers.

The painful hold on her shoulders loosened and his arms gathered her close. She shifted into the tautness of muscles, the angularity of bones, the heat of flesh that devoured every inch of her until they became one entity, moving, breathing, seeking only one thing. Blessed unity.

In that moment Jake ripped away the bonds that kept him chained to his unknown past, finally truly admitting both to himself and Allie that no matter what, he loved her, could not bear to lose her. Lorena's clawed fingers tore at him in one last desperate effort to drag him into the familiar black pit which might well be the only place she existed. He shook them loose; images that had visited and revisited him in so many forms, faded into nothing.

This was real, this moment in which he held the woman he loved in his arms. He could no longer deny that, for if he died tomorrow he would have missed out on holding her, making love to her, spending an hour, a day, a week, a month with her. What did it matter as long as they were together now, for this instant?

They would find the first church they could and get married, and however long it lasted would be fine. Life itself had no guarantees. Why should he expect any for the two of them?

Reluctantly he pulled his lips from hers. "Marry me, Allie. If there's a church at Fort Union or we can find a padre or preacher somewhere, it doesn't matter. Anyone who can join us together for however long we have. Will you do that?"

She touched his mouth gently, as if to make sure he had spoken. Her dark eyes brimmed, caught twinkles of starlight in their depths. "Oh, yes. Say it again so I can make sure I'm not dreaming. Ask me again, Jake, please."

He grinned, felt good all over, despite the aches and pains of the beating he'd taken from those wild Apaches.

"I'll say it again and again. Marry me, Allie. I love you, Allie, marry me, marry me, marry me."

She laughed. "Oh, yes."

"Say it again," he teased, then lowered his mouth to hers so that she couldn't have uttered a word if she had wanted to.

After a long while they took each other to the bedroll beside the fire, hands and mouths exploring with love's frantic grace.

He unbuttoned her shirt and turned her so the firelight played over her firm breasts when he slowly pulled the fabric aside. He kissed each nipple gently, reverently, the touch of his warm, moist lips sending shards of icy fire through her.

"They are so lovely. You are so lovely." He moved a lock of her long hair forward so that it trailed over her breast. The rosy nipple peeked through and he traced it with the tip of a finger. He covered the other in the same way, the golden strands of hair spread like a fan hiding a treasure. Slowly he lay her backward; the lovely young breasts shielded as if by silken water. He nuzzled through the layers and took an exquisite bud in his mouth.

Fingers of desire laced through her, brought a cry that faded to a low moan. She fumbled with his buttons, but could accomplish nothing as his hungry mouth sent wave after wave of ecstasy undulating through her until her body rocked with it. She could only hang on, fists filled with the flannel of his shirt.

Trailing his tongue downward, he moved to the belt around her waist and worked at the buckle even as his kisses branded the flesh there. He tore open her pants and slid them down over her hips to accommodate his searching lips and tongue.

He would not hurt her, could not bear the thought of causing her even the slightest bit of pain. To make her his forever, though, meant pain, and perhaps that was as it should be. Life was hard. He feared it would be even harder for her with him. First he would make her feel so wonderful that perhaps she might be able to ignore that instant of sharp, intrusive entry. Why must the first joining of a man and the woman he loved cause her pain?

He groaned, need overriding caution. He remembered the way Lorena had . . . oh, God, no, not Lorena. Not now. He didn't remember, he couldn't. All the same he wondered briefly if he had taken her virginity, too. Even worse, had he taken her life?

Face buried in Allie's firm belly, the smell of her around him like the fall of honeydew on a cool night, he fought off the images. They would not come now; they could not. He would not allow it.

Hands spanning Allie's hips, he took deep breaths. The dark one hovered, he could feel his heartbeat, hear his thoughts. Damn him to hell.

Allie threaded trembling fingers through his hair. "What is it? Jake, what is it?"

He turned his head, lay a stubbly cheek on the soft mound of her stomach and dragged in great drafts of night air.

"Only that I love you so very much it hurts."

"Then make love to me. Now. Don't stop, please, Jake."

He wanted to make love to her, he did. It was all he wanted. Bloody scarlet images danced at the edge of his vision. He tried to blink them away. Horror uncoiled deep in his gut, drove away his desire, the hardness of his passion.

She cupped his face in both hands, moved his mouth where she wanted it to be and whispered to him softly, rolling gently against the heat of his breath, the gentle nip of his teeth, his warm tongue.

"It's me you love, Jake. Only me. You and I, we belong together. Tonight and always. There's nothing back there, so don't look back."

He responded with caution, darted his tongue out and tasted of her sweetness. This was Allie, the woman he loved. The only woman he loved.

She gasped. "Yes, oh my sweet love, yes."

Taking great care, she unfastened his jeans and freed him of the binding, stiff fabric, moved her hand until she held him, firmly. In her palm the heat, the pulsating of his blood, set fire to her passion, but she held it in check. At any moment he could pull away. If he did that now, she would never be able to do this again, not with him, perhaps never with anyone. With tender nibbles and languid movements of his tongue he teased her into a blinding, light-struck desire, and she could no longer think of anything but having him inside her.

"Now, my darling. Now it's time," she whispered.

He said her name as he moved over her, slipped inside like the moon slips into the embrace of velvety midnight. She cried out with a brief jagged pain, sighed as it trickled away, renewed the cry while passion overrode her.

Patiently, gently he took her on a long, exquisite ride she prayed might never end. She swayed faster and faster to reach its apex because she could no longer be denied. He soared with her, kept her at the crest of the tumult as wave after wave broke over them, then carried her delicately from the peak, a sense of dazzling wonder enclosing him.

Samantha Lee

Lying wrapped in her arms, Jake eyed the evil vision that hung disguised by the night. Crouched out there in the dark, it threatened to destroy him forever. Someone tiptoed near, but it must be his imagination, for his demon had no body and made no sound except deep within his soul.

The dark one would not win this final battle, he would have no part of it. He had made love to the woman he wanted to have forever, and now he held her in his arms. His life had been renewed, he felt clean and bright and hopeful. They were safe, both of them, from the wicked intentions of his lurking memory. He would not remember. He did not care, there was nothing back there for him. He would remain this man he had become, for this man had the love of a beautiful, wonderful woman.

"Allie, are you okay?"

"Oh, don't bother me." A soft, barely audible purr.

"Mmmm. That's fine." He shifted his hip just a little to get off a small rock, but was careful not to pull away from her.

"Jake?" Her voice crooned with spent passion.

"Hmmm?"

"Did you . . . I mean, I've never done this before. Was it as good as it should be? Do I need practice?"

"Beats me," he said.

She knocked at his arm weakly, wiggled her butt up tighter into his groin. "Tell me."

"I'll show you if you keep that up. Perhaps, Allie, we could practice just a bit more. One never knows."

In the long perfect silence sparked by the crackle of the dying fire, Allie laughed down deep in her throat. Sublime moments suspended in time kept them captive for a while longer in that perfect world.

"Well?"

He sighed. "Women," he said softly, fondly. God, it felt good to have someone to hold, to love, to know. "I guess I'll have to be honest with you. This was my first time, too."

252

"Naw, Jake. Really?"

He chuckled at the tone of her question. "Well, in this life, at any rate. First as far as I can remember. If my body has done it before, my mind doesn't remember. So, I guess you could say I'm an emotional virgin . . . or, I was, until a few minutes ago."

"Well, you must have remembered something, because that was the most wonderful experience I've ever had."

"I'll be damned, me too." He nuzzled her neck until goose bumps feathered up her spine. After a long while, in which she thought he might have dozed off, she said, "Jake?"

"What now, woman? Can't you just leave me to recover?"

"No, really. Will it always be that way?"

"Probably not. We'll get old and tired."

"Then maybe we'd better put in a lot of time while we're still young and agile, don't you think?" She wiggled her hips again, felt him rise against her, and turned so that they were face to face. "Now, Jake, would be a good time to start that practicing you talked about."

He raked hair away from her face. "Not a bad idea." Desire rekindled and he nipped and tasted of her delicious lips. This was what it was like to be secure, content, happy.

They must have slept sometime during the night. He remembered drifting off once surrounded by the musky smell of her, awakening to a late moon splashing them in silver, and making love to her once again. It felt as if they floated in warm liquid where everything was ethereal, almost as if they had come together while they slept, never fully awakening, but sinking with ecstasy into the final beatific storm of love. He stored the moments of that most blissful night in the big empty space in his brain where the memory would mark the true beginning of their life together.

Eli could not bear it one instant longer. His Allie, the woman he had loved before anyone else, crying out with passion in the arms of that bastard, Ethan Hollingsworth. A cold-blooded

Samantha Lee

murderer, and he had his hands and mouth all over her, and her liking it. Eating it up like some love-starved spinster.

It was all he could do to keep from leaping from the shadows of the wagon where he hid and beating the man senseless. But there was the ten thousand dollars to think about.

Patience. That's all he needed. Soon enough Jake would be in prison where he belonged. He could wait.

He clamped both hands over his ears so he couldn't hear her moans of delight, and hunkered over himself to still the fury that drove his own desire. He longed to hold her, to fasten his mouth savagely onto her breasts, to plunge deep inside her over and over until the world spun out of control and she screamed with a terrified pleasure.

Much later, he crept through the sleeping camp, the ache in his gut only made bearable by the thought of his ultimate revenge on both of them.

When Jake and Allie moved out the next morning, their lives were forever changed, made whole, by what had happened the night before. Allie thought later that it seemed the cruelest of ironies that when they were the most content, the worst thing would happen.

Brady's letter caught up with them while they were still in Colorado Territory, but New Mexico was just out of sight. The caravan had been pestered by small raids by the Kiowa, and the traders had dared to breathe easier when they spotted civilization, rowdy as it might be. This time perhaps they would move into New Mexico with only the Apache and Commanche to worry about, which, Lord knew, was bad enough. To the south, the Mescalero Apache had left the reservation at Bosque Redondo because of trouble with the Navajo, and the Chiricahuas had joined them. Indian trouble loomed, and everyone was nervous at the news.

Defoe had the letter from Brady delivered to Allie as they settled for the night. Everyone built fires and dragged out heavy coats and more blankets against the crisp air of the mountains.

Jake and Allie sat within the warmth of the flames, a single blanket wrapped about them, unabashedly snuggling.

"Oh, that's nice," Jake murmured. "And how about this? Still cold?"

"I haven't been cold since you moved under here with me. You can keep doing that."

He held her breast and tweaked the nipple lightly. "Are you all right with this, Allie? I mean, we really aren't married. People are talking."

"What people talk about has never concerned me. I want to wait until we arrive in Santa Fe, Jake. Our new home. That way, every year on our anniversary we can return to the church where we said our vows and renew them. And when we have children we can show them the exact spot on which we stood when we promised to love each other for an eternity. It will make everything just perfect. I don't want to get married out here on the trail somewhere, in a place that will mean nothing. And, yes, I'm all right with it. I am spoken for, and you can't imagine how that makes me feel." She nestled her head into his shoulder and looked forward to crawling into the bedroll with him.

He rocked her gently. "Oh, yes, I do know how that makes you feel. Sometimes I'm frightened by the enormity of my own feelings. Afraid it might be too good to last."

"Don't talk that way. Nothing will happen. We won't let it."

He shuddered, pushed away the apprehension.

And as if in reply to his dread the messenger appeared with the letter, sorting it from a handful he carried. For a long while after he left, they sat apart and stared at the tattered and soiled thick vellum envelope sealed by Brady's hand. Was the news good or bad, or perhaps just newsy and of no importance to Jake's dilemma?

She finally shrugged. "Only one way to find out."

"Open it," he said hoarsely. "Read it out loud. I don't want to even look at the words."

"You sure?" She held it close to the flames. "I could burn it, we could forget it, forget her, forget everything but us."

Samantha Lee

"Oh, God, you don't know how I want to." He put a finger lightly against the rich paper, took a deep breath, shook his head vehemently. "Open it."

With trembling fingers she worked the wax seal with a curlicued B pressed into it from the tab and slipped out the letter, unfolded it and tilted it toward the firelight. A carte de visite fell out into the dust and lay there, ignored for the moment.

"Dearest friend Allison Caine. I will get to undoubtedly your most important questions first, as I can sense the urgency in your written words, dear child. I have enclosed information you requested about the stereoscopic camera, but I feel it more important to relay the sad details about the tragedy of Miss Lorena Waring, a debutante and heiress here in our city. For if you have come upon a man who carries her picture, you could be in the greatest peril. I will begin at the beginning."

Allie glanced at Jake, wet her lips and wished she could throw the damnable thing in the fire. It was too late though, much too late. So she swallowed harshly and continued reading, sensing his foreboding in the stiffness of his shoulder against hers.

"The Waring family, well-connected in this city, had two children. The boy, Lansford, known fondly as Lanse by family and friends, attended Yale University. Though quite wild in his youth, his pranks were always covered up by his parents' money. Oh, he wasn't really a bad boy, but there were a few unsavory scrapes that any other young man might have paid for with jail time. Not so his beautiful young sister, Lorena. She was adored by everyone and quite the belle of the capital. She got herself engaged to a dreadful fellow by the name of Ethan Hollingsworth, a friend and schoolmate of her brother's at university. Soon after the engagement was announced the two young men had a falling out over something that may have happened between the three young people. No one seems to know for sure. Lanse joined the Union Army and was never heard from again. He is presumed dead.

256

"*At any rate, if you are in the company of this dastardly Ethan Hollingsworth, then run for your life, my child. For it is strongly suspected that he murdered poor Lorena. No one knows the why of it.*"

As if punched in the stomach, Allie gasped, her voice breaking.

Beside her, Jake said under his breath, "Oh, God. No. No."

She shuddered, acutely aware that he peered over her shoulder, breath coming as harshly as if he'd been running a race.

"Wait, Jake. Now just wait. Let me finish it."

"Finish." A dead monotone.

She began to read again, her voice quivering:

"*She was found in her own bed, and I will spare you the gory details, dear Allie, but suffice it to say it was a vicious act, and Hollingsworth was never to be heard from again. As you know, my dear, so many have gone unidentified and buried in mass graves, that no one may ever know what happened to either of the young men. The parents live in seclusion, their lives ruined by this double tragedy. If you know something of this man. I beg you to contact the authorities. A price remains on Ethan's head. I have included a picture of the unlucky couple which I took for them upon their engagement. It, too, is a carte de vis- ite, and I apologize that there is no tintype or daguerreotype available that would show a clearer image.*

"*Also enclosed is the address of the Waring family in case you would care to write to them, but I would not suggest it, my dear, for they are devastated and would no doubt be unable to shed any further light, for they refuse to discuss the incident. And who could blame them for that?*

"*Well, that is all I can add to the story, except to tell you that the photograph of the beautiful Lorena which you sent to me was taken by me upon her coming out scarcely a year before her tragic death. I hope you do not mind that I passed it on to her parents, since you did not know the girl and would surely have no use for it.*"

He wrote then about the camera and Allie stopped reading. The pages fell into her lap. Neither she nor Jake spoke. The fire crackled, and mist drifted from their mouths into the cold night air.

Finally she glanced down at the picture lying on the ground. It took every ounce of her strength to pick it up, and twice she fumbled with numb fingers. Moving it so the firelight played across the figures, she saw that the man in the vague, impressionistic photo had dark hair cut to the fashion of that day and a full beard of the same color. The camera had captured him totally solemn, staring into the lens. The girl beside him was recognizable as the same one in the small photograph Jake had carried with him. The man, however, could have been Jake or someone else. The beard, the somber expression and the gauziness of the out-of-vogue carte de visite made it impossible to tell for sure. No doubt Jake had changed physically during his terrible experiences in the war, and even since.

He took the photograph from her trembling grasp, leaned closer to the fire. His fingers shook so he could barely hold it still to get a good look.

Fear rose like a ball of fire to choke him. "Look, it's not me, Allie."

She leaned forward, studied it closer. Much as she prayed he was right, it could well be Jake.

He echoed her own silent thought. "But why did I have the picture? Even if it is me, that doesn't mean . . . God, that doesn't mean I killed her."

The forlorn quality of his tone ripped at her heart. She gazed up into his terrified, wide blue eyes. Abruptly they darkened and his voice hardened. "Goddammit, Allie, that doesn't mean I killed her."

"No, no. Of course it doesn't." She shivered, for he was beginning to scare her more than the news from Brady had done. Her voice trembled when she went on. "It's just some dreadful, terrible mistake." She wanted to touch him, to put her

258

arms around him, to kiss him, but could do none of those things as she struggled with an overpowering tide of emotions.

Why couldn't he simply remember and clear this up? How could he be so stupid as to not even know what had happened? Immediately she flung away those unfair questions, studied him silently. Thought of what he had been through, the time spent in Andersonville when he lived under worse conditions than an animal; and later how he'd roamed the country searching for something to connect him back to the real world. She could not, would not desert him now, when he would need her more than ever. But, in sticking with him, would she be putting her own life in jeopardy? For if the man Jake had once been had indeed killed Lorena Waring, a woman he was supposed to have loved, what would that mean for her, whom he claimed to love?

He stumbled to his feet, backed away from her, and as she stood, intending at last to go to him, he cried out as if wounded by a bullet.

"No, get away. Don't come close, Allie. I forbid it. Stay back."

"Jake, stop it. It's not you. It can't be."

"It very well could be."

She thought he would bolt and run, this time for good, but he slumped there in the wavering firelight and gazed upon her with a deep sadness clouding his features.

"Jake, Jake," she whispered. "Listen to me. Whatever happened, you aren't the same person. What happened to you, if you were this man, has changed you, made you the man you are now. A man too kind, too gentle to ever do such a terrible thing. Please, please, don't leave. Stay and we'll find out more, we'll get this straightened out. If you leave, Jake, I'll follow you. I swear I will. Wherever you go, I'll follow. I won't let this happen. I won't."

She was filled with despair that this dreadful news could have come when they were about to start a new life, so furious she wanted to scream, to lash out, to hurt someone the way she was hurting, the way he was hurting.

Her next words were hurled at him, so that probably half the camp heard them. "You've got to stop running away, you stay here and we'll fight this together."

He held out a hand. "Just don't come near me, Allie. You hear me? Don't come near me. I'll stay with the train, but I won't travel with you, I won't sleep near you, I won't ride near you or eat with you. Though God knows I don't know what good that will do."

She nodded, relief coursing through her. It was better than him leaving. Perhaps better all round. For if they remained together before they knew all the truth, would she be able to lie in his arms, let him make love to her without thinking that those same, dear hands might well have driven the life from another young woman? Would her fear and doubt show in her eyes each time he held her close?

She nodded vigorously. "We'll write for more information. There must be some way we can find out for sure who you are, now that we know this much. We'll prove you aren't this Ethan Hollingsworth, or if you are that you didn't kill Lorena. Something, Jake. There's got to be something we can do."

"I'm damned if I know what," he said, turned and walked away into the darkness.

She stood for a long while, shoulders hunched against the cold and the despair, then carefully gathered the sheets of the letter and the picture, and stored the bundle in a wooden box in the wagon where they would be safe but out of sight.

Chapter Seventeen

The caravan plodded resolutely south. The grandeur of the Sangre de Cristos notched the crystal blue sky to the west, green grass that had been belly deep on the stock faded subtly to olives and grays, a portent of the desert to come.

More times than not, over the next few days, the scenes Allie viewed through the lens of her camera were seen through tears. She felt as if Jake had died and she grieved for that death much as she had mourned the passing of her family. An aching numbness set in, blocking out all that happened around her. Again she had lost someone she held dear, and the pain was a vivid reminder of those earlier losses. Would life always take from her that which she wanted the most?

Sometimes she would spot Jake on his long-legged mare, Stetson scrunched down so that the wide brim shadowed his features. At such moments she would be overcome with a need to rush to him, to leap onto the horse's back behind him and dig in her heels. She would press her aching breasts against the warm, taut muscles of his back and lock both arms tightly around his waist as the mare raced away. Such a foolish desire caused her to moan with emptiness and despair. She tried to imagine where he slept, what he ate, and managed to worry about that as well. She missed him terribly.

As the caravan drew closer to Fort Union, excitement increased like the palpable, throbbing heartbeat of a beast. Even that did not lift her spirits.

Eli Martin dropped by unexpectedly one evening. Allie did not welcome him and the meeting was short and terse. But he returned the next evening and the next. He didn't mention Jake, yet obviously the word had gotten around that the two of them were no longer together.

Her sorrow was such that she could no longer exhibit any anger toward Eli. His betrayal meant little to her, for she looked back on their earlier relationship for what it was, a youthful escapade, a flirtation. It soon became evident that Eli did not regard the courtship in the same way. Despite her deliberate aloofness, he continued his visits, almost as if he were once more courting her.

"You've become quite a beautiful woman," he said one evening. "One who should not be traveling alone."

"I prefer it that way. Tell me, Eli, why are you here? Why are you going to Santa Fe?" The coincidence of his presence in Westport at the very time of her arrival appeared questionable.

"For land. I've been quite lucky since leaving Missouri, and find I have some money to invest. There is land there for the taking. Thousands of acres up for grabs to the smartest, the quickest. You would do well to invest, yourself. It would please me to help you. It's the least I can do, since you seem to think I have wronged you in some way."

She nodded, but didn't rise to the bait. Their earlier relationship was no longer a subject she cared to get into. "I understood that the land in New Mexico is held under land grants and cannot be bought and sold."

He chuckled, but there was no humor there, only an underlying wicked intent. "I came by a few sections at the gaming tables, with the promise of more to settle a sizeable debt owed me. There are those who have managed to get around such antiquated foreign laws. Mexicans have no idea of the value of their land, nor do they have the slightest notion what to do with it. Men with a great deal of power as well as money always find ways."

She eyed him with distaste. "You mean steal it, don't you? There was a time, I'm ashamed to say, when I thought I loved you, Eli. Now I thank all that's holy for your departure before I could do something so foolish as to marry you."

His eyes clouded, muscles rippled along his jaw as he visibly held his temper. "Everyone gets along in this world the best way he can. Take your friend Jake, for instance."

Caught by surprise, she snapped, "What do you know about Jake?"

He didn't reply but gazed past her to where a rider sat a horse some distance away. She recognized him immediately as Jake, keeping an eye on her and her visitor. She didn't know whether to be angry or relieved.

Eli turned his attention back to her, shrugged. "It's not my place, but if I were a lawman I would have him trussed up. The word is he's a killer, and it's only a matter of time before the law catches up with him."

"That's a lie. Where did you hear that?"

He smiled, and she saw that he had been goading her for precisely the very reaction she had given. A memory, a bit of an overheard conversation taunted her, then faded. He went on and she lost the tantalizing thread.

"All I know is I should be very careful if I were you. If word should find its way back to Washington that he is with this caravan . . . well, you might be in as much trouble as the man who calls himself Jake. Why don't you ask him who Ethan Hollingsworth is? It seems to me that his memory loss is quite a convenient ruse."

She flinched, her heart growing cold and still, a stone thrown in deep water. Afraid she would say something to give Jake away, she kept quiet.

"You know, Allie, you always were a sucker for a stray, especially if he's wounded." He rose, and bent to touch her cheek.

She drew back sharply.

When his eyes blinked she knew he was on the verge of losing his temper. The effort for control was clear in his voice. "Habit forming, isn't it? Caring for others. He's not your father, sweet girl, and you can't make everything right by pretending he is."

Tears filled her eyes and she wanted to punch him in his smirking face. "You filthy liar. Get away from me, and don't come bothering me again or I'll speak to Defoe. He'd as soon shoot you as look at you, and now I think I know why. Go, and leave me alone." In the midst of her own anger she almost got hold of what she'd been trying to remember, but once more it slipped away.

Eli settled his hat carefully before turning away, taking enough time to let her know he didn't care what she thought, it was all his idea to leave.

The next day the caravan reached the Canadian River. A young rider carried the word to each wagon, and he stopped to chat with Allie. Single women were rare on the frontier and the men found her presence appealing.

"Don't you worry, none, ma'am," he said with youthful charm. "It's a natural rock crossing, makes fording the river slick as peeling bark off a log. *El Vedo de las Piedras*, they call 'er. Safe as being held in your mama's arms. Almost as if old mother nature decided to give us a break. Might as well have built us a bridge of stone. Piedras, that's rock or stone, and she's flatter than a fritter clean across the river. Upstream is sand deep enough to bury a good-sized wagon, and downstream is a big old canyon, but our bridge'll do us just fine. Crossing'll slow us some, so you just take 'er easy." He tipped his hat, spurred his horse into a fancy dance and rode off.

Shading her eyes, Allie gazed into the distance at a growing formation, its shades of sienna brilliant against the crystal blue sky. It was as if some giant hand had uprooted an enormous bluff from the distant Sangre de Cristos and planted it in the center of the flat plains. The massive rock resembled a tremendous covered wagon sitting atop an earthen pedestal. She learned it was called Wagon Mound. What a perfect opportunity for a stereoscopic camera, for the wide panorama spread before them was almost more than the eye itself could appreciate. Perhaps the one she had arranged for Brady to ship would have arrived in Santa Fe by the time she did. How exciting to capture the wonders of the Southwest with such a marvelous camera.

Allie had not mentioned Jake in her brief missive to her friend in Washington, D.C., just assured him she did not know Ethan Hollingsworth, let him know she wanted the stereoscopic camera, thanked him for his trouble and enclosed a few bills, promising the rest as soon as she could send it.

When her turn came to cross the Canadian on the natural bridge, she briefly studied the wide river and the wagon ahead, then smacked the reins smartly on the mules' rumps. A rider moved into view at her side and she glanced over to see Jake. Her heart trembled and she bit at her lower lip to keep from crying out his name. Without glancing at her, he rode into the water, captured the leathers on the lead mules and led them across.

Then he rode off, not sparing her even a moment to enjoy his nearness or to thank him. The action cut deeply. No matter what was going on, he could have spoken to her.

After they camped she saddled Ringo, mounted and spurred him across the flat river valley in a wild gallop. Wind whipped through her hair and cooled her fevered body. The dry air carried the tart/sweet fragrance of the distant desert sage they called *chamisa*. She wished she could ride on forever, bathed by the sun as it slipped below the Sangre de Cristos in a burst of brilliant golds and pinks and oranges to leave her in darkness. And then on through the velvety black night, her way lit by myriad glittering stars, and accompanied by rhythmic hoof beats and the lonely thunder of her heart.

She would never get over Jake, not if she lived out here in this glorious country the rest of her days and never laid eyes on him again. Not if no one ever spoke his name, would she forget his touch, his kiss, his compassion. Her love for him was as vivid as the sunsets, as sweet as the *chamisa*, as powerfully eternal as the mountain peaks.

Abruptly the stallion's muscles tensed, he tossed his head, screamed into the wind, and danced to a halt, shoulders trembling.

She leaned out along his damp neck, lathered in sweat, and whispered in his ear, "What is it, what do you hear, Ringo?"

Though she listened while the great horse shifted restlessly, there was nothing but the wind kissing her face.

Jake eased the mare deep into the umber shadows cast by silver-leafed river willows to gaze at Allie, outlined against the lavender sky. He shouldn't have followed her out here, the two of them so far from the caravan, entirely alone. But Allie had no business out here either. There were Apache and Commanche about. Their sign was everywhere, and they wouldn't be past grabbing a lone rider, man or woman, just for the horse he rode or what he might be carrying. While Jake feared the dark man who dwelled within his soul, he was frightened as well that Allie might get hurt riding out alone at night. He could not stop loving her, didn't know a way to change it and wasn't sure he wanted to. He might well ride alone the rest of his days remembering their love, keeping it close, savoring the taste of her lips on his, the satiny smoothness of her skin, the heady fragrance of her hair after a day in the sun and wind. She would always be more real to him than Lorena.

Distracted with such thoughts, he was startled to see that she had vanished. What had happened to her? Oh, hell, he'd probably drifted off in one of his fits and she'd ridden back to the caravan minutes or even hours ago. A lot of good he'd do her if she really needed help.

He made a kissing sound to the mare and rode up the slight incline into the open.

Her voice came at him out of the darkness. "So it was you."

His heart lurched and the mare stiffened, threatened to buck. "Dammit, Allie, don't sneak up on me like that."

"It was you doing the sneaking, not me. At first I was frightened, thought maybe I'd been a fool and let myself get cornered by one of those savages. What are you doing, Jake? If you're going to follow me around, why not just ride with me?"

"I saw you leave—I didn't want you out here alone, that's all."

"So you decided to come with me. Oh, that's great. You won't come anywhere near me with all those people around . . . oh, Jake."

"Don't be afraid. I know it was stupid."

As always, his reaction caught her off guard. He was the only man she'd ever known who readily admitted to his own shortcomings, even if they weren't absolutely true. Sadly, she shook her head. "I'm not afraid of you," she said softly, and knew she meant it.

"Maybe you ought to be."

It annoyed her that he would beat up on himself that way. "Why don't you stand up for yourself once in a while? You don't always have to agree when I criticize you."

"I don't, not always."

She laughed despite herself. "There, that's better." She drew a deep breath, almost couldn't let it go for the pain in her chest. "Oh, Jake, please, this is all so foolish. You know I love you."

267

In the ensuing silence an owl hooted off toward the river, a melancholy accompaniment to their conversation.

"I love you, too," he said in harmony with the great night bird.

"Then—"

"No, I can't." A harsh interruption of the mood.

She leaped from the palomino, reached up to him. "Walk with me, just walk, that's all. I promise to run like hell if you start acting crazy. This is so ridiculous, Jake. I'm armed."

"You trying to tell me you could shoot me?"

Without replying to the question, she stood her ground, gazing up at him with her hand upraised in a silent plea.

"Goddammit," he said under his breath, but he dismounted anyway, because he couldn't ride away and leave her there alone, and she wasn't about to back down. He could tell that from the look in her eye. "You always have had a stubborn streak, Allie."

Nodding, she reached out to him once more, the ivory flesh gleaming in the dusk. For a moment he stood there, the mare's reins in both hands. Time halted, all sound disappeared and he stumbled forward, as if he had tripped over something invisible. He let the leather slip from his fingers and took her hand to ground himself to earth. The touch, as vibrant as lightning cutting a summer sky, sent them into each other's arms with soft cries.

Her fingers twined in his thick mane of hair, she sensed his anxiety, spoke as he pulled his mouth from hers. "Oh, don't be afraid, please don't. I need you so, and you need me, I know you do."

Face wet with his tears and hers, he kissed her warm neck, drew in the tangy fragrance of her hair, her flesh, and tried to still the sullen warning from deep inside himself. It chilled him to the core. Killer. Fool. Madman. Run, it said, run, run. But desire stampeded through him like a herd of wild mustangs. Accepting her trust and love because he could do no less, he locked her within his arms, his mind and body crying out for her, swaying with the rhythms of her passion.

With a languid, hypnotic ease, they made love in the grass under the darkening star-kissed dome of sky, the immense purple peaks of the Sangre de Cristos bearing witness, as they had for millennia.

The black night cloaked them, and the grass, bruised by their love-making, exuded the fresh tang of life into the clean, crisp air.

Sometime later when he opened his eyes, Jake felt rested, exhilarated, as if he had slept a healthy sleep uninterrupted by vivid dreams. Allie lay on his arm breathing softly against his chest, golden hair fanned over her bare shoulder and down across one naked breast. He took a strand in his fingers and held it there, hand trembling slightly. Then he lay his palm against the side of her neck, thumb at the jaw line. Under his touch her pulse throbbed steadily. Such a delicate lifeline, how fragile and vulnerable was this woman who entrusted herself to him even knowing what she did.

Awe transformed his fear and he kissed her cheek. How could he have less faith in himself than she did?

Her eyelids fluttered, she purred and shifted so her mouth moved to his, her body cradled once again by the man who must possess her.

They didn't return to the wagon until dawn silvered the morning sky. As they rode, thunder rumbled over the Sangre de Cristos and they watched a dark storm cloud stalk majestically over one peak, then another. Rain freshened the dry air, puffs of moist wind kissed their faces, the horses kicked up a fuss and darted here and there. Jake laughed and Allie joined him, feeling as if her heart might burst with happiness. Everything would be all right now. The storm was over.

They reached Fort Union on a hot summer day fighting a burning wind that might have blown through the gates of hell. Tempers had grown short among the teamsters, for the trail had been difficult. An unusual number of repairs had become necessary, and all were eager to lay up awhile at the trading fort, a great, teeming city within a high stockade.

Once the caravan had settled within sight of the fort, Allie and Jake rode in to learn if her shipment of plates had arrived. Her ears rang with the constant hammering at the forges set up in the giant wagon-repair shop. Enormous stacks of buffalo hides dried in the sun. Signs, either painted crudely or burned into slabs of wood, directed visitors to the hospital, the first one they had seen since leaving civilization, and the various shipping offices; directives to both a jail and chapel shared the same post. Under construction was the mechanic's corral. There was a long line of officers' quarters, and soldiers as well as traders moved to and fro in bustling activity.

She thought of asking Jake to marry her here, and in that way bind him forever to her. Being an honorable man, he wouldn't then flee so easily. But that would be very unfair. In the back of her mind, she thought perhaps it wasn't so much the unfairness of such an action, but that she wasn't quite sure enough of who he was yet to marry him. That was by far a better reason for waiting than the one she admitted to. So, when they passed the chapel she gripped his fingers tighter, but said nothing.

Inside the Russell, Majors and Waddell offices, they were directed from one clerk to another until one finally located a bill of lading for the photographic plates and confirmed that the shipment had, indeed, arrived.

He told her she could pick up the crates at the warehouse anytime, as soon as she paid for the shipment. She pulled a leather pouch from her pocket, fingered out a small roll of bills and counted off the correct amount.

The clerk, a short, balding man with tiny round glasses perched on a bulbous nose, glanced at Jake when Allie paid the freight bill. It was easy to see he was used to dealing with the male half of a couple.

Unperturbed, Jake looked away and began to size up others in the large room. Occasionally he would wonder if he knew this face or that or did someone know him? Everywhere he went it was the same. After Brady's letter, it might be better if he never solved the puzzle of his own identity. It was entirely possible he was wanted for murder back in Washington, D.C. Did such information reach this deep into the frontier? Was there a wanted poster nailed up in every sheriff's office in the West with that bearded face of the carte de visite on it?

Allie tugged at his sleeve, breaking his reverie. The clerk led them to the door. He stepped out onto the covered porch and pointed to where wagons were at that very moment waiting in line to be loaded.

"Your shipment is not destined to go out on another freight wagon, so you can pick it up there, next to where those wagons are loading, the first door on the south." He pointed and Allie nodded.

"You headed for Santa Fe?" the man asked before she could walk away.

"Yes."

"Could 'a had it shipped straight through, saved yourself the effort."

She smiled at him. "I appreciate that, but I needed the plates now."

"Glass plates. Photography plates?" the man questioned. "You yourself take pictures?"

She nodded, but she sensed Jake's eagerness to be gone and wondered what was wrong with him.

"Haven't never met a woman photographer before. Did hear of one, though. Some gal that went west into California. Hear she's quite successful."

"Yes, I've read of her. Eliza Withington in Ione City. Perhaps someday they'll put my name in a newspaper for something I've done." She held out a hand to him. "Well, sir, thank you very much. We'd best be going now."

"Say, now, if anything got broke, you make sure and let us know. Russell, Majors and Waddell prides itself on good service."

A man moved along the walkway, his military stance stiff. He wore a butternut shirt from a Confederate uniform. Jake turned with Allie just as the man drew even, and halted abruptly.

"Hey, Captain, is that you?" he asked, sharply bright eyes studying Jake's face closely. "My God, sir, I thought you were dead."

Jake staggered, fingers biting into Allie's arm. He couldn't find his voice to question the man, but finally managed a weak, "Do you know me?"

The soldier leaned to one side, then the other. "Well, I thought . . . but, now I'm not so sure. Damn if you don't resemble Captain Hollingsworth, but on closer inspection . . . no, I guess not. I apologize, sir. You just gave me such a start.

"Here I am going along sure that the Captain died at Shiloh and I see you. Well, you can imagine my surprise. But, naw. Even without the beard, the captain had a more resolute look about him you don't possess. Well, you don't get to be commissioned without that stern quality, do you, sir? I do beg your pardon, sir. Ma'am."

The man glanced at Allie, touched his hat and walked away. Allie couldn't help but notice that he turned once more to study Jake before shaking his head and moving around the corner.

Jake's jaw muscles rippled and he paled as if he had seen an entire regiment of ghosts. His fingers continued to grip her arm until she winced.

"Jake, you're hurting me. My God, Jake." He looked as if all the blood had drained from his face. But more than that, his expression was that of a man who has just lost everything. "Ethan Hollingsworth. That's the man Matthew Brady wrote about, the one that . . . "

He let her go. "I know. Let's get the hell out of here. Now."
He hurried off without waiting to see if she followed.

Jake felt as if he had been poleaxed. The man knew him, all
right. Of course he had changed. Strength had become weakness in the years since Shiloh, and that was why the soldier
couldn't quite recognize him. Somehow he had survived and
been carried off to Andersonville. Everyone thought him dead.
But that soldier saw in that brief encounter remnants of Ethan
Hollingsworth, who was suspected of having killed his fiancée,
Lorena Waring. Remnants Jake suspected had existed within
him ever since Allie had read him the letter from Matthew
Brady.

He remembered things, terrible things that all too easily
could prove him to be that killer.

The noise of the crowd intensified until he wanted to cover
his ears and shout. Frustrated and angry, he elbowed and shouldered his way through the milling throng, moving farther and
farther ahead of Allie. What a fool he had been to think he could
remain with her and be happy. There were debts to settle and
only one way for him to settle them. He must return to Washington, D.C., and face up to the accusations, pay what he owed for
such a terrible deed as murder. He no longer had to search for his
identity, he had found it. Be careful what you pray for. Wasn't
that an old warning oft repeated by those much wiser than he?

Without waiting for Allie, he mounted the mare and rode out
of Fort Union. He would gather his sparse belongings, and this
time he would not be brought back. Not by some roving outlaw
Allie might send to fetch him, not for all her begging and pleading, not for the wishes of his own heart.

He was dismounting at the wagon when he heard her coming, the thundering hoof beats of the galloping palomino
matching the beat of his terrified heart.

Without glancing in her direction, he started to throw
together his bedroll and supplies.

She grabbed his arm, yanked at it. "What are you doing?
Where are you going?"

"Washington. I'm going home, Allie."

"No, I won't let you do that. They'll hang you."

"And well they should. I killed her."

"I will not believe that. I don't care what you say. Killing just isn't in your heart. Dammit, listen to me." She hung on him as he stood from his task, forcing him to stop or drag her along.

He gazed down into her eyes, steeled himself against the pleading, the suffering. "It's no use. I've been headed in this direction all along, Allie. Even as I rode farther away, I've been going back. We both know that. There isn't anything we can do about it."

She sighed, nibbled at her lip, glanced over her shoulder, then back at him. "All right, if that's what you have to do, then all right, but I'm going with you. And there's no way you can stop me short of shooting me."

"Dear God, Allie, don't even think a thing like that."

She touched his cheek and he flinched away, filled with sorrow for the pain he caused her with everything he did.

"Don't. Don't touch me. Don't look at me like that." He clenched both fists, lifted them from his sides as if to pummel his own chest, but held them there, rigid.

Tears poured from her eyes and she clasped his fists. It was like touching knots of iron, but she didn't pull away. "Listen to me. You are not a man who could kill. I know that just as I know that I love you more than I do life itself. Maybe in your past you were this Ethan Hollingsworth, and maybe that man you were did kill Lorena. But that man died on the battlefields of Shiloh. The soldier was right. Ethan Hollingsworth is dead and you are Jake. A gentle, caring man; the man I love. The man who has held me through the night when I didn't think I could go on, the man who asks for nothing in return for whatever he does.

"When I met you I was so filled with hatred and anger I could hardly deal with each day. You changed that for me, you made me see that life is precious. Remember how you could make me laugh with you, no matter what was going on?

You've stopped laughing, Jake, and I'm sorry for that. I want to bring back your joy, just as you brought mine to me. Don't deny me that right. For what you gave me, Jake, I want to give you something in return."

She lifted her shoulders, moved her hands along his taut arms. "So if you insist that you are going back 'home,' then I'm going with you. I'd rather you didn't try to stop me, but if you do, I'll follow you anyway. And every night when you camp, you'll see the glimmer of my fire close by, and you'll hear me cry and call your name. And in the night, after you've fallen asleep I'll come to your bed and lie beside you so you won't be alone. So I won't be alone. We've both been lonely much too long, and you can't deny me this, because I won't allow it."

He watched her in silence for a moment, his blue eyes moist. When he blinked, a single tear escaped and trickled down alongside his nose. She stood on tiptoe and kissed the droplet away. His clenched arms loosened between them, crept around her until he held her against the hammering of his heart.

She almost collapsed with relief, but he supported her and found his voice at last.

"I will not ruin your life," he said hoarsely.

"Your leaving is what will ruin it. Just hold me, love me, be with me. Together we'll figure something out."

"God, Allie, you are something, you know that?"

"Of course I am. But then, you are, too."

"Well, I must be, or how could a woman like you want to keep me around?"

She chuckled, her throat still raw with tears.

It was getting dark and Jake gazed over her shoulder at the trail north, the road which he ought to be traveling. He could wait. For now, he could stay with her. But sooner or later he would have to go back and face the consequences of that dark man's actions. He wished he could simply remember it all and how it had happened, then he wouldn't feel so bad paying for

Samantha Lee

the deed. As it was, he felt like an innocent man would pay for
the killing done by a man who for all intents and purposes, was
dead. Allie was right when she said that. The murderous Ethan
Hollingsworth was dead, but that didn't release the Jake he had
become from guilt.

Once he and Allie were settled in Santa Fe and she had her
business going, and maybe didn't even need him so much anymore, he would head back east and take care of this business.
For he knew if he didn't, it would haunt him the rest of his life,
and hers too.

276

Chapter Eighteen

On the final lap to Santa Fe, Allie and Jake spent incredibly happy days. As if they had both shut out the truth, they moved into a fantasy world in which they worked and played, laughed, cried and made love. She took photographs of him that only she would ever see, and after a while he took some of her. And he learned the business happily, denying the possibility that he would never practice it with her.

Together they would huddle under the black drape of the camera, so close together they might have been one, her showing him how to set up each shot through the lens, him kissing her lightly at every opportunity. And when the heat from the noonday sun soaked their bodies in perspiration, they would find a secluded creek and bathe each other, sometimes getting so erotically involved they would almost miss the departure of the train. As water became scarce, their baths were performed around a wash pan after dark, and most times the ritual led to another, even more ancient one.

It was an idyllic, achingly brief time, for Santa Fe appeared much too soon, as far as Jake was concerned. For reasons he didn't completely understand, arrival at their destination filled him with dread. Something would change forever there, he sensed.

On the other hand, Allie looked forward to a home of their own and a business together, never dreaming Jake had other plans.

On the last night on the trail, with Santa Fe just over the next rise, haircuts were in order. All around the camp, men performed the chores on one another followed by trimming beards or shaving.

Allie watched the activities that were obviously traditional for those traveling the caravan, then rose without saying anything and went to the wagon, where she dug out a pair of cutting shears. Snipping them loudly, she approached a wide-eyed Jake.

"Don't worry," she told him, "I won't take too much off. You've been needing this for a long while."

He scrubbed a hand over the top of his head, recalling the thin patches of hair that had adorned his filthy scalp when he'd come out of Andersonville. Since then he'd been scrupulous about keeping it clean, combed and uncut.

Allie reached for a long strand, held it out and snipped the scissors in the air.

He flinched, shut his eyes and shuddered.

"You're shaggy as a buffalo," she teased. "Just let me at this."

He pulled away, gripped her wrist. "Okay, on one condition. You cut mine, I cut yours."

She tossed her palomino mane. "Hey, no. I'm a woman. Women are supposed to have long hair. It's our crowning glory."

He hunched his head down into his shoulders. "What about my crowning glory?"

She giggled like a girl. "You really want to talk about that just now?" *Snip, snip* went the scissors.

He cringed. "Never mind. You win, but I just want you to remember one thing."

Stretching a long strand of dark hair between two fingers, she asked, "What's that?" and snipped off several inches.

"I love you, and I wouldn't do anything to hurt you. I just hope you feel the same."

Frivolously she kissed the top of his head, and made another cut.

"Ouch!"

"That didn't hurt. Don't be such a baby. Hold still."

"You're balding me."

"No, I promise, I'm not. Just a little trim. You'll see. And when we're done I'll give you a shave."

"Wait a minute. I may be dumb enough to sit still for you chopping off all my hair, but if you think I'm going to let you scrape my face with a sharp instrument, you're crazy."

She moved her fingers through the soft, shiny hair. Remembering how it felt lying across her bare breasts when they made love, she couldn't resist placing a gentle kiss just above his ear.

"Hey, none of that. You'll get distracted." His head tilted forward some more and she put her palm under his chin to lift it.

"Allie," he said in a soft, faraway voice.

Concentrating, tongue between her lips, she didn't answer right away.

"Allie," he repeated, more urgently.

She felt the shudder go through him as he tensed. "What? What is it?"

"My God, Allie. I just remembered something."

She took him by the shoulders to keep him from falling on his face. This time, though, he did no such thing, but instead sat straighter and grabbed her wrist, turning to stare at her.

"I just saw Ethan Hollingsworth. Lying . . . he . . . he was dying. Oh, God, Allie, he's dead. I saw him plain as I see you this minute. And there was gunfire, cannons, men shouting, screaming in agony, smoke everywhere. He held out a hand and he was giving me something. I reached for him, I actually saw my own hand hovering over him, and then there was a terrible explosion."

"Go on."

He shrugged, licked dry lips. "That's all. It was all gone in that brilliant flash, but I felt . . . I felt this terrible pain in my leg, in my head. Allie, he died and I was there." He wrapped his arms around her and she felt him trembling with excitement. "Don't you understand what that means?"

Without answering, she held him that way for a long while before he spoke again, his voice soft in her ear.

"I would have left a long time ago if I hadn't loved you so much, if I hadn't felt that you were the only connection I have in this world. Everything else is locked up back there in the darkness somewhere. I've been selfish enough to hang onto you, and that's not fair, I know. I want so much to do things for you, to make your life better, easier, not to be always the one who needs . . . who needs . . . always, I need you.

"But do you see what this could mean? I've never felt like this man, Ethan. It hasn't seemed right somehow, even though I do keep remembering her . . . Lorena. And something terrible happening. Do you think maybe I'm not him, maybe I'm someone else? Do you think that's possible?"

She kissed his stubbled jaw. "You are my Jake, that's who you are, and I love you. I need you as much as you need me. I thought we had settled that. You're probably going to start remembering a lot of things now that you've quit fighting it. Wonder why that is, Jake? Before you knew anything about what might be your past you fought every memory by blacking out. I really think it was your way of stopping the return of those memories that may be too horrible for you to face. Now that you know about Lorena and the murder, the awful things that happened—"

He stopped her with a kiss. "Now that I love you." He moved back a little, cocked his head. "Do you really think that's what caused the blackouts? That I just didn't want to relive it all again?"

"Oh, I don't know, but you haven't had one in a long while. And a few minutes ago, you acted just like you always did when one was coming on, only instead you recovered a memory. What I really think is that I'd better finish cutting your hair because you're going to look pretty silly with one side six inches longer than the other."

He nodded and returned to the log on which he'd been sitting. "Go ahead, then. Cut it all off. It's you who has to look at me."

She worked in silence until piles of shorn hair black as crow's wings lay scattered on the ground around their feet.

Putting the shears aside, she combed through the shoulder-length locks that hung in soft waves. "There, you look wonderful."

She fetched a mirror and rocked back and forth, arms clasped behind her while he studied himself. When he lay aside the glass he was smiling, for he had seen not Ethan but himself, whoever he might be. Without a word he turned, picked up the scissors and started toward her. "Want it this length or shorter?"

She yelped and darted behind the wagon.

He laid down the shears and went after her, catching her up in a bear hug that lifted her off her feet.

Arms tight around his neck, she thought she had never been happier. "Oh, Jake, we're almost home. Almost home."

"I know, my sweet, I know." Once again the apprehension took hold, but he shoved it away. He might not be this Ethan fellow after all. There was hope, and he clung to it.

"There's a church there in Santa Fe. A very old church. We can be married there."

When he didn't say anything, but lowered her to her feet, she let go and gazed up at him. Clouds shuttered his blue eyes, his expression was grim.

"What? What is it? Tell me."

He shook his head, kissed her on the forehead. "I wish . . . oh, it's nothing. I was just thinking."

"Well, don't. That can be dangerous. As soon as we find a suitable storefront for the studio and get things set up, people will start to come in for their portraits. We'll go out on the desert and up in the mountains and take stereoscopic pictures. I know they'll be popular back East and we'll make lots of money and have lots of children and be very, very happy."

She knew she was babbling, but couldn't stop herself. Smiling, he gazed into her eyes with adoration.

Seeing his expression, she broke off in the middle of her next thought, cupped his jaw. "Don't shave till morning. I like the feel of your whiskers on my bare skin."

That afternoon they rode in the wagon seat together on the long downslope that led into Santa Fe. From all around them bull whackers popped their whips and shouted loud greetings.

As they passed through the great arched gateway to the city, the cry went out, *"Los Americanos! Los carros! La entrada de la caravana!"*

Barefoot, shouting children ran beside the moving wagons, their feet slapping on the firm red clay of the road. The houses were made of mud, as were the walls that surrounded the grassless yards. In some, cactus grew and trees lined what appeared to be canals trickling with water.

Allie gasped when she saw groups of Mexican women in their colorful dresses and long, loose black hair puffing away at thin, brown cigars.

On and on went the caravan, working its slow, creaking way into the center of town and to the Palace of the Governors. A covered walkway surrounded the wide plaza. Defoe drew up his wagon and climbed down to make the mandatory call at the palace for customs and duty payment. Trading wagons stretched far behind him in a long, colorful line.

They had safely crossed on the Santa Fe Trail. Allie could scarcely contain her excitement.

282

"What do you want to do first?" Jake asked.

"Let's get down and walk around. I want to see everything. I want to taste the food and breathe the air and smell the wonderful smells. I thought it would be hotter, being on the desert, but feel that breeze."

"It's because we are so high, ma'am," came a familiar voice.

She shuddered. Eli Martin, dressed in his best finery, tipped his hat. "I am happy to say we all made it in one piece. And your companion has rejoined you. I would be pleased to buy you both a refreshing cold drink in the cantina. I would like to speak to you about that little matter we discussed earlier."

"What matter was that?" Jake asked.

"Nothing we are interested in," Allie snapped. "Come on, Jake, let's get down and look around."

Deliberately she turned her back on Martin and followed Jake off the opposite side of the wagon.

Eli watched them go, then drew a long, thin cigar from his pocket and lit it, eyes squinting against the smoke. Somehow he had to eliminate this man from her life and remain without blame. If she had a hint that he was responsible for Jake's arrest, she would never forgive him. He could kiss all his plans goodbye.

He would have Allison Caine, and this time nothing would stand in his way.

Jake tucked Allie's hand in the crook of his elbow and they moved through the milling crowd. "What was that all about?"

"The man's a fool and a crook, stealing land from these people. Someone should stop him." One day soon she would tell Jake all there was to tell about Eli, but not yet, not on this glorious day. It was too perfect to ruin.

"Perhaps we ought to inform someone in authority," Jake said.

"That's not a bad idea, though I doubt it would do much good. He claims it's been going on for years, stealing from the land grants given these people hundreds of years ago. I would assume they all know about it and look the other way."

"Or can't stop it," he added.

They moved slowly past the artisans, their wares spread on colorful blankets along the walkway in front of the governor's palace. Silver and turquoise jewelry of both Indian and Mexican design gleamed against the handwoven patterns of the woolen blankets. Masses of people touched and bartered with the artists sitting against the wall behind their displays.

"Let's look at the stores." She took Jake's arm and they moved from the covered walkway on down the street, strolling past small store fronts, many of which were empty. Occasionally an iron gate opened into a small garden off the square and within, an adobe dwelling.

As they cut across the road toward the center of the plaza, one of the traders from the caravan drew his wagon up before an empty store. He and a few Mexican youths began to unload cargo, precious wares from the Americanos, into the store.

"Let's go talk to him," Allie said.

Together they approached the trader, whom they had known slightly during the trip. He was a friendly but gruff fellow, a big man with sandy hair and a mud-colored beard. He seemed only too glad to stop and chat with them while his helpers continued to unload crates and kegs of hardware: nails, saws, hoes, spades and knives.

He directed them to the proper officials, and by nightfall they had arranged to rent a small hacienda set back in a tiny, overgrown yard. They got it cheap because most traders preferred the stores that opened directly onto the covered walkway. This one had a high wall, an iron gate and an unkempt yard to pass through before one could enter the house itself. It was little more than twelve feet wide, but probably twenty feet or so deep. They would sleep in the back on their bedrolls.

She gathered several grown boys eager for work to help them unload the precious cargo of glass plates and equipment, and when it came time to eat supper, they cooked it on a small fire in the yard. Across the way a woman made large round loaves of bread and slid them inside an outdoor oven using a long wooden paddle. Allie decided she would learn how to make bread in that way as soon as possible. The fragrant aroma of burning pinon and baking bread seasoned the cooling night air.

Earlier Jake had bought some delightful fruit that resembled elongated peaches with no fuzz on the skin. He laughed when she asked him what it was. "I have no idea. I can't remember what they called it."

After they finished eating he sliced one of the golden smooth fruits in half and shared it with her. When she raised it to her mouth sticky juice ran into her palm and down the side of her arm. The slick, sweet pulp filled her mouth with a delightful, tart taste, its coolness bathing her throat.

"Isn't this wonderful? We're going to have to learn the language as quickly as possible. I love listening to it, but I need to know what everyone is saying. They're so carefree. Oh, isn't this a beautiful place? I can't wait to begin taking photographs."

Jake laughed and leaned toward her, mouth gleaming with juice. "Yes, it is indeed a wonderful place, but only because we're here together. Any place would be wonderful."

"That's true," she replied. "But not so wonderful as this."

They had been there a little over a week when the lawman from back East came to town and fulfilled Jake's earlier premonition.

Allie saw him ride in late one evening, and at the time thought little about it. Only later, after all the trouble, did she remember even seeing him. Things happened like that sometimes, she thought. Just crept up on you unawares because life had a bad habit of waiting until you least expected trouble before swatting you flat with it.

Oddly enough, it was Eli Martin who spilled the beans, stepping into the cool, dim interior of her studio early the next morning. She was not happy to see him even before he made his pronouncement.

He just moved right into it without much more than a hello. "Lawman from back East rode in last evening. Looking for a fella name of Ethan Hollingsworth. Says he's wanted for murder." Martin paused a moment, glanced at her with his penetrating eyes, then went on. "Too bad you didn't see fit to heed my earlier warning."

Allie couldn't find her voice. She opened her mouth to shout at Eli. No one could make her angry so fast as this man who had once stolen her love. Nothing came out but a croak. It was as if the floor had fallen out from under her, the air that supplied her lungs had been sucked off somewhere and her heart had ceased to beat.

Where was Jake? What had he said when he limped off this morning? Something about . . . dammit, she couldn't think. She could remember very clearly the spark in his blue eyes, the way he had turned around one last time and given her a wave and how she had wanted to shout with joy because they were together.

"Are you feeling poorly?" Martin asked, and peered at her solicitously. "Could I get you a drink?"

"Out," she finally croaked. "Get out." And then before he could leave, she asked, "Did he say who he is, who sent him? I mean, does he know this Ethan Hollingsworth?"

Eli grinned, an evil sneer that did not express gaiety. "Knows him on sight. And he has a picture. Ain't very good. But I expect he'll get his man, don't you?"

She swallowed noisily, wanting rid of him instantly, but at the same time needing to hear what he knew. "Did you see it?"

He raised a bushy eyebrow. "It?"

"The damned photograph."

"Ah, yes, that. Well, I wasn't exactly being included in on the discussion. You might say I just happened to be nearby."

"Eavesdropping, you mean."

He nodded once, curtly. "Whatever. At any rate, I would think you might notify your friend that he'd best make himself scarce for a few days. Seems I was right. He killed a young woman a few years back." Once again that penetrating stare. "I tried to tell you, or have you known all along, and that just made him more attractive to you? Listen to me, Allison. I'll help you if you'll let me. I'll help you find a place for him to hide out till this is over."

Pain shot through her chest. "Get out of here, now, you bastard. You stay away from us, from both of us, or I'm liable to shoot you myself." She turned so he wouldn't see that she was near tears. Clenching her hands together to stop their trembling, she repeated her request. "I said leave. This is none of your business. None at all. Why do you keep bothering me?"

He shrugged dramatically. "I'm just the messenger. Just remember what I said. If you need help. You are misjudging my motives because you're still angry about what happened. Think about it."

When at last she turned around, he was gone.

They won't find him, she thought. He really doesn't look much like that picture, the one Brady sent. No one could even recognize him from it. And hadn't Jake said that he no longer believed he was this man, Ethan? Eli said the lawman knew Ethan on sight. He would see right away that Jake wasn't him. Wouldn't he? Her mouth felt dry as the desert wind.

She moved to the open doorway and squinted into the morning sun. Where was Jake? Why hadn't he come back? Suppose they had caught him already. Seen him out walking the street, taking a bit of fresh air. Pounced on him, shoved him to the ground, beat him mercilessly. Why had this happened now? Only this morning they had talked about getting married soon, in the Chapel of St. Francis. Now he could be dead and she wouldn't even know it.

God, she had to stop this, had to find him, warn him so he could get away, so they could get away. Together. She moved along the square, peering into each darkened interior, greeting merchants vaguely, asking if they'd seen Jake, then moving on.

He had left on foot, to take a walk, he'd said. To buy some pomegranates and mangoes, he'd added, and kissed her and then that little jaunty wave goodbye. They kept their horses at the stable until they could find pasture to rent. Maybe he had heard about the lawman, and already ridden away. But without seeing her again? She couldn't believe he would do that. Still, it was possible, if he thought he was running for his life. In that case, he would come back for her as soon as he could.

After one complete turn around the square, she arrived once more at the door of the studio. Even as she entered she knew the place was empty.

Behind her someone cleared his throat and she jumped, heart drumming until she felt faint.

"Excuse me, senorita."

With a composure that surprised her, she turned to face the visitor. "Yes? May I help you?"

She faced Major Don Juan Sena, the local law enforcement officer whom she had met casually a few times on the street. With him was a small man in dusty clothing sporting a badge on his chest, a six shooter on one hip and a rifle held casually at his side.

"Don Juan Sena. I am the sheriff of Santa Fe."

"Yes, yes, we've met."

He nodded, turned to his companion. "This is—"

The smaller man interrupted, "Samuel L. Hooten. United States Marshal, ma'am. We're looking for a man by the name of Ethan Hollingsworth. A Mr. Eli Martin said you could tell us where he is."

Allie backed away, the bottom falling out of her world.

Jake moved along the back of the stores that fronted on the square. In case Allie had a client, he didn't want to barge in at the front, so he shoved the back door open a crack to peer in. If no one was there with Allie, he would rush in and put his arms around her, draw her so close to his heart neither could catch a breath.

The mutter of men's voices drew him up short and he listened. It didn't take long for him to realize what had happened.

They had come after the killer Ethan Hollingsworth, just as he had expected ever since he and Allie arrived in Santa Fe.

Inside, he heard her speak sharply to the two men, the sound of tears in her voice.

He didn't wait to hear more, but moved away quietly, not even bothering to close the door. His first thought was to head for the stables, saddle the mare and ride out. Yet no matter the danger, he would not simply abandon Allie without a word. She feared that over anything else, and he couldn't do it to her.

Instead he made his way toward the Chapel of St. Francis. He would send her word somehow and she could come to him there. Together they would figure out what to do, though he already had a sense of what that would have to be.

Carefully he moved across the courtyard and slipped inside the small adobe chapel. For an instant his eyes saw nothing but sunlight-bathed walls at the front of the church. Then they adjusted to the dimness.

Wooden pews sat on either side of a single aisle that led to the altar. The floor was clay, worn unevenly firm by the feet of the faithful over the past two hundred years or more. On the adobe walls to his right and left hung hand-carved symbols, each with a candle sputtering beneath. The thick fragrance of burning wax filled his nostrils. Across the front of the church was a railing and hanging on the front wall, an enormous tapestry depicting saintly figures in golds and blues and reds. A Mexican woman, head and shoulders covered by a black mantilla, knelt at the altar. Otherwise the church was empty.

Awe stricken and breathless, Jake stood there yet a moment longer, eyes drawn upward toward the gigantic hand-hewn logs that ran the length of the high ceiling. He was surrounded by a tranquility of such enormity he could scarcely bear it. Then without warning, he heard Lorena's voice, cracking the silence as if she stood next to him. He almost turned to look, but found he couldn't, for he was being drawn forward by an unseen force he couldn't fight. As he moved the woman at the altar rose, rearranged the black lace over her hair and started toward him.

Instead of growing closer, she reached out both hands to him, then spread them wide and disappeared.

He nearly fell to his knees, reached out and grabbed the smooth back of one of the pews to keep from going down.

"Lorena?" he whispered.

"Lanse," came a disembodied voice. The name bounced through the empty church and back at him from all sides. And then immediately following, "I forgive you."

"Forgive you, forgive you, forgive you," came at him from everywhere.

He clamped both hands over his ears and swallowed a hollow shout that burned his throat.

Eyes squeezed shut, he clearly saw Lorena's tear-streaked face, heard her say, "I'll never forgive you for this. I never want to see you again. I love him and you can't stop me. Go away and never come back."

He stumbled again, this time fell to both knees on the hard, uneven floor. Ignoring the vicious pain in his leg, he hunched forward, shoulders heaving.

What did it mean? What had he done to her? And why had she called out her brother's name and not his? Lansford Waring was surely the Lanse to whom she referred. Frantically, he looked around the empty church. The apparition was gone, if it had ever been there at all. Had he gone mad and conceived the entire episode? If so, what was next? He had no idea where he should go, what he should do.

Perhaps he ought to just give it all up. Here and now, in this holy place where he might at last find peace.

Chapter Nineteen

In an effort to compose herself following the marshal's question about Ethan Hollingsworth, Allie offered the men a glass of cool water from a pottery pitcher and took one herself. As she drank she thought she heard a sound from the back of the studio, and darted an anxious glance in that direction.

Don't come back now. Jake. Don't. The plea obviously was answered, for no one was there.

When she didn't reply right away to Hooten's question about Ethan Hollingsworth, he took a step forward, handed her back his empty cup. Small as he was, she felt intimidated by his power. Whatever action he took could very well alter her life forever.

"You are?" He had the robust voice of a much larger man.

"I? My . . . I'm sorry, it's just that you startled me. You'll have to forgive me. I was busy and didn't hear you come in." She held out a hand and tried to appear friendly and unconcerned. "I'm Allison Caine, from Missouri. I've only been here a short time. Did you want your photograph taken? You'd make a wonderful subject."

He glanced around, appeared confused by her question.

"Sorry, no. We're here on business. The Hollingsworth matter." His tone verged on a sharp command.

"I'm afraid I don't . . . " She trailed off, waited for his reaction. What more could she say?

The man took a photograph from his pocket, not like the one Brady had sent, but another clearly of the same man. Ethan Hollingsworth, hat cocked to one side and a rakish grin visible from within the dark beard.

Her heart lurched and she could not speak as she studied the photograph. He looked nothing like Jake did now, but . . . no doubt the war had changed him, and the beard disguised his facial structure. She simply didn't know anymore.

"Well, do you know him?" Hooten obviously had little patience.

When she cleared her throat it sounded grotesque to her ears, as if she might be getting ready to spit on Hooten. She peered up into his face, back at the photo. "I . . . no, I don't. Who is he?"

"Mr. Martin said he resembles the gentleman who traveled here with you. I believe he said his name was Jake. I wonder, could I speak to him? It won't take but a moment to clear this up."

"I . . . no, I . . . he isn't here."

"Could you tell me where I could find him?"

"It isn't him," she lied, eyes pooling.

Marshal Hooten sucked at his teeth. "Good, then I will finish my business with the two of you quickly. If you'll just tell me where I can find this Jake."

"I don't . . . I don't know."

"He has left the city, then?"

"I . . . no, of course not. He merely went for a walk and hasn't returned."

"Ah." Hooten glared at her. His granite stare told her he knew she was lying.

She tried to sound calm. "I'll tell him you're looking for him."

"Tell him it would be in his best interest to present himself at Sheriff Sena's office the moment he returns." Hooten again touched the butt of his well-used Colt. "If he does not, I will find him. Would you tell him that, ma'am?"

Pain rose in her chest and she clenched both fists hard against her thighs, nodding her head but unable to speak.

The men left without bidding her good day.

Her head reeled; apprehension sucked air from her lungs. She had to find Jake, warn him, help him get away.

Hurrying to the back where she kept the Colt, she hastily buckled it on and stepped through the back door. Avoiding the plaza, she approached the stables and eased inside. After a few moments her eyes grew accustomed to the darkness, and she checked the stalls. Both the palomino and the mare were there.

If for some reason Jake had learned of the marshal's arrival and left town, he'd done it on foot. Because of his bad leg, she doubted he would do that.

The boy who watched the stable said the owner was next door at the cantina, but she understood very little else he said.

With a few hand signals and her poor Spanish she solicited his aid in saddling Jake's mare while she was busy with the palomino. A few minutes later she led the horses along the back alley to the studio and tied them there. She soon had supplies and bedrolls tied on, and moved one last time through the cool, dim studio. The thick adobe walls kept the room pleasant all day, but the front window let in very little light. She had managed to procure a couple of chairs and they stood in shadow along with other pieces of equipment and the camera on its tripod.

How could she leave before she even got her business started? How could she stay here without Jake? She could do neither, but she must choose, and the thought grieved her beyond reason. When her father died she had learned the true meaning of stark loneliness, even welcomed it for a time, but she knew that she wanted never to experience such a thing again.

When Jake returned they would ride away, maybe go up into the mountains, or head south for Mexico. She would not let him go alone, and she would not remain here alone. She might as well cut out her own heart as do either. They were each half of a whole. If he suffered so did she, and he felt the same. The single being they had become could not survive without both of its parts. She could not wait for him to come—she must find him, and soon.

Knuckles rattled on the back door, a furtive, almost scratchy sound. It was Jake!

She flung open the door to face Eli Martin.

"No!" she shouted, and tried to slam the door against him, but he was too quick and blocked it, forcing his way inside before letting it close.

"I've come to help you, Allison. Don't be a fool."

"Help me? You don't want to help me."

"Yes, yes I do. Listen to me." He took her shoulders in a tight grip, but she refused to look at him. "I'll help your Jake escape. Take me to him and I'll get him out of town and on his way to Mexico."

"Why would you do that?"

His grin was sly. "For you, Allison. I'd do it for you, if you stay here with me. You'll only slow him down. He'll get killed somewhere because he's worried about protecting you. An outlaw on the run doesn't need a woman."

She twisted in his grasp. "No, I won't do that."

"They'll kill him, Allison. Sena and Hooten. Look at you. You know what I say is true. They'll corner him somewhere in Santa Fe and shoot him down like a mad animal. At least with me he'll have a chance."

"You bastard." She spat the words into his face and kicked him in the shins.

He cringed, but held his ground. "Of course, my dear. But nevertheless, you have no choice if you want him to live."

"I'd rather burn in hell than spend a minute with you."

"God, Allison, you've become quite the spitfire. I can see taming you will be most interesting and enjoyable." He laughed. "If I live through it."

"You won't live to see it!" She darted around him, tried to get out the door, but he grabbed her arm.

"I'm the only chance he has, Allison. Take me to him. I'll get a wagon, smuggle him out of town, meet you somewhere, anywhere you say. You bring his mount and supplies. You can tell him goodbye and watch him ride away. Safe and alive. You stay with me. It's the best deal you'll be offered today. They're out there looking for him this very minute."

Her throat filled and she couldn't speak. Anger and despair drove her to distraction. She choked out a reply. "I don't know where he is."

"Oh, surely, Allison, you don't expect me to believe that."

"I don't care if you believe it. It's the truth."

He regarded her through squinted lids, finally nodded. "Find him, then. Surely you have some ideas."

She tried to think, to swallow all emotions and concentrate. She'd find him all right, and they'd get away. Where would he have gone? The evening before he had talked of the beauty of the local churches. He had even wondered aloud if in his forgotten life he might have been religious. And they had discussed the chapel of St. Francis and their plans to wed there in a few weeks. Could he possibly have gone there? It would be like Jake, and it was a place to start.

"All right, I'll see if I can find him," she agreed. It would get rid of him, at least temporarily.

Eli could see he wasn't going to get any more out of her. He'd just have to follow her and play it by ear. He'd be damned if he'd lose her. If she found Jake, that crazy son of a bitch Ethan would kill him without blinking an eye and he'd be clear of any blame in her eyes.

"You make the arrangements with him, then meet me back here and I'll have a wagon ready," he told her.

Samantha Lee

Without replying, she hurried out into the plaza.

As she headed for the chapel she noticed Sheriff Sena and
Marshal Hooten moving along in the deep shadow cast by
buildings on the opposite side of the street. Before they spotted
her she moved into the doorway of a storefront. They turned a
corner and disappeared. At that moment she spotted Jake. He
crept from behind a nearby adobe wall and scurried into the
small chapel, moving as if he already knew he was being
hunted. Rather than call out, she hastened to follow.

Inside the church she waited a few seconds for her eyes to
grow accustomed to the darkness between herself and the
golden light that splashed through the windows across the altar.
His shadowy form moved to the altar and knelt there.

Before she could join him he leaped to his feet, spread both
arms and staggered backward to bump into the first row of
pews. Abruptly, he shouted something and stumbled frantically
up the aisle, never turning his back on the altar, but feeling his
way with both hands.

Allie froze when he clamped both hands over his ears and
fell to his knees, for she'd seen the gun belted around his waist.
How out of place it looked, that weapon of death on his hip.
Horror nailed her to the spot. She couldn't make a sound or
move.

Jake heard a secretive scrape of boot soles in the darkness at his
back. An ethereal light bathed the altar where the vision of his
sister Lorena had vanished, and out of the smoke of battle, the
stench of the slaughterhouse that had been Shiloh, walked his
boyhood friend, Ethan. He held out a clenched hand, opened it
to reveal the small carte de visite of Lorena. The one Lanse had
taken off him at Shiloh.

"Why did you betray me, Ethan?" Jake whispered, voice
hoarse with tears. "Why did you kill her?"

The man regarded him in eerie silence. He could hear his
own breathing, count the heartbeats thumping against his tem-

ple. For an instant he prayed to be caught up, to rise and disappear into the light with Lorena. Put an end to this nightmare.

He palmed the butt of the pistol, pointed it at the illusion that strode toward him. "I told you if you hurt Lorena I'd kill you."

"I didn't hurt her. She begged me for what I had to give, just like I said she would. It didn't hurt a bit. I guess you wanted a little of that yourself, is why you're so mad."

The old anger flared, nearly blinding Jake. "I should have killed you on the spot."

"But instead you told Lorena, and what did she do, dear Lanse?"

Told him she'd never forgive him if he interfered. He remembered clearly the scene, and leaving her lying on the bed sobbing, brokenhearted. He never saw her again.

"Why don't you kill me now, Lanse?" The question echoed from the high walls.

He raised the pistol from its holster, peered into the shadows of the little chapel. "Get back, stay away. I'm armed," he yelled.

Allie found her voice at last, called his name. He was making so much noise, someone would hear. She crept toward him, saying his name over and over under her breath.

Before she could guess at what he might do, he turned and aimed straight at her.

She ducked behind a pew. He wouldn't shoot her, he couldn't. Could he? Did she even know this man well enough to answer that question? When he didn't fire, she eased up enough to see what he was doing. At that moment two men burst through the doors of the church.

"Everyone hold it. I'm a United States marshal. Just hold it, and no one will get hurt."

Jake shouted, "I didn't kill her," and jerked off a shot toward the back of the church where the two men had entered.

Immediately two shots boomed out in response.

Allie jumped out into the aisle, putting herself between the lawmen and Jake, and screamed. "Stop, don't. Please don't shoot him."

"Allie? Allie, get out of the way," Jake yelled. He had no intention of killing the lawmen, but he couldn't let them hurt Allie or take him. Memories of the horrors of Andersonville prison pounded in his brain like bleeding wounds. He would not live a day in prison, that he knew with absolute certainty.

With a shout he shouldered Allie aside, raised the pistol as if to fire at the lawmen.

Scrambling to get her footing, Allie grabbed out, felt the fabric of his shirt sleeve slip through her fingers and threw herself at him with an unholy shriek. "Don't shoot him. Jake, stop, please stop. Oh, dear God, won't you all stop."

Miraculously, she tripped him, sent him tumbling into a pew. That distracted the lawmen and for a split second they didn't fire. Then it was too late because she was once more between them and their target. She threw herself on top of Jake where he lay sprawled in the wooden pew.

He couldn't catch his breath and they lay there a few seconds before Allie rolled off and came to her knees.

Between gasps for air, he asked, "You okay? What were you thinking of? They would have killed you."

"I . . . know. That's . . . all . . . I . . . "

"Oh, Allie, I'm so damned sorry."

Hooten and Sena stood over them, guns still drawn, but no longer threatening to pull the triggers.

Jake stirred, sat up and turned glimmering eyes toward her. He drew in a jagged breath. "I won't go to prison. Allie, I can't." With a trembling hand he jammed the barrel of the pistol under his jaw.

"Stop that," she cried, and knocked it aside before he could thumb back the hammer.

Half crawling, he stumbled to his feet and made for the front of the church. Hooten shouted, took off after him.

"Leave him be," Sena yelled. "There's no other way out."

Relentlessly both men tracked him down the aisle, and a shaken Allie followed.

At the altar Jake dropped to his knees, and the light shone around him like a halo.

"Oh, dear God, I remember. Allie, I remember."

He twisted around, back against the railing.

She ran to him and without rising he wrapped both arms around her waist and buried his face in her stomach. The heat of his breath soaked through her clothing, she threaded long fingers in his hair and held on as if he might vanish at any moment.

"Allie?" The whisper echoed eerily in a stillness so dense they might have all been holding their breath. "It wasn't me . . . he . . . did . . . it. I received a letter from my father telling me. It must have been a few weeks after I saw Ethan dead at Shiloh, and took Lorena's picture. That's when I was wounded, while I was reading my father's letter, not earlier when I found Ethan. Oh, God, Allie. He told me about how they'd found her body, and everyone thought Ethan had killed her, but he'd disappeared." He hugged her tightly, couldn't go on.

Only seconds ago he had tried to kill himself, now he sounded almost normal. Or what passed for normal with Jake. Relief poured through her and at the same time fear. He wasn't Ethan, but would he ever be Jake again?

"Please, you've got to help him," she said to Sena, who hovered behind her, regarding Jake with puzzlement. "That's not him in that picture. I swear it isn't. Look at him, take a close look."

Sena appeared to be ignoring her, but Hooten moved around to grab Jake's other arm, the one she wasn't hanging on to.

She wanted to fall down on her knees beside Jake and pray in this hallowed place, plead with God to spare this man and give him peace, but so much was happening so fast.

The marshal spoke. "Sheriff, let's get these people out of here. Give me a hand with this one."

Jerked free of Jake's grasp and placed aside by Sena, anger overcame her better sense. "Damn you, you bastard," she said, and punched the sheriff square in the mouth. She had little time to be amazed at her own action. Pain shot up her arm and the hand began to throb. She hugged it against her chest and sucked air noisily.

Even as Sena let out a belated howl, blood poured from his nose and soaked the front of his uniform. Jake pulled free of Hooten and put his arms around Allie. The marshal grabbed at Jake, then moved to the aid of the sheriff, then turned once more toward Jake. Clearly he couldn't make up his mind which was more important. When Jake continued to stand still and fuss over Allie's busted knuckles rather than attempting to escape, Hooten went to his companion and tended to him.

Allie and Jake waited, arms around each other until the confusion abated and Sena concentrated on his broken nose.

Hooten finally turned his attention back to the couple. "Now, young lady, you behave yourself and let us take this man with us. You come along and we'll get things straightened out. And it might be a good idea if you gave me that Colt you're carrying in case you decide to do more than belt someone."

She stepped from Jake's arms, gave him a tentative smile and handed over her weapon. Sena on one side, Hooten on the other, they escorted their prisoner from the church. Allie trailed along behind. They would soon see. Everything would be all right. Oh, God, what if he didn't love her? What if, when this was over and settled, Jake no longer existed?

Her heart went out to him as he limped along between the two men. After what he had been through, the threat of jail must be terrifying for him.

The odd entourage made its way to the governor's palace, attracting a good deal of attention. Several children followed and peered through the glass window of the jail. Allie didn't spot Eli anywhere in the crowd. A doctor was fetched, and he soon had Allie and the sheriff patched up. Both looked as if they'd come through one hell of a battle.

300

Holding a white handkerchief to his swollen, purple nose, Sena abraided Hooten, his words barely discernible from between folds of the blood-stained cloth.

"This man must be placed behind bars immediately. He should not be out here with the young lady. It is clear that she loves him very much. Ah, such a wonderful thing, to be so loved by the beautiful senorita that she is willing to, how is it you say? To sock me and go to jail for him.

"You are one lucky man, senor," Sena said to Jake. "But I fear that we must still arrest you."

Allie grabbed Jake with her unbandaged left hand, as if that might somehow keep him from being imprisoned. She was surprised that they weren't going to throw her in a cell too, considering that she had busted a lawman right in the mouth. Sena acted as if he actually admired her, even though he sported a broken nose.

Hooten objected. "I don't think that will be necessary, sir. This man is not Ethan Hollingsworth. I knew him personally. He was a good two hands shorter, his hair some lighter . . . even the bone structure isn't right and the eye color certainly isn't. The difference in coloration isn't evident in a black-and-white likeness with a beard on the face, but I knew the man, and I tell you, this isn't him." In the gloom of the office the marshal glared insolently at Jake as if he blamed him for not being the one he sought. "Just who the hell are you, sir?"

Grim lipped, Jake didn't answer. Allie made a fist of her good hand and glared at Hooten.

Sena moved to hold her back. "Now, now, young lady. We know you are distraught, but you must not hit this man as well."

Jake nearly burst out laughing. A great dark cloud had lifted from his soul, and he grew dizzy with relief. He nodded and hung on to her arm. "I know who I am. I remembered, back there in the church."

"I told you. I said you weren't him," Allie insisted.

Hooten ignored her, stared at Jake. "If this isn't one hell of a note. I come all the way out here to this godforsaken country to pick up a killer and I'm to go home empty-handed? What about you, young woman? What do you have to say?"

Jake prodded her in the ribs and said low in her ear, "Want to bust him one, too?"

She felt like laughing and crying, all at once. He sounded the same. The world suddenly looked like a much brighter place.

Squaring her jaw, she said, "Tell them who you are." *And tell me you still love me.* She swallowed the silent plea and waited.

"Ethan is dead. I'm Lansford Waring. Lorena was my sister."

The marshal studied him, then said, "Come over here in the light where I can have a closer look. I'm damned if you ain't right, I think. But that can't be. Lanse Waring disappeared, was assumed killed in the war. If he had lived he would have come home by now, unless . . . "

"Unless he had no memory," Allie supplied.

The room grew quiet, broken only by the sound of breathing.

In the tiny hotel room across from the jail, Eli nervously watched the man with whom he'd made a devil's bargain. Ethan would shoot him on the spot if he ever guessed Eli actually had no solid proof Ethan had killed Lorena.

Ethan Hollingsworth kicked a chair aside and cursed, then pulled his weapon. "I ought to shoot you where you stand, you stupid bungler. Now he's in the hands of the law. How hard would it have been to shoot him? Be done with this whole mess."

"You won't shoot me. You'll do just like we planned unless you want to be strung up for murder. And when this is over, twenty-five thousand dollars buys my silence and the proof of your guilt. We made a deal and you'll keep your end or hang." Eli wiped perspiration from his face with a white handkerchief. "It's not too late. Whether they turn him loose or put him in jail, we can still get to him."

"And in the meantime?"

Eli decided the man might be educated and rich, but he sure was one dumb jackass when it came to reasoning things out. "The two of you will have a shoot-out in front of her. I'll produce the evidence that he killed his sister. Who'll believe anything he had to say? He was nuts all along, out of his head. Even Allie will finally believe it. I can see to that. It'll blow over, I tell you, unless you cross me and I back him up. I'll take care of everything. Lanse Waring killed his own sister. The girl is mine, and you ride off an unwanted man, free to go home to the arms of your loving and very rich family. And I disappear with my twenty-five thousand dollars."

"And the reward? Who gets that?"

"The Waring family ain't gonna pay no reward for the apprehension of their dead son. Besides, what do you care? You got more money than you can ever spend. You gotta decide, you want cleared of murder and revenge against this Waring, or you want a few measly pesos?"

"Okay. I'll gun down the son of a bitch. I want to see his face when he realizes who I am and what I did to him and his sister. He left me to die at Shiloh and it's only by the grace of them bushwhackers who found me that I'm alive at all. If we hadn't been wearing the same colors, they'd have finished me off. I owe this bastard big, and I intend to pay up."

Chapter Twenty

The two men slipped from the shadows of the alleyway beside the Palace of the Governors, Ethan trailing along so close Eli could smell his whiskey breath. One end of the palace housed the jail that was strongly barred and bolted. Eli had expected the sheriff to lock Waring there after dragging him and Allie across the plaza. He couldn't believe his luck when the couple strode right past him arm in arm, her tucking her head against his shoulder. The son of a bitch!

After they passed, Ethan asked in a husky voice, "What do you think he told them? Why the hell did they let him go?"

"How would I know? Come on, let's see where they're headed. You'd better take care of him quick, cause if I have to watch her simper up into his ugly face one more time, I'll shoot the bastard myself and let the chips fall where they may."

They followed Allie and Jake back to the studio, Eli muttering all the while about that bastard touching his woman, seeing how they had their arms all wrapped around each other, her leaning so close, him tilting his head to say something that made her laugh. He couldn't wait to watch what was about to happen, and it would be perfect. Allie would have no idea he had anything to do with it, and after a reasonable time he'd take her to his bed.

When the two paused to open the door of the studio, Eli had to grab Ethan's arm to keep him from confronting them right there.

"Don't be a fool. We can't create a scene. Got to do this right, with just her as a witness."

Ethan jerked free, pulled his revolver and stuck it in Eli's gut. "Who you calling fool?"

Despite nearly choking on his fright, Eli whispered, "Think, man. Let's not mess up now. You want to spend your life a wanted man?"

This maniac could shoot him down with little provocation, and go in there and kill both of them. Just for the fun of it. He had to keep reminding him of the consequences of such action. Ever since they'd struck a bargain, Ethan in handcuffs and both on the way back to St. Louis where Eli would collect ten thousand dollars from the Waring family, he'd had his hands full with Ethan. How the man had survived this long he couldn't figure.

Inside the studio Allie lit the oil lamp, surprised that her fingers remained steady enough to do so. Since the incident in the chapel, she'd been much calmer than she had a right to be. Perhaps it was because Jake was free at last. Even if he were someone else, he still wanted only her. Lanse Waring or Jake, she had to believe he was the man she loved, the man who loved her.

He caressed her, his touch light and feathery along the back of her neck and over her shoulders. She moved tranquilly into his embrace, lacing the fingers of both hands into his hair.

"I love you," he said against her mouth, then captured her lips with the moist silkiness of his.

"Lanse Waring loves me as much as Jake did?" she teased when she could finally catch her breath.

305

Samantha Lee

"More," he said. He unbuttoned her shirt, taking his time, entranced by the play of golden lamplight over her burnished flesh. He would make love to her tonight as the man he was, the best of both Jake and Lanse, with no dark caverns filled with fearful secrets to plague him.

There would be time to tell her about his past, all the time in the world, and he would never leave her. One day soon they would have to journey back east and see his family, after all the years they had thought him dead. But here was where he belonged, here with her in this land of serenity, where he had finally found peace.

She moved in his arms, stiffened. "Listen, did you hear that?"

One hand cupping her bared breast, he tilted his head, heard nothing. He bent to take the erect nipple between his lips. She tasted like *chamisa* brushed by a pinon-scented desert wind. A woman who was not all sweet and cloying but a bit wild and free. The kind he would never have found had he not become a man like Jake, and he thanked God for that time which he had once detested, the time he had wandered, searched and found at last this woman to love.

"Jake, didn't you hear that? Someone's outside."

He tasted the sweet, warm mound of her breast, spoke against the soft skin, "A dog maybe, or just someone passing by on their way home from the cantina. Take that off." Fingers hooked along the top of her chemise, he tugged it down to free her breasts completely, breath coming in gasps now because he wanted her so badly, ached for her to the center of his being.

Then he heard the noise too, but by the time he reacted it was too late. The back door slammed open, then shut, and he barely had time to shove Allie out of harm's way before the man burst from the dark bedroom into the studio, a long-barreled revolver clutched in his left fist.

The old fear came back in that instant when Jake realized that he might have to die and lose her after all. "Who are you?" he rasped. No sooner had he asked the question than he knew

306

the answer. His dark visions had returned. "What do you want?"

"You. All I want is you. But don't be fooled, I'll kill her, too, if you even twitch one little hair," the apparition of his boyhood friend said.

This man's words echoed from the past. "Marry her, what makes you think I'm going to marry her?" And the laugh, so cruel and vicious.

"Ethan?" he blurted, blood roaring in his ears, the smell of the battlefield thick in the room as he remembered the last time he'd seen this man who was once his best friend. "I thought you'd been killed."

"And did little to prevent it, either, my friend." Ethan's lips curled in a sneer.

Had Allie not reacted in fear, Jake still would have believed this an illusion. But she saw Ethan, too, and held Jake's arm in a vise-like grip.

For a moment he couldn't speak. Ethan. Alive? How could this be?

"Move away from him, lady. Now!"

Finding his voice, he begged, "Let her go. Whatever it is you want with me has nothing to do with her. Let her walk out the door and I'll do anything you say."

"No, I'm not leaving," Allie said, clearly puzzled. "This is Ethan? I thought—" Fingers worked to adjust her disheveled clothing.

Ethan interrupted. "Obviously, I'm not dead. You both talk like you have a say in what's going to happen. Well, you don't." The last words issued like iron hot from a forge. Eyes the color of lead shot glared at them.

At his side Allie shuddered and moved her arm. The sheriff and Hooten had given them back their guns; she wore hers on her hip and it was out of Ethan's sight. Jake wanted to look at her, warn her, but couldn't take his eyes off this man he'd once loved as a brother.

"Ethan, my God, what's to become of you?" Fresh grief for the loss of his sweet, trusting sister remained as raw as if she had died today and not years ago. And this man, his friend, had killed her. Allie hugged his arm, reminding him that here was another woman he loved, and he could not, would not let Ethan destroy her as well.

He clenched and unclenched his fists, the gun on his hip as natural as an extension of an arm to ex-soldier Lanse Waring. "Don't make me kill you, Ethan. Put the gun away and ride off. That'll be the end of it, I promise."

"No. You don't understand. It's me or you—it has to end here in this room, with one of us dead. Someone has to take the blame, don't you understand that? You have to pay for killing your sister."

"No!" Jake's hand twitched over the revolver's butt, but how could he begin his life with Allie by killing this man? This bitter shell of his boyhood friend, a ruined man who had almost destroyed his life, and now accused him of being responsible for Lorena's death. An immense sorrow replaced the hate, the thirst for vengeance that belonged to another life.

Jake held out a hand. "Ethan, dammit, give it up. You don't want it to end like this."

Ethan's visage darkened, fingers tightened around the grip of the forgotten revolver.

Colt drawn, Allie made her move, Jake grabbing at her, knocking her off balance. Ethan moved swiftly and back-handed her across the face, sending the weapon flying.

Blood pounding in her ears, she staggered backward against the table, almost toppling the lamp. Her cheek throbbed but it was nothing to the hammering of her heart when she glimpsed the anger that suffused Jake's face. She watched helplessly while his hand went for the revolver on his hip.

"No, don't," she screamed, but it was too late.

In a flash he whipped out the gun. To her horror Ethan fanned the hammer of his own weapon. And then both men froze, as if each was unable to make the final decision to take the other's life. In that instant's hesitation, Allie threw the lamp, striking Ethan in the chest and knocking him off balance. The gun in his fist went off, shattering the front window. Jake fired almost at the same time. She choked on the stench of black powder, and for a moment could see nothing through the smoke and darkening shadows.

Then she saw Jake, kneeling beside his friend, tears streaming down his face. He reached out a hand to her and she went to his side. Blood blackened Ethan's shirt high on the right shoulder. Allie squeezed her eyes closed and said a little prayer. He was alive. Jake hadn't killed him, and for that she would be eternally grateful.

Sheriff Sena and Marshal Hooten rushed in accompanied by a flustered Eli Martin. Doing his part, he had gone to fetch the law, expecting to find Lanse Waring dead and Ethan Hollingsworth triumphant when they returned.

"We heard shots. What has happened here?" Sena asked.

Rising and pulling Allie up and into his arms, Jake said wearily, "That's Ethan Hollingsworth. He killed my sister."

"Yes, marshal, that's true," Eli Martin said. "I followed him here, and came and got you. That means I get the reward. Let's see, that was ten thousand dollars, wasn't it?"

Hooten eyed the bounty hunter. "I'm afraid there'll be no reward for you, sir. The governor has brought charges against you in an ongoing investigation into fraud and deception. You'll both be sharing the same cell until I take this man back to St. Louis."

For a while it looked as though Eli Martin might make a play for his gun, but his shoulders slumped in defeat and he said nothing. Allie turned away from the man she'd once loved and took Jake's arm.

"Come on, let's get some fresh air while they clean up the place."

Together they walked out onto the square, and hand in hand gazed up at the star-tossed sky.

"I'm sorry about . . . about what happened," she told him. "I didn't want you to have to . . . " The rest of the words caught in her throat.

"I know, Allie, and I'm grateful. He would have killed us both. I'm glad he's alive, but for me the friend I knew and loved died at Shiloh. That man in there wasn't him, hadn't been for a long time. What happens to people, do you suppose, that they can start out one person and become another?" He paused, held her close.

A velvety dark silence caressed them.

She looked up at him, smiled. "Sometimes that's a good thing."

In that moment she sensed a calmness settle over him, and embraced it gladly. In the twinkle of star shine, he gazed down at her. The gleam in his eyes told her all she needed to know. He was her Jake, and always would be.

Author's Note

By the late 1800s there were 10,000 women working in the field of photography in the United States. While many were employed by men in studios, most were actually doing the work themselves. To some it was a hobby, to the rest, a profession. All over the country women like Allison Caine turned out artistic photographs, but very few are recognized by history.

Julia Margaret Cameron was a middle-aged photographer creating portraitures in the 1860s. In 1857, Eliza Withington set up a studio in the mining town of Ione City, where she made stereoeographs and images of the town and its mining operations.

Though Matthew Brady was best known for his photographs of the Civil War, he employed many operators who took a large percentage of the pictures later credited to him. His assistant, Alexander Gardner, actually set out on his own during the war. Brady owned two studios in New York and one in Washington D.C. in which he employed women for retouching and coloring because they were cheap labor.

Jesse and Frank James, along with the Younger brothers, were known to have been quite active in Missouri during the time Allie took their portraits. It would be nearly ten years before they would ride to

Northfield, Minnesota where they pulled off the notorious bank robbery that ripped apart the James Gang forever.

About a year after Clay Allison brought Jake back to Allie, he died of a brain tumor. Many experts claim that the tumor explained his sometimes outrageous behavior, such as riding his horse into saloons to shoot up the place.

As the creator of this work of fiction, I took artistic license with only one specific locale. The rock bridge which the caravan crossed on its way to Santa Fe is actually located on the Cimarron Cut Off and not on the main trail, but I was so intrigued by descriptions of the crossing that I could not resist including it in *Images in Scarlet*. I hope historians will forgive me.

All historical facts are as true as my research would allow. Any mistakes are mine alone.

Samantha Lee

MIDNIGHT SUN

AMANDA HARTE

Amelia Sheldon has traveled from Philadelphia to Gold Landing, Alaska, to practice medicine, not defend herself and her gender to an arrogant man like William Gunning. While her position as doctor's assistant provides her ample opportunity to prove the stubborn mine owner wrong, the sparks between them aren't due to anger. William Gunning knows that women are too weak to stand up to the turmoil of disease. But when he meets the beautiful, willful Amelia Sheldon, she proves anything but weak; in fact, she gives him the tongue lashing of his life. When the barbs escalate to kisses, William knows he has found his true love in the land of the midnight sun.

___4503-6 $5.50 US/$6.50 CAN

Pirate

Connie Mason

Determined to ruin those who kept him from his heart's only desire, handsome Guy DeYoung becomes a reckless marauder who rampages the isles intent on revenge. But when he finds his lost love, and takes her as his captive, he will not let her go until she freely gives him her body and soul.

__4456-0 $5.99 US/$6.99 CAN

BEYOND BETRAYAL

CHRISTINE MICHELS

Disguised as the law, outlaw Samson Towers travels to Red Rock, Montana, where he finds the one woman that can knock down the pillars of his deception and win his heart—a temptress named Delilah Sterne. While the lovely widow finds herself drawn to the town's sheriff, the beautiful gambler suddenly fears she's played the wrong cards—and sentenced the man she loves to death. Her heart in danger, she knows that she must save the handsome Samson and prove that their love can exist beyond betrayal.

___52264-0 $5.50 US/$6.50 CAN

TEXAS PROUD

CONSTANCE O'BANYON

Rachel Rutledge has her gun trained on Noble Vincente. With one shot, she will have her revenge on the man who killed her father. So what is stopping her from pulling the trigger? Perhaps it is the memory of Noble's teasing voice, his soft smile, or the way one glance from his dark Spanish eyes once stirred her foolish heart to longing. Yes, she loved him then . . . as much as she hates him now. One way or another, she will wound him to the heart—if not with bullets, then with her own feminine wiles. But as Rachel discovers, sometimes the line between love and hate is too thinly drawn.

___4492-7 $5.99 US/$6.99 CAN

Dorchester Publishing Co., Inc.
P.O. Box 6640
Wayne, PA 19087-8640

Please add $1.75 for shipping and handling for the first book and $.50 for each book thereafter. NY, NYC, and PA residents, please add appropriate sales tax. No cash, stamps, or C.O.D.s. All orders shipped within 6 weeks via postal service book rate. Canadian orders require $2.00 extra postage and must be paid in U.S. dollars through a U.S. banking facility.

Name_____
Address_____
City_____ State_____ Zip_____
I have enclosed $_____ in payment for the checked book(s).
Payment <u>must</u> accompany all orders. ☐ Please send a free catalog.
    CHECK OUT OUR WEBSITE! www.dorchesterpub.com

Cougar's Woman Ronda Thompson

On the journey to meet her fiancé in Santa Fe, Melissa Sheffield is captured by Apaches and given to a man known as Cougar. At first, she is relieved to learn that she's been given to a white man, but with one kiss he proves himself more dangerous than the whole tribe. Terrified of her savage captor, she pledges to escape at any price. But while there might be an escape from the Apaches, is there any escape from her heart? Clay Brodie—known as Cougar to the Apaches—is given the fiery Melissa by his chief. He is then ordered to turn the beauty into an obedient slave—or destroy her. But how can he slay a woman who evokes an emotion deeper than he's ever known? And when the time comes to fight, will it be for his tribe or for his woman?

___4524-9 $4.99 US/$5.99 CAN

Ariel's Dance

Chloe Hall

On the recreational world of Mariposa, every form of exotic pleasure is available—along with every vice abhorred by Dekkan's people. But the interstellar diplomat has no need to fear such tawdry temptations—until the night his special hormone-inhibiting patch begins to fail and he meets a sexy butterfly dancer named Ariel. Barging into her dressing chamber seeking a stolen family heirloom, he seems so deliciously naive to Ariel that the firebrand decides to have some fun. But giving Dekkan his first taste of desire has unexpected results: Suddenly her own heart is at risk.

___52285-3 $4.99 US/$5.99 CAN

Dorchester Publishing Co., Inc.
P.O. Box 6640
Wayne, PA 19087-8640

Please add $1.75 for shipping and handling for the first book and $.50 for each book thereafter. NY, NYC, and PA residents, please add appropriate sales tax. No cash, stamps, or C.O.D.s. All orders shipped within 6 weeks via postal service book rate. Canadian orders require $2.00 extra postage and must be paid in U.S. dollars through a U.S. banking facility.

Name_____
Address_____
City_____State_____Zip_____
I have enclosed $_____ in payment for the checked book(s).
Payment <u>must</u> accompany all orders. ❏ Please send a free catalog.

Love Just in Time

FLORA SPEER

After discovering her husband's infidelity, Clarissa Cummings thinks she will never trust another man. Then a freak accident sends her into another century—and the most handsome stranger imaginable saves her from drowning in the canal. But he is all wet if he thinks he has a lock on Clarissa's heart. After scandal forces Jack Martin to flee to the wilds of America, the dashing young Englishman has to give up the pleasures of a rake and earn his keep with a plow and a hoe. Yet to his surprise, he learns to enjoy the simple life of a farmer, and he yearns to take Clarissa as his bride. But after Jack has sown the seeds of desire, secrets from his past threaten to destroy his harvest of love.

___52289-6 $5.50 US/$6.50 CAN